*continued . . .*

# uncertain allies

## mark del franco

ACE BOOKS, NEW YORK

**THE BERKLEY PUBLISHING GROUP**
**Published by the Penguin Group**
**Penguin Group (USA) Inc.**
**375 Hudson Street, New York, New York 10014, USA**
Penguin Group (Canada), 90 Eglinton Avenue East, Suite 700, Toronto, Ontario M4P 2Y3, Canada
(a division of Pearson Penguin Canada Inc.)
Penguin Books Ltd., 80 Strand, London WC2R 0RL, England
Penguin Group Ireland, 25 St. Stephen's Green, Dublin 2, Ireland (a division of Penguin Books Ltd.)
Penguin Group (Australia), 250 Camberwell Road, Camberwell, Victoria 3124, Australia
(a division of Pearson Australia Group Pty. Ltd.)
Penguin Books India Pvt. Ltd., 11 Community Centre, Panchsheel Park, New Delhi—110 017, India
Penguin Group (NZ), 67 Apollo Drive, Rosedale, Auckland 0632, New Zealand
(a division of Pearson New Zealand Ltd.)
Penguin Books (South Africa) (Pty.) Ltd., 24 Sturdee Avenue, Rosebank, Johannesburg 2196,
South Africa

Penguin Books Ltd., Registered Offices: 80 Strand, London WC2R 0RL, England

This is a work of fiction. Names, characters, places, and incidents either are the product of the author's imagination or are used fictitiously, and any resemblance to actual persons, living or dead, business establishments, events, or locales is entirely coincidental. The publisher does not have any control over and does not assume any responsibility for author or third-party websites or their content.

UNCERTAIN ALLIES

An Ace Book / published by arrangement with the author

PRINTING HISTORY
Ace mass-market edition / May 2011

Copyright © 2011 by Mark Del Franco.
Cover art by Jaime DeJesus.
Cover design by Judith Lagerman.

ISBN: 978-0-441-02040-9

ACE
Ace Books are published by The Berkley Publishing Group,
a division of Penguin Group (USA) Inc.,
375 Hudson Street, New York, New York 10014.
ACE and the "A" design are trademarks of Penguin Group (USA) Inc.

PRINTED IN THE UNITED STATES OF AMERICA

10  9  8  7  6  5  4  3  2  1

*For Jack, as always*

# 1

Nighttime in the city made me feel at home no matter where I was. The sun went down, and the city changed, became its own dark twin, rich with mystery and surprise. The interplay of light and shadow, the garish and the mundane, produced stark contrasts that changed my perspective of the world. Details stood out in the pooled light of streetlamps that were lost clutter in the daytime. Faces became cloaked with meaning or menace. Mysteries deepened, too, the unnoticed receding into the unseen.

Maybe that was my way of romanticizing the Weird, the decrepit Boston neighborhood I called home. It looked abandoned during the day, the tired dumping ground for the shunned fey—the fairy folk from Ireland and Germany. At night it came alive, filled with humans and fey folk hustling for one thing or another, partying too hard, staying too long, and pushing themselves to the limit. At night it came alive, which meant that sometimes someone ended up dead.

That's what Convergence brought to the world. When Faerie merged with modern reality a century ago, it brought not only fey people but all of their hopes and hatreds. Dan-ann fairies ruled from Tara in Ireland and looked down at all the rest of the Celtic fey. Teutonic elves occupied significant parts of old Germany and threatened war at every turn. Caught between them were the refugees from the old ways—the solitary fey that didn't fit in with the mainstream. They spread across Europe and the Atlantic, hoping for a better life than they had known. Instead, they ended up in places like the Weird while the usual power players moved into the upper echelons of human society.

I had spent my professional career seeking justice for the fey. Connor Grey was the go-to guy for crimes involving fairies and elves or any other fey species. I was one of the best—maybe the best—investigators the Fey Guild ever had. The Guild was the administrative arm for High Queen Maeve at Tara and leader of the Celtic fey. When I lost my druid abilities in a fight with an elven terrorist, I got kicked to the curb. That's when I learned the Guild cared only about the Guild, the rich, and the powerful, and I had been a pawn in its political schemes without realizing it. I spent a year moping, watching my friends, my home, and my money disappear. For another year, I helped the Boston police department solve crimes that the Guild could not care less about—crimes against the weak and the powerless rungs of fey society. I didn't help the Guild or the police anymore, not really. Now I did favors. That was a kind way of saying no one wanted to give me official sanction. I had screwed up a lot of plans for a lot of powerful people in the last year. Now, I helped people I trusted and hoped that my trust wasn't misplaced.

Eorla Kruge Elvendottir was one of those people. She had tried to find a way to unify the Celtic and Teutonic fey and failed. She defied her cousin, the Elven King, and broke away from his rule. With her own court in the Weird, she vowed to take care of anyone who needed it and leave ancient rivalries behind. When she received reports that people were going missing and a strange blue light marked their disappearance, she asked me to look into it.

I had spent the evening chasing rumors, loud noises, and flashes of light. The light came from essence, the energy that bound everything in the world together. As a druid, I sensed the nuances of essence and could recognize things by their unique signatures. Except hunting essence in the Weird was an exercise in frustration. With so many fey living here, sorting out trails was a painstaking process. I was good at it, but tonight wasn't successful. Whatever was causing the disappearances was as elusive as my reputation.

I was on my way home when I spotted a Boston police car parked beside a pile of broken concrete. The Tangle lay beyond, the section of the waterfront that made the rest of the Weird safe and secure by comparison. This end of the neighborhood was a burned-out husk, the epicenter of a night of fire and riot a few months earlier. Little remained of the businesses that had managed to survive. Where the Tangle was a nest of intrigue and danger, the area next to it had become a wasteland of nothing. Even electricity was spotty—a few streetlights remained standing, but the buildings were clothed in darkness without even a hint of a squatter's candle. The hard white light of an arc lamp made finding the crime scene easy.

A building had once been where I stood but had collapsed into a heap of rubble from the heat of fire. An unsecured strip of crime-scene tape fluttered in the wind. I climbed over the first pile of soot-stained bricks and brittle mortar. Light shone from behind the next pile, dark shadows cutting through the beam of the arc light as people passed in front of the lamp. I threaded along a narrow wedge of space too filled with debris to be called a vacant lot.

"Something about not crossing a police line not apply to you, Grey?"

The dark shape of a uniformed police officer stepped into view from the side of the pit. Officer Gerard Murdock directed his flashlight at me, forcing me to turn away. "Hey, Gerry."

He moved closer. "I asked you a question."

I tried to squint past the beam of light. I knew Gerry—I

knew all the Murdocks—through their brother Leo, a homicide detective with the Boston police force. Gerry's tone didn't sound like he was joking. "Eorla asked me to check things out, Gerry. What's going on?"

He had his hand on his holstered gun. At least, I thought it was holstered. "I don't care what some trumped-up elf queen wants. Get out of here before I get clumsy."

To be kind, Gerry had what might be described as an anger-management problem. His father—who had been the police commissioner—was murdered under odd circumstances, and Gerry wasn't happy the case had not been resolved yet. "I'm just doing my job, Gerry."

"Do it someplace else," he said.

I held my hand up to block the flashlight beam. "I'm sorry about your father, Gerry, but I didn't kill him. You know everything that happened that night. I know you read the report."

He inched closer. "Yeah, well, of the people who were there, two are dead, one's in a coma, and you used to sleep with the other. Excuse me if I'm having a hard time with your credibility."

For months now, I had been letting his attitude slide. His father was dead. I wasn't lying when I said I didn't do it, but I did have an unwitting role in the events that led to it. It made me feel guilty, so between that and respecting his grief, I took the taunts and accusations. "Gerry, I told the truth. When Manus ap Eagan wakes up from his coma, he'll confirm it."

He sneered. "Really? He's going to confess to murder? That I'd like to see."

Except for their father, I liked the Murdocks. I was getting tired of tiptoeing around Gerry's temper and tired of him. "Yeah, well, I don't see you so quick to confess to murder."

Gerry dropped his flashlight and grabbed me by the front of my jacket. He bent me back, keeping me off-balance. "You listen to me, you punk bastard. I don't give a damn about you. You want a bullet in the head, you keep talking."

I smirked. "You wouldn't be the first Murdock to shoot me."

I read his body language wrong and didn't see the arm moving. He punched me in the face, his fist sliding off my cheekbone. I pushed him off me, and we stumbled away from each other. He pulled his gun.

"I miss something important, Gerry?"

Detective Lieutenant Leonard Murdock stood on the pile of bricks I had come down. If it wasn't for Leo, I would have died now and then. I've returned the favor. We were gym buddies first, then work partners, then friends. Why he stuck by me after the mess I brought into his life baffled me, but it meant a lot. With his hands in his pockets, Leo stared down at his brother. Gerry glared at him, then at me. He holstered the gun and stalked off. Leo picked his way down the pile. "I see you're making friends as usual."

"I didn't start it," I said.

"I didn't say you did, Connor. Gerry's been a little temperamental lately," he said.

I touched my fingers to a tender cheekbone. Nothing felt broken, but the eye would darken by sunup. "A little? He hit me, Leo. Why the hell isn't he on desk duty? He shot Moira Cashel."

Moira was the reason Scott Murdock, the police commissioner, was dead. He was going to kill her and ended up shooting me by accident. Gerry killed her during the riot that happened afterward. Leo and I walked toward the crime scene. "The force is shorthanded. All internal investigations are on hold."

"You need to talk to him, Leo. I didn't kill your father," I said.

He looked tired. I didn't blame him. "I know. I will. Why was he in your face anyway?"

"Eorla asked me to check out some disappearances around the Tangle, and I ran into this on my way back. Gerry wasn't happy to see me." Eorla Elvendottir had stopped the riot and brought calm to the neighborhood, at least calm by the Weird's standards. In the process, she broke away from the Elven Court and set up her own, making the Weird her particular area of protection. The human government was having a little problem with that. It didn't get the connection between Eorla's standing up for the Weird and the fact that humans did little to protect the people down here.

"Then we're both here to work. I'll talk to Gerry. Stay out of his way for a while," he said.

Some terrible things had happened to Murdock—to all the Murdocks—because of me. Leo told me he wasn't going to hold them against me. He said that what had happened might have been my fault in a sense, but I wasn't to blame. Other things, other people, had their parts in it. Knowing I wasn't to blame didn't help my guilt. People were dead, people Murdock cared about. I was part of it and didn't know how to fix that. At least Leo believed me about what had just happened with Gerry. Even with a bruise forming under my eye, I had to let it go and let him handle it. "Okay. Let's do this."

I wasn't the only person Eorla had sent to monitor that the Boston police did its job without prejudice. Across the pit, a red-uniformed elf stood out like a signal beacon against the pale gray sky, one of Eorla's men. Near him, a thin tree fairy, her skin a pale gray, hair a thick-layered mat, shuffled along the ground.

Down in the shallow hole, the dark figure of Janey Likesmith busied herself around a dead dwarf. A Dokkheim elf, Janey was the sole fey staffer at the Office of the Chief Medical Examiner. I admired her dedication. The fey cases the Guild didn't want landed on her desk, and since the humans didn't know what to do with them, she had to handle them alone. After the insanity that had almost burned down the Weird, she had more than her share of bodies to sort through. The Guild gave token help, and the OCME focused more on the human remains its staff knew how to handle. Janey needed a break, but I didn't see one coming anytime soon.

She had spread a small tarp a few feet from the body; her travel bag, from which she withdrew instruments and laid

them at the ready, was open. The police officers at the next
crime-scene tape let me pass under without hassle. I picked
my way down the slope. Janey smiled at Murdock before she
looked at me, the cool night air steaming her breath from her
mouth. "Happy Yule."

I returned the smile as I crouched next to her. "A few
months late."

She kept the smile. "I haven't seen you since the beginning of the year. Despite everything that's going on, Connor,
the return of the light is something to look forward to. That's
what Yule is for."

All the fey celebrated Yule with variations on the basic
theme of renewal in celebration of the days getting longer.
The Teutonic fey focused on peace and the future. I didn't
know the specifics of Janey's Dokkheim clan, but peace
wasn't a bad thing to hope for. "You're right. Happy Yule."

The dead dwarf didn't look like he had found much peace
and happiness. He knelt on gravel, hands slack to either side
and his head dropped back. Milky eyes the shade of raw oys-
ter stared at the sky, and his mouth gaped in horror or shock.
As I shifted closer to the body to search for any obvious
wounds, the black mass in my head pulsed low and steady,
like a headache coming on, or—more accurately—a bigger
headache. I always had a headache.

The black mass plagued me. MRI scans showed a dark
shadow in my brain but nothing tangible. A spell feedback
during a fight had left the mass behind, and it had damaged
my ability to manipulate essence.

At first, the mass gave me headaches. Then it started to
move around, change shape, and hurt like hell. Not long ago,
the mass changed again, seeming to have a will or purpose
of its own. Sometimes it extended from my body in a way
I didn't understand, but its effect was clear. It drained essence from whatever it touched, and if it touched people, it
could kill them. I could kill them. There was no separating
me from it in the eyes of the world. Whatever happened to
the dwarf caused the dark mass to react.

Janey set thermometers around the body to get base readings. "I don't think he's been here long. No obvious animal damage, and he's still in rigor. Hard to tell with a fey death, though. If essence is involved, it complicates the physical readings. Plus, this pit creates its own microclimate. We're out of the wind, so the temperature will scale differently in here."

"Isn't this a bit late for you?" I asked.

She scribbled a note on her pad: the time of my arrival and where I entered the pit. "I heard the call as I was going off shift and came out to get it done. I would've gotten the call anyway. Everyone's backed up."

What she didn't say is that no one from the OCME would have responded unless no other crimes were happening—a rarity—and her job would have been that much harder with a processing delay.

At the lip of the pit, the ash fairy huddled on the ground, her head twitching from side to side. To the non-fey, she appeared to be a crazy person sniffing the ground, but the fey recognized the behavior as sensing for the trail of someone. Indentations in the sand led up the slope near her. "Has anyone been that way? I think we have footprints."

Janey grabbed her camera. "Good eye. I'm the only one that's been down here."

We climbed out of the pit the way we had come down and circled toward the indentations. The ash fairy peered at me from beneath her dark tangle of hair, then shuffled back as I approached. She pointed a long, pale arm toward the ground. "Dead earth. Doesn't feel right."

All living things emanated essence, the energy that keeps the Wheel of the World turning. Tree fairies were attuned to their clan trees and the earth. Some fey sensed essence as druids did, saw it as shapes of color with a secondary vision that human science hadn't figured out. People left traces of essence on whatever they touched, even in the air. The longer they remained someplace, the more essence residue accumulated. The footprints leading out of the pit and across the empty lot didn't shine with essence light. The earth surrounding the prints wasn't missing its natural essence, making the prints themselves stand out even more. They had no telltale essence signatures that would identify the person or species. Someone powerful was responsible for removing the essence—or responsible for helping someone else do it.

Janey photographed the area. "So this is likely a murder."

We were in the Weird with a dead dwarf that didn't get reported by whoever was with him when he died. The odds were slim that he died of a heart attack. I gave her shoulder a squeeze. "I'm going to look around. I'll let you know if I see anything else."

She inhaled, resigned. "I'm backlogged, so I don't know when I'll get to this autopsy."

"You always do your best," I tried to reassure her with a smile.

Murdock skirted the edge of the pit. "Find something?"

"Nothing, actually, and that's the problem. Essence is missing where it shouldn't be missing." From the spot where the footsteps exited the pit, Murdock followed me as I traced the faded spots across the lot.

"I thought everything had essence. How can it be missing?" he asked.

We reached the broken sidewalk and squatted closer to the ground like the tree fairy had done. "Suppressing essence is possible. Powerful fey, like the Danann fairies and the Alfheim elves, can dissipate essence, scrub an area to eliminate any trace of it."

Murdock turned back toward the pit. "Why would someone that powerful be down in the Weird?"

I pursed my lips. "Why does anyone come down here, Leo? The powerful fey may not live down here, but they do stuff here they don't want people to know about."

The blank trail ended on the sidewalk. The area was one of the worst hit from the fires and rioting during the winter solstice. Buildings were left nothing more than their façades, their main structures slumped behind. They needed to be knocked down. That didn't stop people from picking through the remains for anything valuable. They wouldn't find much. The intensity of the fires had destroyed everything. I didn't have much to offer Murdock either, not when the initial clue at the scene was nothingness.

A few blocks away, a burst of blue light lit the sky over the Tangle, the section of the Weird even people who lived here feared because of its deserved reputation for lawlessness. "What the hell was that?" Murdock asked.

I narrowed my eyes as the light faded. The essence was strong enough for Murdock to see it with natural vision. "I've been chasing it all night. Witnesses say it's like a fast-moving cloud that sweeps up people."

"Anyone killed?"

Death was only a matter of time in the Tangle. "Not yet. Lots of missing, though."

An awkward silence settled between us. "I thought I'd run into you at the hospital," I said.

A slight smile creased his face. "Are you spanking me?"

I shifted on my feet. "Sorry. That was passive-aggressive."

He chuckled. "Yeah. And that's one of your better qualities."

I frowned. "I was just asking."

"Oh, lighten up. Yes, I've been to the hospital. Almost every day. Believe it or not, they have morning visiting hours."

I was on friendly terms with late-night breakfast at dawn. "I hate seeing her like that."

He sighed. "A silent Meryl is a terrible thing."

Meryl Dian and I were in a relationship of a sort, but what that sort was eluded me. I didn't know if it was love or if I didn't know what love was, but we had something intense going on. During the riots, she'd gotten caught in some kind of spell backlash and had been in a coma ever since. For months, her brain activity had been so minimal, it didn't even register. All I knew was I missed her terribly and wanted her back.

"We should have lunch," Murdock said.

We hadn't done anything as normal as have lunch together in weeks. Despite what he said, it was hard not to feel like he was freezing me out, and I couldn't say I blamed him. "I'd like that."

We stepped back as a medical examiner—a human one—arrived. "It never ends, does it, Leo?"

"Nothing lasts forever, Connor. Things won't always be like this," he said.

After everything that had happened to him, Murdock could still say something like that. Hope drove him and a faith I didn't have. I tried to hang on, though. I didn't think I had a choice. It was either that, or let the bad guys win.

# 2

I spent the morning running down contacts, but I didn't get much information for all my efforts. Morning wasn't the most popular time of day in the Weird. As I walked the streets, I realized that I had begun to not notice the damage done by the riots a few months earlier. The Guild and the Teutonic Consortium had pitted the Dead and the local solitaries against each other in another of a long chain of proxy wars between the two monarchies. The tension between the two groups flared into a night of rioting that grew while the Weird burned around them. The Guild and the Consortium had lost control of their factions and turned on them, threatening to annihilate the neighborhood.

If Eorla hadn't stepped in, a bloodbath would have resulted. With Meryl's help, she calmed the rioters and stood up to the Guild and the Consortium. A disaster might have been averted, but damage had already been done. Parts of the Weird, a place already falling apart, were now in ruins. And I had almost stopped seeing it. When people stop seeing the neglect around them—decay sets in, and things fall apart. I hoped enough people kept their eyes open.

As the sun approached noon, I strolled over the Old Northern Avenue bridge toward the financial district—the only bridge left over Fort Point Channel. The other two bridges lay underwater, slumped and broken. During the riots, they had been destroyed by the solitary fey to stop the National Guard from attacking the Weird. The tactic had worked for the most part, but now it made coming and going into the neighborhood difficult. While the government argued about liability and responsibility, no one worried about the inconvenience. At least the Oh No bridge, held together by twisted and warped iron girders, saved a one-mile walk around.

The atmosphere in the lobby of the Rowes Wharf Hotel had changed since the last time I was there. Then, it had bustled with tourists and businesspeople on the downtown side of the channel. Now, it served as the waiting area for Eorla Elvendottir's administrative offices. Across town in Back Bay, people waited in poor weather conditions outside the Guildhouse or not at all in front of the Teutonic Consortium consulate. Treating people with dignity and respect was a nice change of pace for the fey. Eorla wasn't paying lip service to her ideals.

No one stopped me. Two elves followed me across the lobby at a discreet distance, both in the green livery of the Kruge clan, which Eorla had led since her husband was murdered. After years of working for the Celtic-run Fey Guild, it felt odd to have elves providing me with protection. They used to be the enemy. Most of them were, but the line between who hated me and who hated me more was getting blurred.

Boston was under martial law. It had to be. When half the city went on a rampage and the other half was terrified, no one complained about curfews. Despite all the security, I didn't need to show identification. Everyone in the building knew my name, and most people knew my face, one of the perks of being suspected of causing the disaster. It wasn't because I was popular except among a select group of people. Those people weren't popular either.

Eorla held court on the third floor of the hotel in a meeting room that had been decorated to reflect an elven sensibility—woven tapestries featuring woodland scenes and large oaken chairs with intricate carvings lined the walls. Down the center, a long, wide, wool carpet in deep green led to a library table where Eorla received visitors. Courtiers—there was no other word for them—busied themselves along the perimeter of the room, reviewing documents and comparing notes.

A wood fairy stood by himself in front of Eorla. His crackled gray skin gave him a forlorn air, but all his clan looked like that. ". . . and I've lost everything, ma'am."

"I can't replace what you've lost, but I can give you work. Can you work?" Eorla asked.

The fairy lowered his gaze. "I can if it will give me a home."

Eorla gestured to an aide. "We need help shoring up damaged buildings. Some of your clan are already lending their skills to the effort. You'll be provided room and board while you work."

The fairy bowed. "Thank you, ma'am."

Eorla had formed a court that wasn't divided between Celtic and Teutonic fey. She accepted people from all backgrounds and species as long as they understood her goals. She wanted to bring the fey beyond their eternal bickering and find a new path in the modern world. She had tried to do that through the elven Teutonic Consortium, then the Celtic Guildhouse, but she was one woman against entrenched bureaucracies. In the firestorm of the riot, she had discovered she didn't have to make change from the top but could make something happen from the bottom. Fey were flocking to her cause—particularly the solitaries of both the Celts and Teuts, who never caught a break from either monarchy.

The aide escorted the fairy to the side of the room as I approached the table. "Not that I'm against it, but how long can you afford to do this?"

Eorla looked up at me with amusement. Many fey, including elves, had skin tones that diverged from the human norm. Sometimes it was disconcerting. Eorla's skin glowed with a subtle green light, a result of containing the spell that had driven people to riot. Green wasn't a color that appealed to me; but on Eorla, it had a strange effect of enhancing her beauty with a warm tone that accentuated her upswept dark hair and deep brown eyes. "You'd be surprised at the income resources that have appeared. More than a few people support what I'm doing—even among the Celts."

Many people supported her cause, but the big money was waiting to see how Donor Elfenkonig would handle what was essentially Eorla's personal revolt against his rule. "I hope it's enough."

She gestured at the paperwork on the table. "I hope it's temporary. After everything that's happened here, I hope the Guild and the Consortium see the error of their ways and change."

"What are the odds?"

Eorla chuckled. "I have more hope than you do, Connor. Change works faster when it's a long time coming. How did things go last night?"

I shrugged. "Couldn't catch a break. No one's talking down near the Tangle. I saw the essence everyone says shows up before people go missing. It moves fast. I haven't been able to get a good tag on it yet, but there are definitely some of the Dead involved."

"They do continue to be a problem," she said.

The Dead had harassed the city for months. They had arrived from the Celtic land of the dead and become trapped in Boston. They were a rambunctious lot, prone to violence—no surprise since each day they woke fully healed of their wounds from the previous day, even fatal ones. People who were already dead had little to fear. They didn't like authority figures either. "I think they've retreated to the Tangle. I haven't seen them in other parts of the neighborhood."

Eorla glanced at Rand, her bodyguard, who kept tabs on everyone near her. I didn't count many elves as friends, and, while I didn't know if Rand was one, I respected the hell out of the guy. In the short time I had known him, he had stepped up in ways I hadn't expected. Consortium guards weren't known for defying the king, no matter if they were attached to other royals. A flutter went through the air, indicating that Eorla had done a sending, a mental communication much like telepathy but keyed to personal essence. Rand ushered everyone out of the room, then took a relaxed stance facing the door halfway down the carpet.

"I'm having trouble bringing people in that end of the neighborhood to my cause. I was hoping you could provide some insight," she said.

I sat on the corner of the desk. "No one has ever had much luck with the Tangle, Eorla."

"Our goals are aligned, are they not? The Tangle wants to operate outside the influence of the Guild and the Consortium," she said.

I shook my head. "The flaw in your thinking is that you're assuming the Tangle doesn't want to be the way it is. It already operates outside the law. That's its point, and no matter who's in charge—even if it's you—it will still fill a need outside the rules."

She leaned back and steepled her fingers. "I hadn't thought about it in that way. I wonder, though, that they would not prefer to operate as they do with the knowledge that they won't be interfered with?"

"Maybe. But it really is a free-for-all down there. You have no one to make a deal with," I said.

She arched an eyebrow. "Connor, I think you are a smart man, but you are not a warrior. When a group has no leader, that is the perfect time for one to arrive."

When Eorla made a comment like that—or any of the Old Ones who lived in Faerie—it reminded me that I was dealing with people who had lived in warring, often brutal, times. Growing up in Boston, in a democratic system, I tended to forget that majority rule wasn't the only way to gain power, only one that did it with a lot less bloodshed than war.

"I'll keep that in mind," I said.

She rose from her seat and went to the window, gazing

toward the horizon. To the east lay the harbor, sparkling in the midday sun. To the south was the Weird, dim, gray, and sad, a jumble of warehouses and office buildings that had seen better days.

"It doesn't have to be this way," she said.

"It's what gets me up in the mornings," I said. I didn't always believe that. Once upon a time, the Weird had no more concern for me except as a place to get a little down and dirty. The lives of the people who lived there weren't an issue when I was flying high and having fun. I used to think people lived their lives by choice. Losing my job and my abilities—my world and way of life—changed all that. Not everyone in the Weird was there because they wanted to be. Not all of them chose to put themselves in a failing situation. Discovering how much the power elite caused their plights made the matter worse to me. It didn't have to be this way.

Eorla slipped her hand into mine. "I check on her every day."

She meant Meryl. Eorla and Meryl had worked together to stop the rioting in the Weird. They succeeded at Meryl's expense. When Meryl volunteered to help Eorla, she made me promise to take revenge if she died. She didn't die. She didn't live either. I didn't know what to do about it. I wasn't sure Meryl would appreciate the nuance. She'd want me to kick someone's ass. The fact that Eorla followed Meryl's progress despite everything else she had to deal with told me that she cared. Whether she cared because of me, or on principle, didn't matter. She cared.

"I know," I said. I squeezed her hand, and she returned the pressure.

# 3

Outside the hotel, a bus trundled up Atlantic Avenue toward Avalon Memorial Hospital. I hitched a ride, deciding to visit Meryl earlier in the day than usual. I didn't like being at the hospital when lots of people were around. Too many people and too many rumors flying around the floors dragged me down, so I visited people after hours.

The dark underbelly of the elevated highway slid by above, sunlight peering in through the occasional gaps between girders and nearby buildings. The highway formed an enormous barrier across the city, cutting off the North End from the rest of the neighborhoods. It stood ten stories high, double-decked and rust-cancred green—the other Green Monster in Boston. The more well-known one was the wall towering over left field at Fenway Park. At the ballpark, you could get beer. Under the elevated, you could get mugged.

The bus cut through an intersection and rocked side to side as it settled in at the Haymarket stop. Like so much Boston transportation, the route didn't quite take me to where I wanted to go. Waiting for a connection would take longer than hoofing it, so I walked the final blocks to Cambridge Street.

An old brick building overlooking the river had been home to Avalon Memorial Hospital for decades. When the fey got sick, they went to Boston for the best healing expertise. Gillen Yor was chief of staff, and no one knew more about fey medicine than he did. He had been High Queen Maeve's personal physician until he left for the States. She wasn't happy about that. He didn't care.

I passed through the main entrance, its lintel carved with apples dangling from trees in a nod to its Faerie namesake. Avalon was an island, a place of healing, shrouded in mystery. The island didn't come through during Convergence, when other parts of Faerie merged with reality. The fey did the next best thing and opened hospitals that specialized in essence-related maladies and injuries.

The elevator doors opened on Meryl's floor, and the scent of dill and lavender tickled my nose. It said something about my life that the odors of a hospital had a familiarity that had become a comfort for me. Hawthorn, birch, latex, and bleach mixed in an aroma that meant hope and healing. Healers did the best they could with the knowledge they had, and then some. They didn't always succeed, but AvMem was the best bet for most anyone.

Last year, a tainted form of essence had infected the fey down in the Weird. The Taint caused anyone who encountered it to lose control and become violent. It was a major factor in the rioting. With Meryl's help, Eorla absorbed the Taint and contained it. In the process, they had been bombarded with the Taint and fell into comas. Eorla woke up. Meryl didn't. Since then, she had been in a trance state, with no explanation or cure in sight.

Essence was a tool with no will of its own. Depending on the user's intent, it could heal or kill. In the main hallways of AvMem, stone wards dampened ambient essence. The stones were infused with spells to reduce interference with the delicate precision of healing spells that operated in patient rooms. Powerful wards made even the trace of essence disappear, but those took time and ability. AvMem's wards ran a middle ground—strong enough to dampen wayward essence from interfering with healing spells but not so strong that the ability necessary to create them wasted energy, which was why I sensed body signatures as I came out of the elevator, a strong one in particular. I quickened my pace to Meryl's room.

Seated with his back to the door, Nigel Martin cocked his head to the side as I entered, sensing me as I had sensed him. Meryl faced me from a chair opposite him, her stare the same vacant stare it had been for months. I walked around the bed and stood between them.

"What are you doing in here?" I asked.

Nigel tipped his head back, his hands propped on a cane between his knees. The past year had aged him, more white in the dark brown hair that swept over his ears to the nape of his neck, more lines networked in the crow's-feet of his eyes. As much as I wanted to dismiss the stress he had been under, I had a momentary pang thinking that my former mentor was getting old. It was momentary, though. Nigel and I weren't on good terms.

His eyes narrowed. "Your body signature becomes more a mystery to me each time we meet, Connor. Are you in any pain?"

I'd had my own accident with a spell backlash. Almost three years earlier, I was hunting down a terrorist by the name of Bergin Vize. I caught up with him at a nuclear power plant north of Boston, and all hell broke loose. Vize had a ring of power—what it was for I still didn't know—and a feedback loop with the reactor caused an explosion. When I woke up, I had no ability to manipulate essence anymore and the shadowy black mass in my head. It hurt like hell, but as far as I was concerned, it was no longer any of Nigel's business.

I gave him my back as I tugged Meryl's hand. She didn't have any awareness of her surroundings, but she responded to some stimuli. I slipped my hand along her arm and guided her back to the bed. As she settled against the pillows, I faced Nigel. "I asked you a question."

He flicked an eyebrow in annoyance. "There are those,

believe it or not, Connor, who seek my help. Gillen Yor told me he cannot detect any brain activity, yet she isn't vegetative. I came to see for myself."

I used my sensing ability—the only ability I had left—to check Meryl. Other than her dimmed body signature, I detected nothing different from my last visit. "Did you do anything to her?"

He shook his head. "Why does my friendship with her bother you so?"

I frowned. "I've had your friendship, Nigel. It's a fickle thing."

He considered me with a measured stare. "If that's the way you feel, I wouldn't be too sure of your newfound friends if I were you."

I pushed Meryl's chair farther away from him. "Eorla? Is that where you're going to go? If it weren't for her, Nigel, things would be worse, and you know it. She's the only person from the Guild who has done anything to stop the fighting between the Celts and Teuts."

The corner of his mouth drooped as he went to the window. "Her role at the Guild is a technical matter. She is as much the Elven King's creature as Bastian Frye."

I would have loved to see him say that to Eorla's face. Bastian Frye was the Elven King's master spy and assassin. Eorla liked him less than I did Nigel these days. "And whose creature are you, Nigel?"

That time he smiled. "I might ask you the same question."

"I am no one's creature," I said.

"Really? Do you ever wonder how it is that you ended up fighting the Guild when it was hunting Bergin Vize? Or how it is that you stood at Eorla's side when the Weird burned down? Do you not find that at all curious?"

I sighed. "Still seeing Teutonic Consortium agents in the shadows, Nigel?"

He peered at me with one eye open. "Still pretending they're not there, Connor?"

"I don't pretend anything. I'm trying not to get killed in the cross fire," I said.

"You almost killed a few hundred people in the process from what I heard," he said.

I snorted. "I figured Ryan macGoren would go running to you. How is the Acting Guildmaster these days? Has he changed his shorts yet?"

He became solemn, the lecturing old mentor who knew better than I did. "Concerned, Connor. He's concerned that something potentially dangerous is falling into the hands of the Elven King."

"And what might that be?"

"You." He smiled at my surprised reaction. "Deny they have offered you asylum. Tell me that old fool Brokke hasn't whispered his vague portents in your ears." I didn't answer him. Both things had happened. Brokke was a dwarf who had a formidable talent for reading the future. Nigel bobbed his head. "Precisely."

"So now that I'm supposedly dangerous, you're interested in me again? Are we friends again, Nigel?"

"Your petulance is childish," he said.

"And your arrogance is insulting," I said.

He walked toward the door. "There are fools that believe the Wheel of the World turns, and we hang on until we drop. When you move beyond the framework of someone else's definition of what the Wheel is, Connor, you stop being a creature."

That was the Nigel I remembered, the man with whom I argued through many a night of beer and wine, who expected me to listen to myself as much as him. That Nigel was my mentor and, I'd thought, my friend. That man vanished when my abilities vanished. I was a tool for him before that and didn't have the brains to realize it. He had even tried to kill me since then, although Briallen, the true mentor in my life, didn't believe that was his intent. She wasn't there. She didn't see the deadly essence strike aimed at my head, blocked only by Murdock's intervention. "I'm going to ask you again, Nigel. What are you doing here?"

He paused at the door, glancing at Meryl. "I came to visit a friend, Connor, and perhaps to help her in some way more productive than tucking her into bed."

I stared out the window after he left and watched wind-chopped waves whip past on the Charles River. The warmth of my breath fogged the glass, revealing a circle with a dot in the middle that someone had doodled. I added two eyes and a smile, glancing back at Meryl. She didn't react, of course, but a small part of me hoped she would. I slipped onto the edge of the bed and held her hand. "He's a jerk no matter what you say."

Her face remained slack, her eyes fixed on the ceiling. Silence wasn't one of Meryl's strong suits. Seeing her on a bed without a sharp observation or comment was like not seeing her at all. Something had driven away her mind. Gillen Yor, High Healer at AvMem, hadn't been able to break through the silence. Maybe I was wrong to resist Nigel's help, but I worried that he would make matters worse.

Meryl's hair had been dyed a fiery red. She changed the color regularly, but dark roots had appeared since she had been in the hospital. "Your dye job's growing out. I'd fix it, but you probably wouldn't like it." She didn't answer.

A nurse stopped short in the doorway. "I'm sorry, I didn't realize anyone was in here."

I hopped off the bed. "I was visiting. Do you know if Gillen Yor is around?"

The nurse pulled a cart into the room. "He's down at the desk. Can you excuse us a moment?"

"Sure."

I found the nurses' station empty. Glancing down, I noticed the file rack for the floor patients. As casually as possible, I craned my neck to see into nearby rooms for Gillen Yor. I pulled Meryl's file. It was nosy and a violation and wrong, but she didn't have anyone acting as a health-care proxy. I skimmed through the notes, deciphering Gillen's scrawl as best I could. I didn't understand most of it—trance sessions, spell orders, and essence ward boosters mixed with standard physical care like saline fluids and electrolytes. No eureka moments.

Gillen Yor yanked the chart out of my hands and shoved it back in the rack. "Mind your business."

I hadn't sensed him come up behind me. Even as I turned toward him, he relaxed the body shield that had hidden his essence. He had snuck up on me on purpose. "I'm sorry."

Gillen was over a foot shorter than me, a strange man with a halo of gray hair circling his bald spot. He pulled at the hair often when he was thinking. Staring up at me, he tilted his head to the side. "No, you're not. You want to know what's going on, ask me."

"Okay, what's going on?"

He slipped his hands into his doctor's coat and shrugged. "Nothing. No responses to anything yet. Nigel gave me some things to think about, but I'm not confident."

"If it's coming from Nigel, I'm not either," I said.

He peered at me with his usual angry attitude. "I don't give a damn about your personal opinions, Grey. If the Elven King himself gave me an idea I thought would work, I'd damned well use it."

I tamped down my own anger. Given Gillen's personality, there was no competing with him in the annoyance department anyway. He didn't care what I thought, didn't care what anyone thought. He lived and breathed the healing arts and was the best druid healer alive. I was his biggest failure. For years, he had been trying to figure out the dark thing in my head. With Meryl, he had another mystery on his hands, and I suspected he blamed me for it. "I didn't mean . . . I don't know what I meant."

He shook his head. "You look like hell. That thing in your head looks like a dagger. Does it hurt?"

Like Nigel, Gillen was a powerful enough druid to scan me from a distance. Touching made the exam more refined, but it wasn't always necessary. "No. Well, yeah, but no different than usual."

"I saw video of what you did down in the Weird. Actually, I didn't see a damned thing, but darkness. Can you control it?" he asked.

At one point during the riot, I lost control of myself. I thought Meryl was dead, and a fury built inside me that I didn't know I was capable of. I remembered the dark mass spiraling out of me, becoming a huge cloud of shadow that sucked up essence in its wake. It happened so fast and I was so angry, I don't know if I made it do that or if the darkness took advantage of my mental state somehow.

I closed my eyes, touched the dark spot in my mind with a mental nudge from the essence in my body signature. The dark mass didn't move or respond in any way. I opened my eyes. "Not now. I might have then. I don't know how."

He grunted, pulling his hair on one side as he stalked off. "Stay out of my files, Grey."

Back in Meryl's room, the nurse had gone. Meryl was in the chair by the window again, staring at the glass. The smiley face had been wiped away.

I nudged Meryl legs closer to the chair and pulled at her hand. She rose on unsteady feet. I led her out of the room and to the elevator. She responded to touch, to pushes and pulls. Gillen suggested that I take her for walks and give her exercise she wouldn't get lying in a hospital bed. The walks made me feel like she was okay. Whatever was wrong, she was still in there, remembering how to walk and how to eat and how to breathe. To my layman's mind, that was more than reptilian brain.

Meryl was lost, but not gone. The woman I knew—and loved—was inside this silent shell. If I had faith in anything, it was in her will to survive. I was going to be there for her.

# 4

I wandered through the deep end of the Weird later that night, testing the air for essence. For weeks, the strange cloud of blue light had been sweeping the neighborhood, a rush of essence that surged into being as if out of nowhere. In its wake, people disappeared. Eorla had expressed concern because a number of Teutonic fey were among the missing. She worried that it might be overzealous supporters of her cause against the Consortium and the Seelie Court.

At first, I considered it might be a new form of the Taint, the virulent corruption of essence that had driven the fey mad. Eorla had been powerful enough to dominate and contain it. I saw no sign that she had been affected by it or that it had become loose again. The Taint was gone. Whatever this new problem was, it was its own thing.

My main challenge was finding it. I had seen it in the distance a number of times, but by the time I reached each location, it had vanished. It followed no decipherable pattern, and while many of its victims were dwarves and druids, plenty of other fey went missing, too. It was hard to get a handle on how many. People in the Weird received little attention from the police when they reported someone missing. Over time, a culture of acceptance evolved, unexplained disappearances another part of what it meant to live in the neighborhood.

Tonight, I had seen it once a few blocks away, a flash of bright blue roaring across a small intersection. There was no trace of it by the time I reached the corner. The intersection was in an out-of-the-way corner of the neighborhood, off the main streets, where few people lived and fewer businesses operated. The four buildings that sat on the corners of the intersection were boarded up, dark and empty observers over an abandoned street.

Druids have a talent for total recall. If I found an essence signature, I could file it away in my memory and recognize it if I ran into it again. Whatever this blue thing was, it was a kind of essence that left no trace behind. I had nothing to tag and had never seen anything like it.

The air had a sharp tang to it, like the aftermath of someone's firing concentrated essence as a weapon. Essence itself was absent, much like it had been at the murder scene last night. As I moved along the sidewalk, I picked up faded essence from the Dead, which resonated differently from the living.

Essence dissipated in open air. The one consistent thing I had been finding at the sites of the blue essence was old Dead signatures, the faded remnants of their passage. Recognizing a specific essence, I could estimate how long ago the person had passed through. The degradation in the essence intensity gave me a time frame much like Janey Likesmith could estimate how long a body had been dead by taking its temperature.

I suspected the blue essence was following the Dead. In every location I knew, I had found old essence. What I couldn't make sense of was the time frame between the Dead's passing through and the blue essence following. The Dead essence had faded much earlier than the blue. I stepped off the curb and crouched in the gutter. Drawing on my body essence, I boosted my sensing ability to examine the Dead essence. The dark mass in my head wouldn't let me access essence outside my body, but it let me use my sensing ability without any pain. I had learned that seeking essence was what the dark mass did. It wasn't doing me any favors. If anything, I was doing it one.

With my heightened sensing, the Dead essence burned brighter, allowing me to see farther along the trail. Even that tapered off to nothing a few feet away. I was stumped.

A pink light burst into the air in front of me, and the twelve-inch-tall figure of Stinkwort—Joe, to his friends— made a wobbly somersault. Joe's a flit, one of the small fairies no more than a foot tall. His wings were longer than he was, a bright pink that he was as self-conscious about as his real name. I've known him all my life. He drinks more than anyone I know, doesn't care if I yell or snore, and has more going on in his head than I dare to contemplate.

"Ah, there you are, my friend, in the gutter where you work best," he said.

I stretched to my feet. "If it wasn't for gutters, we'd never see each other."

He blinked his wide eyes at me. "That's very touching."

"Have you seen this blue essence that's been showing up?"

He tilted his head from side to side. "Up where?"

"Here. Around the Weird. Flashes by, and people disappear," I said.

He pursed his lips and hovered in a circle. "Are you sure they don't disappear because you show up? I noticed that happens a lot with you."

Joe was one part friend, one part reality-checker, and lots of parts drinking buddy. We tore each other down like only best friends can do and still be friends. That also means sometimes we didn't have the same conversation we thought we were having.

I wasn't finding anything I hadn't seen before and decided to call it a night. I walked toward Old Northern Avenue, with Joe flying upside down beside me. "Doesn't that make you dizzy?" I asked.

He laughed. "Sure, but if I get sick, I'm in the perfect position not to get anything on me. You should try it."

"I can't fly, Joe," I said.

He righted himself. "Oh, great. Another thing for you to complain about."

"Will you stop? I'm not in the mood," I said. He pouted but kept silent. We made it to Old Northern without another word. "I'm sorry I snapped," I said.

"I know," he said.

He flew beside me, sometimes a few feet ahead, sometimes wandering off to the side. A small smile stayed on his lips, as if he were thinking of something amusing.

"You're not mad?" I asked.

He flipped backwards in an arc in front of me. "You had a bad day. It happens. Not my fault, right?"

"It's more than that. It's Meryl and Nigel and a dead dwarf," I said.

He frowned in concentration. "Was this at a party you didn't invite me to?"

To this day, I never know if he was serious when he said things like that. "Different things, but related. Nigel wants to be friends again."

"And that's"— he peered at me—"nice?"

"Suspicious. He saw what happened when the black mass came out of me during the riots. I think his wheels are turning about how to exploit it."

"Well, that's his job, init? You need to stop trying to make him into something he's not. *You* thought you were friends. You weren't. You worked together. Nigel isn't anyone's friend. Haven't you noticed?"

I stopped walking. "How do you do that?"

He hovered in place. "Do what?"

"Point out the completely obvious that I miss?"

He chuckled as he grabbed the pole of a street sign and spun around it. "Oh, that's easy. You think too much. That's from Nigel, always looking for motives and such. Every-one knows how he is, so everyone acts like him when he's around. Getting sucked up in his world is part of his world. He needs to get laid."

Flits have a voracious appetite when it comes to sex. "That's not the answer to everything, you know," I said.

He waggled his eyebrows at me. "It's the answer to enough things to make it worthwhile."

"Not for me anymore."

He landed on a destroyed telephone box. "Connor, you've changed. What happened to that guy who used to have fun?"

I had changed. Once, I would have brushed off the snubs and the drama and gone on my way. The difference was back then I could afford to. I had money, power, and influence. With any one of those things, life was easier. Once they were all gone, I realized not everyone lived like that—more, that most people never had a chance to live like that precisely because of the people who lived like that. It didn't have to be that way. It made me angry often and, yeah, depressed, but I didn't think I wasn't fun to be around.

"Am I really no fun anymore?"

"Only when you're awake," said Joe, then grinned from ear to ear. He started wringing his hands. "Oh, woe is me! The world is so awful. People die, and everything is shite, and it's all my fault."

I glared at him. "Not funny."

He hovered up and snapped his fingers in my face. "No kidding. You know what's going on other places? People are nervous and scared and looking for comfort. And you know what happens next? Lots of sex and alcohol, and you're moping around like a schoolboy on a date with his hand."

I rolled my eyes. "Wow. I can't believe you'd take advan-tage like that, Joe. That's a new low even for you."

He pulled his chin in. "Me? *I* tell *them* I'm nervous and scared. You would not believe the action I've been getting."

I laughed, not just because it was funny but because he was that serious, which made it funnier. "Somewhere along the way, the world went seriously wrong."

He sighed. "Again with the everything-is-wrong."

Exasperated, I spread out my hands. "All right, all right, I get the message. I'm no fun. I complain. I'm a pessimist. No one likes to be around me. I get it already."

Joe looked at me with a solemn face. "Boy, do you have a self-esteem problem."

Laughing, I batted at him, but he flitted away. "I can't win with you."

He clapped his hands and rubbed them together. "Is that an invitation to poker?"

I shook my head in defeat. "You win. Where to?"

He flapped his wings and spun in a circle. "Oh, the places we'll go!"

He zipped ahead of me on the sidewalk. Sometimes, having Joe as a friend was worth doing the wrong thing for the right reasons.

# 5

In a booth halfway to the back of the Rose Rose the next day, I nursed a mug of coffee. Somehow, despite all the riot mess that had happened right around the corner on Old Northern Avenue, the old bar and grill hadn't been damaged. Having one thing in my life remain the same was small comfort, but I took it where I could.

Midday in the Weird was the start of the day in the neighborhood. The only people showing energy were the waitstaff as they hustled late breakfast specials to customers making a grudging attempt to face the day. I sensed Murdock enter behind me, his body signature an unmistakable combination of druid and human. He hung his coat on a peg and slid into the booth. "Is it bright in here?"

I took my sunglasses off. "I had a long night."

Murdock sipped a soda I had ordered for him. "Were you looking into those essence surges?"

"For a while. I met up with Joe later, had a few beers."

Murdock seemed off, distracted, as he skimmed the menu.

"I wanted to talk to you about something. Bernard is going to run for city council in the fall."

Bernard was the second oldest Murdock sibling and a police officer who wanted to make a transition into civilian life, if politics could be called civilian. I didn't know him well since he worked down in Dorchester, the large Boston neighborhood to the south. "His wife must be happy he's getting out."

A waitress refilled my coffee and took our food order.

"She is, but you might not be," he said.

I leaned away from a sunbeam that was playing havoc with my headache. "Meaning?"

Murdock met my eyes. "Meaning he's not going to be a fey advocate. He's going to be saying things you're not going to like. I wanted you to hear it from me before you get all why-didn't-you-tell-me on me."

The coffee tasted bitter, but I drank it. "You make me sound whiny."

With practiced indifference, Murdock checked out the bar. "You are sometimes."

I let the comment slide. I *was* whiny sometimes, like when I got bad news when I have a hangover headache and the caffeine hasn't kicked in yet. "Isn't that going to be a problem for him?"

"It'll probably be a plus in the current situation," he said.

The waitress reappeared and landed a burger the size of my head on the table with a plate of fries. They smelled like heaven. "So what happens when people find out Bern's half-druid?" I asked.

For years, the Murdock family believed that their mother, Amy, died in a car accident after Kevin, her youngest, was born. She didn't, and she wasn't a human named Amy. Through my natural tendency to rip people's guts out, I had exposed the whole sorry tale.

A druidess named Moira Cashel had glamoured herself as Amy Sullivan, met and married Scott Murdock, and bore him children—five sons and two daughters, all cops except Kevin, who became a firefighter. When Scott Murdock found out who—and what—she was, he disowned Amy and threatened to kill her if she ever again set foot in Boston. The commissioner was a Catholic of the old school who believed the fey were demons. You weren't supposed to marry them, but threatening to kill them was okay.

Twenty-plus years later, Amy returned in her true identity of Moira Cashel. She seduced Scott Murdock—again—and brought about his downfall. Scott tried to kill her, but the Guildmaster, Manus ap Eagan, killed him in what I hoped was an accident.

Murdock rearranged his grilled chicken sandwich on his plate. I had a twinge of guilt at all the fat and oil in front of me, but my stomach demanded that a night of beer be salved with salt and fried food.

"That's what I wanted to talk to you about," he said.

He became intent on his sandwich and avoided making eye contact. "Damn, Leo. You haven't told them, have you?"

He dropped his sandwich on the plate and slumped in his seat. "What am I supposed to say? Mom was a lying druid who abandoned her kids, then came back to cause Da's death? And, oh, by the way, Gerry, that was her you shot in the face?"

In the confusion of the riot, Gerry Murdock had fired on Cashel and killed her. It wasn't quite cold blood—she was breaking the law—but it wasn't the cleanest police shooting. I didn't think Gerry murdered her like I had taunted him the other night. It was an accident, an impulsive act that shouldn't have happened. I dropped my gaze. "Danu's blood, Leo, I didn't mean it like that."

He picked at his fingernails. "I'm sorry. It's just . . . I don't know what to say or do. They already think you had something to do with my father's death. What are they going to think when they find about . . . the other thing?"

The other thing was a big thing. I had had an affair with Moira when I was much younger and, unbeknownst to me, was the catalyst for the breakup of the Murdock marriage. I didn't know Amy was married. I was too dumb to suspect it.

I was blinded by my emotions, too young to understand the difference between hormones and love.

Once Scott Murdock found out about the affair, the rest of Amy's—Moira's—secrets came out. I wasn't privy to all the details of that because I didn't believe Moira was who she said she was until too late. "Leo, I can't begin to know what you or your family are going through, but don't hide this from them. Your father lied all those years about your mother and became a bitter man. I don't want that to happen to you."

A pained smile flickered on his face. "I don't want to make a choice between family and friends."

I faked throwing a fry at him, but they tasted too good to waste. "There is no choice, Leo. Besides, I'm used to a Murdock or two hating me. It's my shit, not yours. I'll deal with it."

"Right now it's easier to blame you than my dad. Maybe they'll come around," he said. Maybe, but I doubted it. I wasn't a particularly close friend of the family to begin with and had made more than one faux pas around them. Being involved in the deaths of both their parents was not high on anyone's list of friendship criteria. It was a miracle in my book that Leo still talked to me. He told me he didn't blame me and that it was more important to forgive my involvement. It was a matter of faith for him. I didn't want to let that friendship go, but I didn't want it to cause more pain in his life either.

When I had first met Murdock, he asked me to help him with some minor fey-related crime cases, giving advice and pointing him in the right direction. His body signature read straight-up human, no doubt about it. We partnered on what came to be known as the Castle Island case. Murdock got hit with a spell backlash. His body signature started reading druid, and he also began to exhibit fey abilities like a body shield and physical strength. For almost a year, I had beaten myself up thinking I had caused the problem and that somehow his health might be at risk.

Since Moira Cashel died, Murdock's body signature had become more druidlike. I wasn't an essence expert, but the logical conclusion was that the stronger signature was some-how related to her death. I had sensed something fey around Gerry the other night, too, but other fey were around then, and I hadn't thought to probe. For a lot of reasons, I hadn't been around his other siblings. I had no idea if their signatures had changed, too.

"Has anyone else shown fey abilities?" I asked.

He frowned. "My brothers and sisters? Why would they?"

I finished the last of my fries. "Leo, since Cashel died, your body signature has been more intense. I thought maybe I was getting a more precise reading on you because of my own ability issues, but now I think I'm sensing your true essence for the first time. And if your abilities have increased, then maybe something might show up in the rest of your family, too."

He became still, staring at the table as the thought sunk in. "I didn't consider that. Damn."

"I'm no expert, but Cashel might have used a masking spell on her children that failed when she died. It wouldn't surprise me given your father's feelings about the fey. I think we should talk to Briallen. She's the essence expert."

Upset, he rubbed at his mouth. "This isn't a sneaky way of getting me to see a fey doctor again?"

On more than one occasion, I had tried to get Murdock to see a fey healer. He refused, content that the fey essence he exhibited wasn't a problem. He was right in one respect. The essence hadn't affected his health except to make it bet-ter. What had worried me were potential long-term effects. Now that we knew his mother was fey, I was more concerned about his use of ability than his health. "I am suggesting you talk to someone who has experience as a druidic mentor, Leo. Briallen taught me more about understanding my abili-ties than anyone."

He didn't look happy. "All right, I'll talk to her."

"I'll make the arrangements. In the meantime, I'd keep an eye on your brothers and sisters. If they manifest essence abilities, it could be dangerous without training."

We didn't speak for several moments. Murdock wiped a

napkin around the table, then crumpled it on his plate. "My parents were married before you met Moira, Connor."

"I know that," I said.

He leaned forward, staring in my eyes. "I'm saying it happened before you came along, Connor. She lied to him before you were even part of the picture. Do you understand what I'm saying? This would be happening to me if you and I had never met. It's not your fault no matter how much you want it to be."

Uncomfortable and uncertain, I shifted in my seat. "I never said I wanted it to be."

"You didn't have to. Stop trying to fix things all the time. You have to know when to let things work out on their own."

Joe had said as much the night before. "I'll try. You know it's not my nature."

He slid out of the booth and put his coat on. "Yeah, well, I'm planning on not letting nature control how I live my life. You should give it a try."

# 6

The angry drone of my apartment intercom sliced through my brain like a buzz saw. Hangovers and unexpected visitors made a bad combination, especially when the visitor announced himself as a messenger from the Guild. I took my time getting down to the front door. Guild messengers were notorious for their imperiousness, so rushing wasn't going to make the encounter any better. He handed me a request for my presence at a meeting with Acting Guildmaster Ryan macGoren. True to form, the messenger didn't wait for a response before spinning on his heel and leaving.

By the time I returned upstairs, Briallen verch Gwyll ab Gwyll had left a message that she was sending a car for me. She had been a member of the Boston Guild almost since its founding, so it was no surprise she had received an invitation to the meeting.

A little more than an hour later, the two of us sat in a black car inching its way down Tremont Street. I missed having driver service. The Guild disability checks didn't cover it, and neither did the retirement benefits.

Briallen had been prickly from the moment she got in the car. On the opposite side of the seat, she cocked an eye at me. "Stop fidgeting."

"I am not," I said.

"You're picking at a scab. That's fidgeting," she said.

I chuckled. I *was* picking at a scab. A small cut on my hand that I didn't remember getting had healed over, but a sliver remained behind the skin. "You need to relax."

"I am relaxed," she said.

She was lying, of course. Briallen verch Gwyll ab Gwyll did not like to be taken by surprise, and being asked to the Guildhouse on short notice by Ryan macGoren was loaded with the potential for surprise, especially when she found out I was on his dance card, too. I was suspicious of whatever he had in store, but I had nothing else planned for the afternoon. "I'm only going because you said I should," I said.

"Since when have you ever done anything you're told?" she said.

Briallen had been my mentor during my teenage years. I had lived at her house a good portion of those years, under her rules. I had been on my own for a long time now, but sometimes she forgot I wasn't a teenager anymore. I would never admit that I enjoyed it, like when it allowed me to tease her as if she were a cranky nanny. "Maybe if you told me the right thing to do, I would do it."

She hit me with a playful slap on the arm. "Fine. Don't talk until we're leaving."

"What if someone asks me a question?"

She sighed. "Do you see? Do you see how you don't listen?"

Stress showed in the tautness of her face. Druids weren't immortal, but they lived a long time. Briallen was close to a century in age, maybe older if she had lived in Faerie. Many of the Old Ones claimed not to remember Faerie. Briallen would never answer the question about herself, preferring to keep people guessing. She was ageless to me. She didn't look a day over fifty, her rich chestnut hair worn short, not a touch of gray in its waves.

The Guildhouse rose into view as we entered Park Square. The building had started out life in the eighteen hundreds as an armory, a solid granite fortress for an army cadet group that preceded the National Guard in pre-Convergence Boston. When the group fell on hard financial times after Convergence, the Guild bought the place for its Boston headquarters.

Manus ap Eagan had overseen the reconstruction in those early years. He had expanded the concept of druid hedges—essence barriers—into the formidable shield dome. When activated to the extreme, it was visible as a wall of thickened air, impenetrable to everything short of bunker-buster-level bombs. The fey knew how to protect themselves. The dome acted like a body shield for the building, a transparent layer of essence that protected the Guildhouse from attack. Rumor had it that even a nuke would only dent it. High Queen Maeve loved the idea, particularly early on, when humans were more antagonistic to the arrival of the fey.

In time, floors were added, and the building grew over the Boston skyline, flouting the laws of nature and local zoning. Towers, sky bridges, and random wings joined together in a mishmash of Victorian, Gothic, and fairy architecture. Essence defied the forces of physics, allowing for tall towers to be anchored by slender buttresses or steep-gabled additions to hang off the building with little physical support. Beautiful in a surreal, amusing way, the building had become one part monolith and one part confection. I shuddered to think what a pretender like macGoren would do to the place if given the chance.

The car engine coughed and recovered as we passed through the shield dome. Engines didn't work well around essence. Brownie security guards in dark maroon uniforms that offset their pale hair and tawny skin gathered along the sidewalk in front of the lobby. Their security role included community relations, which meant making it clear to the local community that if it didn't comply with their directions, the guard could go boggie. A brownie in its boggart aspect was a fearsome thing, all tooth and claw.

Today, the guards remained attentive and at ease. They

worked the street level since the people they encountered were human and solitaries, not powerful in the essence department. They might take Briallen down if there were enough of them, but few were powerful contenders. They had nothing to fear from me, of course, provided the black mass in my head stayed put.

I helped Briallen from the car out of courtesy. She was no invalid. As we walked under the portico to the main entrance, something tickled against me, and my body shield shimmered. It wasn't a full shield anymore, small patches here and there, and malfunctioned by triggering on its own.

I paused in the archway beneath the great dragon head carved above the lintel. Gargoyles once clustered on the ceiling and columns of the portico. They were fey in the sense they were sentient stone, even the ones that didn't look human or animal. They appeared after Convergence, moving without being seen, speaking to people on rare occasions. No one ever sensed essence from them, though, which made them an interesting puzzle. They were attracted to essence and sought it out. Every Guildhouse had them anchored to the walls and ceilings. The Boston gargoyles were all gone now. They had moved to Boston Common and taken up residence around a giant stone pillar there that generated enormous amounts of essence.

Briallen glanced at me, but I shook my head. Whatever I was sensing must have been a new security measure. "This isn't a trap. Tell me again this isn't a trap," I said.

"It's not a trap," Briallen said. Her expression held a touch of uncertainty, which didn't make me comfortable. She had nothing to fear, but over the last months, the Guild had been trying to arrest me for one bogus reason or another. Why I was such a threat to them baffled me. I had been involved in more than one major disaster in the city, but I hadn't caused them and had always been on the side that ended them. Yet the Guild acted like I was the primary reason for all its troubles. I was more than happy to blame myself for stuff. I didn't try to imprison myself as punishment for it.

We rode the elevator to the seventeenth floor. Guild security agents, powerful Danann fairies in black uniforms and chromed helmets, their diaphanous wings undulating, waited for us when the doors opened. Security agents were the mobile powerhouses of protection for the Guild. They were strict, forceful, and aggressive in their jobs. Conversation wasn't their strong suit.

"Please follow me to the Receiving Hall," one of them said.

Surprised, I murmured to Briallen, "The Receiving Hall? We're meeting in the Receiving Hall?"

Briallen licked her lips in distaste. "This is so Ryan. You know he needs his ego stroked even if he's the one doing it."

The Receiving Hall of the Guildhouse served as the room of state for official duties of the Seelie Court. When the Guildmaster sat in the hall, for all intents and purposes, he or she was the voice of the Court and spoke with Maeve's authority, a privilege with a double-edged sword. No one wanted to speak for Maeve and get it wrong. To my knowledge, Manus ap Eagan, the current Guildmaster, didn't like to use it. Since he was in a coma and had left no one to act in his stead, no one was around to stop macGoren.

The agent escorted us to another set of elevators. With the additions to the building, elevators were scattered about in order to access odd sections and floors that didn't reside in a standard vertical. "He's not Guildmaster. Nigel should be Acting Guildmaster."

"Nigel resigned the position before Manus went into the coma. You were there the day he did if I remember correctly," she said.

Manus liked having Nigel as his second because he knew Nigel didn't want the job. If he had any idea that macGoren was acting as de facto Guildmaster, he would have awakened from his coma without outside help.

"Then you should do it. You were Guildmaster once," I said. Briallen had been Guildmaster a few times in Eagan's absence, but not in my lifetime. As the twentieth century progressed, she had found other interests and kept her hand in local affairs only when reason demanded it.

Brownie guards opened the doors to the hall. "I wasn't asked, and I have better things to do right now," she said.

"No one asked macGoren."

"Let it go, Connor. It's a thankless job that no one except Ryan wants. No one can do a good job at it unless they commit. Let's hope Gillen Yor figures out how to wake up Manus before Ryan does something stupid," she said.

Ten flights higher, we exited onto a narrow concourse in a tower that hung over empty space. We entered a sky bridge that connected the tower to the main part of the building by an intricate mesh of steel holding together a hallway of glass walls and ceiling. The rounded bank of windows to either side showed an amazing view of the Charles River to the north and Boston's outer harbor to the south. The stark exposure left humans feeling uneasy, but the fey were not afraid of heights.

The bridge joined the Receiving Hall in a seamless transition. A grand medallion design in the floor marked the threshold, a mosaic of stones set with Maeve's favorite sigil—three cups arranged in a circle, one each in bronze, silver, and gold, embossed with birds, symbols of her penchant for bestowing valuable gifts at a great price.

In the hall proper, tall narrow windows of leaded glass let in light that reflected off a gem-encrusted ceiling. Between the windows, pilasters shaped like trees rose, their branches splitting in a uniform symmetrical pattern to form the ceiling vaults. Crystal lanterns hung from the branches and threw subtle golden hues. Power radiated throughout the room, the power of the Seelie Court and the power of essence. It was the heart of the Guildhouse, shimmering with essence in every nook and cranny.

MacGoren, at least, had chosen not to claim the Guildmaster's chair at the far end of the hall. Instead, he sat at the head of a table that had been brought in. His pale wings spread up and to the sides, their surfaces shifting in hues of red and gold. He did his best to appear formidable, but his innate smugness prevented him from succeeding. Since coming to Boston, he had become a major player in the city and the social scene, his good looks and money opening doors with ease. I had noticed younger Danann fairies on the street mimicking his hairstyle, wavy plaits of blond that stopped at the shoulders.

MacGoren had Maeve's blessing, which made his rise swift and easy. Manus ap Eagan had been ill for the last few years, and Maeve wanted him to step aside for macGoren. As an underKing of the Seelie Court, Manus was entitled to choose when he wanted to retire, but he had refused. He might have been ill, an odd occurrence among the powerful Danann fairy clan, but he never seemed to think he would die, a more rare occurrence. His falling into a coma allowed macGoren to take advantage of the situation.

My second surprise of the day was finding Eorla seated to macGoren's left. Rand stood at attention several feet behind her, his gaze in a constant sweep of the room. He trusted the Guild less than I did. Nigel sat to macGoren's right. While he declined to run the Guildhouse, he always had a hand in the governing of the place. Unlike macGoren, he didn't care what his official title was or whom it impressed.

Briallen leaned on my arm as we approached. "Be on your toes because I may not be able to advise you as openly as I'd like."

She assessed the two empty seats, then sat next to Nigel and across from Eorla. MacGoren's lips dipped in annoyance as I took the chair at the opposite end of the table from him. We didn't like each other. I knew about a few skeletons in his closet. Nothing that Maeve didn't know, but he would have bad press to deal with if I went public. I hadn't. He didn't know I wouldn't. If I did, I would lose any advantage I had over him.

"I suppose I should thank you for coming," he said.

"Don't hurt yourself," I said.

Briallen shot me a warning glance. "What's this about, Ryan? Where's Melusine?"

Melusine Blanc was the director who represented the interests of the solitary fey. She was a water sprite, strange and quiet. Neither the Celts nor the Teuts called her an ally, which gave her more power in close voting. It was unusual for her not to show for a board meeting. The dwarf representative wasn't there either, but I had never heard of his attending a meeting. I didn't even know who the current one was. The Guild board of directors had become a strange collection of people, which made Manus's role challenging, what with all the conflicting agendas. If Manus had to grapple with them, MacGoren didn't have much hope.

"This isn't a board meeting, per sc," macGoren said.

Eorla folded her hands on the table. "Nevertheless, Melusine sends her regrets."

I chuckled at her small smile. Since declaring the Weird under her protection—and the solitaries that lived there—Eorla had in effect become their representative. Melusine might have objected, but she didn't. She probably liked the power Eorla brought to the table. Eorla had shown a little of that power by making it clear to macGoren that Melusine had spoken to her, not him. I did like her style.

"Then what is this?" Briallen asked.

MacGoren pushed a folder toward me. "A compromise."

Inside the folder was a series of legal documents with my name written all over them. I skimmed the first few pages. "You're having the charges against me dropped?"

MacGoren had done some political maneuvering to discredit Eagan, part of which was helping the local and federal police accuse me of a long list of felonies. Eagan knew what was going on and managed to turn the tables on him. He didn't have time to clear up my legal problems before he collapsed. I wasn't sure he would have. I appreciated the problems Eagan caused macGoren, but I had to look over my shoulder every time I left the Weird and Eorla's protection.

"In exchange for your agreement to hold the Guild harmless for any past actions," macGoren said.

I didn't have a prayer of holding the Guild legally responsible for anything they did to me. I was broke, and it had the power and resources of the Seelie Court behind it. That didn't mean I wasn't going to expose their actions when I could, but a courthouse wasn't going to be the best route for me. "Seems easy enough."

"There are contingencies involved," he said.

The other shoe dropping was expected. I made a show of boredom as I flipped through the documents. "Such as?"

"You will submit to the jurisdiction of this Guildhouse, present yourself for examination by Nigel Martin, and assist us in bringing Bergin Vize to justice," he said.

Of all the things I could have predicted, being offered a job wasn't on the list. "You're hiring me back?"

He pursed his lips. "I wouldn't put it that way."

I glanced at Eorla. Vize wanted her protection, and she had refused to grant it so far. The issue was eating her up, I knew, since she had raised the monster as her own son. MacGoren was sending her a message that the Guild hadn't wavered from its intention to take Vize out at the first opportunity. "I have no idea where Bergin Vize is," I said.

"Finding him should be a keen motivation for the benefits we are offering you. I understand you have personal reasons for pursuing him as well," he said.

I pushed the folder back. "I'm not signing. I'm done playing the victim in Guildhouse games, macGoren. Let the feds arrest me. I'm sure you don't want it public that you bribed a police commissioner and were instrumental in causing the riots in the Weird, to say nothing of a few other things I know you want buried. I can make those charges disappear on my own if it comes to that."

He smiled. "I had nothing to do with Scott Murdock's choices. Unfortunately, he is dead. There is no connection to me."

I smiled back. MacGoren didn't know that the commissioner had had quite the heart-to-heart with his son Leo before everything went to hell. "Maybe. And maybe the commissioner confessed to a credible witness about what happened. You do know that Eagan knew what you were doing? He never told me his sources, but I'm sure they won't remain quiet for long either."

By the expression on his face, he didn't know Eagan

was onto him. He looked at Briallen. "Unless this matter is resolved, Lady Briallen, you run the risk of harboring a fugitive."

Briallen shifted in her seat, chuckling low. "Me?"

"I have reports that you have entertained this man at your home knowing full well the charges against him," he said.

"Is that why I'm here, Ryan?" she asked. "To blackmail me into pressuring Connor to sign? You're playing way out of your league. I don't answer to you or the human government and never will."

With a languid undulation of his wings, macGoren settled back in his chair. "I'm sure Maeve will be interested in your position. I believe she is quite keen to have the matter of Connor Grey settled."

Briallen eyed him with impatience. "Threatening me with the wrath of the Seelie Court, now? You really don't know what you're doing. Go ahead. I'm a member of the Court, and you're not. Maeve will have to move carefully against me if she wants to maintain support."

Unflustered, MacGoren arched an eyebrow. "Nigel?"

Nigel cleared his throat. "Sign the papers, Connor. We may not agree on things anymore, but I do not wish you ill. Unlike Briallen, you are not a member of the Court. If you don't sign, the High Queen will accuse you of the murder of Ceridwen underQueen. I have that from her very lips. Ryan's shenanigans won't even come into play."

I fell back in my chair. Vize had killed Ceridwen, and everyone knew it. The High Queen didn't like me, but I didn't think I attracted enough of her attention to resort to framing me for murder. "Is this how you make friends again, Nigel?" I asked.

He scoffed. "I'm trying to save your life, Connor. Sign the damned papers. You want to go after Bergin Vize anyway."

"Since you know that, Nigel, then you know I don't need or want the Guild's permission to do it. The only thing you need my agreement on is to be your guinea pig, and that isn't going to happen," I said.

Eorla leaned down and retrieved a briefcase from beside

her chair. She placed it on the table. "Is that everything, Ryan? Are you finished?"

MacGoren narrowed his eyes as he stared at the case. "The offer is firm."

Eorla opened the briefcase and withdrew some papers. She handed a set to Ryan and another to me. "I believe the offer is moot."

Briallen leaned over to see the documents. I skimmed through them, trying not to laugh. Briallen smiled as I handed them to her, and she passed them to Nigel. The U.S. attorney general was suspending the investigation and dropping all charges against me. MacGoren went white with anger, his wings flickering with points of red essence. "When did this happen?"

Eorla closed the briefcase. "This morning. I would have sent it over by messenger, but since you called this meeting, I thought I'd save the expense and deliver them personally. I believe we are done here." She nodded to Briallen and Nigel. "I trust you both will have good days."

She lifted the briefcase and walked down the hall, Rand following close behind.

Nigel tossed the papers on the table. "Maeve will make her accusation, Connor. You won't be able to stand against her." He didn't threaten. I almost believed he didn't want it to happen.

I stood. "Tell Maeve to bring it on, Nigel. I will blow her accusation out of the water." I looked at macGoren. "I guess I'm done, too. Thanks anyway, macGoren. How's Keeva, by the way? She should be having the baby any day now, right?"

Keeva was my old Guild partner. She and Ryan had had an affair, and she had returned to Tara to have the baby that resulted. He glared at me. "Get the hell out."

Briallen wasted no time joining me at the elevator. When the doors closed, she let out a peal of laughter. "That was brilliant. I have never underestimated Eorla and her resources. She knows how to keep things entertaining."

I laughed, too. "I should be angry, but that was so perfect, I can't be."

"I don't know what Maeve sees in Ryan," Briallen said, as we arrived in the lobby.

"What we just saw—a lapdog to do her bidding."

She slipped her arm through mine as we walked to the car. "I am concerned, though. Nigel wasn't playing along. Maeve is gunning for you. She won't stop until she's satisfied."

"What the hell is it, Briallen? I know I've interfered with a few of her plans, but she wants me dead?"

Briallen settled into the backseat. "I don't know. Maybe it's about Ceridwen. You were there when she died in Maeve's service."

As an underQueen of the Seelie Court, Ceridwen had come to Boston to interrogate me. A series of events led to her death, which sent the entire Seelie Court into alarm. "Maeve betrayed her, Briallen. She left Ceridwen alone without help, and that's why she died. Ceridwen made me promise not to tell."

Briallen gaped, something I did not believe possible. Briallen always knew more than she let on, and this was something she didn't know. "Now I see the problem."

"And why I'm calling her bluff to publicly accuse me. If the other underQueens and -Kings find out, Maeve is in deep political trouble," I said.

"Can you prove it?" she asked.

"More than you know," I said. Ceridwen may have died, but she had returned as one of the Dead, trapped on this side of the veil instead of moving on to the Celtic afterlife. I didn't tell Briallen because Ceridwen had asked me to keep her existence a secret. She was in hiding somewhere in the city. If I needed her, it would only be a matter of time for her to hear about it.

"You do have a target on your back, Connor. You have to be careful."

I slumped in the seat. "Great. I thought you were going to say you'll talk to Maeve and tell her it's all a mistake."

Briallen looked away, her face troubled. "The mistake is hers, Connor. One, I think, we will all end up paying for."

# 7

Hours later, I was alone, leaning against a wall, my back to the door as I watched the action at the pool table at Yggy's bar. Low-hanging lamps illuminated the game in a stark circle of light that didn't reach much beyond the table. This early in the evening, the regulars played each other, moving the action along with a gesture or nod before sending their shots into pockets with a sharp clack. The real money to be made would happen later, when the newbies showed up and tried to beat them. A subdued murmur ran through the crowd. The loud voices that accompanied liquor-loosened tongues were hours away yet, as people settled in with early drinks and companionable conversation.

The old dive gave calm refuge to fey of all stripes in the Weird. If you had a beef with someone, you had to take it elsewhere, or you found yourself banned by Heydan, who ran the place. Heydan kept his own counsel, and an appearance outside his office was rare. I knew who he was but had never had the pleasure of a real introduction. Meryl knew him somehow. I was curious about that, but there wasn't much value in asking her. She wouldn't share it unless she wanted to, and so far she hadn't. Of course, under the circumstances, I might never hear that tale. I pushed the reminder of her condition aside and tried to focus on the pool game.

After leaving Briallen at her house, I had wandered back to the Weird, contemplating the strange path my life had taken. Back in my days as a Guild investigator, the twists and turns of the ruling classes were not a part of my world. Sure, I met the players and partied with them, which was social, and questioned them, which was work. I was never, though, a part of the political apparatus. Despite my high standing, I didn't have any influence because I wasn't interested. I saw now that Nigel had used me more than once as a political tool, but that was doing my job regardless of the political ramifications, not doing my job to create them.

Yet, now that I had no ability—or even an official job—I was called into meetings with Guildmasters and high druids, given ultimatums by fairy queens, and tempted by elven spies to do their bidding. For the last year, I had found myself pulled into one monarchial plot after another through no intention of my own. I thought I was doing a job—like assisting Murdock on a case—or helping a friend—like sharing information with Keeva, my old Guild partner. The next thing I knew, the world was blowing up around me, or people were trying to kill me.

Dwelling on the unanswerable was not my forte. I preferred concrete problems, like why this mysterious blue essence seemed to be connected to old Dead essence. I had put the word out that I would be at Yggy's tonight, and I wanted to see Banjo, a gruff guy who had helped me out a couple of times and knew the lay of the land when it came to strange happenings in the Weird. He was also a dwarf, so I hoped he might know something particular about the recent disappearances given that so many of his people were missing.

Banjo hadn't shown yet. At a glance, no dwarves were in the bar. The problem with arranging meetings with people you didn't have direct contact with was never knowing if they had gotten the message. If they showed up, great. If they didn't, you didn't know if they'd decided not to come or had never gotten the message. It took patience.

A slender solitary sat next to me on a stool. Her skin had the dark yellow coloring of the mountain elf clans, her hair a brittle patch of brown that looked like bramble bushes. She watched the game with no emotion, a short plastic cup in her hand. Unlike the other loners in the bar, she didn't check out who was coming and going but kept unwavering attention to the gameplay in front of us. She nursed her drink with brief sips.

An hour drained away with my second beer, and I ordered another. The bar became louder and more crowded. More serious pool players arrived, the casual amateurs fading to the sidelines. Every once in a while, I did a sensing sweep for Banjo.

The mountain elf spoke into her cup. "He's outside on Oh No. Follow him, but don't talk to him until he says it's okay." Nothing about her posture indicated she was talking to me, but no one else was nearby. She watched the game and finished off the last of her drink, then spoke without looking at me. "Banjo says he hasn't got all night."

For whatever reason, Banjo didn't want to come inside the bar. He and the solitary were exchanging sendings, so I guessed he didn't want to engage in a conversation right then. I slid my almost empty glass mug onto a ledge and pushed out of my position against the wall.

Halfway across the floor, a tremor prickled against my feet. It hadn't been that intense, but by the curious looks on some faces, others had noticed it, too. The office door swung open. Heydan paused in the doorway, prominent ridges of bone curling from his temples to the back of his head. His concerned glance swept the room before settling on me. A fine touch of essence wafted against my face, subtle enough not to disturb the dark mass in my head. Heydan's forehead relaxed in thought. He stepped back and closed the door. Meryl once said Heydan watches and listens for something, but she didn't know what. An uneasy feeling told me he might have heard what he had been waiting for. I didn't like that he looked at me.

I spotted Banjo as I left the alley that led to Yggy's at the end of the next block of Old Northern Avenue. He didn't acknowledge my presence but walked away deeper into the Weird. I followed, comfortable with the clandestine behavior. When you worked in the bad end of town, trying to find out things someone else didn't want you to know, people tended to be careful. After several blocks, he ducked into a store surrounded by shuttered businesses.

Instead of a bell ringing when I entered, a moan of pleasure sounded. Different Desires catered to the erotic toy market. Being in the Weird, it offered goods and services not found anywhere else. At the entrance, a subtle incense that prompted the desire for sex wafted over me. My body shields flickered but didn't activate. Sex apparently didn't threaten the black mass.

A dreadlocked kobold with long, beaded hair dyed three or four colors worked the register. The Teutonic kobolds had a vague relationship to Celtic brownies except their passive and aggressive natures were more integrated. The cashier had a bland expression tinged with annoyance belied by a soft voice as she explained the benefits of lubrication to the lone customer in the store.

Silicone products filled the shelves in an impressive array of shapes, sizes, and colors. For the right price, every need could be met with something that vibrated, pulsed, pumped, rotated, glowed, flashed, or undulated. Books and DVDs lined the back wall, featuring action that required a scorecard for the uninitiated.

Banjo perused the leather goods, sorting through belts, straps, and harnesses studded with steel nubs and spikes. He tested the tensile strength of a strip of leather. "What do you think? Buckles or snaps?"

"You can go tighter with buckles, but you can get out of snaps faster."

Bemused, he arched an eyebrow. "Really? Do tell."

"I've been a few places, seen a few things." The fey had

few sexual hang-ups. When they weren't at war with each other, they threw themselves into pleasures of the mind and body without the same taboos and restrictions so many humans had. I had been to my share of parties. Having said that, dwarves could be prudes, but only in comparison to other fey.

Banjo pressed his lower lip out in consideration and picked up a matching set of cuffs and collar. The kobold finished her sale and escorted the customer out the door. She called over her shoulder. "I'm going on break. You got ten minutes. Don't steal shit."

Banjo continued looking at harnesses. "I wonder if they do custom work."

"Yeah, they do," I said. He glanced at me. "So, I've heard. What's with the cloak and dagger, Banjo?"

He replaced the harness and crossed his arms. "People seen with you tend to end up in the hospital or the morgue."

"That's a little exaggeration," I said.

He cocked an eye at me, then went back to browsing. "What do you want, Grey?"

"I was wondering if you had heard about this blue essence that's been tearing up the neighborhood," I said.

He pursed his lips. "Heard about it. Seen it, too."

"And?"

He shrugged. "Why ask me?"

I followed him around the end of an aisle. "You're the closest thing I have to a connection down there. You guys aren't the friendliest bunch."

He strolled along the aisle and picked up a rather large box that contained a lifelike facsimile of an unexpected body part. "Depends on how you define friendly. For instance, I don't have to be here, ya know? I don't have to tell you that someone's looking for seers and scryers simply because some elf queen sent you down here, right?"

"You're absolutely right. What else might you not want to tell me about seers and scryers?"

He pulled out a pair of half-glasses to read the back of

the box. "Someone's offering big money to talk to any dwarf who has been here for the last century."

"Why dwarves?"

He replaced the box and picked up something I didn't recognize. It had its own remote and lots of buttons. I tried to read the label over his shoulder. "Resonance. Dwarves have been here a long time."

"Come again?"

He cocked his head at me. "You used to scry, right? You got better at it, didn't you? At least until you got all screwed up?"

I did my best not to feel insulted. "Sure."

He nodded once sharply. "It wasn't only skill. Scrying's about time, and spending time in one place attunes your ability to the time of that place, makes your scry better. Don't they teach you anything in those druid camps you guys go to?"

They didn't teach me that. Dwarves and druids had a long history of competition over who were better at predicting the future. "So, whoever is looking for dwarves wants to have as clear a picture of the future as possible?"

Banjo winked. "Now you got it."

"But that's what everybody wants," I said.

"Yeah, but not everyone has the cash to pay for the real deal," he said.

Contrary to popular belief—or hope—scrying wasn't an exact science. Seeing the future was about possibilities. The best scryers—who were few and far between—knew how to read the consensus of their visions and turn possibilities into probabilities. They weren't exact, but they were better than most everyone else. "So someone has a lot of money to spend."

"That's the rumor," he said.

Banjo was one of the best scryers in the city. "You biting?"

"Nah. Money like that is dangerous. Bad things happen to you if the payer doesn't like what they hear," he said.

"Wait a sec—that dwarf that ended up dead the other night—did he take the bait?"

"Could be. He was a long-timer. Not very talented, though. Maybe that's why he ended up dead," he said.

"Or maybe whoever killed him didn't want what he knew going anywhere else," I said.

"Well, that strategy might backfire. Dwarves are used to being taken advantage of, and when they are, they disappear. Notice many around lately?"

"Are you saying this blue essence is related?" I asked.

"I'm saying not everyone missing is lost. Know what I'm saying?"

"Is that why you didn't come into Yggy's?" I asked.

Banjo made a cutting gesture. "Nah. That place feels bad lately. Too many refugees from bars that burned down or something. It's not the same."

"It's Yggy's. It's never the same," I said.

He picked up a large bottle of massage oil and dropped a few bills on the counter. "Yeah, well, change isn't always good."

# 8

I grabbed lunch at the Waybread the next afternoon. The place was cheap and didn't attract many locals, which was fine by me. From the size of the lunch crowd, though, the restaurant wasn't attracting much of anyone. Between the police clampdown and the media scaring the public about the Weird, neighborhood businesses were suffering.

As I ate a burger, I mulled over the conversation with Banjo. While it was obvious that he had concerns about being seen in public, Yggy's had always had a strange collection of patrons. Banjo's not wanting to be seen there said more about him not wanting to be seen at all than it did about the bar. On the other hand, he knew this blue essence seemed to be targeting dwarves, so I couldn't say I blamed him for being cautious.

Dwarves always looped me back to Eorla. The clans were secretive, had their own rules, and, like Banjo, were not keen on talking to Celts. Eorla had asked me to check out the blue essence. It stood to reason she might know more than she said. We were friends but not always confidantes.

I left the Waybread with a satisfying bloat in my stomach. I didn't get nearly the gym time I should, but hiking everywhere I needed to go helped. The Rowes Wharf Hotel made for a good jaunt to work off some grease. When I entered the lobby, a cluster of Eorla's house guards surrounded me. They said nothing, maintained a discreet distance, and escorted me to her meeting room. The extra security hinted that something more was going on. When the guards left, Rand let me into the room.

Eorla rose from her worktable and kissed me on each cheek. "Thank you for coming."

"After what you did, how could I not? You left the Guild-house so quickly, I didn't have a chance to thank you properly," I said.

She made a dismissive gesture. "When you are privy to political scandal, it's easy to make investigations go away."

"Still, you didn't have to do it. Why did you?" I asked.

"Ryan macGoren needed to see that I have my resources. Besides, what he attempted to do to you was wrong, never mind everything else," she said.

"Maeve might not take kindly to your helping me."

She shrugged with a smile. "All the better. My sources tell me that she is already nervous about me."

I inhaled and held the breath a moment. "Eorla, I have to be blunt. If you're going to ask me to leave Bergin Vize alone, I can't promise that."

She nodded. "Ryan called me to that meeting to hear his bribe. I think he truly expected you to take the deal. There was no downside for you. By formally committing you to apprehending Bergin, he thought he would drive a wedge between us."

"You know I want Vize taken into custody," I said.

She placed her hand on my forearm. "Despite my personal feelings, Connor, I understand your motivation and accept as it as valid. I may not pursue Bergin or encourage you to do so, but I would be foolish to think I can protect him from everyone. He's done what he's done and will answer for it one day. That is the Wheel of the World."

I bowed my head. "Well, thank you anyway. It's one less thing for me to worry about."

She resumed her seat at the table. "Well, then, how about something new? I have a special visitor, who has been waiting all morning. I thought you might be intrigued to meet him."

"That you think that intrigues me. Who is it?"

"Aldred Core, one of Donor's advisors. I have no doubt threats will be involved. It should be entertaining. Would you like to stay?"

"With an invitation like that, how can I refuse?" I asked.

Eorla gestured to Rand, who positioned himself in front of the table and faced the entrance. I wandered to the side of the room, uncertain where to stand. Two men entered, one I knew. An ancient elf dressed in the traditional dark blue robe of a shaman glided forward in a smooth gait. Bastian Frye was the private counselor to Donor Elfenkonig, who ruled the Teutonic fey from his fortress in Germany. Bastian and I had never met until recently, but we went way back. When I was a top agent for the Guild, he led the opposition from the Teutonic Consortium. We had tried to kill each other, directly and indirectly, about a dozen times apiece over the years. We didn't hate each other, though. It was business.

The other man piqued my curiosity. He wore the formal dress of an elven courtier, a vermillion tunic over black pants. Gold braid wound about his shoulders. On his chest, he wore a series of ribbons that might have impressed me if I knew what they were for. A thick gold chain, with a large blue gem amulet pierced by a gold sword, hung around his neck. He radiated power, both in his bearing and his essence.

The two men paused when they reached Rand. Leaning on his staff, Bastian bowed stiffly. "Your Royal Highness, I present the Baron Aldred Core, ambassador of His Majesty, Donor Elfenkonig."

Despite denouncing the Elven King, Eorla was still a Grand Duchess of the elven royalty. Propping her elbows on the arms of her chair, she steepled her fingers. "How pleasant to see you again, Aldred. It has been many years, has it not?"

He bowed enough not to give insult. "It is a pleasure, as always, Your Royal Highness."

"You must be tired from your trip. Bastian, fetch a chair for my guest," she said.

Frye showed no annoyance but retrieved one of the large oaken chairs. Eorla enjoyed treating him below his station. Aldred lowered himself into the chair, glancing at me, then Rand. "I have communications from His Royal Majesty. Might I share them with you in more private circumstances?"

Unimpressed, Eorla leaned back. "So shy, Aldred? What topic would we speak of in private? Shall we share confidences on how you've risked treason against the crown you hold so dear? Or shall we perhaps discuss your rather creative forays into the royal accounts?"

Amused, Aldred licked his lips. "I would tread lightly on the issue of treason if I were you."

She arched an eyebrow. "I have done no treason, sir. Perhaps His Majesty has been ill informed as to my words and deeds. Speaking of deeds, Aldred, did the king ever discover your dalliances among his women?"

Aldred shifted in his seat. "You do no good thing to distract us."

Eorla twisted her lips into a smile. " 'Us,' Aldred?"

He set his jaw. "I speak for His Majesty."

Eorla chuckled. "Indeed. Enough pleasantries, then. Let us speak plainly with no need of privacy or subterfuge, shall we . . . cousin?"

Bastian stiffened by the ambassador's side. Aldred murmured a chuckle. "I warned you she would not be so easily fooled, Bastian. You have always been perceptive, dear Eorla."

His face blurred and shifted in a rainbow smear of color. The fey used spells and amulets to create glamours to change their appearance, sometimes minor improvements, sometimes complete identities. Aldred's face lengthened along the jaw and widened at the forehead. A deeper glitter appeared in his dark eyes, and, pinned tightly against the back of his head, a short-cropped ponytail appeared. His essence shifted, the removal of the glamour revealing his true body signature.

Donor Elfenkonig pursed his lips in amusement. I had to admit that a small thrill went up my spine. I had met many high-powered people over the years, but being in the presence of the Elven King of the Teutonic fey was fair cause for being starstruck for a moment.

"It has been many years, cousin. You look well," he said.

"As do you, dear cousin. To what do I owe this unexpected pleasure?" she asked.

The corner of Donor's lip curled down. "My condolences on the premature death of your husband. Had I known Alvud wished to be buried in this country, I would have surely made plans to attend his funeral."

From what I knew, Donor despised Alvud Kruge. The late Marchegraf was an internationally known diplomat and frequent critic of the Teutonic Consortium. Eorla's marriage had found ill favor in the Elven Court. She didn't care. Like now, seeing this man smile at the mention of her husband's death, she didn't show the least bit of annoyance. "Thank you, cousin. I appreciate the visit. Shall I call for a car to take you back to the airport?"

Donor sighed with an exaggerated disappointment that I was sure struck terror in his Court. "As much as I would prefer it, I have other pressing matters to attend."

"Such as?"

"Come, come, dear cousin. You realize the position you're placing me in."

Eorla mimicked his casual pose. "I resolved a situation that demanded resolution. A situation, I might add, that had more than a little to do with the intrigues of that pet assassin behind you. He hid Bergin Vize among the solitary fey, which led directly to the riots that tore apart this city. I stopped the riots and prevented a confrontation that would have led to more bloodshed. That blood would have been on your hands, cousin. You should be thanking me."

Frye hid his feelings well when he needed or wanted to. It was what made him good at his job. I'd heard enough about interactions between him and Eorla to know their mutual animosity was rich and deep. Donor smiled with feigned apology. "Mistakes were made, I grant you, cousin, but Bastian has always had our best interests at heart."

Eorla frowned. "That's the crux of the matter, though, cousin, isn't it? Your best interests and the crown's best interest are not one and the same thing."

Donor let annoyance cross his face. "You dare to criticize my rule in my own presence?"

"I dare to criticize your obsession with returning to Faerie. The Wheel of the World has turned, cousin. We are here. We need to move past this death match with Tara and find a new way in this world. You do the Consortium no good by setting us against the Seelie Court."

He narrowed his eyes. "And you think defying my rule is the answer? You have no idea of the situation you've caused. Maeve suspended the protocols of the Fey Summit. She's moving her troops around like a drunken slattern. One misinterpreted action by either of us could spark a war the likes of which these humans have never seen."

Eorla pursed her lips. "Then you have better things to do with your time, cousin, than sit here accusing me of treason."

He leaned forward. "Maeve thinks I'm using you to distract her."

"Maeve's not stupid. Frye tried to drop an army on her, but you claim not to know about that either," I said.

Frye took a step forward as Rand's hand landed on the hilt of his sword. He didn't draw it. Donor didn't look at me. "I don't believe we've met, sir."

"No. We haven't." I didn't give him the courtesy of telling him my name. I had no doubt he knew who I was.

Donor leveled his gaze at me then. Sound faded as our eyes locked. In the void left behind, the pumping of my own blood filled my hearing. A pressure mounted against my skin as Donor's eyes flickered with white light. I had experienced something like it once before when I encountered a vision of High Queen Maeve. Donor was analyzing me somehow, a mental ability I had never realized the powerful fey had.

The dark mass in my head shifted, a dense yearning behind my eyes that welcomed the attention. The pressure eased as Donor's eyes widened in surprise. I sensed the field of the spell he was using, the dark mass pushing outward with a pulse of pain. I wanted to reach out and grab Donor's essence, wanted to feel the strength of it and pull it into myself. It was a feeling of yearning and desire that burned in my chest and groin. I wanted his essence to sate the desire. I didn't like the feeling, didn't like that it reminded me of what I had done during the riots. I had spent the last few months suppressing the yawning want that could only be satisfied by more essence.

My left arm burned with cold. I had a tattoo of tree branches that wound around my forearm, formed out of spelled silver. It reacted to the Elven King's probe, igniting with essence. The tattoo channeled the essence inward, enhancing my body essence. The dark mass scuttled on spikes of pain, dancing around both Donor's spell and the silvered essence from the tattoo. An avenue opened in my mind, a path between the silver and the black, a calm space where there was no burning cold or heat. I focused on it and tapped my body essence, shoving back at Donor's touch.

He flinched, surprise flowing off him, which faded even as I noticed it. Frye's staff glowed with an evergreen light. Donor waved him back, staring at me with curiosity. "You are another problem, Mr. Grey. An intriguing one."

I shrugged. "Sounds like you have a lot of problems."

Eorla dropped her voice. "Does it ever occur to you, Donor, that you might be the cause of your problems?"

Donor continued looking at me for a few seconds before turning to her. "And does it ever occur to you, dear cousin, that your own wants and desires are meaningless? Have you learned nothing by your father's failure? The crown is mine, Eorla. You will never have it."

Eorla surprised the hell out of me by laughing. "I don't want your crown, Donor. I don't need your crown. Our fathers died at each other's hands for a kingdom that does not even exist anymore. Convergence took it all away. The crown is meaningless, Donor. You haven't realized that yet. Neither has Maeve."

His face became unreadable. He stared at Eorla, but whether they conversed by sendings, I couldn't tell. "I came here to offer forgiveness, Eorla. I understand your actions occurred under stressful conditions. Our people are stronger when we are united. You weaken both of us against a common enemy with this adventure."

"Yet I strengthen many, many more, cousin," she said.

Donor compressed his lips. I'd bet he didn't encounter resistance to his wishes all that often, especially to his face. I doubted there were many besides Eorla who could do it either. "Think on this, cousin. Think on this with care. My hand in friendship is a much wiser choice than the alternative. I will give you a brief time to reconsider your path."

He stood and reactivated the Aldred Core glamour. For now, I supposed, it suited his purpose for the outside world not to know that the Elven King was in the city. Frye fell in step behind him. Eorla gestured for Rand to follow them out the door.

Eorla exhaled. "That was not as difficult as I anticipated."

I shook my head with amusement. "I can't imagine what besides threats from the Elven King would be difficult for you."

She waved her hand. "Oh, he had to do that to save face with his weaker supporters in the Consortium. He may be a strong king, but he is only as strong as the confidence of his followers. I'm more interested in the real reason he's here. I felt what happened between you."

I closed my eyes. "It's bad enough I have Maeve watching my every move. The last thing I need is the Elven King doing it, too."

She quirked an eyebrow. "Don't let him fool you, Connor. He's afraid of her as much as she is of him. That's what the Fey Summit was all about—putting on a conciliatory face to cover their fears. He wants to know if her interest in you will help or hurt him."

"You know I'm not a fan of either of them," I said.

She rose and walked to the window. "And that's what he fears about both of us. Come here. I want you to see something."

She handed me a pair of binoculars from the window-sill and pointed across the harbor. The main part of Logan Airport was out of view, but the ends of the runways near the water were visible. A large plane with the Teutonic Consortium symbol painted on the rudder sat on the tarmac off to the side, far from the terminals. I lowered the binoculars. "That's a troop transport."

Eorla hummed in agreement. "Odd choice of travel for an ambassador to the crown, don't you think?"

"What are you going to do?"

She crossed her arms and stared out the window. "Watch for now. See who moves where. He's not likely to seek the Guild as allies, but he will do his best to remove me as a threat. The humans are as leery about that plane as I am. There's another plane filled with U.S. Marines at the other end of the field. Donor is here for a reason. Why he is here is more important than what is in that plane at the moment."

"Until the fighting starts again," I said.

She shot me a look. "You know I will do everything I can to prevent that."

"Except submit to him," I said.

She tilted her head toward me with a slight smile, curious rather than angry. "Is that a criticism?"

I shook my head. "Not at all. Standing up to monarchial power has become a hobby of mine lately. Be careful, Eorla. You can't predict everything."

We stared at the view, lost in our own thoughts.

# 9

Briallen sent word after I left Rowes Wharf that she was free for the evening. Between her schedule and Murdock's, setting up a time to run tests on his body signature had taken a few days. Even though I had suggested the idea, I was apprehensive that Murdock wouldn't take the results seriously. I had no doubt he was part druid—his mother was. What I didn't know was whether his heritage would be a good thing or a bad one. I worried because untrained abilities had a knack for going wrong at the wrong time. Murdock liked to take things as they came, but abilities were not something to ignore.

To distract myself for the remainder of the afternoon, I walked to Avalon Memorial to take Meryl for one of our strolls. I knew her condition wouldn't be any different. Someone would have called me. Being with her calmed me, though, and helped settle my mind about the evening to come.

I guided Meryl up the wide path on Boston Common that ran along Beacon Street. The tall trees that lined the way had begun to bud but remained bare. Meryl moved in a stupor, her gaze sightless. She responded to pressure on her arm, walking when prompted, stopping when held. Sometimes it felt like a game, like she was pretending to be silent and uncommunicative. It wasn't a game, though. She didn't respond to my voice or anything auditory. A motorcycle roaring past, children laughing, dogs barking brought no reaction. I watched for a sign in her eyes or a flinch from a startling noise, but saw nothing.

The concrete basin of the Frog Pond sat empty, a forlorn puddle of water in the depression where the drains were. I didn't know why it was called that. The only frog I had ever seen was a bronze statue on the edge of the basin. The city filled it with water on occasion. In the summer, people waded in the water, little kids splashing in the one foot or so depth as if swimming. In the winter, ice-skaters took over the space, even this year, despite the cyclone fencing erected on the hill side of the pond.

Tall, majestic trees once ringed a Civil War victory column at the top of the hill. The spot had been an oasis in the center of the park, a quiet area above the main paths where people sat and read or enjoyed the view. Last fall, it had become ground zero for a catastrophe that unfolded. The veil between worlds opened between here and TirNaNog, the Land of the Dead. For the first time since Convergence, the Dead roamed the earth again, causing all sorts of havoc. When dawn arrived, the veil refused to close. One thing led to another, as they say, and the top of the hill imploded. The victory column vanished, and a huge granite standing stone pillar from TirNaNog appeared in its place. The stone vibrated with essence, attracting gargoyles from all over the city, turning the top of the hill into a garden of tormented stone.

"I guess that's my fault, too," I said.

Meryl didn't respond. If she had, she would have told me to get over myself. It was what she did, and it was what I needed. I wrapped my arm around her, slipping her head into the crook of my shoulder. It felt good to have her there, and it felt wrong to have her nonresponsive. Pulling away from me I could take; pulling tighter I could enjoy. This nonresponsiveness was wrong in so many ways. Wrong because it violated Meryl's inherent nature. Wrong because somehow her condition was a result of my failure. Her choice, but my failure. I kissed the top of her head. She hated when I did that, drawing attention to my height over hers, kissing down at her. I loved that it irritated her, and I suspected she enjoyed it, but denying it was also part of who Meryl Dian was.

I led her away from the gargoyle-cluttered hill and empty pond basin, helping her up the stairs to Beacon Street. We cut up Joy Street to where Briallen lived around the corner on Louisburg Square, an exclusive address behind the State House, prim formal town houses staring at each other over a locked oval park. It was a pretty, cultured block with who knew what went on behind closed doors, especially at Briallen's house. She had lived there for years, the political and financial fortunes of her neighbors ebbing and flowing around her house, which never changed.

The pleasant odors of dinner filled the entry hall as I removed Meryl's jacket for her. Briallen came out of the kitchen, a dish towel in her hands. "How'd it go?"

"Fine. We walked around the Common and back," I said.

Briallen brushed stray hairs back from Meryl's face, a motherly gesture that surprised and reassured me. Briallen and Meryl had a thorny relationship filled with challenge and verbal sparring. It wasn't that I thought Briallen didn't care about Meryl. It was more a pleasant surprise that at the end of the day, all their disagreements were put aside.

"Well, physically, it probably was a good thing. She has more color in her cheeks. I already brought food upstairs for her in the guest room. Why don't you make yourself useful in the kitchen while I feed her?"

She took Meryl by the arm and led her up the stairs. Smiling, I watched them go. The two of them were the most important women in my life, both prone to giving me orders. I wasn't sure what that said about me, but it did amuse me. I did as I was told, went to the kitchen and washed the dishes in the sink. I had spent my teenage years in Briallen's house learning what it meant to be a druid. I also learned that not doing my chores brought swift punishment. To this day, I made a mental inventory when I walked in Briallen's house, checking if the stairs needed sweeping or the woodwork needed polishing. Not that any of that carried over into my apartment. The slob I was at home was an obvious reaction to my youth.

As the steam rose from the sink, I longed for those days, wanting to shout back through the years to warn my younger self of what was to come. I liked to think I would have done things differently. I doubted it, though. The thought was nostalgic at best. Like everybody else, I made decisions based on what I thought made sense at the time. Listening to some crazed older version of myself was probably not something I would have thought made sense.

I finished the last of the pots as Murdock arrived. "Tell me he didn't cook," he said as he followed Briallen into the kitchen.

"You're safe," she said.

"Hey, I make a mean mac and cheese," I said.

Murdock placed a bottle of French wine on the kitchen island. He knew it was Briallen's favorite. "Emphasis on the mean."

"From scratch. No box," I said.

"Can't prove it by me," he said.

Briallen patted my shoulder. "You do make a good one. He's not always wrong, Leonard. Hard to believe, I know."

I made a show of sighing. "It's going to be one of those dinners, isn't it?"

Briallen handed me a knife and loaf of bread. "Don't worry, dear. We'll find something else to talk about besides you."

Good-natured ribbing aside, meals at Briallen's house rarely lacked for interesting conversation. We managed to avoid talk of destroyed neighborhoods, decaying political structures, and the deaths of too many people. It felt normal, listening to Briallen talk about her students at Harvard or Murdock recommend books he had read. He favored romance novels and, of course, police procedurals. If the two genres ever overlapped, he would be in heaven.

The respite lasted until dinner was over. We went upstairs to the second floor, where Briallen had a small workroom. She and Murdock settled on stools facing each other, and she took his hands in hers. "I'm not going to do anything that will hurt."

He smirked. "Not the first time someone's said that to me."

She smiled. "Not the first time I've said it either. Close your eyes."

"Is this the part where we tickle him?" I asked. Briallen glowered at me. I held my hands up. "What? I can't make silly banter, too?"

"Emphasis on the word 'silly,'" Murdock said with his eyes closed.

"Fine," I said.

When Briallen closed her eyes, my essence-sensing ability registered the room coming alive with essence. Fey homes have more essence by virtue of their owners. Add someone like Briallen into the mix, and the essence levels escalated. Since we were in her workroom, color glowed and flared from every surface. Briallen performed research and experiments in the room. The bookcases vibrated in dark blues and golds, parchments and paperbacks hinting at spells and chants. Boxes made from wood or cloth or glass gave off unique signatures, some made to restrain particular types of essence, some having their own inherent patterns.

Briallen burned bright gold and white as she tapped her body essence. Murdock glowed, too, his crimson body signature flickering with red and yellow points of light. When I had met Murdock, he'd read completely human to my senses. Since the day he was hit with the spell backlash at Castle Island, his essence read more druid than human. When the changes started a year ago, I had worried about the ramifications for him. He, on the other hand, took them in stride. He exhibited some fey abilities, and his essence strengthened but remained human. In the past few months—since the death of his mother—his body signature had intensified.

White light flowed from Briallen's hands onto his. The light separated into delicate filaments that wound their way up his arms. His essence flashed red in response as his body shields flickered on. "Relax, Leonard."

"Sorry." The shield essence faded.

Briallen's essence surrounded him, long, lingering strands tapping his body signature here and there. Murdock's body shield flickered on and off as the exam proceeded, but Briallen didn't need to remind him to relax again. He had been practicing control of the shield, and I was impressed by how far he had progressed on his own.

For the better part of an hour, Briallen poked, probed, and manipulated his essence, chanting and muttering as she worked. I had experienced much the same process many times over the years. To someone who couldn't see essence, it wasn't that interesting, an exercise in one person touching another. For me, it was like watching someone play an instrument. My essence-sensing abilities had become acute, almost painfully so, and for the first time I saw how someone of Briallen's skill worked with essence. She moved it through Murdock's body, tapping essence nodes like a tuning fork, making their bindings dance like reflexes. I never realized the complexity of a single body signature until her work exposed my ignorance. Her precision showed me why I hadn't sensed anything more than human from Murdock when I first met him. The druidic essence markers were there, subtle but strong, bound so delicately into his dominant human body signature, I would never have known what to look for.

With a deep exhale, Briallen dropped her hands in her lap. "That's it. Time for drinks."

She hopped off the stool and crossed the hallway to her second-floor parlor. A small blue fire burning in the grate flared brighter as Briallen poured glasses of port, essence dancing through the air and boosting her body signature. I hadn't realized she used the fire as an essence source. We settled into the armchairs facing the flames.

Briallen held her glass up. "Slainte."

Health, of course. We toasted it all the time, but this time it was more than mouthing the words. We tapped glasses.

"First, let me say, there is nothing wrong with you. Your essence is fine and healthy," Briallen said.

Murdock shot me a satisfied look. "I've been saying that all along."

"A stronger essence shows through a weaker one. You can't hide druid essence under human. How is it possible we didn't sense it before Castle Island?" I said.

Briallen sipped her port. "Leonard doesn't have a druid essence separate from a human essence, Connor. He has his own unique signature, one that reads more human than not. He's human, but some essence pathways read druid. For all her flaws, Moira Cashel was a talented druidess. If I can think of a spell to suppress the druidic aspects of Leonard's essence, I'm sure she could."

"By why didn't we see it before?" I asked.

"I think when you boys were caught in the spell backlash at Castle Island, Moira's protection spell was probably damaged. When she . . . died . . . her spell did, too. Whatever her motivations in other matters, she was trying to protect her children," said Briallen.

"That's the part I don't understand," Murdock said. "When we worked the Castle Island case, you said interbreeding between species caused problems, that the kids didn't live past puberty."

Case studies showed mental and physical defects whenever two different fey species interbred. The more unlike the species, the greater the chance that progeny wouldn't survive. "They don't most of the time," I said.

"Moira had seven children. We're all fine," he said.

I used my recall to review the case studies I had read back then. Druids looked human. We blended in without any problems, which was one of the ways Moira fooled her husband. "None of the cross-species cases we saw were druid/human. Maybe that has something to do with it," I said.

Briallen tilted her head back in thought as if searching

the ceiling for an answer. "Gillen Yor was researching cross-species children."

I glanced at Murdock. "I know. That's where I got my original data from."

"You never told me that," he said.

I nodded. "I didn't exactly ask him, and I know how you get about stuff like that. Does it matter now?"

He shook his head in exasperation. "I guess it doesn't. It still doesn't get us any answers."

Briallen gazed into the fire. "Sometimes we look for answers when we should be looking for questions."

"Like what?" I asked.

"Like why Scott Murdock? Of all the men Moira could have picked, why him?" Briallen asked.

"Are you saying it wasn't accidental they met?" I asked.

"I'm saying she married a man whose death is causing an international incident. I'm saying one of her sons has helped you stop some catastrophic events. And I have to wonder why?" Briallen asked.

"She knew something. Maybe she had a vision of the future," I said.

"Why would she want a future where my father ends up dead? Or herself? That doesn't make sense," Murdock said.

A thin, bitter smile creased Briallen's face. "Welcome to the fey world, Leonard. Even our own lives mean little in achieving our goals."

She stared at the fire in a way that made me wonder if she was warning Murdock or lamenting her own fate. Briallen had lived through a lot, and no matter how much she danced around it, I believed she was an Old One. She knew pain and sorrow in Faerie and hoped to see an end of it here.

I didn't think that was going to happen for any of us soon.

# 10

After dinner, I left Briallen's house and found a quiet place down near the Reserve Channel, a small dive, long and narrow. Timeworn wooden stools lined the bar, old Colonial-style chairs surrounded pitted tables and a three-piece band crammed into the corner next to the bathroom. The patrons slunk in and out, not furtive, but tired and dejected, the type of clientele for which drinking was a necessity, not an entertainment. It was the kind of place people went when something rocked their world and not in a good way.

A fairy from one of the lesser Celtic clans stood at the microphone, singing a song of loss and more loss while the band played melancholy flute and drum. She must have had a decent voice once, broken now by drink and who knew what else. Fairies, especially Dananns, had a weakness for alcohol that turned into a problem with no effort. The rasp in her voice worked for the room. Scattered applause broke the silence whenever she finished a song.

I sat on a stool in a dark corner. I didn't recognize anyone, but that didn't mean no one would recognize me. Between those who remembered me from my publicity-rich Guild days and those who had more recent grudges, I had too many people to avoid. Staying home was easier—and safer—but sometimes wallowing alone in a room with other wallowing people fit the bill.

Learning that Murdock was okay was a good thing. For months, I had hoped that the answer to what had happened to him might provide a clue to a cure for me. If he could develop abilities, maybe a way existed for me to get mine back. I didn't get the answer I had hoped for. Murdock was fey. There was no work-around. The dark mass was in my head and would be in my head until I figured out what it was or I died. With any luck, the two things wouldn't happen at the same time.

Something rustled in the garbage can near me in the corner. I slid away from it, not wanting a rat jumping out at me. The Weird lay hard by the harbor, and rats were more common than dockworkers. During the day, you might catch a furtive movement in the shadows, but at night the little furries ventured about with little fear. An always-dark bar was like a home away from home.

A thumping sound came from the barrel, and I moved off my stool. I wasn't afraid of rats. I was afraid of what a startled rat might do. They avoided people, but they had tiny brains and didn't know the difference between someone trying to avoid them and a big scary mammal looming over them.

A crumpled ball of paper popped out, then an empty beer can. The barrel wobbled as something inside shrieked. I backed away as it fell over with a loud crash, newspapers and more cans scattering onto the ground. Heads turned at all the noise as a bright pink ball of essence shot across the floor and hit the wall.

"I'm trying to be inconspicuous here, Joe," I said.

He rubbed his head. "There's a big brown rat in there with the longest tail I've ever seen."

I picked up a brown-paper shopping bag, rolled up and dangling its broken rope handle. "This rat?"

Joe made a show of dusting himself off. "It was dark."

I tossed at him. "What the hell were you doing in there anyway?"

He straightened with dignity. "Looking for you."

"In a trash barrel? What would make you think . . . never mind." It took me a second, but I saw the setup.

Joe fluttered to the stool and sat down. "What are you doing here?"

"Pondering the meaning of life and the Wheel of the World," I said.

He peered off at the dark bar. "Really? The beer's that cheap here?"

"Yeah," I said.

Joe banged his fists against his forehead. "Can't you get drunk like a normal crazy person?"

I righted the barrel and glanced around. After the initial noise, the bar patrons had gone back to staring into space. "I don't think I'd fit in this barrel."

Joe pouted, letting his eyes grow wide with sadness. "I wish I could ponder life, too, but my hands are empty."

"Would you like a beer, Joe?"

He grinned. "Why, yes, I would love to discuss philosophy with you, kind sir."

A strange vibe swept the room, an air of tension that prompted people to look toward the exit. Drinkers at the bar shifted in their seats, leaning toward each other to whisper. Joe flinched and squeezed his eyes shut. "Ow! People need to tone down their sendings."

"I'm not getting anything," I said. I couldn't do sendings anymore, but I could receive them. Whatever was happening, no one thought I'd be interested.

Joe shook his head. "Another fire. Big one over on the haul road."

Ever since a quarter of the neighborhood had burned down the night of the riots, people had been jumpy. The bar was on the edge of the burn zone, and while some might argue not much was left to burn, that wasn't a joke to people who lived and worked nearby.

"Is the fire department responding?" I asked.

"Lots. It's a big one. Do they have nuts here?" Joe asked.

"Just one. Let's go check out the fire," I said.

Joe gave me a horrified look. "But the beer is here."

"We'll get some later. Promise," I said.

Outside, a muddy orange light smeared across the night sky, never a good sign when it came to fires. I hurried down the sidewalk, dodging puddles and broken cement and made it to the haul road in two short blocks. Thick smoke plumed off the top of a warehouse. From the number of units on the scene, the fire had gone to at least six alarms. On the corner, an elf in a green uniform stopped us. "This is a secure area. You need to move on."

"I'm here on business for Eorla Elvendottir," I said. It wasn't quite true, but he didn't need to know that.

"No one gets in. Move on," he said.

I stepped around him, while Joe circled my head. "I'm Connor Grey. I work for Eorla. You can check with her or Rand."

My body shield flickered on as I sensed the elf charging his hand with essence. In a blur, Joe had his sword out and in the guy's face. "He said you can check with someone, got it? Or do I have to play tic-tac-toe on your face?"

The elf glared but dropped his hand. "I will remember this."

"Good," said Joe.

Flits were not to be underestimated, to be sure, but seeing such a large being back away from Joe was damned funny. We left the guard on the corner, glaring at us. "Tic-tac-toe?" I asked.

He nudged me with an elbow and winked as his sword vanished behind its cloaking glamour. "Yeah, good one, huh?"

"As always, buddy." Joe liked movies. His taste showed in the lines of dialogue he picked up.

As I picked my way over thick yellowed fire hoses, I spotted Murdock next to an EMT truck. "Hey, Leo. I didn't expect to see you down here."

The fire lit his intent face in harsh yellow. "A call went out about a break-in. We're still shorthanded, so I thought I'd back up uniforms if they needed me."

Several fire trucks lined the front of the building. Every ladder truck was in service as plumes of water rained down on the burning building. A misty halo lingered in the air. "Is that Kevin's unit?" I asked.

"Yeah, first one in as usual," Murdock said.

The last time I had seen Kevin Murdock was on his station's ladder truck the night of the riots. He was the youngest Murdock, and that night he looked like a lost boy, bewildered by the carnage around him.

Two firefighters appeared in the front entrance. They staggered a few feet, pulling off their helmets, then leaned on their knees, coughing, as EMTs rushed to their sides with oxygen. "Looks intense," I said.

"They're having trouble venting. Something about the insulation," he said.

The granite front of the building was covered with elaborate carving that resembled a forest. Over the door, a damaged sign carved into the lintel indicated the building was a stone-quarry supplier. "Why would someone break into a stone supplier? It's not like you can shove a slab in your pocket."

"Won't know until we question him. Best we can tell, he set the fire to cover his escape," he said.

"He?" I asked.

Murdock shook his head. "He's still in there. We had to pull our guys out when the fire started. Firemen are on search and rescue now."

The radio inside Murdock's coat screeched and garbled. He had it tuned to the firefighter frequency. I never learned to understand a word on those things. "What's going on?"

Murdock lowered the volume. "They're pulling out of a section of the building. Too much heat."

"Did they find the guy?"

Murdock played with the radio tuning. "I think so. Sounds

like it was some kind of fey. They're talking about a shield blocking them."

The wind shifted and dumped a pall of oily smoke down on us. My eyes teared up. The radio squawked. Murdock tensed as he adjusted the signal. "What's happening?" I asked.

"Something collapsed," he said. Firefighters in full gear stumbled from the shattered doors. He walked toward the confusion near the front of the building.

I followed him. "Why are they coming out?"

Murdock waved me silent as his scanned the firefighters. "Kevin has the perp. I don't see him."

He hurried to a group of men near the chief's car. Words were exchanged that looked pretty animated. Murdock's body tensed, and he thrust an arm toward the building. An argument ensued, several men stalking away in angry disgust. More followed them, pulling back from the building. Murdock shoved his way past them. I caught him near the front of the building. The heat from the fire pressed against my face. "Where the hell are you going?"

"The building's destabilized. The chief won't let anyone else in," he said.

"But what about . . ." I stopped at the look on Murdock's face.

"Kevin and two others are trapped in the back," he said.

The firefighters nearby had removed the masks, horror and anger etched on their faces. They took care of their own. They didn't leave each other behind. Every once in a while, a fire comes along that doesn't give a damn about that.

Murdock paced closer to the building. I grabbed his arm. "Leo, let's think this through."

He shook me off. "I can't let this happen."

"Do we have his position?"

"Rear loading dock. The exit's blocked."

I stumbled after him down the side alley. Between the smoke and hose spray, I lost sight of him. "Leo!" He didn't answer. As visibility went down, my sensing ability responded. In the haze ahead, his body shield faded into the distance. I struggled to keep up with his retreating crimson essence light.

Behind the warehouse, the air cleared enough for me to see without tears filling my eyes. The neighboring building had collapsed, leaving rubble that blocked the alley. Ladder trucks at either end poured water against the back wall of the warehouse while firefighters rushed to remove fallen masonry in front of a buried exit door.

Murdock and I scrambled onto the pile. Stone dust clung to my hands as I grabbed cinder blocks and bricks. The dust bonded to my body signature, a residual effect from an encounter I'd had with a troll. With a twinge of pain, I forced the dust off. It returned at the next touch of stone. I ignored it. It wasn't painful and helped me grip the stones we were throwing aside.

*Door's blocked.*

I spotted another of the green-liveried elven guard watching from a nearby pile of bricks. "No kidding. Think you can lend a hand here?"

The elf tilted his head. "I am an observer for Her Majesty. I do not intervene."

I grunted. "Then stop with the sendings. It's distracting."

"I have not sent anything," he said.

No other fey were around except him. "You didn't do the sending?"

"No, sir," he replied.

I frowned. "How long have you been in Eorla's service?"

He lifted an eyebrow in disdain. "Who might you be, sir?"

"Connor Grey."

He gave me his back. "I am in Her Majesty's service. I do not answer to anyone but Her Majesty."

Something didn't feel right about the guy. I walked around in front of him. "There are people trapped in there. I need you to hit that wall with elf-shot, and I want you to do it now."

He stepped around me. "I will consult with my captain."

I grabbed his arm. It was a dumb mistake. He let out

a sharp flurry of German, and his body shield activated, bouncing my hand off him. He lifted a hand burning with emerald essence. A surge of pink essence seared between us as Joe slammed his feet into the guy's nose. The elf toppled off the pile of bricks.

"Ya got a problem, bub? 'Cause I'm looking for one," Joe said.

Keeping his hands charged, the elf got to his feet. Blood trickled out of his nose. "Interfere with me again, and I shall strike you down."

Joe menaced around his head, bursting in and out of sight, confusing the hell out of the guy. "You think so?"

The black mass in my head shifted, responding to my rising anger. I braced myself against it with my body essence, grimacing with the pain. "We don't have time for this. If you're not going to help, get someone down here who will. I know your face, and Eorla will hear about this."

The black mass pressed with a palpable hunger for the rich glow of the elf's essence. I resisted the desire to relax my will and let the darkness rise, angry that I had to let the man go. With enough rationale, I could let the darkness absorb his essence, justify it by judging his failure to act and receive the uncomfortable pleasure of his essence coursing through me.

The elf wasn't all that impressed with my threat, but he kept his eye on Joe. He dropped his hand and hurried up the alley. Eorla was going to get an earful when I talked to her next.

"You okay?" Joe asked.

"Yeah. Can you follow him for me? Something's not right about him," I said.

"You'll want to discuss it over a beer later, right?" he asked.

"As always," I said. He saluted and blinked out.

The burning warehouse building glowed with the ambient essence of the Weird, a dull, dirty white that wasn't full gray. My sensing ability didn't allow me to extend through walls, but I was able to detect a faint shifting essence. Someone was moving inside. Since the firefighters were human, the one thing strong enough for me to pick would be the fey suspect. If the suspect was alive, that might mean the firefighters were, too. "I'm getting moving essence hits inside, Murdock. They're still alive."

He focused on the task in front of him without stopping to acknowledge me. We cleared the top off the mound of debris and exposed the door. Frustrated, I slumped back on my haunches at the sight of the hinge. "Dammit. It opens out. We've got to get more people back here."

Murdock threw a brick at the exposed edge of the door. The brick exploded with the force of his throw, denting the metal. Something banged against the inside and a sending hit me hard enough to knock me off-balance.

*Can't breathe. Open, dammit.*

I scrambled down the rubble and flattened myself against the brick wall. The stone tickled like static as it bonded to my skin. The body signatures on the other side pushed against my senses like bubbles of pressure. "Here. They're right here. Someone get a ram."

Hydraulic pressure rams were standard equipment on fire trucks. Two firefighters ran down the alley toward the nearest ladder truck.

"Get out of the way."

I pulled myself off the wall, flakes of brick embedded in my skin. Murdock stood fifteen feet away, his body shield rippling with intensity. The firefighters weren't even to the truck yet. "Where's the ram?"

"You're looking at it. Move."

Murdock ran at the wall. I jumped away as he slammed into the building. The reaction force knocked him off his feet as chunks of brick flew in every direction. Murdock pulled himself up, one side of his face a speckled bruise from the hit. Body shields deflected force, but they didn't stop it. Head down, he slammed his shoulder into the bricks. The wall sagged inward, mortar cracking and falling in clouds of dust.

"Leo, the ram's coming," I shouted.

He charged the wall again. Bricks broke free, falling inside the building. Thick, black smoke coiled out of the hole Murdock had created. I grabbed the edge of it and yanked more bricks away.

"Move," Murdock said.

"It's enough, Leo. You're going to hurt yourself." He hit the wall right next to me. I ducked as bricks cascaded down. Murdock tripped and fell again.

A raw, burned hand appeared from inside and pulled away bricks, then a gloved hand joined the task. We coughed and gagged as thick smoke continued to roll out. When the hole was large enough, I grabbed the next hand that appeared and pulled. My eyes burned with the smoke as I hauled out a firefighter. Momentum carried me backwards, and we rolled free down the slope. Someone inside flung an arm through the hole, and Murdock grabbed it.

I half dragged the firefighter from the building, and we fell on the uneven ground. Firefighters swarmed around us. Beneath the clouded face mask, Kevin Murdock struggled for breath. I pulled his headgear off. "Easy, easy. Breathe, Kevin," I said.

Kevin rolled onto his side and coughed up black phlegm. An EMT helped me walk him to where medical equipment waited. Chaos reigned in the EMT triage site. Boston police struggled to keep gawkers and news reporters away from the firefighters as they were being treated for smoke inhalation and burns. No lives had been lost as far as I could tell.

We lowered Kevin onto a gurney. An EMT came to my side and tried to open my jacket. "Are you okay?"

I shrugged him off. "I'm fine."

I pushed closer to Kevin's gurney. Kevin lay on his back, an oxygen mask covering his face. I wasn't going to take that as a bad sign. Even inhaling small amounts of smoke damaged airways, and he had breathed in plenty. It didn't mean he was in critical condition. He lifted his head as an EMT checked his vital signs. When he saw me, his face turned into a snarl. He ripped the mask down. "Get the hell away from me."

Surprised, I backed away from the gurney. "I wanted to make sure you were all right."

"Not interested in your concern."

I looked at the EMT. "Is he okay?"

Kevin tried to sit up, but the EMT held him down. "I'm fine. I know what you did, you bastard. Get away from me."

Now I understood that his reaction had nothing to do with the fire or his injuries. "Kevin, this isn't the time, but I'm sorry. For everything. We're all victims of circumstance here."

His derisive chuckle faded into a cough. "I've heard enough about the shit you've caused to understand your circumstances, Connor. Get the hell out of here and stay away from my family. You got it? Stay away, or I'll make you regret you ever set foot in our house."

"I'm sorry." Stunned, I walked away. I understood his anger, but I didn't expect it while I was saving the guy's life. I backed off. Like I had said, it wasn't the time. He was injured and tired, and what happened, happened. I didn't want to provoke him because I didn't know how to defend myself.

To make matters worse, when the hole opened in the wall, I realized I wasn't hearing the sendings from the burglary suspect, and when I pulled Kevin out, my body signature interacted with his. Whatever having mixed-race parents was doing to Leo, it was doing tenfold to Kevin. He read druid without a hint of human body essence. I decided he wasn't exactly in the mood to hear that.

I found Murdock on the far end of the alley with another group of EMTs. He glanced at me as soon as I neared, and I wondered if it was coincidence or if he had sensed me. His face was swollen on the left side and his forehead had a bruise, signs of body-shield impact. He hadn't hit the wall with his face, but the shield diffused the force and propagated it against his entire body.

I waited while the EMTs finished with him. "Kevin's okay," I said.

He worked his shoulder. "That was the idea."

"I'm going to make a wild guess and say you told him about Moira," I said.

"He's not your biggest fan right now," Murdock said.

I frowned. "He blames me, too."

Murdock looked up me. "He grew up without a mother, and his father was murdered. You were there at the beginning and the end, Connor. He's having a hard time separating that from who was to blame."

"I guess it's a rule that at least one Murdock hates me at all times."

"At least," Leo said.

"I'm sorry," I said.

"Stop saying that," he said. He wasn't angry, but his tone said how tired he was.

"There's something else, Leo. I'm reading a druid body signature off Kevin, a powerful one. More than yours," I said.

Murdock dropped his head back. "Damn. Can we get ten minutes without something blowing up?"

"Are you going to tell him?" I asked.

He winced as he rubbed at his head. "I'll have to, won't I? I don't recommend going anywhere near Southie for a while."

The EMT returned. "You're next, Officer."

Murdock lay back on the gurney. "They want X-rays. Any fey mumbo jumbo I should tell them about?"

I shook my head. "Your anatomy's the same as always, Leo. I'll call you later."

He closed his eyes and let them wheel him away. News vans and curiosity seekers crowded the sidewalks out front. I cut across the street to avoid the reporters looking for someone to interview. The last thing I needed was getting my name in the news again in a story about a fire in the Weird.

Kevin Murdock's angry face played over in my mind. He was a kid, the youngest member of his family. He had never known Moira Cashel as his mother. She left town not long after he was born. But he knew his father. I didn't know what that relationship was like, but Scott Murdock was his father.

Even Leo, who disagreed with the commissioner on so many things, mourned the man. Death was a lot to process under normal circumstances, but to be dragged into the fey world at the same time had to be overwhelming. I tried not to feel hurt by what was said, but it stung. It stung because deep down, I agreed with him. Without having an inkling as to what I was doing—what I did—I had screwed up an entire family. I didn't know how to answer for that or even if I could.

# 11

A few hours of brooding drove me out of the apartment in search of a drink. Half my favorite bars in the Weird were gone, casualties of the firestorm that had swept through the neighborhood. I wasn't all that welcome in a number of the remaining ones. People blamed me for a lot of things that had happened, not least of which were the fires and the shootings and the riot. I might have had a noticeable ego in the past, but even I would have had a hard time rationalizing my ability to cause that much damage. Maybe some of it, but not all.

I went to a variety of bars for a variety of reasons. I went to quiet dives where I could sit at the bar, stare into my beer, tap the bar top for another without having to speak, and go home nicely drunk and depressed. I went to loud dives where I could hang on the bar, watch people in various stages of joy or desperation, and go home nicely drunk and bemused. Some places I went because I was being social, others because of the food, and still others for the eye candy. I rarely went to clique bars like a sports or leather place. I preferred the places that a sports fan can hang out with someone in chaps and not find it the least bit ironic or odd. Sometimes, I needed a space with no judgments, no demands, and plenty of indulgence.

Which brought me right where I needed to be that night, a dark, nameless club that was invitation only. One look around the place revealed that wasn't something to be impressed with. I sat at the dim end of the room, a Guinness warming on the table as I watched a state senator smile into a cloud of fairy dust. Protocol dictated that I did not see him, did not know him, and that was fine. We all needed a place to escape sometimes. Some people needed to cross lines. Some lines needed to be crossed. Druids liked to live by the code of "do no harm," which in politics often translated to "no harm, no foul," even if the action was a bit foul.

Carmine slid into my booth, a mixture of scents wafting off his clothes, smoke and sex and liquor, the stale funk of a night of partying. With Carmine, it was always a party. He owned the bar and several others, provided party services for a steep price and coveted discretion. He smiled in the darkened booth, tiny sharp teeth flashing against his deep red complexion. "Connor, my friend, it pleases me to see you drink, but not with that look on your face."

"I've had a bad run the past couple of days."

He chuckled. "I might have heard about that. I'm beginning to think I might need to learn a trick or two from you about how to end an evening."

I sipped my beer. "Avoid armored tanks."

"Yes, I imagine they are a bitch to park," he said.

A thin elf, skin blue and stippled black, delivered a flute of champagne to Carmine. He checked my drink, then glanced up with a smile. Changes in essence around him radiated soothing calm with a touch of desire. "Anything more?" he asked.

"I'm good," I said.

Carmine watched him with the assessing gaze of a marketer looking through the eyes of a consumer. "He's very good, don't you think? Subtle work. He has this lovely trick of making people feel like they had no plan to come in and end up in the back room."

I took a long swig of my beer. "Sure. Not wanting to take responsibility for your actions is not all that surprising. Blame it on someone else. No recriminations."

Carmine tapped the champagne flute along his teeth. "Imagine—some people hate themselves for enjoying themselves."

I grunted. "I could use a little of that kind of hate."

Carmine draped himself across the booth, leaning on the edge of the table and propping his foot up on the seat. "Connor, Connor, Connor. Self-pity doesn't become you. I thought you had gotten past that."

I slumped back, rested the beer on my hip. "I'm responsible for a lot of dead, Carmine. I'm not happy about it."

"The Wheel of the World turns as It will, Connor. I have the scars to prove it," he said.

Carmine had the right to say it. Some of those scars he wore were because of me. Mistaken identities will do that to a person. I dropped my head back. "But I'm sick of hearing that stuff, Carmine. I'm sick of people doing shit and shrugging it off as fate or the Wheel or bad luck. I did shit. I'm trying to make up for it. I want to. Instead, all that happens is people biting my ass for reasons that have nothing to do with me."

At first, I thought a trick of the light darkened the booth, but then I realized the darkness clustered around Carmine. He sipped long on his champagne, his tiny sharp teeth a slash of white in shadow as a feral yellow glinted in his eye. "Do you know what I do, Connor? Truly know? Do you know the price for the services I provide? I hold a mirror up to people's desires and give them what they think they want. I give people what they want and make them pay for it. But the price isn't coin, Connor. That's the surface, the lie, if you will, that we hide behind to salve our consciences. What lies beneath is the soul of the matter, everyone's soul. The Wheel of the World turns, but people make It turn. and the Wheel responds by turning as It will without regard to our petty desires or hopes and dreams. It turns the way It will, sometimes random, sometimes true, and that is the fate we all must face. It turns, Connor, and gives us the chance to keep It turning for good or ill. We always have a choice. Taking responsibility is one choice, but it isn't the only one. Not taking responsibility turns the Wheel, too. Either way, no one gets away with anything because there are always changes and results, ramifications and consequences."

His voice became one with the shadow around him. "You're not angry about the Wheel. You're not angry about people not taking responsibility. You're not even angry about the things you've done. You're angry about time, Connor. Time reveals answers and not always when we want them or if we want them. That's the Wheel, too. Time will come and go in time enough for what you need. Patience rewards, but action satisfies. Choose between them carefully because they, too, will cause more time still. Choose your time."

The shadows dissipated. As Carmine stopped speaking, the music in the club became louder, and the conversational voices around us rose in volume. I inhaled as if I had remembered to breathe. Carmine stared at me now with a pleasant smile, the horned ridge of his eyebrows lifting in thought or a challenge to deny his words.

I stared back, letting what he said sink in. "Yeah, that's not making me feel better."

He laughed in a staccato of high barks. "You say that as if that was my intention." He pulled a small granite block from his pocket and placed it on the table. "Touch it," he said.

I rubbed my finger across the top of the cube. A short flash of essence danced up my arm and slipped into my face. Blood rushed to my head, a warm flush that spread throughout my body. My heart beat in my ears, a soft, thick pulse that reminded me of a soothing drumbeat. My skin tingled as the rush faded. We called them blushies when I was a kid. I chuckled. "I haven't played with those in years."

Carmine tilted his head to the side. "Then you've missed

some interesting modifications. No headaches, for one. Timed release. Intensity controls. They've come a long way."

The idea was tempting and no more unusual in the fey world than drinking. "Thanks, Carmine. I think I'll see where the night takes me."

Carmine slid out of the booth as pink essence flashed in the air. Joe wobbled above the table, oversize sunglasses pressed against the bridge of his nose. "It's dark as the bottom of a keg in here," he said.

I glanced at Carmine, but spoke to Joe. "The glasses, Joe. Funny you showing up here."

He settled to the table, removing the glasses and staring at them as if he'd never seen them before. He tossed them over his shoulder into the next booth and cocked his head at Carmine. "Dare I think that's a bar behind you, Master Red?"

"Your powers of observation astound as always, Master Pink." Carmine placed a plastic red card on the table next to my elbow. He nodded at the stone cube. "We have a wide selection of those. Consider yourself my guest for the rest of the evening, Connor. The rooms in the back are at your disposal."

"You don't have to do that, Carmine," I said.

He bowed. "Of course not, but sometimes I do things I think are necessary at the time." He nodded to Joe. "Master Pink."

Joe tapped his head and bowed. "Master Red."

Carmine strolled away as the waiter reappeared. He placed a small chair on the table for Joe, two mugs of Guinness in flit glasses beside it, and a full pint in front of me. Joe picked up a mug and draped himself on the chair, dangling his feet over one of its arms. He raised his mug. "To the good red man!"

"To Carmine," I said, and tapped.

Joe hummed as he surveyed the bar. "Busy in here."

"Carmine called you, didn't he?"

He looked at me with half-closed eyes. "I would have been here soon or later, making the rounds. You think you're the only morose guy bitter at the world that I know? I have a schedule, you know."

Joe knew my ancestors, stood beside them on battlefields and watched people die over the right to lands that didn't even exist anymore. It was hard to feel like my issues were important around him. Not that he didn't care what I was going through, but he had a way of reminding me that I wasn't alone and that anything that was happening now had happened before and will again. It was the Wheel of the World. I chuckled as I drained my glass and pulled the new pint closer.

"How'd you make out with the elf?" I asked.

He downed his glass and picked up the second. "Very strange. I lost him. One moment he was there, the next gone. Never saw an elf do that."

"Did he ghost?" I asked. The fey, especially ones with strong body essence, had the ability to move at extreme speeds.

Joe feigned an insulted glare. "Do you really think someone ghosting can get away from me?"

I shrugged. "Just asking."

"Nope. He turned a corner and vanished. Not a trace of essence left behind. It was like he fell in a hole."

I grunted as I drank my beer. "I wish I could fall in a hole."

Joe grinned. "I feel a bender coming on."

"That, my friend, sounds like a perfect idea. I don't want to think about tomorrow."

He downed his second mug and sighed. "See, now, in the same situation, I can't wait to see what happens."

Amused, I crumpled a bar napkin and tossed it at him. He tilted his head and used his toe to nudge at the card Carmine had left. "Are you going to use that? I've heard rumors about some interesting new entertainments."

Meryl's vacant stare flitted through my mind. She wouldn't care if I lost myself in some mindless recreation. Depending on the situation, she'd toss me out the door to go play if I was not on her agenda for the night. I didn't want to, though. Tonight, it would have felt like an indulgence and not in a good way. Beer was enough for what I needed right then. I pushed the card closer to Joe. "I'm not in the mood. Take notes for me."

He spun the card on the tip of his finger, cheating by using essence to keep it aloft. "Oh, I'm sure Carmine has video."

# 12

I woke with a gasp as cold water poured on my face and spilled down my neck. I hunched forward in the darkened living room, a headache blooming at the sudden movement. My body shields flickered but receded as my sensing ability picked up the body signature beside my futon.

"Ass," I said.

Murdock smirked down at me, a half-empty water glass poised in his hand to drip more water on me. "Rise and shine, grumpy."

I wiped the wetness from my face with my hands and winced when Murdock turned on the lights. Sunlight peeked through cracks in the plywood and plastic barrier that served as my replacement window. During the riots, Guild agents had smashed their way in to arrest me, and the landlord wasn't in any rush to replace the glass.

I swung my feet to the floor and made my way to the bathroom. My head felt like it followed on a tether about two feet behind. A flutter in my stomach tried to get my attention, threatening to become a rush of something trying to get out of my body. I stood in front of the john, steadying myself with one hand against the wall as I relieved myself. "You could have called," I said.

His voice echoed in from the living room. "I did. And I rang the buzzer, but you didn't answer. Seemed like a good idea to check if you were on the run or dead."

I shuffled out of the bathroom and slipped on some black jeans from the floor. I was pretty sure they were the clean ones. "I guess I was in a deep sleep."

He eyed me with amusement as he washed the glass. "I guess technically that's true."

I pulled a clean T-shirt out of the laundry basket. It was clean. I knew for sure. "What's that supposed to mean?"

He leaned against the counter, shaking his head. "Connor, I really don't care you went on a beer binge. What I do care about is that you got dressed and still smell like ass. Go take a shower. I'll wait."

The aroma of bar reek and beer sweat coming off me was not a pleasant combination. I hadn't realized I wasn't the only one who could smell it. "Wait for what?"

"We got an ID on the pit victim," he said.

I pulled the T-shirt off again and shucked my pants to the floor. I lost my balance in the process and almost fell over. "And that concerns me because?"

He smiled and shrugged. "Because you need to do something other than drink and act like Eorla Kruge's errand boy."

A thick silence hung between us as I debated whether to be insulted. Murdock's eyebrows flicked upward, a telltale sign he was more than willing to go toe-to-toe with me on the subject. I checked the rumbling burn of anger in my chest. He was right, a little blunt, but right. I walked back in the bathroom. "Your shirt's ugly."

"And for the love of God, brush your teeth," he shot back.

The hot shower soothed my muscle aches but didn't get rid of my headache, or, at least, the headache I had in addition to my usual headache. It did help me shed the layer of odor. I came out of the bathroom, rubbing my hair with a towel. "How'd the ID happen?"

He didn't look up from the home-design magazine he was reading. I might live in a hovel, but I still appreciate a nice design sensibility I will never see again for myself. "Prints. A couple of minor arrests two decades ago," he said.

I pulled on a clean T-shirt, then a dark gray sweater. "Has Janey done the autopsy yet?"

He dropped the magazine on the floor. It wasn't rude. It landed on the stack of other magazines there. "Since we got an ID, she's going to move it up," he said.

I grabbed my jacket and knit cap. "Ready."

Downstairs, we settled into Murdock's car. "When I said 'ready,' I meant ready to go through the drive-thru at Dunkin' Donuts. You knew that, right?"

Murdock lifted a large foam cup from the console and handed it to me. "Took care of it on the way over."

The cup was warm in my hand, so he wasn't joking. It's hard to tell the fresh junk in Murdock's car from the stale. I took grateful sips. "Do you always stop for coffee when you think someone's dead in his apartment?"

We hopped on I-93 south to take the shortcut to Albany Street in the South End. "I said I was checking to see if you were dead. I suspected you were hungover. Likely outcomes first, you know."

"Is that what they taught you in that online detective course you took?" I asked.

He chuckled. "Drink your coffee, Connor. You're not awake enough to insult me effectively."

I settled back and did as I was told. Despite everything, the fact that Murdock still joked with me was an enormous relief, even if I was the butt of the jokes. I didn't cause the pain in his life, but I had been a part of ripping them out in the open. It wasn't my intention, but it weighed on me.

He was a victim of the Guild as much as I was, more so, really. The Guild used me as a tool, even a weapon, when it suited them. I was the perfect instrument because I believed their lies, thought I was serving some greater good, and, yeah, reveled in the glory and honor thrown my way.

Murdock, though, had never been part of their schemes. He was collateral damage.

He recognized that for what it was and didn't blame me for what happened. I didn't think I'd ever known anyone like him. Joe had proved time and again that he would stand by me, but Joe was, well, Joe. He rolled with everything, didn't dwell on the past or worry about the future. Briallen, as much as she supported me, made it clear there were greater issues that demanded the sacrifice of individuals. I took that as a hint that someday, if she ever had to make a choice, she would actually consider the options. For Murdock, there were no options. He stood by me, and I'd be damned if I didn't stand by him at this point.

I glanced at him. The bruising on his face from smashing into the wall was already healed to a faint red. "You're awfully chipper for someone who had a fight with a wall yesterday."

He glanced over at me with a smile. "I won the fight. What's not to feel good about?"

I forced myself to ask the question I was dreading to hear the answer to. "How's Kevin?"

The smile stayed on Murdock's face. "Good. Some not-unexpected damage, but a few days in the hospital should take care of it."

I frowned at him. "Druids heal faster than baseline humans. Did you tell him about his druid signature?"

"Yeah. You really don't want to know what he said," he said.

I sipped my coffee. "What about the suspect?"

We coasted off the exit for Albany Street. "He's in worse shape. The hospital won't let anyone talk to him for another day or so," he said.

I sipped my coffee. "I don't pity that guy. Being to blame for injuries to fire and police officers is a tough rap to beat."

"You should know," said Murdock.

I gave in and chuckled. I was not going to win with him today.

The Office of the Medical Examiner building had that

bleak cast that made one wonder if it was built to be depressing. The bones of the building hinted at an older, dignified past, maybe not grand, but at least presentable. What existed these days was a pitted structure, graffiti painted over in mismatched shades of gray, windowpanes repaired with cardboard when they weren't sooty, and a much-patched asphalt driveway that led around back to the receiving bays. Despite having a grungy, years-old car, Murdock didn't risk a parking space on Albany Street, so he parked behind the building in someone's reserved space.

The bustle inside the OCME startled me. It had been so long since I had been in the lower level during normal business hours that I had forgotten how many people worked there. Murdock flashed his badge at the security booth. Once inside, no one paid us any attention.

At the far end of the hallway, Janey Likesmith moved with a deliberate step as if she were concentrating on the act of walking. Dark circles under her eyes marred her smooth skin. "Nice to see some friendly faces," she said.

"If Connor's a friendly face, it must be bad," Murdock said.

Janey shot him an uncertain smile.

"It's Whack Connor Day. Feel free to join in," I said.

"Ignore him. He thinks it's Pity Connor Day," Murdock said.

Janey's smile became more amused as she led us up the hall. She dropped it as we entered the autopsy room. A plaque on the wall read *Hic locus est ubi mors gaudet succurrere vitae.* "This is the place where the dead delight in helping the living." I don't know how delighted they were, but more often than not they did provide answers.

The recent riots had produced a lot of death and now, months later, the unidentified and unmissed were being processed. Bodies occupied every table in the room, surrounded by pathology teams, some of them joined by photographers and evidence technicians. At the far end, a draped form lay without anyone attending. It wasn't a coincidence that it was the only body in the room that had a fey body signature.

Janey received no support at the OCME. Dead fey bodies that ended up there were from the edges of society with nowhere else to go. She worked hard to give them dignity and some final recognition that they had once lived. The OCME had Janey on staff because someone had to take the fey cases the Guild didn't want. That didn't mean the humans welcomed her. Janey managed to ignore the politics of the situation a lot better than I would have.

She lifted the cloth off a shallow stainless-steel bowl with a single dull brown stone in it. "I've started the physical but thought you might want to see this."

I used a set of tongs to pick it up. "There's a touch of essence on it."

"Too faint to make anything of it, though. Guess where I found it?" she asked.

"I'm not going to say what I'm thinking," Murdock said.

Janey poked him. "I'm going to pretend you didn't think that. It was in his stomach. I'm not seeing any bruising that might indicate a struggle. He may have been forced, but I'm inclined to suggest he swallowed it on his own."

I turned the stone one way and the other. Except for a lone rune scratched on it that could mean anything, it looked like a plain stone. "You're suggesting he wanted to hide it."

Janey shook her head. "No, that's for you guys to decide. I'm pointing out that the physical evidence might support it."

"What's the issue with the essence?" Murdock asked.

I dropped the stone in the bowl. "It was charged with essence, which makes it a ward stone of some kind. It was meant to do something, but the residue is too slight to figure out what."

Murdock gave Janey a playful bump with his arm. "You called us down here for something that could be anything?"

She bumped him back. "Yes, and something else, Detective. Come take a look."

She led us out of the examining room and down the hall to her office, a cramped space far from the other offices with a ground-level view of the parking lot. She handed Murdock a file. "This is the file for another body found on the edge of

Southie three nights before our friend up the hall. He was a dwarf, too, with little essence on him."

I read over Murdock's shoulder. "That's the other side of the Tangle. Same general location. Same species. Similar body signature status. Sounds like a lot, but nothing surprising for that area of town, no?"

Janey nodded. "True, but it prompted me to review the file. When the first one came in, I took tissue samples for testing because the body had negligible essence that didn't track with the time of death. A little unusual, but not unheard of. The second body has reduced essence in a similar profile. That moves them into something less coincidental."

"Why?" asked Murdock.

Janey leaned against the wall of drawers that held her files. "Because losing essence has a purpose. I've seen this patterning before, particularly in dwarves. I think you have two dead essence sellers on your hands."

Surprised, Murdock looked up. "People sell essence?"

I held my hand out for the file. "Where do you think those ward-stone security systems come from? I have one. Even the governor does. Someone creates the stone wards, installs them in a building, then someone shows up regularly and charges them."

Murdock opened the other file. "They get paid much for that?"

"Some do. Some don't. It depends on how complicated the system is," I said.

Janey opened a drawer and held out a small bag with a stone in it. "Guess what I found sewn into the lining of the Southie victim's jacket?"

I held the bag toward the light. "Same rune marker on it, too."

Murdock grunted in approval. "And two rap sheets that show they knew each other. Looks like we have some other associates here, but no known addresses."

"And I know where to start looking," I said.

# 13

Murdock pulled his car to the curb near the corner of Tide Street and Old Northern. "You sure you want to do this?"

I stared out the dusty windshield at the dark buildings leaning over the street. The Tangle was the worst of the worst of the Weird, a spidery network of dark alleys and dead ends. Essence fights, illegal potions, and strange trades filled the streets. A dark glamour hung over the area, casting shadows even during the day. Law enforcement had given up on it and stayed away. As long as the Tangle kept within its borders, it was allowed to exist.

I stayed out of the area as much as possible. Since the dark mass had appeared in my head, scrying caused me incredible pain. Whether someone was reading the future through fire or water, the black mass recoiled. The Tangle was filled with prognosticators of every stripe—druids and dwarves, the occasional nixie with a knack for weathercasting, and plenty of norns who could take one look at you and know when you were going to die. My head was hurting thinking about it.

"That's why we're doing this together, Leo. Fire up the body shield, buddy, and let's go."

We left the car on Tide Street. Machines didn't operate well in the Tangle. Many fey feared iron and steel because it warped essence and made it operate in unintended ways. In the Tangle, jamming spells stalled engines to keep them away, and good luck trying to get a tow truck to pull a car out without getting stuck itself.

The street narrowed, not an abrupt change from two lanes to one, but a sinuous compression that pulled in the buildings with it. The twilight sky darkened above as the sounds of Old Northern Avenue muted. Sharp points of pain prickled my brain, and I moved closer to Murdock. His body shield filtered out the brunt of the pain.

"This place gives me the creeps," Murdock said.

"It's supposed to," I said.

As if a switch had been flipped, people appeared. The Tangle attracted humans and fey who liked things on the wild side. The people who lived in the Tangle obliged. The more esoteric the need, the higher the price. It was always a seller's market. To enhance their image as talented practitioners of essence abilities, many fey wore traditional clothing out of Faerie. Nothing says genuine like a druid in a robe or a fairy in a diaphanous dress. What some lacked in skill and real ability, they made up for in appearance.

"What is that smell?" Murdock muttered.

Odors filled the air, the by-products of spells. "Herbs and incense. Spell stuff."

"I'm getting a cold or something. My sinuses have been killing me for weeks," he said.

He recoiled as a brownie brushed past him. I didn't notice any particular scent coming off her. "Weeks? That's not a cold, then. Maybe sinusitis."

"Whatever. Something down here is making it worse," he said.

The Tangle was the go-to spot for people looking for something essence-related they couldn't get anywhere else. Drugs were one lure. The fey were adept at creating new highs that slipped past the FDA before the FDA had any idea what they were. Curses were popular, too. The biggest appeal of the Tangle was its secretiveness—no paper trails, no credit cards, and no evidence. If both parties were fey, sendings could be used instead of audible conversations that might get recorded. The main thing to worry about was blackmail, but you bought into that risk if you went to the Tangle in first place.

We turned a corner into an empty pedestrian tunnel lined with brick, wide enough for four people to walk abreast but too narrow for a vehicle. "I thought this was going to be a street," said Murdock.

"It probably is to some people. The streetscape reacts to all kinds of things," I said.

Illusions drifted through the neighborhood. Real buildings and real streets existed alongside glamours of places that weren't there. Who made them and why were mysteries. Some people saw them, and others didn't. They created an atmosphere of uncertainty and the surreal that was part of the unique signature of the place.

Harsh white light lit the end of the tunnel, as if daytime had returned on the next block. People passed back and forth across the archway. We exited the tunnel, and the light vanished. We were back in twilight, in the heart of the Tangle.

The street didn't have a name, but when people talked about the Tangle, the road was what they meant. It stretched anywhere from two to ten blocks, depending on the time of day. The business of the Tangle happened amidst a chaotic group of stalls, booths, and tables. Burning incense, herb-infused potions, and the rank odor of bodies combined into a heady brew. More than a few hooded figures made their way through the crowd, buyers and sellers masking their identities. Murdock sneezed.

We roamed for a while, checking out the merchandise. Selling essence wasn't illegal. Mainstream stores along Boylston offered essence-charged stones for everything from mood modification to high-level security systems. On the street in the Tangle, plenty of ward rechargers were scattered among the other vendors. If you were looking for a lot of essence, enough that would drain a dwarf to almost none, you weren't looking to use it for something strictly legal. The select sellers knew that and kept as low a profile as the buyers. They had to work by sense and feel and learn not to spook a potential client.

After a couple of hours, a dwarf caught my eye. He held a coffee cup, lounging against a wall, watching the crowd in a neutral way that was too practiced to be casual. A sharp-eyed customer—or Guild agent—would notice the difference. His gaze lingered on single people—buying essence for the wrong reason was not a group activity—skipping the obvious groups and fey who didn't need his services.

An elf in the livery of Eorla's house guard wandered over and stood next to him. They eyed one another but didn't speak, at least not aloud. I gestured with my chin. "That's interesting."

Leo and I separated a few feet as we approached. The elf saw us first and lost himself in the crowd. Confused, the dwarf turned and spotted us. He dropped his coffee and made for another pedestrian tunnel. We let him get around the corner before Murdock rushed forward and grabbed his arm. The guy struggled until I flanked them, and Murdock let go. Dwarfs are strong, damned strong. I wouldn't have been able to hang on to the guy for more than a few seconds before he shrugged me off like a gnat. Murdock's strength level had become astounding even by druid standards.

"Leave me alone," he said.

"We just want to talk," I said.

Incredulous, he frowned at Murdock. "To a cop? You gotta be joking."

"No joke. We need some info. It's about the two dead dwarves," I said.

His gaze shifted to either end of the enclosed alley. "I had nothing to do with that."

"Not saying you did. We're looking for information," Murdock said.

The dwarf craned his neck to see over our shoulders.

Rubberneckers were checking us out from the main drag. "You are killing my cred. You want to talk, then walk me outta here like I'm a badass and you're badder," he said.

Happy to oblige, Murdock grabbed his arm again. At the end of the alley, we pushed through the cluster of people that had gathered. The dwarf made a show of looking unhappy, which was fine. The crowd flowed around us, some shouting at us, and not encouragement. Law enforcement in the Tangle was not welcomed by many.

The crowd closed in tighter. The dwarf yanked his arm from Murdock and shoved me out of his way like a rag doll tossed aside by a child. The push sent me barreling through the crowd. The dwarf darted back the way we had come, with Murdock close on his heels. The dark mass in my head shuddered as Murdock's body shield slipped away from me. Ignoring the pain, I ran after them.

Scrying essence bombarded me from all sides. Every step I took intensified the pain in my head. Darkness crept into the edges of my vision as I fought off a faint. I pushed on, focused on Murdock ahead of me. Relieved, I entered the field of his body shield, and the pain diminished.

The dwarf darted into another pedestrian tunnel. The sudden dimness blinded me after the illumination of the street. I struggled to maintain my footing. Ahead, the dwarf ran toward the exit, but Murdock was nowhere in sight. He had to be there. His body shield was protecting me. I shouted his name and received a muffled response. We were caught in some kind of glamour, invisible to each other.

Murdock's shield slipped on and off me, the pain in my head telling me when I was falling behind. With a burst of speed, I ran into the next street. Murdock reappeared, ahead and to my left side, as we chased the dwarf ran down a jagged path of undulating pavement.

The street stretched, elongating into an impossible long path between tall gray buildings. Far overhead, the stars burned in a narrow strip of sky. Shadows came alive and oozed across the street. I navigated by essence light, the buildings and street etched in faint white shot through with shades of the green and blue. I passed Murdock as the dwarf pulled farther ahead.

"I can't see," Murdock's voice echoed from behind me.

"To the left. Stay with me," I said.

Darkness danced in the air at the far end of the street, long tendrils that undulated and waved across the pavement, weaving itself into a web. The dwarf stopped running, his hands out to either side in uncertainty. Surprised, I skidded to a halt. Murdock knocked into me, and we jostled away from each other. "Why'd you stop?" he asked.

I pointed. "Can you see that?"

Something slithered out of the darkness and reached for the dwarf. He turned to run, but a strand of darkness wrapped around his torso and pulled. The dwarf lifted off his feet and screamed.

Murdock pulled his gun. "What the hell is that?"

I grabbed his arm. "Don't shoot. You'll hit the dwarf."

He aimed the gun and walked forward. "We can't just watch."

I wasn't watching. I was fighting off a surge of pain in my head. The dark mass shifted and burned with heat. I fell to one knee as normal vision vanished. The street became a black void. Murdock glowed like a red flame, and, beyond him, the emerald essence of the dwarf flashed and flickered in the air.

I pushed myself up. "Murdock, wait."

He paused, glanced over his shoulder, then swung his gun toward me. "What is that stuff? What do you want me to do?"

The dark mass was bleeding out of my eye. I held my hand out in a calming gesture, concentrating on forcing the darkness back inside. "It's the thing in my head. Stay away."

Gun focused on me, he circled, a look of horror on his face. "What should I do?"

"Nothing. Stay out of reach."

The darkness in the street swirled with deep violet light. As I forced myself to walk toward it, the dark mass in my head flexed, a finger of pain running along my jaw. The vision dimmed in my right eye as pressure built behind it. I caught the wall as I lost my balance. Pain swarmed the right side of my head. I went blind and tripped as the dark mass sliced out of my right eye.

The darkness in the street loomed over me like a claw. It paused, tendrils of black vapor waving in the air. The blade of darkness from my eye splintered and reached for the tendrils. The two strands of darkness connected, and a concussive jolt like electricity threw me against the wall. The dark mass whipped back inside my head, and I fell.

Murdock leaned over me. "You okay?"

I lifted my head. The darkness in the street had vanished. The street had become dead space, no vestige of essence on it. My head echoed with the emptiness. "Where's the dwarf?"

Murdock helped me up. "Over there."

The dwarf lay in the street, his body signature dim, his gaze fixed on the sky as he struggled to breathe. We huddled over him. Up close, a faint spark of essence remained in him, but I didn't see it lasting long. The pavement beneath him was devoid of essence. "Get him against the wall. He might be able to draw essence from the stone."

I didn't know if it would work, but without a healer, he had little hope of surviving. Murdock helped me move the body into a seated position against the wall. The dwarf's head slumped to his chest. I patted at his face. "Come on, buddy, tap the stone. You need essence."

His eyes fluttered. A feeble trickle of essence came out of his chest as he tried to use his body signature to tap the stone. I scanned the wall and street. The darkness had leeched essence from the surroundings. "This whole area is stripped, Leo. There's nothing for him to pull. Let's get him farther up the street."

With frustrating slowness, we carried him. The pavement was uneven cobbles, and dwarves are heavy.

"I'm dying," the dwarf said.

"Hold on a few more feet," I said.

"She wanted the stone," he said.

A sense of dread swept over me. "Who?"

The dwarf wheezed. "She was in my head. She wanted the stone."

"We have to move faster," I said to Murdock.

"Two druids were chasing me. I don't know who they are," said the dwarf.

"Hang on. We're almost there," I said.

Essence reasserted itself in the street as we neared the pedestrian tunnel. The weight of the dwarf increased with each step. "He's fading, Leo," I said.

A shout rang out, the sound of nearby voices calling a death knell. At the same instant, the dwarf fell from of our hands, his weight too great to hold any longer. I rested my hand on his chest. "He's gone, Leo."

Angry, I stalked away, banging my fist on a wall. I glared up the street, searching for some sign of the darkness. Essence was creeping back into the pavement and the walls, thin and weak. At the far end of the street, a burst of bright blue light surged out of a gap between buildings. It filled the street, moved toward me, then stopped. Indiscernible darker blue shapes moved within it. I took a step, intent on chasing after it, when it gathered into itself and retreated the way it had come. It vanished around a corner.

"Did you see that?" I asked Murdock.

He turned toward me. "What?"

"The blue light I've been tracking. It was at the end of the street. I want to say it was checking out what just happened," I said.

Murdock shook his head. "I missed it. I was searching the body. Look what I found." He held up a stone identical to the ones on the previous victims.

"Whatever he was selling wasn't essence, Leo."

"That dark stuff that attacked you looked like what came out of the *leanansidhe* we found," he said.

The *leanansidhe* were fey predators that survived by absorbing essence from people. Leo and I stumbled into one a few months back. When I said stumble, I meant almost were killed by her. "I was thinking the same thing. Same dark tendrils. Same indigo and violet essence light surrounding it. All this time, I thought she was dead."

"Dead? You never mentioned the *leanansidhe* again after you told Keeva about it. I thought the Guild finally stepped up and dealt with a criminal in the Weird," he said.

I had gone to Keeva macNeve at the Guild. She had taken it upon herself to hunt down the *leanansidhe*. She found it, but it got the better of her. She almost died, which was why she had needed to go to Tara to finish out her pregnancy. "I forgot about it. I never checked to make sure it was dead."

Hands on his hips, he sighed. "We can go tomorrow."

I frowned. "Where?"

He looked up at me. "Where we found the *leanansidhe*. Don't pretend you aren't thinking about it. Promise me you won't go without me," he said.

"She can't hurt me, Leo. That's why the dwarf didn't die right away. My presence interrupted her feeding."

"Promise me," he said.

I glared at him. He was with me when we found the *leanansidhe*. It knocked him on his ass. She wasn't going to be happy to see me after what happened. "Leo . . ."

"I will lock you in a cell," he said.

I laughed. "You will not."

He shook his head. "Fine. I'll tell Briallen, then. Or Eorla or whoever else I can think of who will tie you up and dump you in a corner until you get some common sense."

I chuckled. "You're as stupid as I am."

He grinned. "Maybe, but I have a gun."

# 14

The *leanansidhe* were feared by even the powerful Danann fairies. They fed on living essence, preferring the strong essence of people as the primary source for their needs. They lived in obscurity, hidden away from world, finding ways to survive that might go unnoticed. When they were noticed, they were hunted to death. Few people met them and lived.

I had met one named Druse. She called me her brother. She meant it metaphorically, but she wasn't that far from the truth. After years of no one understanding what the dark mass in my head was, she knew something. Her fey ability to drain essence used a form of the same darkness. She showed me how it worked and how to find pleasure in it. She showed me a side to myself, a desire within, that disgusted me. She showed me how easy it can be to intend to kill someone. Using the darkness, I had tasted the essence of a living person—Keeva, my old partner at the Guild. That was bad enough. What made it worse was that on some level, I recognized what I was doing and didn't stop right away. For that, I was ashamed. Many things I've done wrong in my

life have made me feel guilty, but the night I almost killed
Keeva made me truly ashamed.

When Druse showed me how to use the darkness, I felt
pain, but a pain with a twisted pleasure to it. Druse had
linked her mind to mine and wouldn't let go. When we used
the darkness in sync with each other, we bonded on an intimate level. When we worked in opposition, the individual
darknesses within us rejected each other, and we blacked
out, like what had happened to me last night. I had seen the
darkness kill again, its waving tendrils of shadow sapping
away the life of their victim. The darkness in my head had
responded to it.

The dark tendrils in the alley the previous night were exactly how a *leanansidhe* siphoned essence from people. I had
two explanations for what had happened in the Tangle. Either Druse was alive, or another *leanansidhe* was loose in the
city. One *leanansidhe* in the neighborhood was a surprise—
even a shock. Two stretched the bounds of believability.

The dwarf's dying whisper that "she" wanted the stone
made it more plausible that Druse was alive. She had a stone
ward she was willing to kill for—a rare ward shaped like a
bowl that had the ability to generate essence from its surroundings and return it tenfold. Druse used it to stave off her
hunger during the low periods when she couldn't acquire living prey. The ward stone had a geasa—an essence-enhanced
restriction— that only a virgin could move it. A virgin-only
geasa was old-school Faerie stuff, and the stone was definitely old-school. The essence it emitted had the distinct
signature of the Faerie that existed before Convergence.
A fortuitous blow to the head with that same stone bowl
stopped Druse and, I thought, killed her. If she had survived,
she would want the bowl back and would stop at nothing
until she had it.

After I escaped Druse, I hid the stone with a street kid
named Shay, who had a rather funny advantage in the virgin
department. No one knew Shay had the stone, but Druse was
attuned to it and would find it eventually.

Shay had been through a lot of heartache because of me,

and I didn't want to panic him with a theory. If whatever was haunting the Weird and the Tangle was not Druse, Shay would be safe—or at least safer. Before I told him anything, I wanted to see Druse's body for myself, and the way to do that was to return to her lair. Murdock had known what I wanted to do before I did. I had to go back and confirm whether the body was there.

I waited in the cool early-morning air outside the warehouse where we had first found the *leanansidhe*. Murdock arrived all tricked out in a police tactical uniform but with his regular Boston P.D. jacket over it so there was no mistaking where he worked. I wore jeans and a short leather jacket. "You look like you mean business," I said.

"I do. I'm not walking in blind this time." Druse had been feeding on one of her victims when we stumbled on her in a tunnel. She'd attacked Murdock and knocked him on his ass. She would have drained him to death, too, if I hadn't been there.

The building remained a crime scene after Murdock and I had found skeletons in the basement. Druse had been around a long time before we found her. The Weird was the perfect place for her to operate. Since it was routine for people to disappear in the neighborhood without explanation, she survived without notice for years.

Murdock produced a key out from the pocket of his black tactical vest and unlocked the warehouse door. The inside had not changed since my last—unauthorized—visit. An upper corridor led to a hammered-metal basement door. We descended into the gloom of the basement. Murdock activated his body shield at the bottom of the metal stairs. It burned crimson in my vision. Under normal circumstances, the layer of hardened essence protected him from a fey attack, with the exception of a *leanansidhe*. Heightened essence was what she sought, and a shield served as an appetizer to her.

A narrow passage stretched fifty feet to a tunnel that led to the sewer system. That was the route we used to find the basement when we were investigating another case. Unlike our first visit, the space was empty, swept clean of the possessions and remains of Druse's victims. The police had been processing the large volume of evidence for months.

On the right, a hole broken through a bricked-over archway led to the basement proper, a vast space that was empty when we found it and empty still. At the far end, an opening in the wall gaped like a wound. "You couldn't see this opening a month ago, Leo. The *leanansidhe* had a glamour on it that made it look like the rest of the wall."

He directed the beam of his flashlight into the opening. "It looks clear."

"I've been in there. There's a few blind turns, but mostly a straight shot to her room. Watch out for binding spells," I said.

Despite my foray into the various tunnels around the city, I wasn't a big fan of urban exploration. It was dangerous in general, and in the Weird, it was asking for trouble. Through the hole, the walls and ceiling had a smooth, organic feel to them, an indication that they had been shaped long ago by trolls and dwarves. The path wound deep beneath the Weird, branching off to parts unknown.

"You came down here alone and unarmed?" Murdock asked.

"Yep."

He chuckled in my ear. "Man, you are crazier than I thought."

"Well, I wasn't down here for the best possible reasons." As understatements go, that was a big one. Druse knew things about the dark mass in my head, maybe not how it got there or how to get rid of it, but she showed me how to—and I hated to admit it even to myself—enjoy it. The pleasure it gave me was hard to describe, but the kick and the kink of a sexual addiction didn't come close. No matter how I tried to stop myself, I gave in to the desire at the risk of my life and people I cared about. I had managed to keep it under control all these months by staying away from powerful essence sources.

In the upper section of the tunnel, we passed rooms that were basements to other buildings. As we descended, the path sloping deeper underground, the rooms were shaped out of the earth and became more rough-hewn, empty of trash or other debris. "What the hell is this place?" Murdock asked.

"Boston is almost four hundred years old, and it's riddled with tunnels. Someone's dug a hole in the ground in every one of those years," I said. Access tunnels, subway tunnels, sewage tunnels, utility tunnels, escape tunnels—name it, and there's a tunnel for it somewhere in the city. At least once a month, someone doing construction or renovation stumbles on one or more passageways, some impressive enough to make the news. The ones that don't make the news are the scary ones, small bolt-holes that were used to get out of sight fast and secure.

We arrived at Druse's room without any surprises. At one point, she had rigged the tunnels with binding spells, webs of essence that trapped intruders. Without her, the spells had dissipated. The lack of them raised my anxiety as I waited for an attack that hadn't come.

We stood to either side of the entrance, searching for signs of movement within. A stained-glass lamp had provided the main lighting, but it lay broken on the floor, smashed in the fight between Druse and Keeva. A bare bulb dangling from an extension cord along the ceiling cast enough light to see by after the darkness of the tunnel. Murdock entered first, his shooting arm extended as he scanned the room.

I panned the beam of my flashlight into darker corners. "I don't feel anyone," I said.

Murdock remained in a crouch as he worked his way across the room. "You didn't the first time we met her. Remember? We thought she was dead."

My light picked out the random assortment of furniture Druse had collected over the years. Judging by the volume, she had been down there for a long time. Books lay everywhere. When I first saw the room, the books had no discernible organization—stacks of them on tables and chairs, shoved into leaning bookcases and piled on the floor. That was orderly compared to now. Now, the room was in shambles. It hadn't changed since the night I almost killed Keeva.

"She's not here, Leo. The room hasn't been touched since the night Shay killed her," I said.

He swung his flashlight beam toward me. "What the hell did you say?"

At the back of the room, I slipped through a long fissure in the wall of the room. Murdock followed, his gun at the ready. Inside was a natural two-story chamber, a gap in the bedrock under the landfill far above. In the middle of the chamber, an upheaving of stone rose like a pedestal. Druse had stored the ward-stone bowl on it. Months later, the bedrock glowed with residual essence from the powerful ward. "Shay killed the *leanansidhe*, or at least I thought he did."

Murdock relaxed his stance but didn't holster his weapon. He wasn't taking any chances this time. "Shay? Runaway prostitute Shay?" he asked.

"It's a long story."

"I think you better start telling it, Connor, while I decide if I'm a little pissed off," he said.

I inhaled and closed my eyes. Time after time, I held back information from Murdock, thinking it safer for him or to avoid an argument. Time after time, Murdock found out and read me out about it. This time, I didn't tell him because it was personal. "I didn't tell you because I was embarrassed, Leo. I lost a piece of myself down here. I gave in to something dark inside me that had nothing to do with the dark mass. I want to blame it on the dark mass in my head, but I think that might be an excuse. I had this craving for power I never realized I had. I let it overwhelm me, and I almost killed Keeva because of it. If Shay hadn't shown up, I don't know what would have happened."

"How the hell did Shay get involved?"

I chuckled in derision at myself, caught with another thing I had kept to myself. "Yeah, that's something else I didn't tell you about. I have a dog."

Murdock brought the flashlight beam back to my face. "Are you losing it, Connor? 'Cause I don't understand a damned thing you're saying."

"I don't blame you. I don't understand it myself. There's

a dog. Shay and I call him Uno. He's a fey dog. You've actually been around him, but for some reason you can't see him."

"Okay, you're not convincing me you're not losing it," he said.

I circled around the bedrock. "You've seen fey people vanish in front of you. It's not exactly the same, but something about Uno cloaks him from certain people. I don't fully understand it myself. Joe can see him. That might be because he's supersensitive to essence. Keeva didn't see him when he was standing right next to her. Shay can see him because he's supposed to. The old tales of Faerie say it's a harbinger of death."

Murdock made a slow circuit of the room perimeter. "I'll accept that. God knows I've seen stranger things around you. But if you thought Shay killed the *leanansidhe*, why are we down here?"

I stared around the chamber. "I was hoping to find the body. It happened the night before the riots. After everything that happened, I forgot about it. Can you believe that? I forgot about a dead body."

"A lot happened that night." He looked away. It happened the same night his father died.

"When I saw that darkness stuff in the Tangle, I realized I had screwed up again. I was in denial, Leo. If I told someone what had happened down here, I'd have to admit what I had done. I think I convinced myself I was protecting Shay and keeping him out of jail, but I was really trying to deny what I did."

I walked toward the bedrock. "The *leanansidhe* had a ward stone that amplified essence. She showed me how to drink from it, and it made the dark mass in my head stop hurting."

Murdock shifted in place opposite me. "The dwarf said she wanted the stone. That's why you wanted to come down here."

I ran my hand along part of the bedrock, and the essence

in the stone danced up my arm. "Shay has it. We've told no one else."

As I touched the bedrock, the dark mass shifted in my head, perhaps at the memory of that night, but it didn't push to come out. "Like you said, Leo, the first time we found the *leanansidhe*, I thought she was dead. Her body should be here. The blow to the head must not have killed her. The deaths of those dwarves are my fault. I have to stop her before she kills more people or goes after Shay."

"Now we know who we're looking for," he said.

"Better yet. We know *what* she's looking for," I said.

# 15

I went to Druse's hiding place first because I had to know if her body was there. I had to confirm the facts with my own eyes. Part of it was my nature, which had made me a good investigator once upon a time. The important part, though, was not wanting to scare Shay until I knew for sure what was going on. He didn't need any reminders of that night.

Sometimes I wondered where Shay would be if he had never met me. Almost a year earlier, he had been a minor witness in a murder case Murdock and I worked on. Shay's involvement grew when I made a bad call and asked his boyfriend Robyn to act as a decoy for the murderer. Robyn fit the needed physical description of the victims better than anyone available, and I thought he would be a slam-dunk for finding the killer. I was too right, and he didn't survive the setup. Shay lost his lover and protector because of me. Ever since, I've looked out for him whenever I can.

In life, Shay's boyfriend Robyn was human, a young guy with a tough life that involved drugs and prostitution. We didn't like each other. Robyn was convinced I didn't care, that the only reason I wanted their help was for my own benefit. It didn't help that Murdock gave him an ultimatum—work with us or go to jail. He was killed, maybe by his own arrogance and stupidity, but I set him on the path that led to his death.

Then Robyn showed up again. When he died, he ended up Dead in the Celtic realm of TirNaNog. The veil lifted between our world and his, and he came back to check on Shay. When I collapsed the veil, the Dead that were here became trapped, Robyn among them. Another bad call on my part that I didn't know how to fix.

When I was under the influence of the *leanansidhe*, Shay came to my rescue for a change. The reward for his help was yet another complication. Since he was the only person I knew that could move the *leanansidhe*'s stone, I thought hiding the stone with him would be safe. He wasn't fey, so he couldn't use it. My old partner, Keeva, knew about the stone, but not where it was, and she was off in Tara. Until I told Murdock, Shay and I had agreed to tell no one else he had it.

Now Shay was in danger again, because of me, again. Druse might suspect dwarves had taken the stone and gone after them, but it was only a matter of time before she would find her way to Shay's doorstep. At some point as she prowled the city, she would sense the stone's telltale emanations. I had to move it somewhere that wouldn't put Shay in danger.

Visiting Shay presented a tricky situation. I was being watched by Guild and Consortium agents and who knew who else. Eorla probably had a pair of eyes on me, too. Any unusual place I visited might spark unwanted interest, and I didn't want to draw attention to Shay.

Walking Meryl around town for an hour or so had become a habit, the kind of habitual activity that caused a spy to lose interest and get sloppy. Even better—I took her different places, hoping against hope that a different environment might jog her out of her constant reverie. Wandering into Shay's neighborhood and stopping by for a few minutes was a low-risk proposition that I hoped wouldn't raise eyebrows.

I maneuvered Meryl along the sidewalk with some difficulty. In her trance state, she walked with a simple push and maintained a steady pace until stopped. The problem was that she didn't have any awareness of the surface she walked on. She stumbled with any change in the grade of the ground, lurching forward when the slope dropped and staggering when it rose. Her gait would adjust, then she staggered when the slope changed again. I had some success by holding her arm, pulling up when the sidewalk canted up and steadying her as it fell. Through it all, she maintained the same vacant stare.

When we reached Shay's building, I spent a few moments of weight shifting to convey to Meryl the idea of mounting the front steps. Shay buzzed us in without checking who we were, a practice frowned on by most neighbors. I led Meryl through the tall narrow hallway of the converted warehouse. The soaring walls held artwork in various levels of seriousness. In the public, unsecured spaces, no one wanted to hang anything valuable but did want to convey their talents. A riot of color covered the walls in paintings and drawings in styles ranging from the Renaissance to spray-paint graffiti. Mobile sculptures created with found materials dangled from the ceiling far enough out of reach to discourage easy theft.

Artists rented the space for work studios, and many, like Shay, used them as illegal apartments. It wasn't a bad setup if you didn't mind sharing a public bathroom and begging friends for the use of a shower. Shay opened his door as we reached it. He looked at Meryl with curiosity. "Hi, Connor. Who's your friend?"

I nudged Meryl. "Her name is Meryl Dian."

Shay had one of the smaller studios, about thirty feet long and ten feet wide. He had divided the space with bookcases to form a makeshift kitchen at the door, a sleeping alcove in the middle, and a combination work space–living room at the far end, where the windows were.

As soon as we stepped inside, potent essence registered in my senses. I wasn't surprised. The stone bowl collected essence and amplified it. I was surprised at how intense it had become. With no one or nothing to deplete it for months, it had gathered an enormous reserve.

Shay helped me remove Meryl's coat. "What's her situation?"

It was a diplomatic way of saying it. Shay worked for an institution that provided care to people with mental disabilities. "It's a long story. Why don't we set her up on the couch?"

At the back of the studio, two large armchairs flanked a couch, all of them covered in bold primary-colored slipcovers that weren't the same as the last time I had visited. The coffee table was pushed aside to make room for a large easel and a rolling cart filled with paint and art supplies. The canvas on the easel was an untouched white expanse that glistened with moisture. "I was prepping a canvas. Don't touch it. The base is still wet," Shay said.

I settled Meryl in an armchair next to a box draped with a needlepoint rug. A pale waft of essence welled in the air, and Uno, the large black dog I had told Murdock about, materialized on the couch. He had a true name, as all things do, but neither Shay nor I knew it. The name Uno started as a joke—Shay thought he looked like a hound from hell out of Greek mythology, minus the extra two heads.

The joked backfired on him. Uno was a real hound from hell, the Cu Sith of Celtic legends. When the Cu Sith appeared to someone, it meant that person was going to die. Through an unexpected turn of fate, Uno acted as a protector for Shay instead of a predator. Uno chose to protect me, too. Why, I didn't know, but he had come in handy a few times.

"I hate when he does that," I said.

Shay wrestled with the dog's shaggy head, and Uno woofed in pleasure. "He makes me feel safe. I'm starting to think he's my good-luck charm. Nothing bad has happened to me since I found him. Or he found me."

Shay's boyfriend, Robyn—his Dead boyfriend, Robyn—had sent Uno to protect him. I promised Robyn I wouldn't tell Shay that was what happened. Robyn didn't want Shay to know he was back from the Land of the Dead. He didn't want him hurt again if the veil between worlds opened, and he was forced back to TirNaNog. "I end up in trouble when he shows up," I said.

Shay smirked and went up to the kitchen area. "Funny, I was about to say the same thing about you. Do you want some tea?"

"Sure." I trailed after him.

He filled the kettle and set it on a hot plate. "I was wondering when you were going to show up."

"I've been busy trying not to get arrested," I said.

Shay adjusted his long dark hair over his shoulder and played with it. "I've been waiting for that knock on my door, too."

My memory flashed to the night Shay hit the *leanansidhe* over the head to save me. He had been dazed. The shock of what he had done to another living being overwhelmed him. He hadn't intended to kill her—Shay would never intend to hurt anyone—but it had happened. He seemed to have recovered, but you never really recover from killing someone. Worrying about the body being found must have been rough for him, and I hadn't given the idea a second thought. "That's why I'm here. I went back, Shay. The body is gone. I don't think you killed her."

He bowed his head, folding his arms across his waist. "Uno's been appearing a lot lately. When you buzzed the door, I had a bad feeling."

When Uno first appeared, Shay had been convinced he was going to die. The idea wasn't far-fetched among the fey, but until Uno showed up, no one had seen the Cu Sith since Convergence. He protected Shay—and me—and had been around us long enough to hint that something had changed about its purpose in the World. "I don't think Druse will come after you per se. She's looking for the stone. You should be safe once we move it."

Dubious, he arched an eyebrow. "She'll forget that I bashed her head in? That thing's the forgive-and-forget type?"

I compressed my lips to keep from saying it would be fine. Despite being young, Shay was wise beyond his years and had a bullshit detector most adults never acquired. He had his rough edges, but at heart was a good person. He was exactly the type of person I wanted to protect in the Weird. He deserved a better life. "I don't know, Shay, but leaving the stone here will definitely bring her right to your door."

The whistling of the kettle startled him. He poured out two mugs and handed one to me. "You look tired."

"Things have been a little crazy," I said.

The essence level in the studio changed, a brief dip in intensity before stabilizing again. I sipped the tea, thinking the stone had reacted to the presence of two druids—to say nothing of a Dead dog.

"Are you going to take it now?" Shay asked.

"I can't, remember? You're the only person I know who can lift it." Shay qualified as a virgin on a technicality as far as the stone went. He had never slept with a woman.

He used a fingernail to worry at a chip in his mug. "But you need to move it, right? You want me to take it somewhere."

"I was thinking that old squat you had with Robyn down off Pittsburgh Street, unless you think it's not safe anymore," I said.

"It's safe. No one knew we lived there except Murdock. We never had a problem. When do you want me to move it?"

"I don't want people to see us together, but as soon as you can after I leave," I said.

A spike of pain lanced through my head. I jammed the heel of my palm against my eye trying to push back against the pressure. The black mass jumped. I've learned the meaning of its different reactions and movements, recognized patterns in the kinds of pain it produced. A dull steady ache was normal, daggerlike spikes meant a strong essence was nearby, and a squeezing sensation for when someone tried to read the future around me. Body-numbing pain happened when I was losing control of it because it wanted out. "Does someone in the building scry, Shay?"

He set his mug on the counter and placed a concerned hand on my arm. "Probably. There are a few fey here. What's wrong?" he asked.

The pain ratcheted up, a great multifaceted spike that pounded against my skull as a dark haze drifted across my vision. "I have to leave. The dark stuff in my head is reacting to something."

Shay jumped as Uno let out a piercing yowl.

"Meryl?" I called. I hurried past the bed alcove, my head pounding with heat. Meryl stood at the easel, white splatters down the front of her sweatshirt as she smeared gobs of paint onto the canvas. Next to the couch, the needlepoint rug hung askew, revealing where Shay had hidden the stone ward under an old table. Fierce white essence light jumped from the bowl, arcing into Meryl from across the room. Her eyes and hands glowed as she slapped at the canvas with her hands, the white painting burning with a rainbow of essence. Uno's yowling scaled higher and more frantic.

I staggered under waves of pain. The vision in my right eye vanished, replaced by a darkness littered with jarring flashes. A black bolt leaped out of my chest and tangled with the white essence in the air. As if from far off in the distance, I heard Shay scream.

Essence seared into me, delicious surging essence. It splintered inside me, racing tendrils burning with energy. I had been fighting against the urge to absorb essence for weeks, keeping the darkness at bay, but the volume from the bowl was overwhelming. I couldn't restrain the darkness. I dropped to my knees and shouted at the cold luscious pain. "Get it out of here!" I shouted.

Shay's body signature radiated in a soft purple light. The stone bowl glowed like a brilliant white star as he lifted it. My body yearned for it, wanted to reach out and suck it in. Nothing but white light cascaded across my mind. The star rose in the darkness, obliterating any sign of Shay, then danced away from sight.

My vision muddied, the room becoming a blur of fading color shot through with streaks of light. Intense heat and cold warred in my chest as the dark mass pulsed against the essence that remained. Meryl swayed on her feet, her body shimmering with golden light. Behind her, shapes coalesced into almost recognizable figures, then broke apart in a maelstrom of color. The surface of the canvas spun like the eye of a hurricane, impossibly white, with a dark hole in the center.

The bands of shadow from my chest revolved around Meryl like predators, worrying at the edges of her body essence. Desire rose within me, a desire to goad the darkness forward, make it take what it sought. I struggled against it, fighting against the yearning. With a flash, essence rippled beneath my skin. Something snapped inside me as the light and the darkness met in a blaze of pain. I flew backwards with a force like a gunshot recoil. Meryl crumpled to the floor, the canvas awash with essence.

Spots danced in front of my eyes, blotchy smears of red and black that weren't essence. I convulsed as my sensing ability broke off like a sudden dousing of the sun, and sweet, sweet numbness swept over me.

# 16

A steady throb pounded my temples. I forced my eyes open. From the ceiling, a wavy distorted image of my body lying on something white reflected from thick glass. Behind the glass, a dull gray smear indicated steel sheathing. Around me, the walls, floor, and lone door were lined the same way. Essence didn't travel well through glass, and metal warped it back on itself. Putting the two together created an effective barrier against it.

I lifted my head from a pillow, my brain following the motion a second later. I sat up, holding my forehead to ease the rush of blood to my head. To either side, four-foot stone obelisks shimmered with a pearlescent glow. They reacted to my movement, flashing with a slow whirl that danced through the field around the stone. They were dampening wards to monitor my body signature and prevent the accidental or intentional use of essence.

I was on a bed in a containment room. Hospitals used them to protect patients from outside influences that might disrupt healing spells. Mental wards used them to keep patients calm and protect staff against unpredictable essence bursts. Prisons used them as holding cells. Mine was a holding cell.

The thick glass-coated door opened, and four Danann security agents entered. They fanned out, their wings rising and falling with sharp flashes of blue and white, their hands primed with essence and ready to fire. Briallen came in next, her face set with concern as she approached the bed. Outside the door, Joe fluttered in the hallway. He waved.

"Where am I?" I asked.

Briallen stopped at the foot of the bed. "Avalon Memorial holding area. Do you know who you are?"

I smiled through fatigue. "You know I've been working on that, Briallen."

Tension eased out of her. Briallen had spent a good part of the last few years scolding me for whining I wasn't the person I wanted to be anymore. She took my hand. "I'll take that as a yes."

"What the hell happened?"

She placed her free hand on my forehead. She didn't perform her usual probe but examined my body signature with the gentlest touch of essence. "I was hoping you could tell me. You had some kind of episode. Two agents who arrived on the scene were drained." Her hand slid to my shoulder as panic ran through me. "I said 'drained,' not 'dead.' They're fine. How do you feel?"

"Where's Meryl?" I asked instead of answering her.

"Upstairs. She's fine. Tell me what happened."

I glanced at the guards. "Are they necessary?"

She examined the ward monitors. I wasn't an expert on them, but I knew they measured things like essence outputs and fluctuation patterns. *Are you in control of yourself?* she sent.

My body was sore. My chest ached, and my face throbbed as if someone had punched me, but Briallen wasn't asking about a physical assessment. The black mass in my head smoldered with a heated smoothness, not the jagged edges that appeared when it was agitated. The hungering sensation

wasn't there either. It was sated, for now. I nodded. With
the flutter from a sending, Briallen dismissed the agents. Joe
flew in over their heads as they filed out.

I swung my legs off the bed. "I want to see Meryl."

Briallen steadied me as I stood. "Are you going to tell me
what happened?"

I pushed my way toward the door. "What about Shay?"

She grabbed my arm with a fierce grip that warned me
I wasn't going anywhere. "He called Leonard, then disappeared before help arrived. Do not make me ask what happened again, Connor."

I forced myself to remain calm. "The dark thing came out
of me. It reacted to something in Shay's apartment. I don't
understand it myself."

Worry etched her face. "Then why should I let you leave
this room?"

Dumbfounded, I stared at her. "What do you mean? Am
I under arrest?"

She relaxed her grip but held on. "You've committed no
crime, Connor, but I saw the agents brought in. There are going to be questions. Convince me you're not a danger outside
this room."

Her neutral tone unnerved me. Briallen always warned
me that sometimes personal relationships had to take a backseat to bigger issues. She'd had pain in her past, details she
hadn't shared except to say she did what needed to be done
when necessary. She hadn't cut me any slack when I was a
young kid in training. She wasn't going to now.

I went with honesty. "I can't. I can say that at this moment, you have nothing to worry about."

Not taking her eyes from me, she cocked her head. "Joe?"

He squinted as he fluttered around me, his essence glowing hot pink. Flits sensed essence at a granular level. They
needed to in order to be able to teleport without landing in a
wall and killing themselves. Joe was doing his own version
of a scan. "He's telling the truth, m'lady. I don't see anything
freaky."

I dropped my gaze to the floor. "You don't trust me."

Briallen rubbed my arm. "I don't trust myself."

"I'm okay," I said.

She searched my face, her eyes troubled. "I will let you leave if you promise me you will call me the moment you feel out of control."

I took her hand and kissed it. "I promise."

I thought she wasn't going to accept my word, but she inhaled and nodded as if resigned. "I'll take you to her."

The surface of my skin felt raw and jangly as we stepped off the elevator upstairs. With all the ward baffling in AvMem, there wasn't much essence in the air. The mass vibrated inside me, testing the area for a hint of essence, but it was more standard procedure for the dark mass than any threat it would activate.

In Meryl's room, Gillen Yor stood at the foot of the bed, his fists planted on his hips. He glared at the medical and stone ward monitors as if trying to bend them to his will. Knowing Gillen, he probably was. He cocked his head as we entered, his long, shaggy eyebrows animated. "I'll be bled and drained if I can figure out what the hell is wrong with this woman."

Meryl sat in bed, her blank expression unchanged from earlier in the day. White paint flecked her hair and spots on her hands and face where someone had missed cleaning them. I picked up her limp hand. "Is she all right?"

Gillen tugged at his hair, adding to the cotton-candy halo around his bald spot. "Better than she was. We've got strong brain activity back. It's trance-state, but it's there."

"That's good, right?"

Gillen chewed at his lips as he narrowed his eyes. "It's progress, but there's still not a damned thing I can do to help her."

I winced. "Do you think it's okay to say something like that within her hearing?"

That was a mistake. Gillen glowered with utter contempt. "I do not need some lovesick puppy lecturing me on what is or is not okay to say in front of my own Danu-damned patients, Grey. And speaking of which, who the hell let you out of your cage?"

"His episode is over, Gillen," Briallen said.

He grunted. "Until next time. How did this reaction occur?"

I moved away from the bed. "There was an intense essence surge. The black mass reacted before I could stop it."

Gillen hummed as he scanned Meryl. "That must have been some surge. I've hit her with high enough bursts of essence to kill a troll. What caused it?"

I ignored his question. The fewer people who knew about the stone ward, the better. "Is she going to be okay now?"

He slid his hands into his lab coat. "These trance states can last anywhere from hours to years. Without knowing how the Taint caused it, I have no means to proceed without dropping everything else, and I can't do that."

"So, what? You're giving up on her?" I asked.

He glared. "She's alive, Grey. That's more than I can say the future holds for a lot of my patients. I'll keep working on the problem, but I can't do it exclusively."

I stood shocked in the silence that followed. "You're giving up."

His eyes flickered with yellow light, and a sharp gust in the air slapped me hard on the side of the head. "Don't you dare, Grey. I don't need a patient in a bed in order to treat them. When you start saving lives instead of screwing them up, then you can criticize my methods."

Briallen spoke in a quiet voice. "I'll take her back to my house."

Gillen stared me down like an angry parent until I looked away. "She *is* one of yours, Briallen," he said.

"What's that supposed to mean?" I asked.

Briallen placed the palm of her hand on Meryl's cheek. "We're part of the same Circle, Connor. I understand her in ways no one else does. I may be able to wake her."

Following the druidic path meant being part of the Grove, men and women joining together to understand their place on the Wheel of the World. The masculine and feminine aspects of that journey had their own peculiarities. Briallen was one of the most powerful druidesses in the world. I wanted to believe she could help Meryl, but she hadn't been able to figure out what was wrong with me. I didn't want to doubt her, but I didn't know whether to have hope.

"What do you want me to do?" I asked.

Gillen headed for the door. "Leave. I have enough headaches."

Briallen and I stared at the empty doorway. "He's in a better mood than usual," I said.

She chuckled. "It's a mess here. The riots caused so many essence-related injuries, they've opened an annex."

Seeing Meryl so still, so quiet, tore at me. "Whatever you need to do, Briallen, do it. I want her back."

"What about you?"

"What about me?"

"I saw what happened during the riots, Connor. I saw video footage of a dark cloud that left hundreds of people drained of essence almost to the point of death. What the footage doesn't show is who was at the center of that darkness," she said.

"It wasn't my fault," I said.

She laughed. "Oh, now it's not your fault? After taking the blame for things that weren't your fault, suddenly it's not your fault when it obviously is?"

The black mass pulsed as anger surged through me. "I couldn't control it."

"Bullshit. I watched that black mass move with purpose—with direction. The victims weren't the solitaries and the Dead of the Weird. They were Guild and Consortium agents and National Guardsmen. Those are the people you blame for everything that's wrong. Don't tell me you didn't have control. I don't know how or why you stopped, but don't try to bullshit me that you didn't almost kill those people. Those were *your* victims, Connor."

I hadn't told Briallen everything. I hadn't told her that I had talked to the *leanansidhe*, not after the thing had called me "brother." The thought that we were related, even conceptually, terrified me. "It's complicated."

"It always is," she said.

"Remember the *leanansidhe* I found? Her abilities have something to do with the black mass in my head. I asked her for help."

With cool anger, Briallen glanced down at Meryl. "Did she know about this?"

I looked away. "No. I went alone."

She grabbed my chin and turned my face toward her. "Did you do this to her, Connor?"

I pulled back. "No! How could you say that?"

She set her chin. "How could *you* not tell me about the *leanansidhe*?"

Exasperated, I rubbed at my face. "You're right. I should have told you. I was—I don't know—embarrassed. The *leanansidhe* showed me that when the black mass gets out, the pain goes away a little. She thought she was controlling it, but that's only half-true. I don't want to believe it has a mind of its own, but it has a compulsion that's hard to resist. It makes me want essence, too."

"Is it out of control?" she asked.

I shook my head. "I use my body essence to hold it in check."

Unimpressed, a corner of her mouth curled down. "Yes, I'm sure the two drained agents will appreciate that."

"I was out when they arrived. I think the darkness is afraid of draining me. If I die, it loses its host. Those agents would have died otherwise."

"You're guessing. We need to test it somehow," she said.

"I haven't hurt anyone, and I don't want you to be the first," I said.

"Let me worry about that. I'll call you when Meryl is settled in, and we'll arrange something," she said.

I hung my head. "I need to find Shay. Are you going to stop me?"

For a moment, I thought she might. "Go, then. If you have

any more episodes, I want to know about them. I mean it," she said.

"Okay."

She stopped me at the door, wrapping her arms around me. "I'm worried."

I smoothed her hair. "I know. And thank you. Sometimes I forget to ask for help when I should."

She squeezed tighter, then released me. "Be careful."

"I will."

As I rode the elevator down, I called Shay on my cell, and he answered immediately. "Where are you?"

"I had a problem. Where are you?" I asked.

"I . . . Where you first met me," he said.

Shay had enough paranoia to worry someone might be listening in. "I'm on my way."

# 17

Déjà vu teased at me as I walked down Pittsburgh Street. Less than a year had passed since I first went down the alley behind the warehouses, yet so much had happened. The graffiti-covered buildings hadn't changed, nor the forlorn atmosphere of a place that had seen better times. The boarded-up windows and doors that faced the alley made the buildings look like they had construction barriers. Construction was the last thing happening.

The door to the squat wasn't hard to find despite the way it blended with the others. I checked for observers before tugging on some pine boards, a false barrier to disguise the entrance, a poor man's glamour in a way, no different in intent than an essence barrier. They pulled way from the building, bringing the door with them.

Inside the trash-filled hall, I sensed Shay's body signature and the pure essence of the stone bowl. He hadn't been followed, at least not into the building. The door at the end of the hall opened, exposing Shay in silhouette. "For gods' sakes, Shay, I told you someone might be after you."

He stepped back as I entered the room. "Uno's here. You know he doesn't let anything happen to me."

The big dog sprawled on the bare mattress of one of the two beds. He pricked an ear as I came in, then settled down with his head between his paws. "You shouldn't take that for granted. You shouldn't take anything for granted."

"Like thinking it's safe to let you in my apartment?" Shay never let an opportunity pass for a little sarcasm.

"Are you okay?" I asked.

He placed a languid hand on his hip. "Other than being scared half to death and having a perfectly good canvas ruined, I'm fine."

I spotted the stone bowl on the floor near the wall. As I crouched over it, the black mass in my head danced in reaction to the emanations rising from it. "Do you think it's safe to leave this here?"

"Probably, assuming, of course, a gang of virgins doesn't break in," he said.

Shay had lived in the room with his boyfriend, Robyn. They had been safe, watching out for each other, living under the radar until I came along. Except for the furniture and a ripped maroon velvet curtain that covered some shelving, Shay had stripped the place of personal belongings when he moved into his studio. "Has anyone been in here since you left?"

Shay sat on the bed and ruffled his fingers through Uno's fur. "It's exactly how I left it. We never told anyone we lived here. Murdock knew about it because he followed Robyn home one night to see what he was up to."

"Good. Tell no one about it or the stone. As far as the world is concerned, you never had anything to do with this," I said.

He pouted in amusement. "Until you need it moved again."

"Let's cross that bridge if we come to it."

Shay played with Uno's hair. "You and I both know it's 'when' and not 'if.' What happened, Connor? That black stuff that came out of you was like that night in the *leanansidhe*'s cave."

I sat on the opposite bed. "That's one of the things I'm trying to figure out. I have some clues now. The *leanansidhe* was able to do something similar, and the Guildmaster is affected by it, too."

His eyes went wide. "Is that why he's been sick all this time?"

Manus ap Eagan's illness wasn't a secret, but Shay's knowledge of things fey often surprised me. "I shouldn't have said that, but, yeah, it looks like it."

Uno rolled on his back as Shay scratched him. "I hope you figure out." He buried his face playfully in Uno's fur. "And I hope it's not the reason this guy follows you around."

I pressed my lips tighter, conscious of trying to keep a secret. I didn't think it was fair to Shay that Robyn made me promise not to tell he had sent the dog. The two of them had left some things unresolved when Robyn died. I told Robyn he should resolve them. He said he would consider it, and I made the promise to keep silent. "I'm sorry you got dragged into all this, Shay."

He smiled up at me. "There's nothing sexier than a good-looking man apologizing."

I tweaked his nose. "You are incorrigible. Let's get out of here."

Shay shut off the light, and we left the darkened room, at least, darkened as far as visible light. The essence was building again in the stone bowl, its unique properties amplifying the surrounding essence and gathering in its shallow depression. Out in the hall, Shay showed me a hidden chink in the door to check the alley before leaving. Uno followed us out to Congress Street, then melted into the air. Though I liked the dog, I breathed easier when he wasn't around.

"Take care of yourself, Shay," I said.

He tucked his chin down. "I always do. Call me sometime."

Amused, I shook my head as he walked away. The kid had flirted with me from day one. It was innocent fun for him, and I didn't mind. I needed more fun.

I waited until he was well down the street before return-

ing up the alley and letting myself back into the squat. I
didn't turn the light on, but bathed in the glow of the stone
bowl. The dark mass in my head stretched, a sinuous finger
of shadow pushing at the front of my skull. I gasped as it
pierced my right eye. Blood rushed to the surface of my skin,
igniting the nerve endings in delicious pain. A dark spike
oozed from my eye and slipped into the bowl. Yearning hunger overwhelmed me as the darkness sucked at the essence. I
sank to my knees and hunched over the stone, letting myself
drift off in an ecstasy I couldn't explain and didn't want to.

# 18

I leaned against my building the next morning, a fine rain drizzling against my face as I waited for Murdock. He wanted me to help with an interview that might produce a lead on the dwarf murders. I almost said no because I wanted to sleep in, but his comment about being Eorla's errand boy still burned in my ears. Besides, the way the blue essence had behaved in the Tangle the other night intrigued me. It could be coincidence that it showed up when it did, or it could be related to the murders. If our investigations were riding parallel for a while, it made sense to work together.

When he arrived, I moved a box of paperback novels to the back and hopped in the passenger seat. Murdock handed me a coffee as he turned down Old Northern Avenue and made for the highway.

"You look pretty good for a guy having convulsions yesterday," he said.

"I feel good. Great, actually. Must be some kind of post-trauma endorphin thing." I smiled, then turned to look out the window. Between what had happened at Shay's apartment and spending time in the squat with the stone ward, the dark mass in my head had gone quiet and sluggish. I didn't remember the last time I had felt so good.

"Really?" Murdock asked.

His dubious tone made me paranoid. An edge of guilt crept over me. I didn't like feeling good about how I felt good. Siphoning essence at that level—even if it was from a stone—had a creep factor to it that I didn't want to admit. "I guess."

"You were convulsing when I found you, Connor," he said.

"I know. You said that," I said.

Murdock glanced at me with a frown. "And that doesn't bother you?"

I wanted to slap myself. By trying so hard to appear non-chalant about what had happened, I hadn't listened to what Murdock actually said, which drew exactly the kind of attention I was trying to avoid. "Thanks for calling in the cavalry."

"I had to. I couldn't get near you or Meryl. What happened to Shay?" he said.

"You know Shay. He knows how survive," I said.

The rain began to fall harder as we took the on-ramp to the highway. "Wow," he said.

I glanced over. "What?" I asked.

He let out a long breath in an aggravated sigh. "Is this how it's going to be? Because if it is, you can find some-one else to cover your ass when you need it. I'm getting tired of your keeping shit from me. If you think I'm going to have a problem with something you said or did, then maybe you should start thinking about what you said or did and not about my reaction."

Stunned, I stared through the windshield. The highway traffic coasted by in a mist of kicked-up water. Cabs and tractor-trailers wheeled by, people on business in nonde-script sedans, SUVs driven by people with cell phones to their ears. Everyone going somewhere, doing things, having an agenda. Here I was, in a car with someone who had saved my life, acting like a dumb-ass junkie hiding a habit.

"I am so screwed up, Murdock, I don't even know where to begin," I said.

"Try honesty," he snapped.

Murdock was living proof that someone could have sympathy without pity. He wasn't going to let me off the hook. "The stone ward provoked the dark mass. Shay ran off with it and hid it in the old squat he had with Robyn. That's where I was last night, sucking up essence like it was ambrosia and manna and alcohol all rolled into one. The stone's dead cold now, and the entire time I've been sitting here, I've been wondering in the back of my mind how long it will take it to recharge itself so I can go back and do it again."

"What else?" he asked.

If I weren't so humiliated, I would have been angry. I didn't let people talk to me like he was. I didn't respect most people enough to let them, but Murdock had earned it. And he was right to do it. "I should have told you," I said.

"You need help, Connor," he said.

"No one can help me, Leo. Everyone's tried," I said. Saying it out loud hurt. No one could help. No one knew what was wrong. It was getting worse, and I had the feeling that I was on the road to someone's bashing me in the head in a dark hole in the ground to stop me from killing someone.

"You're wrong," he said. "The *leanansidhe* helped. She showed you something you didn't know. If she knew something, someone else does."

"How am I supposed to find them?" I asked.

"Imagine it's me asking you that, then answer your own question. You're the fey expert. Start thinking fey," he said.

The windshield wipers beat back and forth, a steady rhythm counting the seconds in the silence. "Thinking fey" had a nice ring to it. The dark mass thrived on essence, so it was logical that it was part of the fey world, and the fey world was a lot bigger than Gillen Yor or Briallen. They were smart, knowledgeable people, but they couldn't know everything. No one could. No one ever made a connection to me and the *leanansidhe*, but Druse recognized what was hap-

pening to me right away. It was time to start thinking outside
the box because if I didn't, I might end up *in* a box.

"Thanks, Leo," I said.

"No problem," he said.

I settled in the seat and sipped my coffee. For all my anger at the number of friends that disappeared when I lost my
abilities, I wouldn't trade them for the ones I made after.
Murdock might not pull any punches in the criticism department, but I deserved every one he'd thrown at me. "So,
who's this guy you want to interview?"

"Thekk Veinseeker, the owner of the stone supplier that
burned down," he said.

"You're working an arson case? Just how shorthanded is
the department?" I asked.

"It's about the dwarf murders. I found a connection that's
a little more than curious. Veinseeker has a brother named
Nar. Nar Veinseeker popped up in a couple of old cases as an
associate of both of the dead dwarves down at the morgue,"
he said.

"And you couldn't find Nar," I said.

"Right. Last-known address was a building that went
down during the riot. No one's seen him since."

"He could have died in the fires," I said.

Murdock grinned at me. "Or he could be hiding from
someone trying to kill him."

The idea played around in my mind. If Druse was looking for her stone, why would she be looking for a specific
person? "Banjo said someone was offering big money for
information about dwarves who have been here a long time."

"The *leanansidhe* didn't exactly live in the lap of luxury,"
he said.

"Don't let that fool you. Lots of fey have a ton of cash
they don't know what to do with. They tend to buy real es-
tate, then build a one-room house on it. It's a cultural thing,
different values out of Faerie. It's why goats and cows show
up in the Weird sometimes."

Murdock tapped his fingers on the steering wheel as the

traffic slowed. "Thekk Veinseeker's been in Boston at least since the 1920s. It was in the arson file."

"His brother was probably here then, too," I said.

"Okay. Assume the *leanansidhe* has the money and has been in Boston as long as Veinseeker. What can he do important enough for her to kill?" Murdock asked.

"I don't think 'important' is the right word. We're talking about a person for whom killing is a way of life. It's not important to her. She might be looking for Nar, taking essence as a matter of course, and the deaths are collateral," I said.

"What if I talk this up the chain of command? We're not equipped to handle this. It's exactly the situation the Guild should handle," he said.

"The Guild is not going to do anything in the Weird that looks like it's helping Eorla. Same old, same old, Leo. Just the faces change," I said.

"So the deaths don't matter. Nice. The *leanansidhe* wants the stone, and she wants Nar. What's the connection?" he asked.

"Dwarves are stone fey. They create excellent wards. Maybe she wants him to make her a new one," I said.

"Then why is he in hiding? He's got to know that two of his former associates are dead, and his brother's warehouse went up. Why doesn't he take the deal?" he asked.

I slumped farther into the seat. "Maybe because there's always a price to be paid when dealing with a *leanansidhe*."

# 19

Thekk Veinseeker's house was in a quiet neighborhood in West Quincy, hard by the Blue Hills State Park. Old granite quarries in the area had once produced stone for buildings throughout New England. A number of dwarf families had set up mining-related businesses nearby and lived in the nicer neighborhoods. The quarries were closed these days, but the dwarves who had made homes in the area remained.

Murdock pulled into the driveway and parked near several other cars. Contrary to popular belief, dwarves didn't mind daylight. They did prefer being underground whenever possible, and the architecture of their homes reflected that. A well-maintained garden surrounded several ornately carved stone outbuildings no more than ten or twenty feet square. The outbuildings weren't the house itself but the aboveground evidence of one. Some had doors, but most were windowed to let light into the house below. Landscapers were replacing some broken shrubbery. The structure they had been next to had scorch marks on the side that another group of workers were scrubbing.

Murdock rang the bell. A pale blond kobold no taller than my shoulder answered, a faintly suspicious look on her face. "Yes?"

"Detective Lieutenant Murdock to see Thekk Veinseeker."

Her placid gaze swept over us, then she closed the door. Confused, Murdock looked at me. "Kobolds are not big on social graces. Let's give it a few minutes," I said.

It was a few minutes. The kobold returned and ushered us in. Inside, the granite structure was nothing more than the top landing of a wide marble staircase. The kobold led us down without speaking. I'd been in a few dwarven homes, but this one was more elaborate than any I had seen. The construction was all stone—slates, marbles, and granites— richly carved to resemble wood. I never understood the affinity for nature carvings that dwarves preferred yet avoided in day-to-day life. They liked to look at it but not be in it.

At the foot of the stairs, a wide round entry hall served as the junction for several corridors leading off into dimness. The kobold headed straight across the mosaic floor to the archway opposite and directed us through an open door.

I had a hard time pinning the room down. It was a study or an office or a receiving room. Ornate ribs of granite crisscrossed the ceiling in a series of vaults. Deep red stone latticework filled wall panels between black-veined mustard-colored pilasters. Intricate marble tiles turned the floor into a tapestry of geometric designs. A long narrow slab of granite rested on ebony legs that resembled a wolf's. Shafts of sunlight filtered down from the ceiling at the far end of the room, backlighting the dwarf seated on a large chair carved with woven vines. Two fireplaces flanked the table, tall enough for us to stand in. Fires burned in both, taking the edge off the cool air of the underground chamber. Something felt familiar about the place, but, despite the patchy spots in my memory, I doubted I had ever been in the room.

"Subtle," Murdock said out of the corner of his mouth.

Thekk Veinseeker wore a short quilted jacket of orange silk with dusty yellow pearls sewn into whorls of gold thread, a casual version of the florid outfits that rich dwarves favored. His large, blunt face jarred in contrast, hard lined with thick black eyebrows and bowl-cut hair the color of iron. "How may I be of service, gentlemen?"

"We're here about your brother. I'm Detective Lieutenant Murdock. This is my associate, Connor Grey," Leo said.

Thekk didn't move. "Which brother?"

"Nar," Murdock said.

"I have no such brother," Thekk said.

Murdock and I exchanged glances. "I don't think I made a mistake, sir," Murdock said. "Our records indicate Nar Veinseeker was your brother. I've seen his name mentioned in relation to your quarry business."

Thekk made a face as if Murdock had suggested something perverse. "Nar is no longer part of the clan."

The only thing dwarves held closer to their hearts than profits was family. Extended family grouped into clans and lived as near to each other as possible. They knew each other, knew their businesses and their secrets. "How can he not be a part of the clan if he was your brother?" I asked.

A thin trickle of essence floated through the room as Thekk stared into the fire. Disturbed, the dark mass pulsed in my head. Thekk was scrying, using the flames to sort through possible future events. "Can you not do that, please? It's interfering with . . ." I paused. He didn't need to know my personal issues. ". . . It's making my body shields activate in an uncomfortable manner."

Thekk grunted in surprise, and the scrying field collapsed. "My apologies, good druid. I am a poor host."

"No problem. We were hoping you might tell us if Nar had enemies," I said.

Thekk pushed out of the chair and strode toward one of the fireplaces. "I'm sure he has many. It is not a subject of study for me."

"Why isn't he part of the clan anymore?"

Thekk moved away from the hearth. "He chose profit over his family."

"And the clan booted him out?" Murdock asked.

"There is no shame in making profit. Nar made his by

betraying the clan and refused to tithe as recompense," said Thekk.

We were moving into cultural territory I didn't know well. Dwarves valued loyalty to each other. Other people didn't rate high on their list of concerns, but a member being rejected by the clan had to be about something major. "What was the deal about?"

Thekk rubbed his hand along the edge of the granite slab. "It was so long ago, good druid. I don't recall. It no longer concerns me."

I didn't believe him. Dwarves have long memories. "When was the last time you spoke?"

Thekk folded his hands in front of him. "Seventy years? Eighty? I have no information about him that would be of help to you."

"Let's talk about your warehouse going up in flames," Murdock said.

Thekk sighed. "An unfortunate occurrence."

"You don't seem that upset," I said.

He shrugged. "I should have sold the building years ago. I had the good fortune of insurance. My business has been outside Boston for decades now."

"Someone's been interested in talking to dwarves who were in the city decades ago. Have you heard anything about that?" I asked.

Impatience was starting to show on his face. "Is there a purpose to this discussion? I am a member of the Teutonic Consortium and see no need to answer to Guild agents."

"We're not Guild agents," I said.

"You were, sir. I see it in your bearing and your voice. I have made it clear that the clan has no knowledge of Nar and no interest. His fate has no meaning for us," Thekk said.

"Three dwarves have been killed, and your warehouse burned to the ground. Don't you find it interesting that Nar is linked to all three?" Murdock said.

"I find it sad, sir. Trouble gathers like crows. Nar always had a knack for trouble," he said.

I decided to change the conversation. "What happened upstairs? You've got burn marks on your house."

"I believe the gardeners are clearing unwanted brush."

He had paused longer than necessary to answer the question. "A little aggressive, aren't they?" I asked.

"I am not a gardener, sir. I pay them to do their jobs as they see fit."

"Has someone threatened you?" Murdock said.

Thekk chuckled. "I am a loyal subject of the Elven King. If someone were threatening me, I would pursue it through the Consortium."

"Do you know any of Nar's current associates?" Murdock asked.

Thekk frowned, his thick unibrow rippling into a thicker one. "He lives in that slum in Boston where my warehouse was. Why would I know any of those people?"

A smile twitched at the corner of Murdock's mouth as he offered his business card. "I know what you mean. If you think of something, we would appreciate a call."

Thekk received the card and made a point of reading it. "I will, Detective, but I doubt there will be a need. Will there be anything else?"

Murdock looked at me, but I had nothing to say. "No, thanks."

Thekk returned to the chair behind the slab table. "Have a pleasant day."

Given Thekk's less than warm manner, I was surprised he trusted us to see ourselves out. Once in the receiving hall, though, I sensed subtle essence barriers across the openings to the other corridors. Walking anywhere but up the stairs would have tripped alarms. Either that or they were simple barriers that would prevent us from moving freely through the house.

"That was strange," Murdock said as he pulled down the driveway.

"Dwarves are suspicious of outsiders. I don't know what he was talking about with the clan thing though," I said.

"I wonder why he wasn't telling the truth about the landscaping either," he said.

"It could be a coincidence, Leo. If he cut ties with Nar all those years ago, he probably doesn't know anything," I said.

"You know what I'm thinking?" he asked.

"You're thinking that despite what Thekk said, he knows something about Nar, which means that until something more likely comes along, you will investigate this mysterious business deal that went sore between them until you can rule him out as a suspect," I said.

He pursed his lips. "And what makes you say that?"

"You're predictable."

"I am not," he said.

"Okay, now that I helped you with this interview, I have a favor to ask," I said.

"Uh-oh," he said.

"Shut up. It's easy. I need a motorcycle," I said.

"I want a pony," he said.

"Seriously, I need something fast and maneuverable to chase down this blue essence in the Tangle. A motorcycle's perfect."

"The department would never approve it. They're dealing with inventory loss from the night of the riots," he said.

"I wasn't thinking about the department." Murdock's brother Bar had a bike, but since I was persona non grata with the Murdock family, I didn't think he'd loan it to me. His own brother, on the other hand, would have no problem.

Murdock laughed in disbelief. "I see where you're going. I'll ask, but don't get your hopes up." He pulled off the road and into a Dunkin' Donuts parking lot, parked the car, and leaned back. "Hurry up. I don't want to get stuck in midday traffic."

"Hurry up with what?" I asked.

He grinned. "It's been over an hour since you had your coffee. You want another cup, and need to take a leak. You're predictable."

I laughed as I got out of the car. "Touché, my friend, touché."

# 20

I grinned at the approaching sound of an engine. Murdock had come through with my request for the motorcycle. He coasted the bike to the curb in front of my building and cut the engine. I whistled in admiration. "When the hell did Bar get a Ducati?"

Murdock pulled off his helmet. "About six months ago, I think. I'm surprised he let me take it instead of the Harley. I think he sleeps with it."

I trailed my hand along the front. "A Monster, right?"

"The S," said Murdock.

The bike really was a beast. Even parked, the machine looked like it was in motion, stripped down to the bare bones, not a piece of chrome wasted. I circled around the back to check out the exhaust. "Man, I wish I still had the money for something like this."

"Okay. I got the bike. What's the plan?" Murdock asked.

"I can't catch the blue-essence surge. I tried essence speeding the other night, but it kicked up a storm in my head, and my nose bled for an hour," I said.

"Basically, you want to race around the Weird on a bike," he said.

I tried to look innocent. "Well, I think the blue surge is related to the dwarf murders. It's shown up nearby every time."

Murdock smirked like he wasn't buying it. He handed me a helmet. "Get on."

"What? I thought you were dropping the bike off for me to use," I said.

He shook his head. "No way am I letting you take this bike. Bar would scream if he found out. I didn't tell him you wanted it."

I pulled the helmet on. "This is so not fair."

"You can always try running faster," he said.

I grabbed his shoulder and swung my leg over the bike. "I'd leave you in the dust."

"Left tap, slow down. Right tap, stop. I tap you, hang on. Every helmet bump costs a beer. Got it?" he said.

"Got it. Let's check out the burn district first," I said.

Murdock started the motorcycle as I gripped his waist. To show me who was boss, he tapped my hand and tore up the street. I laughed at my momentary panic at the speed, then settled in for the ride. It had been a while since I was on a bike. We tore up Old Northern, turning heads as we passed.

We cruised up and down side streets, keeping an eye out for a hint of blue essence. Its appearance was a nightly occurrence. Sometimes people vanished afterward, but not every time. Murdock looped through areas where the Dead were known to congregate, since I suspected a connection existed between the Dead and the surge. Every reported sighting I had checked out had faded Dead essence in the area.

"We don't get a lot of calls about the Dead anymore," Murdock said during a pit stop.

The Dead had been major trouble before Eorla contained the Taint. The Taint had heightened their propensity to violence. They had torn apart the Weird, causing mayhem and death. That Commissioner Murdock had been taking bribes to look the other way didn't help, either, but that was something I wouldn't say in front of Leo. "Since the solitaries learned how to fight back, I'm guessing the Dead have decided to keep a low profile."

Murdock smiled around the mouth of a water bottle. "Yeah, a cop loves to hear vigilante justice works."

I laughed. "You know that's not what I meant. The Dead had to learn they have to get along here. They thought they could slaughter people like they did in TirNaNog, and the solitaries had to make them understand that things don't work like that here. Think of it as a cultural conflict that worked itself out."

"Uh-huh. At least we're not finding decapitated bodies anymore. Ready?" he asked.

We donned our helmets and got back on the bike. I hadn't ridden in a long time, and my butt was going to be complaining in the morning. Murdock turned a corner and tapped my hands. I grabbed his waist tighter as he picked up speed. Two blocks ahead, the blue surge swept across the road. Murdock raced the bike up to the turn. I bumped his helmet as he came to a full stop. The alley was empty.

"Missed it. That's one beer for me," he shouted over the engine.

"No fair. I didn't know you were stopping," I said.

"Pay attention," he said. He gunned it up the alley. I tilted my head on the recoil and bumped his shoulder instead of his head. Ten minutes later, the surge appeared in the road ahead, moving away at a good clip. Murdock swerved around a car that had slammed on its brakes. I leaned in to the turn, trying not to think about the sandy grit in the road as the bike tilted.

Murdock righted the bike and ripped it up the street. The surge billowed ahead, dark indigo shapes flashing in and out of sight. It pulled away, gaining speed as we neared. It twisted across the sidewalk and plunged into a building. Plunged, as in vanished through a brick wall. Murdock hit the brakes hard. The rear tire kicked out, and I held on as the force almost threw me. Murdock killed the engine and whipped off his helmet. "What the hell is that?"

"A wall," I said.

"Thanks," he said.

I eased off the bike and approached the wall. It was an illusion. Someone had created a shield out of hardened essence. I touched the facing with my right hand, feeling the essence tingle like static under my fingers. "There's a shield barrier here, a good one. This must be why I keep losing track of them. They must have barriers like this scattered all over the neighborhood."

"They?" asked Murdock.

I looked at him. "They're the Dead, Leo. I thought the surge was following the Dead, but it *is* the Dead. I didn't realize until tonight that Dead essence fades faster than living essence. I was gauging the time frame for the faded essence wrong."

"So you're saying the Dead are kidnapping people," he said.

"Looks that way," I said.

He smirked. "Remind me again about that resolved cultural conflict thing you were talking about."

I got back on the bike. "They're not doing the killing. The *leanansidhe* is. Remember, the surge showed up down in the Tangle *after* the darkness did. Let's circle around the block and see what's on the other side."

Murdock did a slow cruise down the sidewalk. At the corner, the engine jumped in pitch as we turned. We were on the edge of the Tangle, with its engine-killing spells.

Darkness shadowed the block as Murdock coasted to a stop. I hopped off again and found another shield barrier. My finger sank beneath it as I touched it. Suspicious, I pulled away. It didn't make sense for one shield to be softer than the other. Ready for a trap, I placed both hands against the wall, I pushed again. My left hand slipped beneath the surface, but not the right one. I stepped back and looked at my hands.

"What's the matter?" Murdock asked.

"I think my tattoo is letting me through the shield." The tattoo on my left arm was created from the filigree that had once decorated a silver branch. The fey used silver branches to cross the barriers between worlds. I lifted my left hand to the wall and pushed. As my arm went through, it dawned on me that silver branches would work with shield barriers, too. I held my breath and pressed forward, leading with the arm. I passed through the barrier, its essence itching across my skin until I stood on the other side. From my side, the wall was transparent. I could see Murdock frowning, but the look said he couldn't see me. Behind me, the faint residue of Dead essence trailed across a long, empty alley. I went back through the wall to the sidewalk.

"That was freaky," Murdock said.

"It's gone. They either looped back around or left through another barrier," I said.

Murdock scanned the street. "Keep looking?"

"Oh, yeah. We almost had it that time," I said.

The surge teased us as we rode through the neighborhood, a flash in the distance that vanished again and again. We followed but didn't get close. Murdock turned down a narrow lane, and the engine guttered. We had moved deeper into the Tangle, but as far as I knew, remained outside the central area. Murdock goosed the engine. Warehouses loomed to either side, wet and dark, their rooflines curling overhead. Fire escapes tangled into each other, forming a tunnel of metal.

As we continued, the lane lengthened and appeared to run for a mile—impossible for the area it covered. Murdock had to rev the engine more often to keep it going. Illusion twisted our perceptions. What looked like a long, straight lane was more likely a circle. I searched for a break in the walls, some other exit than the false promise ahead. The motorcycle whined and shuddered. With a loud pop from the exhaust, the engine died.

"We've drifted farther into the Tangle than it looks," I said. While Murdock held the bike steady, I got off. The lane stretched in either direction as far as I could see.

He leaned back in his seat to get a look at the engine. "The bike's okay, though, right?"

"Yeah. Once we get it out of here, it should start right up," I said.

Murdock wheeled the motorcycle around toward the direction we had come. "Are we even going to get out of here?"

"We should be okay. Backtracking usually works. It's going forward that's a bitch," I said.

A screech of metal tore through the air, followed by a crash. Ahead, a pall of smoke curled across the street.

"What's the hell is that?" Murdock asked.

"Sounded like someone's car spell-crashed and hit something," I said.

More sounds echoed toward us, tortured metal and rumbling falls. Smoke rose higher, blocking the view. Blue light flickered in the haze. As the light intensified, a churning cloud of essence filled the lane from one side to the other. Behind us, the street stretched even farther than before, with no visible turns or exits.

"Whatever that is, it's coming right at us," Murdock said.

The blue light became more prominent and flared. Deep within it, something moved, a great silhouette of darker blue. The fire escapes rattled and shuddered as the cloud rolled forward. Networks of stairs and landings twisted and pulled from the walls, crashing into tangled, jagged heaps. The blue surge flared and rushed toward us.

"A plan would be a good thing if you have one," Murdock said.

"Park the bike," I said. We pushed it against the wall. I pulled Murdock several feet into the shallow depression of a bricked-over door.

He resisted, pulling his arm away. "I can't leave it there."

I pushed him back against a wall and flattened myself next to him. "We have to. We don't want the bike's metal interfering. This is far enough. Harden your body shield, Leo, and brace yourself. That stuff's going to hit us hard."

Crimson essence blossomed around us as Murdock activated the shield. "I thought we wanted to catch it?"

The ground vibrated as the surge approached with a growing roar. "Catch it, not get run over by it. Whatever you do, don't drop that shield," I shouted.

Murdock closed his eyes in concentration. His body shield shifted, darkening from a rich crimson to a deep maroon, pressing around us in fractured planes. Indigo and white essence billowed toward us. The fierce cloud consumed the entire lane, yanking down fire escapes and tossing dumpsters aside as it passed.

Murdock staggered when it hit, his shield shuddering and bending under a rain of yellow sparks. He steadied himself against the wall, forcing the shield back against the passing wave. With a scream of stressed metal, the fire escape above toppled into the street, narrowly missing us. The surge slammed us against the wall. Murdock's shield heaved and shifted. My body ached under the pressure, black spots flashing across my vision as the dark mass in my head danced in confusion.

A thick plume of indigo essence smudged the horizon, swirling and flickering as it moved toward us. A sound weaved itself into the background noise of the city, subtle but distinct, an uneven hum broken by sharp notes. My ears pricked to them, and my heart raced, responding to some deep memory, a sound of danger like a wild yelp in the night. By the time the sound resolved into the barking that my instinct had already recognized, the low hum rose higher and became the clear call of horns, deep bass soundings that signaled one unmistakable thing: the approach of a hunting party.

Caution forced me back against a wall while curiosity tempted me to lean out. The light grew, its color bleeding from indigo to violet. Figures appeared in the rolling fog, animal and wild human shapes leaping and lunging past.

The cresting wave of essence threw me down. Despite Murdock's shield, I bounced in a hazy blue torrent like a pebble in a flood, my body hitting the wall again and again as the riders and runner swept past. The world turned into a confusion of light and tangled bodies twisting and falling among winged solitaries and running beasts.

The shield buckled, and the blue essence swirled around us. Murdock lifted off the ground and grabbed at a tangle of fire escape as he rose into the air. I grappled with his kicking legs as the surge coalesced around him like a cocoon. Blue haze obscured my sight. A blast of crimson essence burst through, shredding the blue light. The surge retreated up the street, eddies of faint gray mist trailing after it.

A dark figure broke away and wheeled toward us on a massive black horse with yellow-lit eyes. Thick fog rolled along the ground as the enormous beast reared with a thunderous neigh. Its hooves sparked with yellow lightning as the horse came back down.

Behind its enormous head, a cloaked figure pulled the reins in hard, turning a skull-masked face toward me, eyes burning like embers beneath an antlered helm. The rider stared, as the agitated horse pawed in the fog. With a flick of the reins, the rider wheeled the horse and cantered away. The rider lifted a sword, a long blade of red flame, and let out a scream that pierced my chest with its vibration. The rider disappeared back into the haze, fading away as the mob raced off into the night.

Dazed, Murdock climbed down from the fire escape where he had landed and slid to the ground. "I feel like I got hit by a truck."

I crouched in front of him. Taking him by the chin, I shifted his head left and right. Murdock opened his eyes. His skin was abraded, but he didn't appear seriously injured. I didn't hurt as much as he did. He had taken the brunt of the hits. Chalk up another debt to him for saving my ass. "I would have said a train. You should get checked for a concussion."

I moved into the lane, trying to get a good look through the tangled heap of fire escapes. A faint shimmer of blue essence remained, fading as it splashed up the building walls to either side. Light glittered in the distance, but it was a streetlamp. The stretching illusion had vanished, too.

"Damn. There's going to be hell to pay," Murdock said.

I glanced back, thinking he was making a boast, then realized where he was looking. The motorcycle lay under a jagged cage of shattered fire escape. The weight of all that heavy metal had bent the handlebars and metal rods, piercing the engine case. I groaned. "Please don't tell Bar I was on the bike."

At least Leo laughed. "Please tell me you saw someone riding a horse, 'cause I saw someone riding a horse."

I helped him to his feet. "It was a dream mare. You saw them in TirNaNog. It must have escaped before the veil dropped and gotten trapped here on Samhain."

"Who was riding it?" he asked.

"I think it was the King of the Dead."

He grimaced as he rubbed his neck. "Of course it was."

"We just bought a big problem, Leo. If that was the King of the Dead, then that blue surge can be only one thing. The Wild Hunt is in Boston, and as far as I know, nothing can stop it."

# 21

Briallen wasn't home when I let myself into her town house the next morning. I was one of the few people she allowed open access to her home. I scared the hell out of the brownie caregiver she had hired to watch over Meryl. Once the poor woman's claws and teeth retracted, she was quite nice—even apologetic, though the fault was mine. I should have knocked at least.

Meryl rested by the blue fire in the upstairs parlor. By a trick of positioning, she appeared to be staring into the flames when I entered, meditating like a druidess with something on her mind. Her lack of response killed that notion. I kissed her on the top of the head and sat in the armchair opposite, trying not to let melancholy overwhelm me.

"I miss you," I said.

Our relationship was complicated, one part friends, one part lovers, and one part what-the-hell-is-going-on. I had thought a lot about it since she went into the trance. Meryl provoked and challenged me at every turn, daring me to call her my girlfriend so that she could dismiss the idea. She understood me on a level that only good friends did, but would have slapped me upside the head if I compared her to Joe or Briallen. She knew she was more than that. She had her own life, her own ideas, and her own way of doing things that mattered more than anything I said sometimes. While that frustrated me on occasion, I respected the hell out of her and wouldn't have it any other way. When push came to shove, though, she dropped all pretense of indifference and became the strongest ally I had ever had. Maybe I didn't know how to define what we had together because it wasn't supposed to be defined. Or maybe what we had was a real relationship, and I had never had one before.

I read aloud to her while I waited for Briallen, an old tale about dreams and war. I thought Meryl would appreciate it. She was a Dreamer, and her dreams often had glimpses of the future. In recent months, I had had prescient dreams, too, and she had helped me understand how to interpret them. I wasn't good at it, or at least didn't like my dreams' implications. Too often, my symbols and metaphors pointed to death and destruction around me. Reading about someone else's dreams made me realize I hadn't experienced my own in a while. Like so much else in my life, I didn't know if that was a good thing or a bad one.

Briallen swept into the room an hour later, a high flush on her cheeks. "It's a beautiful day. I walked back from the Guildhouse. Did you two go out at all?"

"We've been reading. I didn't want to miss you," I said.

Briallen put down some books she carried and ran her hand along Meryl's arm, causing their body signatures to interact. She brushed back hair from my forehead and placed a gentle hand on my temple. Briallen had raised me and had earned a mother's privilege of not asking permission to touch me. She checked my health whenever she had the opportunity. I closed my eyes as warmth spread from her hand into my head. The dark mass quivered from the touch of her essence. It never reacted to her probing, as if it understood that her touch meant concern.

"It's shaped like a ball of spikes," she said.

"It feels like one. All the essence in here makes it curious," I said.

She glanced at Meryl. "Let's go downstairs. I'll make some coffee."

I touched Meryl on the shoulder as I left. She didn't react.

Down in the kitchen, Briallen pulled out an old percolator pot and rinsed it at the sink. "I'm glad you're here. It saves me a phone call."

I slid onto a stool. "Sounds serious. You never use the phone."

Amused, she pouted her lips as she put the pot on to boil. "I've been talking with Nigel. He has an interesting idea about Meryl. Do you want to argue about it now or wait until the coffee is ready?"

I stared at her, uncertain what to say. She knew my opinion of Nigel. "I hope you have cream and sugar."

"He wants to simulate her trance state on himself and guide her back. I've gone over the spells he's talking about. I think he has a good idea," she said.

"So why hasn't Gillen Yor tried it?" I asked.

"He tried something similar. He can't resonate the essence correctly," she said.

I folded my arms, suspicious. "And Nigel can? Why?"

She sighed. "Connor, you are going to ask all the questions I did, and that's fine. But we have to do something. She can't stay like this."

Frustrated, I rubbed my hands over my face. "I don't understand his interest. It worries me."

"They're friends. Isn't that enough?" she asked.

"Not with Nigel. I was friends with him once."

She lowered the flame on the stove and set the pot to perk. "You have to remove your personal feelings from this. I've gone over the process and the spells. They make sense. I'll be with them the entire time. We can do it in my sanctum."

"I don't trust him," I said.

She leaned across the kitchen island and held my hand. "Don't think I don't know Nigel Martin, Connor. He has a reason for doing this that has nothing to do with friendship. Whatever that is, it's a side issue for the moment. If his idea works, Meryl is more than capable of dealing with him. She's told me so herself whenever I've expressed my own doubts about their friendship."

Meryl never mentioned that to me. "You have?"

She poured out the coffee. "Of course. I've known Nigel a lot longer than you—either of you, I think. I don't believe he's malicious, but that doesn't mean he isn't capricious, and it doesn't mean I'm not cautious around him. He serves the Wheel of the World in a different way than I do. I'm not so foolish to think mine is the only way."

I smirked. "'And you shouldn't either,' she pretended not to say."

She play-slapped my hand. "Exactly."

"When does he want to do this?"

"Tomorrow," she said.

"I want to be here."

She settled herself onto a stool. "Of course. I'm sure Meryl will be happy to see you."

I sipped the coffee, its rich flavor hinting at one of Briallen's secret additives. Everything Briallen made had a little something extra. "The reason I wanted to talk to you is because I ran into something last night. It looked a hell of a lot like the Wild Hunt."

Briallen groaned and slumped against her hand. "Can we have one month when no one starts a new pissing contest? It's bad enough Donor Elfenkonig's in town."

"You knew about that?" I asked.

"You did?" she asked.

We contemplated the countertop. "So . . . anyway . . ." I said.

Chuckling, she sipped at her coffee. Briallen knew more than anyone about what went on among the fey in Boston. She had connections everywhere. While Nigel saw the Teutonic fey as straight-up enemies, Briallen considered them the friendly opposition. "Yes, anyway, why do you think the Wild Hunt is here?"

I described what happened to Murdock and me in the

Tangle. She played particular attention to the description of the rider. "That doesn't sound like Arawn."

In Celtic tradition, Arawn ruled over the Land of the Dead. "He's for real?"

She nodded. "I've met him. I'm sure I would have heard if he was in Boston."

"You've met Arawn, as in 'King of the Dead' Arawn," I said.

"Why does that surprise you? I may not remember everything pre-Convergence, but Arawn is hard to forget. One of the most courteous kings I've ever met," she said.

"Did you just out yourself to me as an Old One?" I asked.

She smirked and lifted her coffee. "I don't know, did I? I don't remember saying when I met him."

"How did you meet him?" I asked.

"That's a story for another time. If the rider you met were Arawn, he would have spoken to you, taken you with him, or killed you."

"So it was an imposter?" I asked.

She pursed her lips and gazed into her mug. " 'Imposter' is the wrong word. The Wild Hunt rises for many reasons, and Arawn doesn't always lead it. How did you run into it?"

"I've been tracking missing persons in the Weird. Witnesses report a blaze of essence followed by disappearances. I thought it might be related to the solitary/Dead conflict because the surge seemed to be following old Dead essence, but last night Murdock and I encountered the surge, and it was all Dead essence."

She squinted. "It's a leap to call it the Wild Hunt, don't you think? I mean, the original hunt was about weather superstitions and enforcing conformity. You're talking about a few kidnappings," she said.

"True—but right now the Weird is full of centuries-old Dead who believe that stuff."

"Aren't they calmer now that the Taint is gone?" she asked.

" 'Calm' isn't a word I would use to describe the Dead, Briallen. Maybe they're more rational in their approach—

and forming a unified band could be evidence of it. There's a guy wearing an antlered helm and riding a dream mare," I said.

"You said people are going missing. Is there a pattern, or is it random?" she asked.

"Mostly scryers and fortune-tellers," I said.

She tapped her nails against the sides of her mug. "People seek the future when the present is unsettled."

"That pretty much describes the Weird," I said.

She arched an eyebrow at me. "That pretty much describes everything right now. I don't have to remind you of the uncertainty around here. We have an acting police commissioner, an Acting Guildmaster, no one directing the Consortium consulate since Eorla left, and Eorla setting up her own court. People are worried."

"But what would the Dead gain by forming a hunt? Tir-NaNog is gone. The Dead have no place to go."

She made a slight swirl of her coffee. "The social structure is destabilized. While people in power struggle to get their acts together, one person has managed to bring order to the situation: Eorla. Maybe the Dead see what she's done and want to duplicate it on their own terms."

"Are you suggesting they're setting up their own version of TirNaNog?"

"Maybe. Or maybe it's another power play by another player," she said.

"People join Eorla willingly. The Dead are kidnapping people. Eorla doesn't do that," I said.

Briallen gave a sly smile as she drank her coffee. "A little defensive about her, aren't we?"

I frowned. "I know you've been talking to Nigel. I didn't think he'd be able to poison you against her that easily."

She poked me. "I'm teasing, but I should point out that Eorla is hard to say no to. People may join her, but there's more fear involved than you're willing to admit."

"And I should point out she's not the only person like that around here, Ms. Gwyll," I said.

Briallen chuckled. "I do take that for granted, I guess.

Anyway, it wouldn't surprise me if someone is rallying the Dead. People down in the Weird might not trust the Guild or the Consortium, but that doesn't mean they will automatically trust Eorla."

"I told her pretty much the same thing," I said.

"And, don't forget, the old gang structure fell apart last fall. Whoever's riding that dream mare might be making a power play."

"Well, if the Weird falls any more apart, there won't be much to play with," I said.

"Something new will form, Connor, maybe not down in the Weird, but somewhere else. It always does. That's the Way of the World. One thing ends, and another begins, but the World goes on," she said.

Briallen and I had an old argument about whether places like the Weird had to exist. She believed they did, that society always had a class of people who didn't succeed for one reason or another. Solving that problem always created a new one in her view. She had no hesitation helping to make people's lives better, but she assumed the same issues would crop up elsewhere. Nigel, though, accepted the existence of places like the Weird as necessary evils. If improving the lot of most people meant sacrificing a few, he could ignore the Weird. A few desperate or dead didn't bother him. Between those views, everybody else fought over turf and power.

"Donor might have a role in this. He's actively campaigning against Eorla with the Guild. Aldred Core has shown up several times warning macGoren that Eorla is a threat."

"She's more a threat to Donor," I said.

"True. But if he can isolate her politically because he says she's dangerous, he forges alliances elsewhere," she said.

"There's a platoon of U.S. Marines at the airport," I said.

"And a frightened human population in the city. Creating more trouble in the Weird would work in Donor's favor," she said.

I leaned my forehead against my hands. I didn't care about Donor or macGoren. I didn't care about their strategies and games. I cared about the woman upstairs and wanted her back. "Do you trust Nigel?" I asked.

She studied her cup. "No, but I trust the Wheel of the World. It's given us a path to take, and I think we should take it. That doesn't mean we shouldn't watch our step."

# 22

Later that afternoon, I waited in a small anteroom at the
Rowes Wharf Hotel. The strange behavior of Eorla's people
in the Weird concerned me. Some seemed to have crossed
the line from not helping to interfering in the community po-
licing Eorla was trying to establish. Keeping fey away from
the warehouse fire when they could have helped or hindering
investigators from doing their work were not the best ways
to create a safer environment. Eorla might have her reasons,
but it was getting to the point where her people needed to
stay out of the way.

Security had been tightened in the building. I had been
asked to show identification even though the person asking
me for it addressed me by name. I didn't take it personally.
They were doing their jobs, and the policy wasn't directed at
me. At least, I didn't think so.

As I watched people stream in and out of Eorla's office,
I realized they were not the usual petitioners and construction people. More security and administrative staff attended

to the room. Their stressed and concerned faces brought to mind Briallen's thoughts about Donor.

Rand appeared at the door. "Her Majesty will see you."

I gave him a playful poke on the shoulder. "You're a receptionist now?"

Elves, in general, were aloof with people outside their social group, and elven guards more so. Rand was no exception to the point of appearing not to get that I was joking. "I won't be serving coffee."

Yet again, he surprised me. His bowed head hid a small smile as he stepped back to let me pass. Eorla sat behind an enormous desk stacked with files and paper. Unlike the receiving room, this office was her working space. The dwarf Brokke perched on the edge of a couch beneath the windows, skimming some documents. He gave me a cursory glance and went back to his reading.

I hadn't figured out what Brokke's motivations were. He claimed to be an advisor to Donor Elfenkonig—and was—yet had informed me about some crucial court gossip in the past. Now he sat with Eorla, a renegade of the Elven Court who had been threatened by the king himself.

Eorla came around the desk to greet me with a kiss on the cheek. "I wondered that we haven't spoken."

"I've been helping the Boston police with the dwarf murders," I said.

She gestured toward the seats by the windows with a drab view of the city's elevated highway. Brokke didn't acknowledge us as we sat in the chairs to either side of him. "Are you having problems with the police?" Eorla asked.

"No, but the case looks like it's leading to something they can't handle. I have reason to believe the murderer is a *leanansidhe*," I said.

Eorla raised a considering eyebrow. I had yet to find something that flustered her. "I haven't encountered one, but I understand they can be debilitating."

I smirked with affection. "Eorla, they debilitate people to death."

Annoyed, Brokke shifted in his seat. He didn't like my lack of deference to royalty, nor Eorla's indifference to it. Eorla chuckled, then hid her mouth with her hand. "Do not tell anyone I laughed at that."

I tilted my head. "Promise. How have you been?"

She leaned sideways in the chair and stared out the window. "Cautious. Donor is trying to persuade the human government to allow him to move against me. So far, he has not met with success. I haven't been able to determine what his true game is."

I gave Brokke a sharp glance as she spoke. He didn't impress her, and she often spoke to him in a dismissive tone when she wasn't ignoring him completely. Her admission in front of him that she knew something of Donor's movements struck me as strange. "After they let the Guild have free rein down here, I can't say I blame them. They're getting enough flak for not moving against you themselves," I said.

She nodded. "For now, it's to their benefit to let me lead the fey down here. They know I'm taking care of things the Guild doesn't, and it eases their burden. I haven't banned them from the Weird, so they can pretend they still have the territory under control."

"Except you don't let them bring anything more than handguns in," I said.

She waved a dismissive hand. "They know that's common sense. They saw what happened when their National Guard came in with tanks. I've kept the neighborhood calm, and that's what they want."

"Is that why your people are keeping the fey away from the police?"

Curious, she cocked her head. "How do you mean?"

"I've witnessed your guards either refusing to help the police or keeping other fey from helping them," I said.

"I gave no such order. In fact, quite the opposite," she said.

Brokke shuffled through his documents. "In life, I find, Your Royal Highness, not everything—or everyone—is who they appear to be. One must look beneath the surface to understand the depths."

Eorla pursed her lips as she tapped her foot. "I see. Donor has been secretly moving his men into the city. A few have attempted to infiltrate our operations. Perhaps you have met some?"

"He's trying to discredit you?" I asked.

She smoothed her long skirt down her leg. "Of course. I know he has been working with the humans. My sources tell me he has been trying to make a side agreement against me with the Guild."

"I've heard that, too. I guess your attempts at getting the Consortium and the Guild to work together are working," I said.

To Brokke's annoyance, Eorla laughed. "I suppose this is an example of that phrase 'be careful what you wish for.' He's been exploiting the fears and suspicions among the people in the Weird. Not all of them trust me yet, especially the Dead."

"The Dead have no interest in anything that doesn't benefit them, and the living have nothing to offer them," I said.

"Which might make them perfect mercenaries for Donor," she said.

"I don't think you have to worry about the Dead. They played that game for the Guild, and it got them a war," I said.

"Anything can be bought for the right price," she said.

I stared at Brokke point-blank. "If only there was someone who had access to the king who might advise you."

Brokke glowered. "His Royal Majesty knows full well my loyalty and my whereabouts."

I nodded toward him. "You let him in your office knowing that?" I asked Eorla.

Her mischievous smile revealed the answer. "I feed him misinformation, and he runs to Donor with it like the trained puppy he is."

Baffled, I stared at both of them. "I do not understand elven politics at all."

Brokke rustled his papers and went back to reading while Eorla laughed. "It's an old game—like all court intrigue. We pretend to be fooled by subterfuge while using it to further our own ends. By saying I give my cousin's dwarf misinformation, I reveal my awareness that he is not to be trusted while making him wonder what is true and what is not."

Brokke sighed. "And I am no one's dwarf."

Eorla observed Brokke with bemusement. "He says that often, and I tend to believe it is the one thing he speaks always true. Brokke may provide counsel, but he keeps his own more often." .

"Maybe he can tell me why one of Donor's men was after an essence seller down in the Tangle?" I asked.

Brokke dropped his papers on the seat beside him. "Her Royal Highness may entertain herself by speaking about me as if I were not here. You may not."

I shrugged. "Sorry. I got confused."

"The Elven King knows Eorla is concerned about the blue essence moving through the Weird. He made the connection to essence sellers before you did," Brokke said.

"Why does he care?" I asked.

"Answers have advantages when you are the only one who has them," Brokke said.

"Did he find any answers?" I asked.

"I don't know, but he will find something. I have seen him in a vision, sure and elated as he moves through this city," said Brokke.

Brokke's visions were what made him valuable to the Elven King. His predictions held up, and that made him dangerous as an ally or foe. He saw truth and likelihood where less skilled scryers saw hints and guesses.

"And then what happens?" Eorla asked. Donor had come to Boston to bring Eorla to heel. Anything that made him happy did not bode well for her.

Brokke shrugged. "The vision fails. I see nothing beyond those moments."

The downside to seeing a future, even for those who were good at it, was that the scryers could not see their own future. Knowing the future changes the future. For scryers, events that included them became difficult to decipher, if not unseeable. When scryers were part of events, thinking about them muddied the vision. "You're going to be there," I said.

He narrowed his eyes at me. "Or you are."

Time and again, scryers had told me that they cannot see me in their visions. The obvious conclusion was the black mass in my head, but how that related to the future—or affected visions of people I had never met—puzzled me. "Is it asking too much to find out what Donor knows?"

Brokke gave me an enigmatic smile. "Not at all. Sharing that answer might be another matter."

# 23

Meryl lay propped up in her bed in Briallen's guest room, her eyes fixed on the opposite wall. Upstairs, Briallen and Nigel prepared the sanctum sanctorum. I played with Meryl's hand, twining my fingers through hers. "I don't know if this is the right thing to do, Meryl, but I don't know what else to do. I don't trust Nigel, but Briallen says this might work. I can't stand seeing you like this, but I'm afraid, okay? I'm afraid you might never come out of this, and I'm afraid Nigel has some motive I haven't figured out. But I can't not do anything. I'll be right beside you, and so will Briallen."

She didn't answer. That would have been too much to ask, never mind too-perfect timing. A cool touch against my forehead preceded Briallen's sending. *We're ready.*

I lifted Meryl's hand and kissed it. "Time to go."

Her weight barely registered in my arms as I picked her up. She curled into me like a child, her head bowed and leaning into the crook of my shoulder. I didn't rush to the fifth floor of the house, worried I'd slip or bang against something. At the top of the stairs, I paused to catch my breath.

Soft yellow light filtered out of a stone arch centered in the wall on the top-floor landing. The stone door stood open, Celtic spirals and knots inscribed over its entire surface. Essence flickered in the swirling patterns, glowing shades of blue, white, and yellow. The door replaced another that had been destroyed last year. That was my fault, but I didn't feel guilty about it. No one got hurt that time, and lives were saved. Briallen never said a word about replacing it. The new door was more ornate than the last one. I was sure it cost her a pretty penny. Not that I could afford to pay her back, but I liked to know my debts. Despite its weight and size, it moved with a bare touch, balanced on carved-stone hinges.

I waited in the doorway as Briallen and Nigel finished their preparations. Dressed in plain muslin robes, they faced each other across a long granite slab that took up the center of the oval room. The room was a jeweler's dream, every surface encrusted with diamonds, rubies, emeralds, and other gemstones that glittered in the light from candles set in niches. The floor tiles had bloodstone and quartz embedded in them. Sapphires and opals—ward gems of a moon worshipper—clustered about the foot of the table. Some stones glowed with their own inner light, evidence of the resonant essence that created a safe environment in the room, sealing it from outside forces.

I had seen Briallen's sanctum once before when she needed me to act as her anchor while she went into a trance. What Nigel had proposed was similar. The problem was that none of us had been designated as an anchor when whatever happened to Meryl happened. The challenge would be getting her essence to latch onto someone, who would then guide her back to the waking world.

That someone wasn't going to be me. Nigel explained his intentions, which depended on a fine understanding of body essence. The dark mass was a wild variable. Without knowing what the black mass was, it was impossible to take it into account in the spells. I understood and had to accept that. It didn't mean I liked it.

I lowered Meryl onto the slab. A thin white cloth over

the table didn't provide much cushioning. Briallen arranged Meryl's arms and legs in as comfortable a position as she could for someone lying on cold stone. Nigel moved to the head of the table and placed his hands on Meryl's shoulders. "You need to leave now, Connor."

He didn't say it with the usual snide tone he had adopted for me. It was a statement of fact. Even without the ritual starting, the dark mass in my head pounded against my skull, eager for the ambient essence in the room. I caressed Meryl's hand and stepped away.

Briallen wrapped her arm in mine and escorted me out onto the landing. "Remember: This will either work or it won't. If it doesn't, we've lost nothing."

I kissed her on the forehead. "Okay. I'll wait in the parlor."

She squeezed my arm and let me slip into the hall. Our eyes met as she pushed the door closed behind me. *It will be fine,* she sent.

More spirals on the door flared as it closed. I reached out, wanting to help, but the dark mass in my head shot a dagger of pain down my arm. It wanted the essence in the door, maybe even in the people on the other side. I clenched my jaw as I backed away, trying to understand how to make the darkness behave. It receded either because of my thoughts or my moving away from the door.

I descended the stairs all the way to the kitchen and made coffee. Trance rituals took time, and I had to distract myself. I brought a tray up to the parlor with some cookies Briallen had made. Only Briallen would think of baking my favorite cookies before embarking on a complicated essence experiment. I wished I was that attentive and organized.

I placed the tray on the table near an armchair by the fireplace. The blue flames burned in the grate higher and brighter than usual. From my years living in the house, I knew they did that in reaction to essence in the house.

I browsed through Briallen's bookshelves. The fascinating thing about her library was that it always surprised. I couldn't count how many times I've looked through her books, yet whenever I approached it with a new question, I

found a new book. Part of that was the sheer wealth of information. Many times, I didn't get beyond the first shelf before
I discovered something I had to read right then. Like now, I
started looking for something on powered stones and instead
ended up seated with a book on dwarves and their customs.

I startled at a noise and realized I had dozed off. My book
had slipped to the floor, but that wasn't what had awakened
me. Something fell in the next room. I hurried across the
second-floor landing to the workroom. Briallen crouched on
the floor beneath a table, rummaging in boxes.

"What is it? What's wrong?" I asked.

She didn't look up. "Nigel is deep in trance. We need
more crystal to anchor him."

I came around the table to help her. "What's happening,
Briallen?"

She looked up at me, tired but pleased. "We found her,
Connor. Her spirit was lost, but Nigel found her. We need to
pull them back."

Relief swept over me. "What do you need?"

"Orbs. Quartz crystal, preferably selenite. Check those
shelves."

I pulled a large fabric box from a high shelf and placed
it on the table, tossing aside paper wrapping. "You used to
keep some in here."

She cocked her head at me. "And you know that how?"

I threw her a guilty look. "I accidentally climbed up there
once and found them."

She shook her head with amused annoyance. "Never
doubt the inquisitiveness of a teenage druid."

I lifted a rose quartz sphere from the bottom of the box.
"Here's the one."

The dark mass in my head spiked as a wave of essence
washed over me. I clutched the sphere to my chest to avoid
dropping it. Another wave hit, crashing over me, and a spear
of black shadow stabbed out of my right eye and struck the
table. Briallen leaped out of the way, backing against the
wall.

The room trembled. Boxes and papers slid from the

shelves. Glass bottles along the windowsill rattled against each other as the worktable danced in place.

"Are you controlling this?" Briallen asked. Her voice sounded far away.

I thrust the sphere at her, and she grabbed it. I slipped to my knees. My right hand curled into a stiff claw of black. Another wave of essence swept over me. I recognized it then, knew it as intimately as my own. Meryl's body signature permeated the air. "It's not me. It's Meryl."

Shadow filled the room as Briallen stumbled out the door. I crawled after her, pulling myself to my feet. Out in the hall, Briallen struggled up the stairs. As the house shook around us, I followed, unsure if I would make matters worse or not. The darkness blinded me on one side but enhanced my sensing ability. The air seethed with essence, roiling clouds of angry colors grinding against each other. As we turned the stairs to the top floor, a concussion of air slapped us back. Briallen stumbled into my arms, knocking me off-balance. We fell, rolling to the landing, our fall cushioned by her body shields.

The shaking stopped. The crazed essence that had filled the air retreated up the stairs. Briallen and I faced each other, our legs tangled where we had fallen. The darkness in my eye withdrew, a thick, painful ooze into my head. A heavy panting sound filled the silence.

I pushed myself up. "Meryl."

I half ran, half crawled up the remaining stairs as I tried to move before my feet were under me. Meryl sprawled on the landing, her head propped up against the banister. She turned her head—my heart raced to see it—she turned her head to look up at me. I fell to the floor and gathered her in my arms. "Are you okay?"

The warmth of her body pressed against me. She didn't move at first, then her arms came up and hugged me. "Why the hell am I wearing a pink sweatshirt?" she asked.

I laughed into her hair and kissed the top of her head. Pulling back, I held her face. "Are you back?"

Her eyes went wide as she focused on me, then looked over my shoulder as Briallen arrived. "I'm fine."

"What happened? Is Nigel all right?" Briallen asked.

Something in her voice—something horrified or angry—made me turn. The door to the sanctum was closed—not only closed but fused shut—the door and its frame one seamless whole. The circular stone had been burned white from essence discharge, a dark spot in the center where the bolt had struck.

Meryl's face pinched in anger. "Screw him. He tried to kill me."

# 24

Meryl sat bundled in a blanket in front of the fire in the second-floor parlor. She sipped tea from a large mug. Briallen watched her either like a concerned mother or a bird of prey. "Sit down, Bree. I'm not going anywhere."

Briallen gave her some space, but didn't sit. "Damn right, you're not. What happened?"

Meryl brushed her hair back from her forehead. "My hair feels weird."

"I wouldn't let them cut it. I thought you would be mad," I said.

Meryl pulled several strands in front of her face and examined them. Her eyes went wide. "Shit. How long was I out?"

"Almost three months," I said.

She sloshed tea on the blanket and almost dropped the mug. "Three months? Are you kidding?"

"What's the last thing you remember?" asked Briallen.

I noticed a slight trembling in her hand as Meryl placed the mug on the table beside her chair. "I was with Eorla down in the Weird. We were trying to contain the Taint. Did it work?"

I nodded. "Completely. Eorla absorbed it all and suppressed it inside herself."

"Damn, that woman's strong," she said.

"You both passed out. I thought you were . . ." I couldn't finish the sentence. Seeing Meryl collapsed on the street, no sign of life or essence, had torn something inside me that night. I lost control and went on a rampage.

"Wow," she said, her voice almost a whisper. We waited as she absorbed the news. "I ain't gonna lie—it hurt like hell. I tried to wall off the pain, but every time I shielded myself, the Taint got stronger. I kept building the protection spell until I couldn't even think anymore. I remember burying myself deeper and deeper in my mind while the Taint rushed through me. The next thing I knew, I heard Nigel calling my name."

"We took you to Avalon Memorial. Gillen tried for months to revive you. Nigel found the way though," said Briallen.

Meryl hummed in understanding. "Not surprised. He told me he was trance-lost once, and he got back by following a powerful essence."

"I never heard that story," I said.

Meryl shrugged. "I'm sure he told you things I never heard either."

Briallen paced in front of her again. "What did you mean he tried to kill you?"

Meryl picked up the mug again, no tremor this time. "I was dreaming, then I felt this jolt that made my head feel hazy. The dream stopped, and I heard someone calling my name. Eventually, I saw Nigel's essence. When I moved toward it, his essence seemed to push me away." She turned to Briallen. "You were there, too, Bree. Why'd you leave?"

"I was anchoring Nigel while he searched for you. When he saw you, Nigel said he needed selenite to boost his essence. He said you were too deep for him to pull you out. I was getting the crystal when you did whatever you did up there."

I pulled my chair closer. "You said he pushed you away."

She played with her hair, checking its length. "I realized I was in a trance, and when I tried to return to my body, he blocked me. Then he tried to rip my mind apart."

"Why the hell would he do that?" Briallen said.

Meryl shrugged. "It wasn't clear. My sense was that he was looking for information. Something he needed to know before he finished me off. Something about you, Grey. Something about an essence source."

I gripped the arms of my chair. Touching someone's mind in a trance state was an intimate process. If someone you didn't invite in gets into your mind, your defenses are limited. "I'm going to kill him."

Meryl batted her eyes at me. "That's sweet, Grey, but I took care of it."

Briallen stopped moving. "Is he dead?"

Meryl shook her head. "Nah. I locked him down in a suspended trance. By the way, nice sanctum you got there, Bree. It should keep him there a good long time."

"You have to let him out," Briallen said.

"No," she said. Her tone said there was no arguing.

Briallen back off. "We'll talk about it later."

"No. We won't," said Meryl. They stared at each other, both defiant. I was surprised when Briallen looked away first. Or maybe I wasn't.

"What essence source?" I said to break the silence.

"I don't know," said Meryl. "I only sensed his intent, not his full thoughts. I was kinda busy trying not to lose my mind."

I took her hand. "I'm glad you're back."

"Yeah, well, don't be too sure about that. I told you I was dreaming. I think the shit's about to hit the fan."

Meryl was the only True Dreamer I've ever met. Her future visions were filled with symbol and metaphor, but she always knew what they meant. "What's going to happen?" I asked.

"The end of the world, I think. Is there any more tea?" She held out her mug.

# 25

Meryl agreed to come back to my place for the night. She didn't want to stay at Briallen's, and I didn't want her to be alone. Going to her house was out of the question still. Meryl never let anyone in her house, not even me. I didn't even know she had a house until we argued about where she would sleep. She had always referred to it as her place. She didn't want me rambling around while she slept, so we went to my apartment. I understood. She was as nosy as I was, but I cared less if she rummaged through my stuff.

We curled on the futon in the living room, Meryl's head tucked under my chin, my arms wrapped around her. "I missed this."

"It feels like yesterday to me," she said.

"Yeah, that was sweet," I said.

She poked me with an elbow. "You have no idea how odd this feels, like time travel or something. Who's president?"

"It wasn't *that* long," I said.

She giggled and shifted in my arms. "You know, people wish they can go to bed and wake up three months later and all their problems will be gone. I did, but now there are new problems to contend with."

"Don't think about it yet. No one knows you're awake except me and Briallen," I said.

"And whoever she's told by now," she said.

I ran my hand along her thigh. "You told Eorla."

"You said she was upset about what happened. A sending was common courtesy," she said.

I tickled her. "Yeah, you're sooo courteous."

She struggled against me, and I stopped. "Yeah, well, the bitch owes me. I lose three months, and she gets to be Queen of the Unseelie Court."

I laughed. "That's a little exaggeration."

Meryl rolled and looked up at me. "Grey? The solitaries and the Dead have rallied to her cause. She took leadership against Maeve and Donor. That's how the Unseelie Court forms. It's a gestalt fey court with attitude."

I traced my finger along her chin. "You're right. I assumed you had to be a solitary to lead the Court."

"Nope. Just angry," she said.

"That must be why Maeve's so freaked out. Donor says she's moving her troops into defensive postures," I said.

"Donor says? Since when do you talk to the Elven King?"

I leaned over and kissed her. "Since he came to Boston to threaten me and Eorla. He's much fatter in person."

Meryl propped herself up on an elbow. "The Elven King is here. In Boston."

"Yeah."

"That's bad," she said.

"Well, yeah," I said.

"No, it's bad because the Elven King was in my dream," she said.

Meryl had a geasa on her for her Dreaming. If someone was in her Dreams, she was compelled to tell them. "Damn. Are you going to tell him?"

She settled down on her side. "Hell, no. I have to tell people what I Dream if I meet them. I don't have to seek them out unless I want to."

"What did you Dream?" I asked.

She didn't answer for the longest time. "I don't remember."

Druids never forget unless, like me, something was wrong with them. "What do you mean?"

"I can see the Dream, but only the shape of it. The details are vague. That's never happened before," she said. She didn't speak for so long, I thought she had fallen asleep. "I'm probably burned-out out from knocking Nigel into the trance."

I debated whether to argue. Meryl liked to choose her discussions, and forcing her to talk about something didn't work. I let it go. I had her back. That was all that mattered. "I wish I had been there."

"I took care of it, Grey. Stop with the he-man thing," she said.

I chuckled. "Oh, that's not it. I wish I could have seen the look on his face when you beat him at his own mind game, then slammed the door on his ass. That bastard lied to me. He said it was safe. I don't care what Briallen says. I'm glad you did what you did."

She leaned over and kissed me. Gods, I missed her kiss. For months I had pressed my lips against hers with no response. I pulled her closer. She nestled down against my chest. "I never trusted him, you know."

"I warned you," I said.

"Yeah, but you were angry and bitter about him. I didn't trust him because Nigel never does anything without an ulterior motive. I liked talking to him, and I learned a helluva lot from him, but I always knew someday he would disappoint me in some despicable manner short of murder. I underestimated him," she said.

"You're a lot smarter than me."

She patted my chest and sighed. "I know."

I poked her, and she laughed. "Why did I miss you?"

"'Cause you were bored," she said.

"I wish."

Her breathing became slow and even. My eyes slipped

closed in the dark. For the first time in a long time, I was happy—allowed myself to feel happy. Despite everything, the one thing I feared was not having Meryl with me. I don't know when that feeling happened and didn't know where it would lead, but I liked it as much as it scared me.

"By the way, Grey, I love the plywood curtains," Meryl said.

I kissed the top of her head. "That's why I missed you."

# 26

A phone ringing in the middle of the night was never a good sign. I groped for my cell as Meryl groaned beside me. The caller ID showed Murdock's number. Meryl mumbled a hello and pulled the covers over her head. Between the months lying helpless in bed and the huge expenditure of essence at Briallen's, she was exhausted. Even powerful druids didn't have the body strength of a Danann fairy. We needed sleep to replenish essence, to say nothing about improving our dispositions.

"We have another body," Murdock said, when I opened the phone.

"Where?"

"The Tangle. You need to see this one."

I dressed in the dark as he gave me directions. He offered to send a squad car to pick me up, but the Tangle was only about a mile off. It was faster to run—maybe walk—than wait for a car to make the lights to my place and back. He didn't say more because he wanted me to have my own first impression. I kissed Meryl's head before I left. She answered with a snore. After months of no reaction, she made me smile.

I jogged down Old Northern Avenue, dogging through late-night crowds on the sidewalk. The party crowds thinned out as I reached the burned-out section of the avenue. No more buildings meant no more business. Boston's World Trade Center and its boat terminal had escaped the fire, but it was locked down for the night. Not far past it was where we had found the first body.

This part of the neighborhood was pretty damaged, but as I neared the Tangle, the rougher crowd that sought its entertainments began to appear. The local gangs had fragmented after last summer, but they existed in small groups. Elf and dwarf thugs eyed each other on opposing corners, flexing their muscles over turf. The groups were smaller, but it was only a matter of time before they started growing and taking over city blocks. Hard-core partiers dressed in leather and vinyl hustled their way along the sidewalk, searching for new clubs and drugs. Solitary fey lurked in doorways, their strange appearances adding an air of menace as they muttered their sales pitches for exotic spells and potions. No matter how beaten down the Weird was, it always managed to rise again in the same desperate ways.

I paused on the sidewalk and faced the incandescent glow of the Tangle. The directions Murdock had given me led a few blocks in. I had to take a deep breath to prepare myself for the next part. I tapped my body essence and activated what was left of my body shield. Hardened essence covered my head and parts of my chest and arms, nothing like Murdock's full protection. My body shield had been damaged in my fight with Bergin Vize. When I met him, I discovered Vize didn't have a shield at all but depended on a blue-skinned nixie named Gretan, one of the small river fey, to protect him.

My shield served as an early-warning system these days. It activated on its own, reacting to heightened essence like a cat bristling with fear. Hardened essence could protect me from the collateral pain caused by scrying, but without someone else's shield, I had to rely on my pathetic remnants until I found Murdock. The Tangle was a nest of scrying. Walking into it was going to hurt.

I took one more calming breath. A street address in the Tangle was pointless since the streets appeared to move. Illusions hid passageways that appeared at certain times or when the light struck from the proper angles. Sometimes the path itself was an illusion that had to be followed in order to find a destination. Murdock had told me to follow a line of dark blue brick buildings and turn up the alley next to the third one.

I found the building with no problem, turned into the alley, and saw a lamppost with a green light. Ten paces past that I walked through a door that looked like the entrance to a building but actually led to another alley. Over my shoulder, the illusion didn't exist—the entrance to the alley wasn't a small door but the typical wide gap between buildings.

People hurried by, huddled in hood-drawn cloaks or turning away from me. Not everyone wanted to be seen in the Tangle. The end of the second alley let out onto a narrow street. Despite people moving in every direction, some fast, some slow, it wasn't hard to find Murdock. The cluster a block away had the obvious appearance of crime-scene rubberneckers.

An electric anticipation filled the air. People ran up and down the street, voices pitched with excitement and anger. Dim light made everything more chaotic as shadows played along the walls. A group of dwarves crowded ahead, shouting in triumph as they shined lights on the wall.

Two patrol officers kept the crowd back. Murdock had his gun drawn and his body shield up. The fey folk around him threw apprehensive looks at the metal weapon. Murdock didn't have the whole beware-of-iron baggage the fey had, and a man with a body shield and a gun confused them. The funny part was that because he always had his gun on him, he had intuitively figured out how to compensate for the essence warp the metal created.

I edged around the crowd for a better view of the wall. At

first, my mind didn't process what I was seeing. It seemed fake, like a strange art installation or even a joke. A thought later, I realized it was no joke.

Suspended a foot or so off the ground, a woman was embedded in a bricked-over archway. Her twisted body protruded from the bricks as if caught in the act of turning away. One arm dangled limp over the sidewalk, the other lost from sight in the wall. One leg had gone through. The other bent against the stone pavement, its foot twisted sideways against the ground. Her head was turned away from the wall, as if she had paused to look down behind her. Long dark hair draped over her shoulder, obscuring her face.

I stopped next to Murdock. "That's not a *leanansidhe*," I said.

"I didn't think so," he said. Even without sensing her elven body signature, I would have known she wasn't a *leanansidhe*. The *leanansidhe* were around four feet tall, and the woman in the wall was nearly six feet. Now that I was close enough, I sensed a barrier shield, not a literal wall. She had started to pass through the barrier, and it closed on her.

Murdock shouted at the crowd to disperse. They moved back but didn't leave. The patrol officers did their best to maintain control, but on a good day, people in the Tangle weren't known for complying with the law.

I lifted the hair from the dead woman's face and froze in surprise. "Son of a bitch. This is Gerda Alfheim."

Murdock shuffled closer. "You know her?"

"I saw pictures of her after the Castle Island fiasco," I said.

He leaned in closer so as not to be overheard. "What did she have to do with Castle Island?"

From her expression, her death had not been pleasant. She was well within the field of the glamour when the barrier spell triggered a shutdown through the door. "She put Gethin macLoren up to what happened, Leo. That's his mother," I said.

MacLoren was a terrorist responsible for the first in the string of recent disasters in Boston. He was mentally unbalanced, a damaged soul whose mother, Gerda, was an elf and father a Danann fairy. Gerda had manipulated her son's desire to heal and used him in an attempt to open a portal into another realm that held some of the scary beings out of Faerie history. It was the first major case Murdock and I had worked together. We both almost died stopping the catastrophe. Gerda Alfheim hadn't been working alone back then. Anger swept over me as something fell into place for me. "Gerda works with Bergin Vize. This changes everything, Leo."

# 27

I wasn't the only person who had recognized Gerda Alfheim.
Word spread through official and unofficial channels, and
law-enforcement agencies from the Guild, the Consortium,
and the federal government descended on the Tangle. A dead
international terrorist garnered attention. I wasn't much interested in Gerda, though. I wanted to know about her ally,
and I knew one person who might put me on a lead to him.

I nursed my third Guinness in a back booth at Yggy's. It
took more than that for me to get drunk enough to be stupid,
but I didn't know how long I would have to wait for Brokke.
I had asked Rand to send Brokke my request to meet. Rand
couldn't promise anything, but he said he would try. Given
Gerda's death, I was pretty sure Brokke's arrival would be
more "when" than "if." Even so, my patience was wearing
thin.

Murdock wanted to be there, but I asked him to let me
handle it. Brokke didn't trust people and was likely to avoid
answering questions with anyone else around. I didn't fool
myself into thinking he trusted me. As a scryer, he liked be-

ing able to see possible futures. Adding Murdock into the mix would increase the variables and shake up the outcomes.

Brokke showed before dawn, slipping into the booth when the bar was loudest, and people were less attentive. A waitress served him a small glass of claret before he had time to settle in. "I didn't realize you were known here," I said.

He sipped. "Yggy's has been here longer than you've been alive, Grey. Some of the staff have been here since it opened."

I went right to the point. "Where's Bergin Vize?"

"I don't know," he said.

"Bull. I know he hasn't left Boston. Why is he here, Brokke?"

Brokke held the stem of his glass between two fingers and moved it back and forth. "That's a different question. He thinks he's saving the world."

"That's not an answer."

Brokke pursed his lips. "You know anything I tell you will have ramifications."

"So will anything you don't tell me," I said.

He sipped the claret, playing it around on his tongue. "In my life, I have seen many things I wish I hadn't. People think knowing the future is an advantage, an opportunity to create something good or avoid something bad. Over the years, I've come to believe that not knowing is better than knowing. People rarely make choices that benefit the future."

People with information always said crap like that. Everyone else was too dumb to be trusted. "I'm not interested in the future. I want to know about the past and the present. You know why Vize is here. I don't believe it's for any good reason. Convince me not to hunt him down and kill him with my bare hands."

"I've seen that possibility. It doesn't end well," he said.

"For him or me?"

"For anyone," he said.

I finished off my beer and signaled for another. "Maybe that's fine by me. Maybe I don't give a damn anymore."

He stared at me with an infinite patience that made me want to slap him. "I don't believe that about you," he said.

I hunched forward at the table. "Fine. Maybe I'll kill him to spite you. A world without Vize has to be better than one with him, no matter what you say."

"A fatal flaw exists in that statement. You assume a world will exist without him," he said.

I scoffed. "I don't buy that anyone's that important."

"It's all ramifications, Grey. Vize's death will lead to inevitabilities. One of them is too dark to entertain," he said.

I gave him a cold smile. "'One of them.' I'll risk other possibilities."

Brokke surprised me by shuddering. "There is truth in your words. I would not have believed it."

I thought I had been bluffing, playing his game of words, but what he said was true. I felt it in my gut. I was more than prepared to kill Vize and damn the consequences. "Now tell me why Vize is here."

"Why has he always come here? He wants to destroy the Seelie Court and return us to Faerie. That has been the goal of the Teutonic fey for over a hundred years."

"The Elven King destroyed Faerie and caused Convergence, Brokke. They're fighting for a memory," I said.

"That's what you've been taught and what you choose to believe, Grey. The Elven King blames Maeve for Convergence. All he wants to do is go home."

"I'm not going to debate politics, Brokke. I don't care who caused Convergence anymore. I'm also not going to let anyone destroy my home to chase a pointless dream," I said.

"You might destroy it if you try to save it," he said.

"Tell that to Vize. What was he doing down in the Tangle with Gerda?" I asked.

Brokke stared into his glass, swirling the claret now and then. He was powerful enough to use such a small surface area for scrying, but I didn't feel anything. One of Heydan's rules for Yggy's was no scrying on the premises. "Vize was helping her recover a stone ward she lost a long time ago," he said.

The idea that Gerda Alfheim had had the *leanansidhe*'s stone bowl at some point didn't defy imagination. If anything, I was more surprised a *leanansidhe* had it than a powerful elf. Many things were lost after Convergence and ended up in odd places. "How did she lose it?"

"Gerda wasn't anyone important years ago. She worked her way through barter and trade before she gave her skills to the Teutonic shadow network. At some point, she came into possession of the stone and sold it without realizing what it was."

Another Guinness appeared on the table. "Who did she sell it to?" I asked.

"I'm aware of your investigation with your detective friend. You already know. Nar Veinseeker," he said.

"And she thinks he still has the stone?" I asked.

Brokke shrugged. "That I could not determine. The most I learned was that Gerda knew him after Convergence and that they had a falling-out of some kind."

"He seems to have a knack for that," I said.

"Then you know more than I. He knows where the stone is. Gerda wants that information," he said.

"Well, Gerda apparently knew something about where it is. She already found the *leanansidhe*," I said.

Brokke's forehead wrinkled. "I saw no *leanansidhe* in my visions."

"They're using her like a bloodhound. She's attuned to the stone. I've seen her operate. Veinseeker doesn't have the stone, Brokke. They want him for something else," I said.

"My visions have shown no connection between the stone and a *leanansidhe*. Tell me what you know, Grey. Leave out no detail," he said.

"The *leanansidhe* survives by absorbing essence. There's a darkness inside her that pulls essence to itself. She uses her ability to feed on that essence as it passes through her into the darkness. She's sensitive to the stone. It draws her to it."

Brokke looked around the busy bar. "I have seen such a creature years ago. Few of them exist, and we can all thank the Wheel for that. I think you are wrong about this. The stone is bound to the Wheel and is too strong to yield to something like a *leanansidhe*. It would be of no use to it. I don't think Gerda was working with one of these creatures."

I had seen the *leanansidhe* use the stone. Hell, she had shown me how to use it. The stone gave its power with no resistance. In Shay's apartment, it had worked with no effort by anyone at all. It was a directionless thing, a producer of raw power for the taking. That Brokke believed otherwise didn't sound right. His reputation for accuracy was based on the truth of his visions. For him not to understand the stone didn't ring right with me. "You seem pretty sure of yourself, Brokke. If the stone wouldn't be of use to a *leanansidhe*, what good is it?"

"When it chooses someone, the wielder has the power to stir hearts to his cause. His followers become formidable warriors, stopping at nothing to achieve the goals of the wielder."

When I had touched the stone bowl, I felt nothing more than the surge of essence. No spells were bound to it. The pure essence flowed without purpose or restraint. I didn't sense that adoring masses were dying to follow me to the grocery store. An uneasy feeling came over me. "Can you describe the stone, Brokke?"

Brokke made a triangular shape with his hands. "I have seen drawings and renderings of it in records across Europe. It rises and falls in both our histories, Grey, sometimes with the Celts, sometimes with the Teuts. No one can say whether it was created by someone or simply appeared at the beginning of time. It's roughly three-sided, about the size of a fist, and made of deep blue quartz. You might say it looks like a heart."

The *leanansidhe*'s stone was carved from quartz into the shape of a bowl—but it was bloodstone, a deep green with splashes of red. We weren't talking about the same stone. "What do they want it for?"

Brokke frowned. "I would think that obvious. It's a faith stone. It inspires people to the cause of the wielder."

I shook my head. "I can't imagine a stone so powerful it would turn people into terrorists. Vize may be crazy, but I don't think he's delusional."

A sudden uncomfortable look passed over Brokke's face. His eyes shifted out toward the crowded bar. "I don't recall saying Vize wanted it for himself."

For once, Brokke was revealing something he knew rather than uttering his usual evasions. He could be talking about only one person. The Elven King would benefit the most with such an artifact, and he conveniently happened to be in town to force Eorla back into the fold. If he could make the faith stone work on her, he would have a potent weapon to use against the Seelie Court. World opinion has always been in Maeve's favor. If the stone worked the way Brokke said it did, Donor Elfenkonig could tip the balance of power in his direction. "Dammit, Brokke. I've been trying to connect Vize to the Elven King for over a decade."

"And you won't this time either, Grey. Donor knows how to distance himself from people like Vize. The stone will be found and out of this city before you or anyone else can do anything about it," he said.

"Have you seen that?" I asked.

He sighed. "The only thing I can tell you is that the stone will be found. What happens after that is anyone's guess. My vision failed two nights ago. So did everyone else's. That happens when profound change is imminent, and the future is in flux."

Meryl had said she couldn't remember her dream vision. The same thing happened to Briallen before the Castle Island catastrophe. Now one of the most powerful scryers in the world was saying he was blind. "I have to stop them, Brokke."

Brokke sipped his claret. "No, you *want* to. It's one of the reasons my vision fails. Your darkness obscures more than your mind."

The sounds of the bar whirled around me. I had been about to shrug off his comment, discard yet another hint from the always-mysterious Brokke. Murdock's words about seeking answers in unlikely places came back to me. "What do you know about it, Brokke?"

"The darkness is a rare thing, Grey, but the *leanansidhe* isn't the only fey that touches it. I've seen it far too many times recently."

"So have I. Something drained the essence from the dwarf victims. If a *leanansidhe* didn't do it, who did?"

He considered me with surprise and annoyance. "Vize, of course. He has the same darkness in him as the *leanansidhe*. It's the same thing in you."

My memory flashed to the *leanansidhe* hissing in the dark. She'd called me "brother." The night of the riots, I saw Vize, saw the darkness in him, and recognized it as the same thing in me. "You're wrong, Brokke. It's not in his head. It's in his hand."

He gestured with his glass at my arm, the one with the silver-branch tattoo, hidden beneath my jacket sleeve. "Does that need to be in your head for it to have power?"

Self-conscious, I slid my arm off the table and dropped it in my lap. It was pointless to ask him how he knew about the tattoo. "How does he know how to use it?"

"How do you?"

I wasn't about to confess my personal involvement with the *leanansidhe*. "Answer my question."

"I have, in a way. You showed him, Grey. When you touched him with your darkness the night of the riots, you disturbed something within him. I was on the bridge that night, too. I saw what happened. The darkness in Vize exploded when you attacked him. You showed him the way," Brokke said.

Dread gripped my stomach. When the *leanansidhe*'s darkness touched mine, I understood her, understood how she used the darkness. I never realized I had done the same for Vize. "What have I done?" I said, more to myself than to Brokke.

"I don't know. Our minds see it as darkness because we can't visualize it as it truly is," he said.

A chill ran over me. "You know what the darkness is?"

Brokke's hand shook as he reached for his glass, his smug self-assurance slipping. "No one knows what is beyond knowing. It exists in opposition to existence. If I could describe it, it would exist in the world. It doesn't exist in the world because it is outside It."

When powerful people showed fear of something, it was a sign to start worrying. "The *leanansidhe* said something like that to me. She said the Wheel of the World has two sides and that we—she—touches both sides."

Brokke eyed me. "It's not a side. It is. It is what was and will be. The Wheel of the World, Grey, is what comes between."

"The Wheel of the World has no end and no beginning," I said.

Brokke shook his head. "What is destruction but the seed of creation? What is creation but the fruit of destruction? The Wheel of the World at once turns infinitely in both directions yet begins and ends. What happens between is the Gap, out of which the Wheel might arise again or not. The Gap was there at the beginning and will be there at the end. It is the source of everything and nothing. It drives the Wheel forward and brings It to a standstill. It devours the Wheel as it creates the Wheel. It is greater than the Wheel and less than the Wheel. It will end us all if we let it and it allows us. It is the place of power from which opposing forces spring and create the Wheel of the World. But the Gap never vanishes, Grey. It shrinks as the Wheel grows and turns until there is nothing left but the Wheel, and the Wheel begins to feed on itself, and the Gap appears anew. We cannot escape it, and it cannot escape us."

His words had the cadence of a chant. He knew this thing, had a sense of it, and there was a sense of truth to what he said. I gazed into my beer. "Why have I never heard of this?"

He made a dismissive sound. "You Celts love to lord over others with your superiority while you wallow in your ignorance. Your people turned away from the truth long ago, Grey, content to indulge themselves with no thought for the future or the past. Do you know why Convergence happened? Because the Celts believed the world would never end because for them it never began. With all your talk of the turning of the Wheel, you and your people act like It turns in place, that nothing was ever different, and nothing would ever change. And that's why you know nothing of the Gap. You know nothing of the past and have no understanding of the future."

Annoyed, I sipped my beer. "You want a religious discussion? I could say the Teuts caused Convergence because of their doom and gloom. When you think the world is going to end, you start acting like it, then you cause it. You create a self-fulfilling prophecy. You sit there and tell me the Elven King wants the faith stone so he can challenge Maeve; and then you want to blame the Celts for the destruction of Faerie? Spare me."

"You cannot stop what is coming. The darkness is beyond comprehension," he said.

"It can be controlled. I've seen the *leanansidhe* use it. If something can be controlled, it can be stopped," I said.

"That thinking, I fear, will bring ruin to us all. No one can control the Gap," he said.

"This isn't an abstract discussion, Brokke. You're telling me that I've handed Bergin Vize a dangerous weapon that can destroy everything. He has to be stopped."

Brokke pursed his lips. "What makes you think I'm any more comfortable that you have the same power?"

# 28

I woke alone at midday. Meryl, praise be, had set up the coffeemaker. She left a note to join her for lunch if I managed to get up before the sun went down. The funny part was she wasn't being sarcastic. We were both night owls and cast no stones in the waking-up-late department. I took a leisurely shower, then walked over the Oh No bridge to catch the subway.

At Boylston Street, the train left me with a screech of metal on metal as it rode a sharp turn out of the station. When no one on the platform or in the token booth was paying attention, I slipped through the break in the fencing near the stairs. I walked the access curbing beside the tracks toward the next station in Copley Square. I had told Murdock that Boston was riddled with tunnels—some official and legal like the subways and some not so much. Not far into the tunnel was a concrete niche that wasn't concrete but a glamour hiding a not-so-official tunnel that led to Meryl's office in the Guildhouse.

Meryl had been with the Guild a long time. She had

worked her way up in the archives division until she became the Chief Archivist. Despite doing important work, she isn't respected by the investigative division the way she should be. I should know. I was one of those jerks once. I knew Meryl before I lost my abilities and made assumptions about her that weren't fair. I thought she was lazy and grumpy. Once I was bounced out of the Guildhouse, I learned she was neither—far from it. Taken advantage of at work, sure, but not lazy. I still think she's grumpier than she claims, but a lot of that has its reasons. I wouldn't have her be any other way.

In the course of her career, she had discovered things in the Guildhouse—beneath the Guildhouse—that had been forgotten or lost. Tunnels layered their way into the earth, complicated mazes of stone and brick that only dwarven crafters could have produced. Long-hidden rooms filled with rare treasures lay dormant until Meryl had found them. She had made a few improvements of her own along the way, like the secret bolt-hole out of her office into the subway system.

As our bond grew, Meryl had given me privileges she gave to no one else—like tuning some of her wall illusions to my body signature so that I could enter or leave the Guild-house unseen. I eased down the steps that led from the con-crete niche. At the bottom, a long, narrow tunnel ended at her office, a bright rectangle of light in the distance.

The wall glamour included a warning anytime someone passed through, so Meryl knew I was coming. She worked at her desk, her face intent as she read her computer screen. Both Gillen Yor and Briallen had given her a clean bill of health, and seeing her back in action was an enormous relief.

From the office side, the tunnel exit appeared to be a blank space between a filing cabinet and a credenza. Meryl spun her chair as I stepped through. I leaned over a stack of manuals and kissed her on the lips. She had trimmed her hair and dyed it lemon yellow

"You look great," I said.

"Comas are very refreshing," she said.

The office was a shambles, filing drawers half-open, with

papers jumbled in them, stacks of reports spilled across the floor, the guts of Meryl's backdoor computer spewed out across the credenza. "What the hell are you doing?"

She blew a puff of air that fluttered her bangs. "Not me. It was like this when I came in this morning. I've been looking for patterns."

I picked my way over a mess of e-mail printouts and tossed a box of old CDs off a chair to sit. "Of what?"

"What they were looking for," she said.

"Let's start with who," I said.

"Let's call it macGoren, et al. Various agents have been in and out, but the directives are coming from macGoren," she said.

"Now the what," I said.

"The who again, actually. You," she said.

"Me? Why would they be searching your office for information about me?" I asked.

She shrugged. "We're boinking."

"We boink?"

"Not for at least three months"—she narrowed her eyes at me—"that I know of."

I chuckled. "No worry. It's been that long." I watched her read through something on her computer screen. "You said Nigel was looking for something you knew, too."

"I did," she said, and kept reading.

"So, macGoren and Nigel both think you know something important about me," I said.

"They do," she said.

"Aaaaand . . . we're not really having a conversation, are we?" I asked.

She glanced at me. "They want their weapon back."

Meryl had made a connection between me and Nigel I had never considered before I lost my abilities. When I didn't understand Nigel's coldness, she pointed out that I was his number one soldier in the fight against the Elven King. When I lost my abilities, he lost what he considered his advantage. "I'm not a weapon," I said.

"But you were a tool and didn't know it," she said.

"Regardless, I'm neither now," I said.

She pursed her lips. "Maybe not a weapon but maybe still a tool."

I scrunched my face at her. "Are you continuing this metaphor or are you insulting me?"

She grinned. "I so love that you're uncertain."

I folded my arms against my chest. "Why does that amuse you so much?"

"Because you used to be this arrogant prick who thought he knew everything even when he didn't, and now you act sorta human, and that baffled look you sometimes get on your face is incredibly adorable," she said.

"And you like to kick puppies, too," I said.

"Gee, Grey. I might be brutally honest, but I don't think I'm cruel," she said.

"So, be honest. What have you found?" I asked.

"A lot of chatter about the night of the riots and what you did at the Old Northern bridge. I have to confess to being intrigued by that, too."

"That's what I came to talk to you about. I spoke to Brokke last night. He thinks I have the ability to access a primordial darkness he calls the Gap," I said.

"Nigel talked about that a lot. It's part of the Teutonic creation myth," she said.

"Do you think it's a myth?"

She shrugged. "What's a myth except a creative explanation for something people don't understand? Something that is cloaked in myth doesn't mean it isn't about something real."

"We don't have a myth like that," I said.

"Myths are created when something is important to a culture, Grey. The beginning and the end of the world isn't something the Celts focus on. We care about the world as we find it, not as it was or will be. The Teuts took a different approach," she said.

"So, Brokke could be wrong," I said.

She shifted her eyes from side to side, pretending to check if anyone was listening. "If anyone ever heard me say this,

Grey, I'd get kicked out of the Grove. Celts are interested in questions about the world. Teuts are interested in answers. Either one could be the right path, but that's not important. Finding a path is. Only you can decide what to believe."

I sighed. "I don't know what to believe anymore."

A small smile slipped onto Meryl's lips. "You know what, sweetie? You just made another step on your own path."

I set my chin. "Then my next step is to kill Bergin Vize."

Meryl stared, a long, blank stare while she turned something over in her mind. Silence filled the room as we looked at each other, as if a turning point had been reached. Whether it was in our relationship or something greater, I couldn't tell, but I felt it coming.

"Let it go, Connor," she said.

"I can't," I said.

"Maybe that's why you should," she said.

"I can't. I unleashed something in Vize that can't be stopped by anyone else," I said.

"What if you release something in yourself that can't be stopped?" she asked.

"I've never wanted to end the world," I said.

"Are you sure? Ever since I've known you, you've been trying to stop something. Every time you do, the world as it is ends and becomes something different, something new," she said.

Her words twisted in my gut. What was change but the end of one thing for another? "That's how the Wheel of the World works," I said.

She looked down, and muttered, "Dammit."

"Yeah," I said.

She looked me in the eye then. "What do you want me to do?"

"First, we call Murdock. Then we hit Vize when he least expects it."

# 29

Murdock pulled to the curb on Tide Street. He eased out of the car, his tactical uniform all black and business, and scanned the sidewalk like a cop. Meryl pushed herself off the wall she had been leaning against and hugged him. "You finally updated your wardrobe," she said.

He hugged her back. "I see that a coma hasn't made yours any more subtle."

Meryl wore her biker jacket over a black lace top. What the neckline hid, the tight fabric more than made up for. Black leather pants and high, flat-soled boots with lots of buckles completed the outfit. She tilted her head and feigned confusion. "What do you mean? This is my running outfit."

"Running to or from?" he asked.

"At," she said.

He leaned against his car and crossed his arms. "What's the plan?"

Meryl looked at me. "You're sure you want to do this?" she asked.

"I'm sure," I said.

She lifted her head, and the subtle flutter of a sending wafted through the air. In the distance, a howl mixed with the sound of sirens. Something primal tugged at me, raising the hair on the back of my neck. Another howl joined in, and another, until we were ringed with the sound of yips and barks drawing closer. A dark shape leaped from a building in the distance and landed on all fours. As it scrambled down the street toward us, more figures appeared from every direction, dark and howling.

Responding to some instinct, Murdock and I backed next to Meryl, who lounged in a casual pose against the wall. Murdock's hand went to his gun holster, but Meryl put her own hand on his arm. "Don't," she said.

The figures bounded closer, bunching together until they formed an arc of rippling muscle and fur. They ranged along the edge of the circle of light, wiry lupine bodies darting forward and back, agitation showing in the orange gleam of their eyes. Some pulled up onto their hind legs and howled against the sky.

The *vitniri* surrounded us. An unsettling merging of man and wolf, they struck terror in everyone who crossed their path. The tang of musk and sweat hung in the air as they jostled each other, pawing and nipping at one another. Their howls and barks receded as one broke through the circle into the light. He loomed over us, peering down his long-snouted face as he licked his tongue across sharp teeth. "We came," he said.

"We need to find someone," Meryl said.

He growled deep in his throat. "Give us a scent. We will find him."

Meryl gestured at me. "He smells like this one."

I resisted the urge to shudder as the *vitniri* regarded me. The *leanansidhe* had called me "brother." I suppose it made sense that Vize could be considered the same. I smiled. "Hi."

He leaned in close, his nostrils flaring. His eyes never left mine as he sniffed, his face hovering over my face. He stopped and exhaled, a rancid odor hitting me as a plume of essence settled on my skin. His lips curled back, and I flinched as a long tongue snaked out and licked my cheek.

He retreated, hunching his shoulders as his body signature brightened around him in a halo of deep orange light. He arched his spine and roared. A cloud of essence burst from his mouth, curling in the night air as the pack around us barked and howled. They danced in the cloud, the essence heightening their excitement. They jumped and leaped down the dark street in several directions. The lead *vitniri* dropped to all fours, howled at me, then dashed up the alley.

I reached up to wipe my face, but Meryl grabbed my hand. "Leave it. It's a tag so the pack doesn't confuse you with its prey."

"Can someone explain to me what's happening?" Murdock asked.

Meryl walked into the street and peered into the distance. "The *vitniri* can scent essence over long distances for a brief period."

"Why the hell didn't you mention this before?" he asked.

She cocked an eyebrow at him. "Uh . . . coma?"

Murdock had the good sense to be chagrined. I couldn't blame him though. The *vitniri* freaked me out a little, too. My body was taking its time settling out of fight-or-flight mode, and I knew what the damned things were. They had protected Vize during the riots without knowing it. With their strong sense of honor, they wanted to repay the error. "How do we follow them?" I asked.

"The alpha will send the location," she said.

"They're not going to kill him when they find him, are they?" Murdock asked.

"The alpha will do his best to prevent that," she said.

" 'His best'?" Murdock asked.

Meryl nodded once. "His best. The pack is in heightened hunt mode. They listen to the alpha, but emotions can get out of hand. Be glad you weren't down here when the Taint was loose."

I paced the sidewalk, alert and anxious. An occasional howl brought me to a stop, and we tensed, waiting to see if Meryl received a sending. She remained still, head cocked toward the sound. The first few times, she shook her head to indicate she hadn't heard anything. After a while, she took to filing her nails without acknowledging the sounds.

An hour later, Meryl stood in the middle of the sidewalk, hands planted on her hips. "Let's move," she said.

Murdock and I trailed after her as she walked down the alley. "Have they found him?"

"They hit two old traces but nothing solid. They're running a grid pattern. This area's clear for a couple of blocks," she said.

As we rounded the corner to the next street, my head buzzed with the effects of scrying. Without being asked, Meryl took my hand and activated her body shield. The shield draped over us, deadening the threat of pain. "No one's getting any good reads on the future lately, mostly static. People keep trying, though."

"That happened before Castle Island, you know," I said.

She glanced at me from under her yellow bangs. "And before Forest Hills and before Boston Common and before the riots."

"I get it, I get it," said Murdock. "Something bad's going down. Can we focus on the problem at hand instead of going all ominous?"

"Just stating the facts," said Meryl.

"Can the facts be more about succeeding than dreading?" he asked.

Meryl started to say something but snapped her mouth closed instead. A reflective look came over her face, and she swung my hand. "They found him," she said.

She pulled me along the sidewalk into the next alley, a sinuous gauntlet of brick and trash. Howls filled the air as we approached the end, the buildings curving over the next street like cupped hands. We stopped in an intersection of six streets, *vitniri* running in circles around a cluster of darkness pressed against the narrow end of a corner building. The dark mass in my head contracted and flared with heat.

"All I see is shadow," said Murdock.

"It's him," I said. The darkness in front of me swelled and undulated against the building, feathering along the cornice of the first floor. Around it, *vitniri* darted and snarled, avoiding its edge. Whenever the shadow shifted, the lupine figures backed away. Whether the alpha held them in check or they sensed danger in the shadow's touch made no difference to me. They weren't going to die because I had asked for their help.

Meryl primed her hands with essence but left them at her sides. "He's using some kind of shield to hide behind. It's being generated by an essence spot near the ground."

I peered into the shadow with my sensing ability. The darkness made a pale white haze seem brighter than it was. It moved and shifted down near the curb. Living essence moved around, not stone wards. "He's got Gretan with him. She has a cloaking ability."

"The nixie who left the bite scars in your neck?" Meryl asked.

"She left scars?" My hand went to the back of my neck. The last time I had encountered Vize, the small blue nixie jumped on my back and bit me. Her tiny claws left their marks, too. I hadn't realized they scarred.

"Upper teeth. She could use an orthodontist," Meryl said.

The dark mass in my head ached as it contracted again. Across the square, a tendril of darkness snaked out of Vize's shadow and stabbed at one of the *vitniri*. The lupine jumped away without being touched as his brothers moved closer on the other side. Another tendril shot out as the first one withdrew, and the shadow shifted. Vize seemed unable to spread his attack, and the *vitniri* used their numbers to keep him pinned. Even though he had the power of the darkness, he was outnumbered. It was a stalemate.

"What's our plan?" Murdock asked.

Meryl hardened her shield as some *vitniri* danced around us. "When you fought him in TirNaNog, I saw a shadow like that appear when you made contact. It knocked you off your feet."

"It hurt like hell, too," I said.

"If you do that again, maybe Murdock and I can subdue him before he regains his balance," she said.

"Not with the nixie shielding him," I said. Vize didn't have a body shield anymore. Despite her small size, Gretan generated a formidable shield for both of them. Meryl would be able to penetrate it, but that would draw their attention and make her a primary target. I didn't want that, not after her coma and not after her doubts about the sanity of my plan. A physical assault wasn't going to get us anywhere.

"Then let's get rid of her." Before I could stop her, Meryl set her stance, stretched her arm out, and fired a tight, intense burst of essence from her hand. It sliced through the nixie's shield and hit the faint hazy body signature dead-on. The shield evaporated as the nixie tumbled out of the shadow, a blur of blue skin and white hair that stopped splayed out on the sidewalk. Vize's image resolved into view within the darkness.

Meryl waggled her fingers. "Damn, that burned."

The nixie didn't move. "Is she dead?" asked Murdock.

Meryl flicked her bangs back. "Nah. Precision stun. Word to the wise, Murdock: Having a kickin' body shield doesn't mean it's invulnerable if someone knows what they're doing."

A plume of darkness raced across the intersection and slammed into Meryl. Her body shield collapsed. She stumbled, and I caught her as she shielded herself again.

"Point taken," Murdock said.

Vize leaned over Gretan, shadows swirling around him.

"Shoot him," I said.

Murdock aimed his gun. I don't know what was sadder about that moment, that I asked my friend to shoot somebody or that he considered doing it. "Bergin Vize, this is the Boston police. Get down on the ground with your hands out."

Vize ignored him as he lifted Gretan from the ground.

Meryl held her hand out for the gun. "I'll do it."

Murdock relaxed his stance but didn't holster the gun. "No. There has to be another way."

"If killing one person could save the world, would you do it, Leo?" I asked.

"No one's that important, Connor," he said.

I stared at the darkness, stared at Vize in the darkness. He stared back, keeping the *vitniri* at bay with feints and starts of shadow, but he didn't take his eyes off me. He acted too calm for the position he was in. He had a plan. I didn't want to give him any more time to execute it. "You're right, Leo, but not the way you meant."

As I walked away from Meryl, her shield slipped off me and the staccato beat of scrying hit my mind. She started to follow. "Please, stay back, Meryl. Leo's right. I started this, and I have to end it. One person doesn't matter."

She put her hand on my arm. "Don't do this, Connor."

"I'm pretty sure I'm the one here he's afraid of," I said.

She pressed against me. "You don't know that. You don't."

I glanced at Murdock. "You can always shoot him if you change your mind."

He shook his head and looked away. "Maybe I'll shoot both of you."

Despite my lack of popularity with the Murdocks, I told myself he was joking. I was sure he was. Pretty sure.

*Vitniri* paced beside me as I crossed the intersection. Several ran close in, their eyes glazed with the heat of the hunt, tongues lolling as they scented me. One or two nipped at my clothing, then backed off, barking in frustration or confusion.

I hadn't seen Vize since the night of the riots in the Weird. Then, he had been a little worse for wear—binding burns, cuts, bruises, and a nice split across his cheek where I had clocked him. He pulled the darkness back, let it rise and curl over us like a canopy. It didn't touch me. Touching each other had ramifications, usually bad ones. That much Vize understood.

He cradled Gretan against his chest. "Odd company you are keeping," he said.

"I'm going to kill you," I said.

"You'll miss the point of all this if you do," he said.

"There is no point, Vize. There never was. It's all chaos and power games," I said.

He arched his eyebrow. "And you're playing and being played. Of course, it's chaos and power. The reach for power always causes chaos. It's the Wheel of the World, Grey. Without chaos, there is no change, and without change, nothing progresses."

"You expect me to believe you're in this for progress? This city is in ruins because of you. You're not going to spread your brand of progress. I won't let you. It ends here."

"You know you can't touch me," he said.

"I don't have to," I said. I pulled the dagger from my boot, the enchanted one that Briallen had given me. It radiated heat, the runes on the blade glistening with pale fire. The air around my hand rippled, and the blade stretched to the length of a sword. I held it with the tip stopping short of Vize's chest.

Unimpressed, Vize looked down at the blade, then back at me. "You think you can kill me. You're not who you think you are."

I pressed the tip against his tunic. "Last chance to surrender."

He lifted his hand, not toward the sword, but toward empty space. "And you."

The air crackled with a blinding white flash of essence, and a spear appeared in his hand. Not any spear, but *the* spear—the one that had disappeared when I closed the gate into TirNaNog. The spear had bonded to me, to my body signature back then. It operated by some arcane set of rules no one knew. Vize had bonded with it, also, and, for some reason, it preferred him to me at that moment.

Vize pressed the tip against my jacket. The dark mass in my head burned against my skull. Spots flashed before my eyes as I tried to fight against the pain they generated. "Where did you get that?" I asked.

With a flip of his wrist that I should have seen coming, he parried the sword away and slammed the spear against the side of my knee. I fell on all fours. The dark mass bulged against the back of my right eye, pressing forward. Vize grabbed me by the hair and wrenched my head back. "I will have the stone, Grey. The only way to stop the Seelie Court is to destroy it."

Streaks of essence-fire rained into the intersection. Vize tilted his head up to watch. "And I am not without allies."

In TirNaNog, a ragtag collection of Celtic and Teutonic fey had joined his cause, some powerful enough to take on Danann fairies and Alfheim elves. I didn't realize how many of them had managed to hide in the city.

Darkness sprang from my eye and hit Vize in the face. The contact jolted me to my feet as it slammed him against the wall. I staggered back as essence seared the air between us.

*Get out of there.* I flinched at the force of Meryl's sending.

*Vitniri* screamed and howled as they scattered. Fairies swept the air, firing down. Solitaries flooded into the streets from the surrounding buildings. Behind me, Meryl and Murdock pushed across the street, their hardened body shields sizzling with the incandescent light of essence strikes.

Vize smiled at me as he pulled darkness around him and Gretan like a cloak, the spear blazing within it like white flame. The dark mass seeped out of my eye. With a shout of pain, I contracted my body essence, helping the darkness release.

The darkness boiled out of my chest in a cloud. It hurt like hell, but I didn't care. I fed it my anger, and the darkness leaped forward, hitting Vize's cluster of darkness like a fist. I flew backwards from the contact, hitting the pavement. I blacked out, my vision, already cluttered, going darker. The blackout lasted a few seconds, my awareness returning to see the backs of Meryl and Murdock over me as they held off attacks from either side.

I pulled myself up a wrought-iron fence. Essence-fire pinned us down, but Meryl's and Murdock's shields held it off. The air in front of us rippled, and Uno's hulking form appeared, his shape swelling in size as he howled against the sky. Fey folk scrambled away in fear. Murdock swung his firing arm back and forth, panic etched on his face.

"What the hell is that?" Meryl shouted.

"I told you I got a dog. A big dog," I said.

The sky lit with a growing halo of blue light that swept

into the square as a boiling haze. Uno pressed against us, forcing us away from the fighting. Shouts echoed against the shadowed walls of a narrow street. The essence billowed toward us, clouds of indigo and white filling the width of the street. It hit Murdock's shield in a shower of yellow sparks. His hardened crimson body shield bent and shifted, forcing itself back against the wave. He had learned how to deal with the essence wave from our last encounter.

Figures ran in the fog, distorted human shapes that leaped and screamed. They swept by us in eddies of blue, essence I recognized. The Wild Hunt had come calling, and it was attacking Vize's allies.

A deep indigo light flickered in the midst of the Hunt. As it rolled closer, people fled in confusion. The shape resolved into a huge figure on a dream mare, its eyes burning with fierce red light. The rider reined the beast and turned it toward us. The horse stamped its feet, bloodred sparks flying up from the pavement. The rider stared down, eyes glowing with flames from a helmet mounted with enormous antlers.

*Follow.* The sending had a rich, deeper baritone that made me shiver. With a jab of sharp-heeled leather boots, the rider wheeled the dream mare about and cantered down the street.

# 30

The blue light of the Dead flickered as the Hunt continued the fight on the next block. Murdock stared after the rider. "Was that a friend?"

"If I'm not mistaken, we've been invited to follow the King of the Dead."

"What, like the devil?" Murdock asked.

I twisted my lips in amusement. "The King's more of an administrator and occasional hunter, but I don't think that means he's the nicest guy around, if that's what you're asking."

"And we want to go meet him because . . . ?" Murdock asked.

I looked back up the street. Uno guarded the sidewalk, his massive bulk obscuring the scene in the intersection. "Given the options at the moment, I say the King of the Dead is the least of our problems. Don't drop your body shield, though."

"Great," he muttered.

Meryl slipped her hand in mine. "You know, usually when we go out, all hell breaks loose, but I don't think it's ever been this literal."

The sounds of the fighting diminished as we walked deeper into the Tangle. Faint blue light hazed the air, the residual trail of the dream mare and the rider. The surrounding walls glowed pale white. The street turned into a dead end.

"Did we miss a turn, or is it an illusion?" Murdock asked.

I stepped up to the end wall. "The rider's essence ends here. It's a glamour." I placed my left hand against the wall and pushed. The concrete bent under the pressure, and my hand slipped through.

"Do I hold my breath or what?" Murdock asked.

"Geez, we were invited, remember?" Meryl said. Without hesitation, she walked through the wall.

"I didn't get the invitation," Murdock said.

"Door glamours aren't that thick. Hang on to my arm and step through without stopping. You'll be fine," I said.

He gripped my arm by the triceps, leaving his gun hand free. "I'm sure Gerda Alfheim was told the exact same thing right before the wall ate her," he said.

The glamour tingled cool over my body as we slid through the illusion to join Meryl. On the other side, light and sound startled me. Murdock was even more surprised than I was. We hadn't heard anything from the street.

A makeshift market sprawled through a cavernous space. Essence-powered lanterns hanging from scaffolding and fire escapes illuminated a winding path through canvased stalls and tents. Herbs and essence spiced the air, and unseen musicians weaved spelled tunes meant to encourage relaxation and camaraderie. The crowd spanned the various fey folk races, with a notable number of dwarves and minor clan elves. A dwarf paused in front of us and bowed with formal courtesy. "My apologies the Hunt gave you trouble. We did not know you were favored. I have been asked to escort you."

Without waiting for a reply, he led us through the tents. The main aisle followed an abandoned trolley track bed. Vendors eyed us, but no one made an attempt to solicit.

"People seem intent on the door we came in," Murdock said.

"I think they're worried about who's coming through next," I said.

"Or isn't," he said.

His comment made me remember the screams up the street. "We don't know what happened back there."

"Something tells me we won't either," he said.

At the end of the vendor stalls, stone constructions jutted from the walls and rose into shadow. From glimpses through open doors, some had the look of barracks about them, compact bedding in rows and bunks. Other build-outs were more private, even elaborate. True to the abilities of dwarves, not a speck of mortar was visible in the joinings of the structures. At the back end, the outcroppings were decorated with carvings of wildlife and trees.

Another glamour blocked the way, radiating a green essence of complex alarm spells and resistance shielding. The dwarf walked through it, his presence triggering another spell that opened the wall as if someone had pulled aside a curtain. Beyond was an enclosed room, a long, narrow space like an audience chamber, lit with torches. A single chair faced us from the far end. The dwarf knocked on a door behind the chair, then stepped aside and waited.

The rider emerged, wearing the long maroon cape I had seen earlier. Back in the street, I assumed I couldn't see his face because of the poor lighting, but now it was obvious that a glamour masked the front of the helm. In any other context, stag antlers and burning red eyes would have generated giggles, but in the shadowed room, they looked damned eerie. A formidable body shield guarded that side of the room.

*Drop your shields,* the rider sent.

"Well, well, well," Meryl said. Amused, she dropped her shield.

"No," said Murdock.

His answer surprised the dwarf, but the rider made no move. We regarded each other until the rider's shield wavered and collapsed. *Since you do not have your weapon pointed at me this time, I suppose I shall take that as courtesy, Detective.*

The rider reached up and removed the helm. Two long, thick braids of red hair tumbled from within as the glamour deactivated. The rider threw back one side of the cape, revealing a formfitting red leathered armor. Ceridwen sat in the chair and propped the helm on the arm. "My apologies for what happened to you a few days ago, Grey. The Hunt should have recognized my ring."

In life, Ceridwen had been a powerful member of the Seelie Court. As an underQueen, she helped decide on who would be High Queen or could campaign for it herself. Maeve sent her to investigate me and Meryl about our role in a different catastrophe. That was the cover story. It turned out she was tracking rumors that Bergin Vize was about to launch an attack on Maeve. The rumors were true, and Ceridwen ended up Dead.

After she died, she surprised me by showing up at my door. She gave me a ring, in token of a promise we made to each other to take Maeve down. "I wasn't wearing it. I didn't want to invite questions."

Annoyed, she shifted in her seat. "That ring represents a great promise, Grey. I trust it has not been tossed in some forgotten drawer."

"In this neighborhood? Are you kidding? I don't even leave lottery tickets at my place." I unsnapped the boot sheath that held my old dagger and slipped the ring off the leather strap. I held it up. "It's safe."

Meryl leaned in. "She gave you a ring? You didn't tell me she gave you a ring."

I nudged her with my elbow. "Behave."

Ceridwen rose with her hand out. I dropped the ring onto her palm. Melancholy flitted across her features as she touched it. It was a fine band of gold set with a large carnelian. She reached for my left hand and slipped the ring on my pinkie finger. "This will keep you safe from the Hunt. They will sense it and know you for a friend. You can use it to seek my audience at any time. It cannot be removed without my blessing."

I tugged at the ring. It wouldn't budge. "I can't wear this, Ceridwen. Maeve is already threatening to arrest me for your murder. I don't need her adding robbing the Dead to the charges."

Ceridwen returned to her chair. "The ring remains. It is glamoured from sight. Someone might sense it, but no one will see it."

Meryl crossed her arms and tapped her foot. "Now you're wearing her ring."

I glowered. "Knock it off."

She huffed, pretending to be annoyed. "Fine."

"What's this all about, Ceridwen?" I asked.

She leaned back. "I'm building an army, Grey."

"An army," I said.

"A reckoning is coming, Grey. Maeve is losing the support of the full Seelie Court. I will have it known how she betrayed me," she said.

"In the meantime, you're kidnapping people," said Murdock.

Ceridwen glanced at him with unconcealed disdain. Murdock had pulled his gun on her once. First impressions were lasting. "No one is here against his will, Detective. We give everyone a choice. Safety with me or a pawn in Eorla's war with the Elven King."

"Sounds more like they're pawns either way," said Murdock.

"My people will always have a choice. The elves do not understand that concept," she said.

"You've never met Eorla Elvendottir," I said.

"You said you would stand by me, macGrey," she said.

"I did. And I will. This isn't the time."

"I disagree. Eorla's people are hunting us down. Her people have harassed mine throughout the neighborhood." She tilted her head in consideration.

"Those are Donor's people. He's trying to create confusion down here," I said.

Ceridwen narrowed her eyes. "Why would Donor care? His problem is Maeve."

"Then why was Gerda Alfheim embedded in one of your glamoured walls? She works for Donor, not Eorla or Maeve," I said.

The dwarf made a noise that drew my attention. He tried

to cover the reaction by feigning disinterest. "Who is this, by the way?" I asked.

"This is my security chief, Nar Veinseeker," Ceridwen said.

Murdock and I exchanged glances. "He's who Donor's been after, Ceridwen," I said.

Ceridwen cocked her head at Nar. "Explain."

Nar remained still for a long moment. "I had no knowledge of this, m'lady. My intent has been to secure our facilities as requested."

"It sounds like your security chief has been hiding information from you, Ceridwen. Someone has been looking for dwarves that were here a century ago. Anyone with contacts in the Weird knows about it. I have it on good authority that it's Nar they've been looking for," I said.

"A curious claim, Nar, don't you think?" Ceridwen asked.

Nar bowed. "M'lady, I do not know this gentleman, but I will not be spoken ill of. Our facilities were being attacked, and I took appropriate measures to protect us as you requested."

"You weren't being attacked, Ceridwen—he was. He's been using your Hunt to protect himself if Gerda caught up with him," I said.

Ceridwen didn't take her attention off Nar. "What did she want with him?"

"Her last victim said she was looking for a stone ward that he knows about," I said.

*We both have held the truth spear, macGrey. I sense you are not telling me everything,* she sent. Ceridwen had brought the spear to Boston, not realizing what it was. Access to it appeared in our minds at the same time, and we struggled over control of it. In the end, it came to me, but not before Vize used it to kill her. And now he had it again. I shrugged and glanced at Nar. I wasn't going to share anything with a dwarf I didn't know.

Nar drew a round polished stone out of his pocket and tossed it to me. "That is what she wanted. Stone wards are keyed to our glamour defenses."

"These alleys and tunnels are our sanctuary. If anyone were to gain access uninvited, we would be at their mercy," Ceridwen said.

I rolled the stone in my palm, feeling the essence cycling within it. It matched the ones Janey Likesmith had found on the dead dwarves at the morgue. I handed it to Murdock. "It's like a pass key through the essence barriers and works with your body signature. It resonates with the same essence as the shield and lets you through if you have it on you."

"Why not change the lock?" Murdock asked.

Nar held his hand out. "We do, but it takes time to modify all the barriers."

Murdock tossed the stone back to Nar. "We found one of these on Gerda Alfheim. Kinda curious it didn't work for her. Maybe you found time to modify one or two?"

"We only defend ourselves," said Nar.

"This is all beside the point. Nar knows that's not the stone she wanted," I said.

"What stone do you believe she sought, Grey?" Ceridwen asked.

"Something called a faith stone. Bergin Vize wants to know where it is, too. That's who your people are fighting back there, Ceridwen."

She placed the helm on the floor and stood, her wings sparking angry shades of red and orange. "Vize is here?"

"I talked to him myself not an hour ago. Your people interrupted the conversation. He has the spear, again," I said.

*Then it seems our interests are aligned once again, Grey. I will have my revenge against the man who murdered me,* she sent.

Nar moved closer to her chair. "He is playing with you, m'lady, to discredit me. He knows how you feel about this man."

"Gerda may have been your enemy, Nar, but Vize is the one you need to worry about," I said.

"The Guild is getting curious, too, Ceridwen. Your security guy is bringing some heavy hitters down on you," said Meryl.

"I will not allow the Guild in my domain," Ceridwen said.

"This isn't your domain. It's a city neighborhood," Murdock said.

"Ryan macGoren is not to be trusted. We will investigate this matter and proceed appropriately," she said.

Murdock shook his head. "After what happened in the Weird, the mayor is not going to allow fey vigilantes to run around outside the law."

"I will deal with the Guild and the Elven King on my own terms, not anyone else's, fey or human," she said.

"I'm still reporting it," he said.

"Then perhaps you should make yourself comfortable until I decide the best course," she said.

Murdock loosened his jacket. "Is that a threat?"

I held my hands up for calm. "Let's bring it down a notch. We're all on the same side here."

"Speak for yourself," Murdock said.

I ignored him. "Ceridwen, don't do anything foolish. You're already planning on taking on the Guild. Talk to Eorla. I can vouch for some of her people, and she's operating under color of law at the moment. Her support will be a lot more useful to you than that of someone who has a private agenda."

"My people come to me because they do not trust her, Grey," asked Ceridwen.

"Donor has been creating that distrust. There's a dwarf named Brokke who can vouch for it. Your people might trust him," I said.

"I know who he is. He's a Consortium advisor, not one of Eorla's people," Ceridwen said.

"Eorla trusts him."

Nar leaned forward. "If I may, m'lady? I do not believe I am the one here with a private agenda."

Ceridwen glared down at him. "I will speak with Brokke and decide for myself, Nar. If Bergin Vize is indeed behind the attacks on my people, there will be hell to pay."

# 31

Not long before dawn, Murdock dropped me off at my apartment. I had to crawl out of the backseat. Meryl considered it a toxic zone and had made a permanent claim on the passenger seat. "Thanks for another quiet evening out with friends," Meryl said.

I tweaked her nose. "When was the last time you got to knock out a nixie?"

She smirked. "Yeah, that part was kinda fun."

I leaned down so I could see Murdock. "Are you going to report Ceridwen?"

"We can't ignore a gang fight shaping up, even if it is the Tangle," he said.

"Can you give me twenty-four hours to broker something between Eorla and Ceridwen? I want the Guild going after Vize, not them," I said.

Meryl groaned and dropped her head back against the seat. "You can't help yourself, can you? It's bad enough you have Maeve breathing down your neck and Vize running loose, but you have to step into a territory spat between two chicks who wished they were queen of the world."

I pursed my lips. "I think that's oversimplifying it a bit."

She rolled her eyes. "Danu forbid that happens."

I leaned in and kissed her cheek. "Did I mention how much I missed you?"

She pouted, then chuckled. "Can you miss me a little more? I'm beat."

I looked across the seat. "Leo? At least don't mention Ceridwen by name. No one else knows she came back Dead."

He sighed and shrugged. "Another day isn't going to matter in this mess."

I tapped the roof of the car. "Thanks, man. I'll call you both later."

I lingered on the sidewalk as they drove away, pretending to see them off. I knew the real reason I didn't go upstairs right away but pushed down the thought. I wanted to go to Shay's squat, hunch over the stone ward, and bliss out on the essence surge. It was a few short blocks away. I could be there and back in less than an hour.

I took a few steps toward the corner and stopped, realizing what I was doing. That wasn't what I wanted. I didn't want to be seduced by need. I didn't want to be too weak to resist. I didn't want to be controlled by something outside myself. I had lived my entire life the way I wanted, not because I could but because I couldn't stand being controlled.

When I had my abilities, I had the ability to determine my fate. Sure, I worked for the Guild, did what I was asked, even stuff I didn't want to do but was ordered to. That was always on my terms. I had options. I didn't have to be a Guild agent. I could have left anytime I wanted. I could have used my abilities for something else.

When I lost my abilities, I thought I lost my ability to live my life my way. It made me angry, made me feel controlled. It took me a while, but I learned I was wrong. If I was controlled by anything, it was my perception of who I was. I had spent the last three years learning that I was more than just a

body with or without an ability. I was more than that. I was
the sum of my experiences. I was my own person. I was who
I needed to be, not what someone else wanted me to be. I
wasn't going to invite in something beyond my control. Not
again. I turned around and went upstairs.

Despite being tired, I tossed and turned on my futon. I
hated that Vize had slipped away. Worse, he had the spear.
It was a powerful weapon, strong enough to seal a breach in
the veil between here and TirNaNog. When it had bonded to
me, I sensed it in my mind even when it wasn't physically
present. When it materialized in his hand, I had felt nothing.
It made me worry that the spear was no longer bonded to me
or Ceridwen, but to Vize.

It came when summoned with an enchanted word of
command—*ithbar*. Ceridwen had revealed the command to
me, thinking only she could control the spear, but it was a
fickle thing. I'd used the command, and the spear left her.
Then, without the command, it left me and went to Vize.
Why it jumped from person to person escaped me. Someone
told me it was a sliver of the Wheel of the World, whatever
that meant. I didn't like to think about Vize's having control
of the spear and the faith stone. I had to find a way around
him. Even if I couldn't control who the spear went to, I still
had a chance to keep the stone away from him.

I gave up on sleep. One person in Boston was key to both
the faith stone and Vize. The whole mess could be stopped if
Donor Elfenkonig laid off. I doubted he would, but I at least
had to explore the option, if only to close that door.

I left the apartment and walked across town to Back Bay.
"Ambassador Core" had chosen to stay at the Teutonic Consortium consulate rather than at the Ritz-Carlton, where his
diplomatic corps preferred to stay when they were in town.
Of course, the consulate was sovereign Teutonic territory
and defended by a contingent of elven soldiers. No doubt
the Ritz couldn't compete with those amenities, which made
the consulate a much more attractive residence for an under-
cover Elven King.

Guards became alert as I turned the corner of Commonwealth Avenue. They had the right to stand on public property, but they had no real jurisdiction outside the consulate. They were an outer perimeter, an early-warning system. They recognized me. I had no doubt. My face was probably plastered in the lunchroom. Before I reached the building, word would spread via sendings that I was coming.

No one challenged me. Through back channels, the Elven King had offered me asylum from the Guild or the U.S. government should I ever need it. Donor saw an opportunity to gain favor with a valuable former Guild agent. I knew plenty of secrets. I found the idea more entertaining than anything else. Despite my troubles, the last person I would make an alliance with was Donor. After my experience with Nigel, I recognized a strategic opportunist when I saw one.

The consulate was a mistake of architecture. Thrust into the middle of a block of Victorian brownstones, the Bauhaus structure was hard to miss. A tall statue of Donor dressed as a warrior guarded the entrance. Now that I had met him in person, I knew the armor wasn't affectation. Beneath the mannered aloofness of a monarch, I had sensed a fighter.

The reception area resembled an upscale mountain lodge. Empty overstuffed couches faced each other in several groupings, as if the elven staff hung around socializing. None did that I ever saw. Uniformed guards waited behind the desk.

"Connor Grey to see the ambassador," I said.

"Please declare any weapons," the senior guard said.

They weren't going to argue or brush me off. Either Donor expected me or wanted to see me for his own reasons. "Two daggers. Don't even think of asking for them."

They exchanged glances a few moments. I had bluffed my way in with weapons last time I was there. They let me keep them, but last time I wasn't visiting the Elven King. I wondered how many of the guards knew the true identity of the ambassador. "You understand, sir, that the current climate prevents us from honoring your request," the guard said.

Elven security wasn't known for its courtesy. Donor must

have been eager. "I will leave one dagger here. The other was a gift I cannot replace and will not relinquish. I will keep it in its boot sheath as long as I am not required to defend myself."

Again, they exchanged glances, the air fluttering with sendings. The dagger was a gift from Briallen, gold-plated handguards and silver-bound pommel encrusted with crystals and gems. The blade had carved runes from different alphabets, bound with spells and essence. Without seeing it, I sensed runes activating in the presence of elves. Briallen never explained how the runes worked—or revealed if she even knew—but they activated on their own according to circumstances.

The senior guard extended his hand. "Agreed."

I handed over my favorite plain steel one and watched it disappear beneath the counter. I could live without it but preferred not to. They led me through the back of the lobby, past the elevators, to a secure section of the floor. A windowless area was laid out with the comfort of a corporate suite. Beyond a well-appointed living room was an empty, sterile office with an oak desk and several chairs, where they left me to wait.

Fifteen minutes later, Ambassador Core entered in full court regalia, the bright red tunic with all the gold bric-a-brac hanging off it. To my surprise, Brokke followed him and seated himself in a corner. The ambassador gestured at the guards to leave, and they closed the door behind them.

"What can I do for you, Mr. Grey?" he asked.

"Show me your true face for a start," I said. I hated games.

Without hesitation, Donor released the ambassador illusion. Instead of the smug face of Aldred Core, the smug face of Donor Elfenkonig stared at me. "Have you considered my offer of asylum?"

"I don't need it. I'm sure you've heard by now that Gerda Alfheim is dead," I said.

Bored, he glanced at Brokke. "I've been apprised of local news, dull as it is."

"Where's Bergin Vize?"

Donor frowned. "Mr. Grey, these are people I have no knowledge of."

"Funny you would forget Eorla's fosterling," I said.

Donor lowered himself into a chair. "I do not concern myself with the doings of all my citizens. Perhaps if you spoke on a subject I do engage, this conversation might proceed somewhere."

"Alfheim's dead, and Vize has added more victims to his body count. They work for you. They always have. They've caused a lot of damage. At some point, it's going to stick to you," I said.

"I doubt that. I won't be held accountable for the deeds of others. Terrorists have their own agenda," he said.

"But they serve yours," I said.

Donor looked down at the desk, his face a mask as he weighed which string to pull. "Many people do. I am not in the habit of rejecting things that have the good fortune of redounding to my benefit. I have heard a rumor that Gerda was looking for something I am interested in. I will not object if it comes into my hands at some point."

"Where is the faith stone?"

Donor gave his head a small shake. "Faith stone? If Gerda sought such a thing and did not find it, I'm sure no one else has."

"As far as you know, you mean," I said.

His arrogant smile was starting to get on my nerves. "True, but I think I would know if someone else found it. I think we all would know," he said.

"Vize has killed at least three of your own people helping Gerda in her little treasure hunt," I said.

He sighed. "Not all dwarves are my subjects, pity though it is, Mr. Grey. Whomever Gerda recruited to help her was her business. If she involved Vize, she sealed her own doom."

"I want Vize," I said.

Donor's gaze shifted toward Brokke. "So do I. I understand he is wanted for high crimes in several countries. As a head of state, his freedom concerns me. I don't know where he is. I no longer understand his motives."

"Do a sending. He'll come," I said.

Brokke shifted in his seat. "He can make sendings but not receive them."

"Then call him on the damned phone. Look, I didn't come here to chat. I want Vize. I don't care if he's useful to you. Find someone else to do your dirty work. His usefulness to you has run out."

"I will be the judge of that," Donor said.

I leaned over the desk. The attempt at intimidation had no effect that I noticed, but it made me feel better. "Then let me warn you. I will hound him until he is in custody. Anything he does will be done with me breathing down his neck. I will disrupt every plan I can. I will expose every manipulation. I will undermine you at every turn, Donor."

He murmured a chuckle. "In other words, Mr. Grey, you will do what you have always done."

"I don't work for the Guild anymore," I said.

He smiled. "Officially."

"At all," I said. "Maeve is no friend of mine."

"I have been at this sport much longer than you, Mr. Grey. Denials from the enemy mean nothing. Affirmations mean less."

"What you and Maeve have going on is not my concern. That was another life for me. I'm not interested in you anymore. What I care about now are four dead bodies, including Gerda, in my town that lead back to you. I won't shed any tears for her, but I'm not going to let Vize run loose."

He arched an impatient eyebrow. "Perhaps you should find out who killed Gerda, then. I'm sure it wasn't Vize."

"Asking Vize a few questions might help. Where is he?"

"He's gone rogue," Brokke said.

"You've lost control of him?" I asked.

Donor glared at Brokke, and I sensed the flutter of a sending. The dwarf flinched but set his jaw. "It matters not."

"I don't believe you. I saw him in TirNaNog. He has an army of followers. That's got to matter to you," I said.

"Those people support my cause, not his. If Vize turns against me, they will not follow," Donor said.

"Really? Like what's happened with Eorla Elvendottir?" I asked.

His cheekbones tinged red in anger. "Eorla and I will resolve our differences. She will have no choice. It is no concern of yours."

"It is if you don't resolve it. Because if you don't, then I doubt you can control Vize's followers either," I said.

The color faded from his face as he resumed control of his emotions. "Enough of this discussion, Mr. Grey. I will not help you find Vize, but I will not hinder you. Now, it is your turn to answer my questions. Why does Maeve fear you?"

"I seem to have a knack for disrupting her plans without intending to. I annoy her, but I don't think she fears me," I said.

"The Wheel of the World turns, and we follow, Mr. Grey. We influence It as much as It influences us. If you obstruct Maeve's influence, then she has reason to fear you. Your absence in the world might clear her path," he said.

"Maeve doesn't turn the Wheel of the World. The Wheel turns, no matter what she wants," I said.

"Among the common people, that is true, but those with real power do, in fact, move the Wheel. We cannot stop It, but we can change Its course for a time. If Vize had succeeded in TirNaNog, the world would be different right now. The dead fairy queen changed the outcome of that encounter," he said.

"Her name was Ceridwen, and you're right. She did change things—for the better. If she hadn't warned Maeve, Boston would have been destroyed, and Tara would be yours now," I said.

"You closed the gate to TirNaNog, not she. That kind of power is what Maeve fears. The ability to take power away is as powerful as power itself. I am beginning to wonder if I should fear you, too."

"Give me Vize, and you have nothing to fear from me," I said.

He rose from the desk and resumed the Aldred Core glamour. "That, I think, is a promise you cannot make, never mind keep. I wish you well, Mr. Grey, but, more, I wish never to meet you again."

As Donor strode from the room, Brokke glared at me. "You fool. You just signed your death warrant."

# 32

After his portentous announcement, Brokke clammed up, fearing the room was bugged. I expected no less from the Teutonic Consortium. The Guildhouse was riddled with listening devices. It didn't bother me so much when I thought they were the good guys. Using a sending, Brokke asked me to wait for him in Copley Square. Not long after I settled myself on a bench near the park, he appeared on the sidewalk along Boylston Street and entered the Boston Public Library. *I will be in the upper stairwell,* he sent.

Since the riots, any number of agencies had people keeping an eye on me. As a high-level advisor, Brokke no doubt had his own spies to contend with. I waited a few minutes, checking if he was followed or I was being watched. The square and surrounding sidewalks were crowded with tourists, businesspeople, and shoppers. Any one of them—several of them—could be working for the Guild or the Consortium.

I crossed to the main entrance of the library and entered the cool quiet of the old building. I climbed the marble steps without hurrying in case someone was, in fact, watching. In the portrait gallery of the third floor, Brokke lingered near the entrance to the special collections rooms. The top floor of the old library received few visitors unless a new exhibit was on display.

"No one is up here," Brokke said. "If you sense someone coming up the stairs, I'm going down the elevator. You can still sense body signatures, correct?"

"I can," I said.

He moved into the gallery space. "You should not have gone to Donor. He will kill you now at the opportune time."

"I'm no threat to him," I said.

"Not in any way you understand, but you will become one. He needs Vize to finish what Gerda Alfheim failed to accomplish," he said.

"Is this faith stone the real deal? Can it really be that powerful?"

Brokke checked over the railing before responding. "It is perhaps the greatest stone ward ever created. Kingdoms were founded with it. Battles were fought over it. It made small men great and great men tremble. It grants the ability to sway men to one's cause with utter fealty."

"So, how does some dumb-ass like Veinseeker end up with one of the most important artifacts from Faerie?" I asked.

Brokke stared at the murals, a series of portraits showing the progression of religious history from paganism to Christianity. The pagans came off like the bad guys. "You are here-born, Grey. You have no idea what Convergence was like. We didn't go to bed one night and wake up the next day in a new world. We were thrown here amidst war and confusion. Our memories were damaged. We didn't know who we were. Most of us still don't. Things got lost."

After a hundred years, Convergence was still reverberating through the world. Whatever had happened between the Celtic and Teutonic fey that caused the merge was still being fought. Old wars died hard. "Veinseeker claims he doesn't have it," I said.

True surprise came over Brokke's face. "You've met him?"

"Yep. He's kind of a jerk," I said.

Brokke worried his hand through his hair. "Then a confrontation is inevitable. The Wheel of the World turns as It will."

I leaned against the railing and crossed my arms. "Really? Because I met the guy? I'm getting a little sick of the cryptic comments, Brokke. You're playing me for something. I don't like being played."

"Meeting Veinseeker pulls you more into Donor's web. You're already connected to Vize and Alfheim. Maeve is watching you. The closer you get to the stone, the closer you come to death at Donor's hand," he said.

"I didn't ask for any of this."

"But you don't walk away either. If enough people walk away, the inevitable struggle doesn't happen," he said.

"Is that what your vision tells you?

He wandered the gallery, looking at the wall murals. "I made a mistake a long time ago, Grey, and I do not want to repeat it. When Convergence happened, I had a vision of the end of everything we know. When I shared my vision, I lost control of it, and now I do not know where it ends," he said.

"You told Vize the vision?"

"Not I, but he knows it and has tried his entire life to fulfill it for the Elven King, but you changed all that."

I crossed my arms. "What does that have to do with me?"

"Knowing a thing changes a thing. My vision has driven Bergin Vize to madness. It could do the same to you," he said.

"That's not good enough, Brokke. I want answers. You warned me that Eorla might die in the riots, and I made sure that didn't happen. She's alive, Brokke. You owe me. Vize knows whatever you're talking about. I can't stop him if I don't know what it is."

Brokke pursed his lips and closed his eyes. He shook his head and muttered, as if arguing with himself. With a sigh, he looked at me. "The spear was in my vision, Grey. You awakened the spear, and it bonded with you. It bonded with Vize as well.

"And Ceridwen underQueen," I said.

"Aye, and her. Something changed after my vision, something dark and unseen. I saw one person wielding the spear, not three. I thought it was Donor. Because of what happened to the spear, Vize thinks the vision was about him, not the king. Now he wants the stone because that was part of the vision, too. He thinks he can return us to Faerie. The only person strong enough to prevent him from keeping the stone is Donor. If you interfere, Donor will lose the stone."

"That doesn't sound like a bad thing," I said.

"Only if the stone doesn't end up in the wrong hands," he said.

"Sounds to me that any hands are the wrong hands," I said.

Brokke snorted. "'Struth."

"It's been hidden all this time. Maybe it should stay that way," I said.

"If only that could be, Grey. These things are tied to the Wheel. They do not stay hidden. The spear, the stone, and the sword have all pushed into the path of the Wheel."

"What sword?" I asked.

Brokke sighed. "The one in your boot. I knew it for what it was the moment I saw it. So did Eorla."

Briallen had given me a dagger. When I found myself in dire circumstances, it changed size and shape and became a sword. I didn't understand the mechanism of it; but when Brokke spoke, I realized it responded during times of great essence being expended. "I didn't ask for that either. It was a gift."

Brokke gave a sharp nod. "And a perilous one. I don't know if you are drawn to these objects of power or if they are drawn to you. For you, everything hinges on what you do with these things. You can keep on this reckless course, or you can discard them."

"I can't walk away when people are dying, Brokke. There has to be another way," I said.

He sighed. "I already gave you another way. Stay away from Vize. These are all signs from my vision, Grey. Faerie was just the beginning. The sword and the stone and the spear are here. It will take only one more thing to destroy everything if you choose wrongly."

# 33

Before the conversation was even over, I knew I wasn't about to walk away even though Brokke did. Voices floating up the stairwell spooked him, and he was in the elevator with the doors closed before I had a chance to turn around. Whatever his visions, I didn't believe everything Brokke said. Like it or not, he worked for the Elven King. A lifetime of experience cautioned me against anything he said.

That didn't mean I ignored him. It didn't take a rocket scientist to understand that the spear was connected to the Wheel of the World. I had seen that in action. My sword was another matter. Enchanted swords littered the landscape in old Faerie. Mine had saved my ass at pretty opportune times, but not in any way that shocked me. Gerda Alfheim's interest in the stone—to say nothing of her death because of it—was as red a flag as could be when it came to the stone, though. Whatever Brokke's motives for warning me away, Veinseeker didn't seem to have that option.

Brokke might have tried to convince me not to get involved, but his words had the opposite effect. Vize was after

Veinseeker. I was after Vize. To track my quarry, I had to track his. Ceridwen had verified enough of what I told her to kick him out. She had made a mistake in expecting Maeve to have her back when she needed it. She wasn't about to make the same one with an exiled dwarf who wasn't invested in her cause. A few well-placed questions throughout the day helped me follow Veinseeker out of the Tangle.

I wanted to pity Nar as I tailed him. He moved like a man defeated and a man on the run. The open air of main streets meant danger, and he avoided them at every turn. Time after time, he slipped into a disheveled building, home to squatters or illicit dealers, and was turned away. Individuality ruled the Weird, but community made it function. Nar had proven more than once that he couldn't be relied on, and no one was willing to take a chance by letting him in.

In the long run, he ended up where so many other fey did in troubled times. With so many bars and clubs destroyed during the riots, Yggy's had seen an uptick in business in recent weeks. The inclusive environment drew Nar at last. Heydan threw no one out as long as they followed the rules.

People packed the place, brought out by the delicious gossip of a dead elven terrorist. Those with a story about Gerda Alfheim found themselves the center of attention and recipient of free drinks. Once he assessed the atmosphere, no one gained more attention than Nar Veinseeker.

He held court in a booth near the pool table, regaling listeners with a tale of how he had duped Gerda Alfheim a century ago. "She didn't know what she had," he said. "Miss High-and-Mighty was dirt poor when I found her in Munich, trying to pass herself off as royalty to any human willing to spot her a dinner or a drink."

"What precisely-like did she offer for two drinks?" someone asked.

Nar winked. "Now there's another tale for another time. She was a scavenger, back then, she was. She was able to find the whiff of Faerie in the Black Forest like a pig after truffles. Back then, the fey sold the least pebble for a song,

amused that the humans would trade gold for shit. She tried
to sell me a lot of cold stone when I noticed a nice piece in
her room. I pretended to feel sorry for her, offered to take it
off her hands for thrice her price, and she took my coin. I
sold it for a ransom price if there ever was one."

"Aye, and lost your clan in the bargain, the way I heard
it," someone called out.

Nar leaned out of the booth, a sour look on his face. "Then
you heard lies, friend. I left the clan because it wouldn't
know a barter from a scam. Where are they now? Hiding in
holes, their quarries silent."

I eased my way among the listeners until I was in Nar's
line of sight. When I caught his eye, I nodded toward the
back. Nar lifted his glass. "She hounded me for years, vow-
ing revenge when she learned what she lost. But I sit here,
while she lies elsewhere. May she burn in darkness."

He downed the drink and slid from the booth. "A moment, good kin, while I make room for the water of life."

People laughed and slapped him on the back as he worked
his way to the bathroom. With the entertainment paused,
they drifted away, searching for other tales or drink refills.
Unsteady on his feet, Nar reappeared from the men's room.
He paused on the threshold, scanning the room. When he
saw me, he smiled as if recalling why he had left the booth
in the first place.

He propped himself on a stool next to me. "I hear you
have your own tale of the witch to tell."

"You need to be more careful. Gerda wasn't working
alone," I said.

He waved a clumsy hand. "She's gone and good riddance.
I haven't breathed so easy in decades."

"Do you have any idea how many unfriendly eyes are on
you right now? Alfheim was working for the Elven King,
Nar. You're no safer with her gone," I said.

He pressed his finger into my chest. "She was in it for
herself, friend. Her cronies have vanished in the night like
shadows. I've checked. They're gone. They know nothing."

"About the faith stone?" I asked.

That pulled him up short. "What's that?"

"The faith stone, Nar. You see? She talked. The Elven King heard. Where do you think all that money was coming from to hunt you down?" I asked.

He rocked on the stool. "What are you looking for? A pay-off? You'll get nothing from me, Grey. The stone is beyond their reach. They'll all get nothing because I have nothing."

"You know where it is. That's what they want to know," I said.

He chuckled. "Even if they knew, they couldn't get it. Maybe I'll sell that, too. They'll pay for nothing when they have their answer."

"You have to trust me, Nar. Bergin Vize is hunting you," I said.

"Trust you? You got me kicked out by the Dead. I wouldn't trust you with the time of day," he said.

"This isn't about me, Nar. Vize is different. You've been making such a loud ass of yourself in here, he's probably waiting outside right now."

"Let him wait. He learned his trade at Gerda's knee. I eluded the bitch for a century. I have no fear of one of her whelps."

"Think, Nar. You're practically asking for him to kill you," I said.

Nar barked. "You know the rules. He can't touch me here. I learned a thing or two from Heydan in my time. Heydan showed me how to keep scum out." He leaned in close, his breath thick with whiskey. "I got a hidey-hole so close it would knock your boots off. Goes right to my bed when I need it."

I did pity him then, a drunken old fool who had no idea the danger he was in. Like me, he had been sucked up in power politics without intending to be. Unlike me, he had no awareness of it, sure he was maneuvering his way out of a simple barter that had gone bad. "Have Ceridwen send someone for you, Nar. You can't stay in here forever."

He waved at a waitress. "That one. Another high-on-her-horse woman who thinks Nar Veinseeker can be used. Well, I used her, dammit. I used her to keep that witch away from me for weeks like I wanted, then I laid a trap for Gerda, and she sprung it. Beautiful piece of work, it was."

"You killed her," I said.

He snorted. "She killed herself. She stole an access stone to try to kill me. No one forced her to walk into that wall."

"You set her up," I said.

He grinned and hopped off the stool. "Damn straight. She's been hunting me for a hundred years, and now I'm free. Leave me be, Grey. You're killing my party."

"At least stay here until I get back," I said.

He bowed and lost his balance, bumping into several people. "Gladly, my friend. The night is long, and I'm short on drinks. Buy me a drink, and I'll spot you a tale."

He stumbled into the crowd, pushing his way back to his booth. I wanted to drag the idiot out of the place, but he would make a scene in the state he was in. Making a scene was against Heydan's rules. Besides, I didn't have the physical strength to wrestle a drunk dwarf out the door.

I lingered in the alley outside, trying to decide what to do. Nar was right that Alfheim's henchmen had disappeared. I hadn't seen the Wild Hunt all night. Ceridwen probably wasn't in any mood to save his ass anyway. I debated watching out for him myself, but I had my own spies on me.

I called Rand and explained the situation. "Can you get someone to make sure he gets home alive?"

"I'll do it myself," he said.

"I didn't want to ask," I said.

He chuckled on the other end of the line. "Right. I'll be there in a few minutes."

Curious, I hung up the phone. Rand's attitude made me wonder what he knew about me, whether Eorla confided in him. He was acting awfully familiar for someone who didn't know me well.

I now knew what Donor and Vize were after. I knew who they were going after to find the faith stone. By keeping tabs on Veinseeker, I had a chance to contain the situation. Rand would watch the rest of the night. I would take over in the morning. Veinseeker was not going anywhere without my knowing about it.

I made my way home to a warm bed and a hot woman.

# 34

I jumped when Meryl bolted upright in bed. In the dim light of the living room, her dark shape appeared featureless and unmoving. "What is it?"

She threw back the covers. "We need to take a walk."

As I was reaching for the alarm clock, we both squinted when she turned on the light. "It's almost four A.M."

She hopped in place getting into her jeans. "Heydan said we should go down to the bar," she said.

I was next to her in an instant, pulling on my pants. "Is it Nar?"

"Probably. He didn't say. He said we—you, actually—would want to be there," she said.

I pulled on a T-shirt. "It's Nar. I wonder why Rand didn't call me." She flashed me a concerned look. "What? Did Heydan say something about Rand? Is he okay?

She disappeared into the bathroom. "He didn't say anything. I was being ominous."

I put on my jacket and held Meryl's while I waited for her. "Should I call Leo?"

She came out brushing her hair. "Let's see what it is. No sense waking everyone up in the middle of the night."

As I locked the apartment, the security wards Eorla had installed for me activated. The elven essence shimmered across the door, an odd sensation for me since I had spent so much of my life fighting the Teutonic fey. We skipped the old elevator and quick-stepped down the stairs to Sleeper Street.

At 4:00 A.M., the Weird was a perilous place. The late-night revelers had thinned, taking the protection of a large crowd with them, and the more mundane working crews had not hit the streets yet. The hard-core partiers were the only ones out, the ones who had no legal jobs to go to in the morning and the desperate still out looking for a fix or an adrenaline rush. They weren't shy, but prone to confrontation or threat to whoever stood in their path. They sensed their own kind on some instinctual level, eyeing each other in the street, granting a wide berth on the sidewalk out of professional courtesy. It wasn't fear. It was respect. Anyone else was fair game.

Meryl waved hello to a group of guys, who waved back with tight smiles. "What are those guys doing on this end of the street?"

I hugged her from the side as we hurried down the sidewalk and kissed her on the top of the head. "Uh . . . the neighborhood caught on fire down the other end, buildings exploded, people died, and martial law went into effect," I said.

Her eyes widened in realization. "Oh, right. I thought a decent club opened around here I didn't know about."

The alley down to Yggy's was empty, the lone light over the beat-up metal door illuminating a small pool of asphalt. The door clanked open, and someone walked off in the opposite direction toward the harbor. Rand drifted out of the shadows as we reached the entrance. "He's still in there," he said.

"Are you sure? We got a sending to come down," I said.

Puzzled, Rand glanced at the door. "He hasn't come out. Yggy's doesn't have a back door."

One of Heydan's rules was that you left through the door you came in. It cut down on games and forced the clientele to behave themselves. No one wanted to deal with the bouncers if something started. "Nar told me I'd be surprised at how close his hidey-hole was. Maybe he has some kind of arrangement with Heydan. Let's see what's up," I said.

Inside, the music filled the bar more than the patrons. Liquor service was supposed to shut down at 2:00 A.M., but no cops ever bothered Heydan. Still, people tended to move on to more raucous venues after hours. Nar wasn't in sight. We went to the back hall, where the restrooms were.

"I'll check," Rand said, in answer to my unspoken thought. A moment later, he emerged and shook his head.

Meryl walked toward a roped-off staircase. "Heydan said the roof."

"I didn't know he allowed people anywhere else in the building," I said.

Meryl glanced over her shoulder. "Yeah, people. Not everyone."

I followed her up the dark stairs, winding through the building. Rand brought up the rear, summoning up a light body shield. The thump of the bar faded below as we passed closed doors, each floor painted black from floor to ceiling and covered with dust. The last flight was steep, and a door to the sky stood open at the top. Outside, years of debris littered the roof, old asphalt embedded with pea gravel. Beer bottles, condoms, broken ward stones, and shattered glass created their own layer of waste. In all the years I had been drinking at Yggy's downstairs, I had no idea so much action happened on the roof.

A small addition leaned against the abutting warehouse. At one time it had served as a greenhouse, maybe a respite for whoever owned the building in the days it had harbored a sweatshop. Now, the south-facing wall was an expanse of dirty, cracked windowpanes, and the door hung askew.

The financial district shone overhead across the channel, office buildings lights on for no one. To the east, signals blinked blue and red on empty runways at Logan Airport. The roof gravel crunched beneath our feet as we walked toward a tall wooden scaffolding, part wood, part metal pipe, that supported old civil-defense horns thirty feet above the roof. The scaffolding was a remnant from World War II, when the East Coast had feared a massive invasion across the Atlantic. The invasion never came, but the horns remained, their original red paint fading over time to black-pitted maroon. Some were still used for emergencies around the city, but I never heard the ones in the Weird go off. They would probably go off constantly if they still worked.

Nar's body swayed in the breeze from the harbor, the leather cord around his neck making a soft squeak as it rubbed against a wooden brace. His right eye had been removed, a stain of blood and viscera trailing down his cheek. A glossy round stone bulged in the socket where the eye used to be.

Meryl had to tilt her head far back as we stood beneath the body. "There are so many bad jokes running through my head right now, but instead I'll question the wisdom of his meeting you in a bar."

"Thanks," I said.

Rand circled around the other side of the tower. "I failed you and apologize. My understanding was that those back stairs were warded, and no one was allowed elsewhere in the building."

"No blame from me. That's what I thought, too. Did you see Vize tonight?" I asked.

He shook his head. "None of the Elven King's operatives entered while I watched."

"Vize has a nixie companion. She can cloak him," I said. Gretan was taller than Joe, but not by much. She might have been able to slip past Rand, but I doubted she had the ability to overwhelm a dwarf.

"I didn't detect any unusual body signatures. I will check the alley again," he said.

"Don't bother. It was Vize," I said.

"What makes you so sure?" Meryl asked.

I gestured at the roof. Meryl sensed essence like I did.

"The dead spots of essence around the tower. Vize used the darkness to absorb his body signature and hide his trail," I said.

"Can you do that?" she asked.

I nodded. I wasn't ready to tell her that I had almost absorbed some of her essence at Shay's studio. "What do you make of the stone in his eye?"

Before she answered, a welling of essence built beneath us like the shock wave of something huge surfacing from within the building. Meryl and Rand felt it, too, and we all turned toward the door. No one came out of the stairwell, but the decrepit greenhouse glowed with a deep blue light that faded. The tall figure of Heydan appeared in the doorway.

I had to admit, Heydan gave me the shivers. The power he emanated was subtle yet immense, like a placid mountain pool that hid unfathomable depths. Ridged bone showed beneath the skin of his forehead, rising from his temples and back over his bare head. His calm, dark eyes beneath a heavy brow focused over our heads at Nar's body. With ponderous steps, he moved out of the ruined greenhouse and joined us beneath the tower, keeping his gaze on the dead body.

"This is deep work and bodes no good thing," he said.

"What happened to his eye?" I asked.

Heydan shifted, moving his body away from tower. "It was taken for what it had seen. The stone conveyed the memory."

I looked at Meryl. "He knows where it is now."

Heydan lowered his gaze to me. "You know what was sought?"

I gestured at the swinging body. "Veinseeker hid a stone of power. A terrorist named Bergin Vize wants it to take down the Seelie Court."

Heydan stepped to the edge of the roof, peering off into the night sky above the harbor. Seeing such a large person one step from the six-story drop made me a little queasy. He remained silent and unmoving for so long that I wondered if he had forgotten we were there. "It is the nature of power to invite its own destruction. Shadows grow and ebb against the future as ever. I listen and wait."

"Do you know where Vize is?" I asked.

He didn't answer for another few minutes, then stepped back from the edge. "I do not know this man. It matters not who he is."

"It matters to me, maybe a lot of other people. I would appreciate the help," I said.

Heydan's deep eyes gleamed beneath his shadowed brow. "I watch and listen. I heard a shadow move like to the one within you. The Wheel of the World turns, and I hear the sighing of Its passage. What say you to a hanging man?"

"I warned him this would happen. He didn't listen," I said.

"No one ever does," he said.

# 35

The sky over the alley outside Yggy's bled gray into black.
Police lights flashed on Old Northern, rubberneckers pressing against crime-scene tape. Gerry Murdock leaned against
a squad car, indifference in his stance though he threw the
occasional glower in my direction. Meryl wrapped her arms
around me inside my jacket to keep warm in the cool morning air.

Next to the entrance to the bar, another door stood open
leading to the building stairwell. Heydan wouldn't let the
police in the bar and disappeared after he opened the access
door. Murdock came down the alley, all pressed shirt and
clean shoes. He didn't stop to talk to his brother. He glanced
at the medical-examiner staff car. "Is Janey here yet?" he
asked.

"No, OCME sent someone else," I said.

He slid his hands into his pants pockets, standing back to
let a beat officer enter the building. "Looks like we have the
same case again."

"Yeah, but this time we know who the killer is," I said.

"Vize?" he asked.

I nodded. "He knows where the stone is now. It's only a matter of time before he finds it."

"Can we use the *vitniri* to track him?" Murdock asked.

"They're not dogs, ya know. You can't point, and say, 'fetch.' They need a reason," said Meryl.

"I wasn't under the impression that reason and half wolves went together all that well," Murdock said.

A tinge of red flushed across Meryl's cheeks. "They're still people," she said.

Murdock smirked and nudged her. "You're so easy sometimes."

"Not in my experience," I said. They both turned to look at me like I had no business interrupting. The look, in fact, reminded me that I didn't. "I want to get ahead of Vize. We've been chasing him. We've been everywhere he's been. Even if he had to kill Nar to get the answer, there's a method to his search that we're not seeing. We're missing the pattern."

"Old dwarves and stone," Murdock said.

Meryl nodded in feigned amazement. "I would never have noticed that."

Down on the avenue, a murmur ran through the crowd. People had turned their attention from the alley to the sky. Above us, three Guild agents swept across the alley and over the roofline of the building. "That's interesting. The Guild hasn't touched a crime scene down here in ages," Murdock said.

"Veinseeker popped up on the alert database," Meryl said.

"Why didn't you tell us he was in the Guild database?" Murdock said.

She cocked an eye at him. "Um . . . because I'm not a field agent on your case, and no one asked me to? And that I picked up the alert from a security sending about a minute ago? And did I mention I've been in a coma?"

Amused, Murdock grunted. "That coma's going to get a lot of mileage, isn't it?"

With a small smile, Meryl tilted her head down. "Would you like to try one?"

More Guild agents landed at either end of the alley and began clearing everyone out. Instead of waiting to be tossed, we walked to the avenue. At the sidewalk, the Boston police were moving their crime-scene perimeter farther out, pushing the crowd back.

Murdock leaned against his car. "Why is it I'm annoyed when the Guild won't take a case in the Weird and pissed off when they do?"

"Because it speaks to your ineffectual nature," Meryl said. They made faces at each other.

"The Guild knows where the faith stone is. That's why they're here," I said.

Meryl nodded. "Veinseeker is flagged in the system for a reason. If you guys haven't connected him to anything else, the stone's as good a reason as any for the Guild to watch for him."

I gave Meryl a playful look. "Can I ask you a favor?"

She sighed. "Yes, I will hack into the system, Grey."

I hugged her. "See? Not everything involves major interdimensional meltdowns."

"Yet," said Murdock. We got in his car and drove past the growing line of Guild agents. At the Boylston Street T station, Meryl remained in the car as I stood on the curb. "Do you need change for the fare?" she asked.

"You're not coming with me?"

She poked me in the chest. "I'm allowed in the front door. If I'm going to be hacking security and someone catches me, I'm not raising questions about how I got in without my building pass registering."

I tapped her nose. "I'll see you in a few minutes."

I entered the station and paid the fare. This early in the morning, the platform was empty and the token-booth agent half-asleep. I walked into the tunnel unseen. The glamour covering the access door to the escape tunnel had an odd resistance but let me through. I was down the stairs and through the passageway in minutes.

Meryl was at her desk before I reached her office. The

room was back in some semblance of order, at least by her standards. The piles of papers and folders that had been knocked over were back in their precarious piles, the chair was unsittable with boxes, and the trashed computer components on her credenza had been replaced and reconnected. "I will get this done with less annoyance if you stop reading over my shoulder," she said.

I perched at the far end of the credenza. "You don't want me to see how you get in."

She smirked. "If you can't figure it out yourself, you don't deserve to know."

She sorted through screens, leaning back now and then as she waited for something to run. "Okay, here's a problem. Veinseeker's alert was assigned by Manny."

"Eagan? The Guildmaster never put stuff in the system himself," I said.

"Maybe not these days. The alert goes back decades. There are even scans of old paper memos in here that predate computers," she said.

I read over her shoulder. "No reason given for the flag."

Another screen popped open. "Here's something: Veinseeker worked on the Guildhouse," she said.

"When? As far as I know, dwarves never worked here," I said.

She shook her head. "Not like that. He helped build the place, Grey. Looks like he used to own a quarry."

"His brother Thekk owned the quarry," I said.

Meryl pointed to an old contract scan. "Not according to this. They both did."

I pointed to the screen. "This doesn't make sense. Thekk drops out of the contract work after major construction was completed, but Nar continues as a security consultant."

"So?" she asked.

"So, Thekk is the one that controlled the business, not Nar."

Meryl sorted through more documents. "This might mean something. Nar helped set up the shield dome."

"Looks like Thekk was cut out of the security contract. I think you found the falling-out between the two brothers," I said.

Meryl peered up at me. "I must have been in the bathroom during that scene, but I'll take your word for it."

"I thought Eagan created the dome," I said.

"He did. Apparently, Nar provided some kind of"—she gave me a triumphant smile—"essence booster."

Cold realization swept over me. "It's here, Meryl. The faith stone is in the Guildhouse."

She looked doubtful. "If it is, no one ever told me about it."

I stepped into the hall. The stone corridor stretched in either direction, leading to room after room of artifacts. "It makes sense—the falling-out between Thekk and Nar, Vize looking for dwarves who were here a century ago, Eagan's alert for Veinseeker. It's here somewhere. I can feel it."

Meryl came up behind me and wrapped her arms around me. "Do you mean feel it like sense it or feel it like gut instinct?"

I turned in her arms. "Instinct. We have to search."

"There are a lot rooms down here and a lot of stone wards in them," she said.

"Brokke described it to me. We can narrow the search," I said.

Behind us, the computer rang with an e-mail tone, then another and another until the beeping sounded like a coded message itself. Meryl's body shield fuzzed around her as she turned off the sound. "Holy shit, Grey. Agents arrested Vize. They're bringing him in."

I went around her desk to see the alerts. "Bull. If Keeva and I couldn't catch him, no one else could. He let himself be arrested. He wants to get inside. The stone's here. We have to find it," I said.

"The holding cells are down here, too," she said.

I went back into the hall. "I have to convince macGoren not to let Vize down here."

"The moment you step off the elevator, you'll be arrested for being in the building unauthorized," she said.

"I'll go back around to the front door. Call Briallen. Tell her to meet me outside," I said.

"Done," she said.

I grabbed her by the shoulders. "Lock this place down, Meryl. Don't let anyone in."

She inhaled and screamed, a bloodcurdling shriek that started high and swept down into a low note. The air became electric with essence, barriers running down the hall. The grind of stone against stone echoed, and the heavy thunk of wood doors slamming. She grinned. "Sonic cantrips. Better than keys."

I kissed the top of her head and dashed through the wall and into the escape tunnel.

# 36

Outside the Guildhouse, I ignored the blank silver stares of Guild agents while I waited for Briallen. The Danann fairies were on high alert, flying a low-altitude surveillance around the building and backing up the brownie guards on the street. The Guildhouse was in lockdown, the primary shield dome over the building hardened and public access forbidden. By luck, I had been inside the perimeter when the barrier came down.

No one walked the sidewalks unless they were wearing a Guild or law-enforcement uniform. Unmarked vans idled on various corners, men and women with no identification moving between them, their telltale black uniforms an obvious sign of federal authorities. Vize had destroyed a nuclear power plant, so it was no surprise the human government was on the scene.

I caught sight of Murdock parked next to a fire hydrant up the street. I found him slouched in his seat, reading a paperback. He placed a bookmark and closed the book. "Don't tell me you're working a detail for the Guild," I said.

He shook his head. "I heard the news about Vize. I wanted to watch a little karma in action."

One of the reasons Moira Cashel had returned to Boston was to capture Vize. If it hadn't been for him, she might have stayed away, maybe waited until Scott Murdock died before she reconnected with her children. Instead, she'd come back, caused the commissioner's death, and was killed by one of her sons. Vize's getting arrested didn't begin to cover the karma due. "I think he let himself get captured."

"I'll buy that. Maybe I should have shot him the other night," he said.

I gave him a sharp glance at the out-of-character comment. "Are you going to shoot him now?"

He cocked an eyebrow. "Are you going to stop me if I say 'yes'?"

I folded my arms and leaned against the car. "You know, I think I would. I don't give a damn about Vize, but I do about you, Murdock."

He gave me a pleasant smile. "I'm here for the karma. I've shot people in the line of duty, Connor. I didn't like it. I'm not about to choose to do it, no matter how much I'd like to."

I squeezed his shoulder. I understood how he felt. I was ready to kill Vize. I would if I had the chance. Murdock's doing it would make me sad. I had failed at times in my life when it came to being a better person, but I counted on people like Murdock to balance out the damage I had done.

Briallen appeared by my side, a whiff of hot essence around her. She had used essence to travel, coasting faster than the eye could see. Dananns did it all the time, but druids used the ability only in a pinch because it was draining. "Hello, Leonard. I hope you're not here to do anything foolish."

He shook his head. "No, ma'am. I'm going to wait here while you folks do the foolishness. You know Connor doesn't have cab fare home."

She gave a tight smile as she pulled me away from the car. "Good. Don't irritate the brownies. They're on edge."

She glanced around the square. "They've cordoned off

the neighborhood for two blocks around, so they're taking this seriously."

"I don't believe for one second macGoren's men captured Vize. Something's wrong, Briallen," I said.

She flashed identification at the Guild agent blocking the sidewalk, and we passed. "I agree. The important thing is that he's in custody. Let's see what our Acting Guildmaster is going to do about it."

As we approached the main entrance, Brokke waited under the vaulted portico.

"I'm surprised they're letting any Consortium agents through security, but for some reason I'm not at all surprised to see you here" I said.

"I asserted my right to enter the Guildhouse as a board director," he said.

That was news. "Since when?" I asked.

He shook his head. "Eorla made me her second."

"You needn't bother. She's on her way," said Briallen.

Brokke narrowed his eyes. "You called her. Why?"

"Because she raised Vize. I don't trust whatever's happening here, but I trust her to keep him from doing something stupid if she can," said Briallen.

Brokke lifted his gaze to the ceiling. Empty spaces spread from end to end, where the riot of gargoyles had once adorned the ceiling and columns. The huge dragon's head over the main door remained. "The gargoyles have all gone to the Common. The essence of the standing stone down there attracts them," I said.

Brokke closed one eye as he stared. "It's not that. It's the dragon."

Briallen strode through the door "I'm not here for an architectural tour."

Brokke hesitated. "Have you ever wondered, Grey, why no dwarf enters this place?"

In all the years I had been associated with the Guild, I had never seen a dwarf on the premises. The dwarven representative on the board of directors refused to enter the building.

If the reason was known, no one talked about it anymore. "What about it?"

Brokke placed his hand on my sleeve. A static of essence danced along my skin and settled on my eyes. Around the dragon's head, faint dwarven runes glimmered in deep green light. "What does it say? I never mastered the dwarven language," I said.

"When Thekk Veinseeker did not feel he had been treated fairly by the Guild, he laid a warning on the door that any dwarf who entered would meet his doom," Brokke said.

He released my sleeve, and the runes faded from my sight. "Is this your way of saying you can't stay, but you'll meet me for coffee later?"

He crossed the portico. "Doom is merely the judgment of our lives, Connor. I have always lived my life knowing it would be judged in the end. I do not fear my doom. If I did, I would rethink my life."

Briallen waited at the elevators, glaring, with her arms crossed. "I'm glad I'm the one with the least interest here."

I kissed her temple. "Liar."

She hit the elevator button. "MacGoren's still using the Receiving Hall as an office. He needs to assert his authority any way he can. Let him pretend he belongs there," she said.

We switched to the second elevator bank and arrived at the thirtieth floor. The doors opened to several squads of Guild agents lining the corridor. The air vibrated with sendings as we were ushered along. An agent opened the large door carved with an oak tree with an interlocking crown of branches. MacGoren waited at the end of the sky bridge in a chair in front of the Guildmaster's seat. For all his pretension, he didn't have the nerve to sit in the official chair. In the crook of his arm, he cradled the Guild staff of office, a short length of ebony wood tipped with gold and topped with a blue beryl the size of a golf ball.

He enjoyed watching us make the long walk down the length of the hall. "You have five minutes. Say what you will and be done with it," macGoren said.

"This is a trap, Ryan. Vize would not walk in here willingly," I said.

MacGoren pretended to dust something off his knee. "A wise man once told me that recognizing a trap was the beginning of avoiding it."

"The point was to figure out what the trap was, not to let it close on you. Nigel taught me the same thing, macGoren. You're about to fail avoiding one," I said.

"It is Vize who is trapped, Grey. He can do nothing within these walls without my permission," macGoren said.

Briallen stepped closer. "Oh, knock it off, Ryan. You aren't Guildmaster, no matter how much you wish otherwise. Only Manus ap Eagan has the power to bind anyone here, and while he lives, you keep the seat warm—and not even the actual Guildmaster seat."

MacGoren frowned, shots of white essence sparking in his wings. Her words stung, as she'd intended. One of the nice things about being Briallen ab Gwyll was speaking her mind when others feared to do so. "I will not allow this opportunity to pass, Briallen. He's requested protection from the Elven Court. Maeve will be pleased with this."

"Delay this until we've had a chance to figure out his game," she said.

From the moment I met macGoren, he had been an opportunist. Whether it was money, power, or status, he put himself first. That self-interest had been his downfall on more than one occasion. "MacGoren, I know Vize better than anyone. He doesn't operate this way. A public ceremony is not his style."

MacGoren leaned back, shifting the scepter into the crook of his arm. "He has nothing left, Grey. Even the Consortium hunts him now. The humans will thank me that he did not fall into their hands."

Briallen scoffed. "Thank *you*? Is that what this about, Ryan? Your vanity? You will never be Guildmaster if you put yourself first. I will go to Maeve to stop this. If she doesn't appoint me Acting Guildmaster, the underKings and -Queens will."

MacGoren affected a bored expression. "Feel free, Briallen. Let me know when she gets back to you."

The doors to the Receiving Hall slammed open, startling us. Aldred Core strode in, his ceremonial cape flaring behind him. I glanced at Brokke, wondering if he knew that the "ambassador" was going to show. He hardly turned to watch Donor approach, which was enough confirmation that he knew what was going on.

"I demand an explanation for the detention of Bergin Vize," Core said.

MacGoren had the common sense to stand, even if he didn't know the Elven King was under the glamour. "Ambassador Core, it is a pleasure to have you here again."

The fury on Donor's glamoured face was anything but pleasure. "I asked you a question, Guildmaster."

"He's not really Guildmaster," I muttered.

MacGoren pretended not to hear and wore that smug look I hate about him. "No, I believe you made a demand, sir. If you wish an official response, there are official channels you may go through."

"This isn't Aldred Core. You're standing in front of the Elven King," I said. Brokke made a small hissing sound under his breath. I ignored him. If Donor was gunning for me, I doubted he had changed his mind.

MacGoren laughed. The idiot laughed. "Really, Grey, do you expect me to believe the king of the Teutonic fey would be here, and I not know about it?"

Briallen held up a hand. "Wait, Ryan. My sources have been indicating the Elven King is in the city. If Connor is saying this is Donor, I believe him."

I turned to Brokke. "Tell him."

Brokke bowed and stepped closer to the window. "I am here as an observer at the request of Her Majesty Eorla Elvendottir."

I flinched as the dark mass reacted to my anger. Brokke wasn't going to help.

"Ask Eorla, then. She knows," I said.

Donor drifted to the window and faced downtown. "The

Grand Duchess is on the march here as we speak. I warned you something like this would happen, macGoren. My people are trying to force her to rethink her actions."

I went to one of the large windows. Plumes of essence radiated near the financial district by the Rowes Wharf Hotel, the afterimage of essence-fire burn. "What are you trying to pull, Donor? Eorla would not attack the Guild."

He gave me a dismissive look. "My name is Aldred Core, sir. I imagine she is mounting a rescue for her foster son. She has always been volatile, as you well know, Guildmaster."

I saw the plan now. Donor wasn't going to let Vize out of his sight, not until he had the faith stone. "Don't listen to him, macGoren. He's setting Eorla up."

MacGoren returned to his chair. "Enough of this. Eorla is the reason you're not in chains yourself, Grey. She may have gotten the federal authorities to go away, but she has never acted in our interests. I would believe her no more than that dwarf standing behind you. I need to get this issue out of the way. If Eorla dares to attack, we shall meet her with firm resolve."

The flutter of a sending wafted across the hall. Guild agents entered, their chrome helmets gleaming as they marched down the sides of the hall. Another squad took to the air and hovered over the rest, their faces focused on the door. Vize entered, surrounded by four druids. Everything else aside, macGoren had the sense to use his toughest security. A small group followed them, local Court hangers-on, reporters and Guild staffers, their faces avid with the excitement of seeing an international criminal under arrest.

The dark mass in my head flared with spikes as Vize approached. He grimaced at the same moment. In the battle between us that had cost us our abilities, we both ended up with the darkness inside us. As it had grown inside me, the darkness had spread inside Vize. His entire arm smoldered with it.

The look he shot me said he hadn't expected to see me there. His usual self-righteousness seemed shaken. I didn't buy it. The escorts stopped him shy of the floor medallion.

He stared at the glamoured Elven King, hate burning in his eyes before he faced macGoren. I didn't buy that either, not after Brokke's refusal to out Donor. They had a plan. "I seek protection from the Seelie Court," Vize said.

"On what basis should we grant you such a thing?" mac-Goren asked.

"I face death at the hands of the Consortium should I return to my homeland," he said.

"That is a lie, sir," said Donor.

MacGoren ignored him. "Many people fear such a fate. Why would the Consortium seek your death?"

"Maybe because he's a mass murderer?" I said.

MacGoren frowned. I was ruining his drama. "I asked you a question," he said.

"Treason, sir. I have failed my king's orders, and he contrives to accuse me of his own crimes," he said.

"And what orders were these?" macGoren asked.

Vize cocked his head back and tried to restrain a smile. "The destruction of the Seelie Court and the death of High Queen Maeve."

Gasps, some genuine, rose from the observers. I saw what macGoren was after. Accusing Donor in public for directing assassination plots against Maeve would take attention away from the missteps the Guild had made in Boston. It was a stupid blunder. The media victory for the High Queen would blow over, but Vize wasn't ever going to provide any real information about his terrorist network, not after all he had done to destroy Maeve. He wanted her dead as much as Donor did.

"What an idiot," I muttered.

*I've been trying to tell him, but he's ignoring my sendings,* Briallen sent.

"These are grievous claims, sir," macGoren said.

Vize bowed his head. "I am ashamed for how I've been manipulated by the Elven King. In humility, I ask for the High Queen's aid."

MacGoren gestured with the scepter. "You ask for protection?"

Briallen cleared her throat. "My lord, as a director of this Guildhouse and a member of the Seelie Court, may I speak?"

MacGoren glared. As much as he didn't want to allow it, he wasn't about to silence Briallen ab Gwyll in front of reporters. "Pray, be brief, Lady Gwyll."

"This man is not known for his honesty. Before you grant him protection, a formal investigation into his claims would be in order."

"I hear your words, lady, and consider them. This man is well-known to the Guild and the Seelie Court. He would not come to us were he not in fear of his life, I think," macGoren said.

"Then arrest him for the crimes of which he is accused, sir. We can assess his words best with deliberation than grant him protection in haste," she said.

He made a point of shifting in his seat to face away from her. "Thank you, Lady Gwyll. We have noted your suggestion and will let the record show it. Bergin Vize, you must know that this protection does not excuse you from any crimes committed against the Seelie Court. Do you still seek protection under this understanding?"

"I do, sir," he said.

*See, I know what I'm doing,* macGoren sent us.

Briallen let me hear her response sending. *Leaving the door open to prosecute him doesn't explain why he's doing this, Ryan.*

MacGoren ignored her as he stood. "I represent Her Majesty, High Queen Maeve at Tara. In her name, I extend you protection. Bow before me in this place and address yourself to the High Queen's seal."

Vize complied, going to one knee before the three cups in the floor tiling. The black mass spiked in my head, and I let out an involuntary gasp.

Briallen took my arm. "What is it?" she asked in a low voice.

"The dark mass is shifting in my head. He's doing something," I said.

Briallen moved closer to macGoren. "Ryan—please—don't go near him.".

A murmur rose among the people who heard her. MacGoren paused, anger building in his face as white shots of essence danced in his wings. "Enough, Briallen. You've said your piece."

He lifted the scepter. "Bergin Vize, I grant you protection of Her Majesty, High Queen Maeve at Tara."

I clutched my head against the pain as Vize rose, a smile on his face. His arm snaked forward as shadowed darkness and wrapped around the scepter. The blue beryl shattered from his touch. Startled, macGoren tried to pull away. With a flick of his arm, the shadow undulated and yanked the scepter from macGoren's hand. Vize slammed the ebony rod down on Maeve's seal in the floor. White essence burst from the fractured tiles and threw me against the wall.

# 37

I stumbled to my knees, gasping as pain sliced through my mind. White light blinded me, pure essence searing the air. The marbled floor pressed hard and cool against my palms as I fought the urge to throw up. The dark mass jumped and shifted in my mind with no discernible purpose, like a trapped animal struggling to escape. I shook my head, trying to clear it, trying to see around me. Several feet away, Briallen crouched, holding macGoren by the shoulders as he pressed the heels of his hands against his eyes.

The light from the floor intensified and rose in a ball of brilliant white. A spot like a deep blue star burned in its midst, smoldering with power. The essence dimmed, coalescing into a piece of triangular blue crystal, its edges flickering with a deep forest green. The white aura diminished as my eyes adjusted, the spot resolving into a stone hanging in the air.

Donor Elfenkonig stared at the stone, cold satisfaction on his face. Vize stood to one side, clutching his blackened arm against his waist. If the pain in my head was any indication,

Vize was fighting to keep his own darkness from escaping. Donor reached out and closed his hand around the stone, incandescent light bleeding out between his fingers. The essence flickered and vanished.

A deep moan rattled through the air. The floor trembled beneath my feet, my vision blotched by the sudden absence of the essence light. Donor turned in confusion as cracks spiraled from the shattered floor medallion. The walls twisted on their moorings, shattering the long ranks of windows. I stumbled, ducking to avoid shards of glass. Winds blew from every direction as the hall was exposed to the outside. An electric static ran through the air.

"The shield dome's down!" someone shouted.

It wasn't true. I forced myself to stand. I sensed that the dome had weakened, but it remained. The release of the faith stone had damaged it somehow. A ripple ran through the floor, and a fissure opened as I struggled to Briallen's side.

"MacGoren's blinded. We have to get him out of here," she shouted above the howling of the wind. Briallen hardened her body shield around her and macGoren. With a screech, the sky bridge separated from its moorings, splitting open to the outside. The floor canted down, and I grabbed Briallen as she lost her footing. We struggled to hold mac-Goren, pulling up as the floor sloped away from the main part of the building. With a gut-wrenching lurch, the floor gave way. I sailed through the air and landed hard on a fractured ledge outside the building.

Above me, the sky bridge remained attached to the opposite tower by thin cabling, but moved in a slow swing away from the main portion of the Guildhouse. On the tower side of the gap, Briallen struggled to hold an unconscious mac-Goren from sliding off the bridge. She secured him against a fallen column.

"Don't move. I'll come get you," she shouted down to me.

A cloud of essence blossomed around her as she rose in the air. Another shudder ran through the building, and mac-Goren slipped from the column toward the broken edge of the bridge. Briallen hesitated, then settled back to pull him to safety. The thick tower in front of me swayed. "Get mac-Goren out of here. I'll be fine."

*We're thirty floors up,* she sent.

"I don't care about macGoren. You do. Get him out of here. I'm going after them," I shouted against the wind.

Briallen stared toward the sky. Guild agents whirled in confusion around the damaged bridge. Another chunk crumbled, plunging through a roof below, which collapsed inward and pulled a section of turrets with it. The center of the hall bridge fell away, smashing into the main building. "You can't stand up to the Elven King," Briallen said.

The dark mass pressed against the inside of my skull, and I relaxed against it. It pierced my eye with searing pain. I coaxed it into dark ribbons that coiled around me, a trick I'd picked up when I touched Vize in the Tangle. "Watch me."

The tower shuddered. Briallen stared at me, fear and uncertainty on her face. *You can control it,* she sent. It wasn't quite true. I could push it in certain directions, but "control" was an overstatement.

"Stop delaying," I yelled, and started climbing. The damage gave me plenty of handholds as I pulled myself toward the remains of the Receiving Hall. Black-clad Dananns swooped in overhead. They tumbled back into the sky as emerald essence flashed out from the ledge, a blast of elf-shot more powerful than any I had ever sensed.

I pulled myself over the remains of the overhang. Behind the Guildmaster's chair, still glamoured as Aldred Core, huddled Donor, with the stone clutched to his chest. His body shield was warping and flashing around him. Vize stood a few feet away, dark shadows slicing the air as they stabbed at the remaining Guild agents.

*I could use some help, Grey,* Brokke's voice reverberated in my head.

I craned my neck, searching the debris.

*Down here,* he sent. I leaned back over the ledge. A dozen feet down, Brokke dangled from a section of broken floor.

He had fused his fingers into the stone. The building shook again, and the stone shifted farther down the side.

"Fuse the slab to the building," I shouted.

Brokke bowed his head against the stone. *Been trying. Too much stone.*

"Hold on. I'll get a Danann," I said.

I scrambled back from the edge. The Receiving Hall was a haze of essence as agents exchanged fire with Donor and Vize. A steady vibration built beneath my feet, and I stumbled again. A burst of essence flashed from the end of the hall. I slipped, rolling back toward the edge.

*Listen to Bastian, but trust Eagan, Grey,* Brokke sent.

Brokke's slab had levered out into space. He pulled a hand free and pressed it into the stone farther up. With painstaking slowness, he dragged himself toward the building. The wall shuddered, and the slab slid. I thrust out my hands, opened my mind to tap into my abilities to extend ribbons of essence and grab Brokke. I screamed as the black mass spiked like claws and shut me down. I fell forward, clutching the edge of the floor.

I watched in horror as the slab broke free. In silence, it tumbled end over end, with Brokke clinging to it. He vanished in an explosion of dust a hundred feet below.

Angry, I knelt back against my feet. The black mass burned with sharp intensity. I held my breath, calming myself. It didn't help. The mass trembled with spikes, piercing my mind again and again. My body essence retreated before it, crumbling under the strain.

White essence jolted through me like a stroke of lightning. A sharp white line appeared in my mind, pulsing with power. I recognized that essence. The spear had reestablished its bond with me. Dizzy, I retreated from the edge and faced the remains of the Receiving Hall. The spear whirled in Vize's hand as he fended off Guild agents. Sliding his grip to its base, he swept the spear around him, scattering more agents. With a pivot, he brought the spear to a stop, point ready for the next opponent, when he saw me.

Planting the spear on the floor of the cleared space, he

wrapped his arm around Donor's. When I had touched Vize with the darkness, he had touched me, too. A primal understanding had passed through our connection. I had learned how to control the darkness like he did. He had learned how to use the spear to teleport like I did. Through my bond with the spear, an echo of Vize's destination opened in my mind, like a tunnel of vibrant, spiraling essence. He was going to teleport away and take Donor with him.

I wasn't going to let him. I stretched out my hand.

*"Ithbar,"* I shouted.

# 38

The spear lurched in Vize's hand as it responded to my command. Our minds pressed against each other, the spear a white streak of essence between us. I focused all my thought on the spear, willing it toward me. Vize fought back, trying to teleport away. The vision clarified as the tunnel locked on its destination. I pressed harder, my will against Vize's. The spear slipped his grasp and launched across the expanse. I grabbed it, and the world fell out below me, twisting and blurring as I hurtled into the tunnel.

I landed hard on my feet, my ears popping in the sudden shift from the wind-torn Guildhouse to a dim, quiet room. I didn't know where I was. It was Vize's destination, not mine. The room appeared to be an office with a bed tucked in the corner. I sensed several elven body signatures, including Vize's, but no one had been there recently.

I hesitated. As much as I wanted to know where Vize had hoped to escape to, I didn't have time to investigate.

I focused my inner vision on the entrance to the Guildhouse. The swirl of the tunnel formed again, and I spun across the darkness to a spot of daylight in the distance. I tripped onto the sidewalk under the Guildhouse portico. A brownie guard shoved me to the side. "Get down! Get down!"

Essence-fire slammed into the roof above. Chunks of granite cascaded into the street, and I ducked behind a column. Shouts drew my attention across the square. A block away, people filled the street—fey folk, yelling and shooting essence at the brownie security guards and police. In the air above them, Dananns and other fairies tangled with Guild agents.

I stood before the shattered front doors under the dragon's head. "What the hell is going on?" I asked.

"The Unseelie are attacking. They have breached the dome," the brownie said. He was fighting his boggart side; but from the length of his claws, he was going to lose it soon. He growled, his jaw lengthening with exposed teeth, and sprinted across Park Square toward the fighting. While I didn't delude myself into thinking Eorla would take me into her confidence, outright battle wasn't her style. She was a diplomat. The attackers weren't her people. They had to be Donor's in disguise.

*Where are you?* Briallen sent. The sending was followed by another, then another, each more frantic than the last, like a flurry of mental voice mails. I didn't have the ability to respond. I debated using the spear to join her, but the tower she was in was now disconnected from the rest of the Guildhouse. Donor and Vize were somewhere in the main section. My strength was fading against the power of the spear. I hated ignoring her, but I had no choice.

I stepped over broken glass into the lobby. A Guild agent by the elevators raised his hand at me. "You may not enter."

"I already have," I said.

The agent's hand glowed white as it welled with essence. I didn't engage him, but opened my mind to find Meryl's essence. My body essence danced along the spear, searching for her as I had done once before, in TirNaNog. This time I knew what I was doing. As the agent's hand released its fire, I let the spear run free, and it pulled me into its twisting tunnel of darkness and light. I landed on the threshold of Meryl's office, taking a step to keep my balance. I was getting better at teleporting.

Meryl shoved her computer mouse away. "Dammit, Grey. I was going to beat my best time."

"No, really, I'm fine. Stop asking," I said.

She grinned. "I knew that. As soon as Briallen told me what happened, I figured out what you did."

"She's okay?" I asked.

"Making her way down what's left of the tower as we speak," she said.

"What's this about an Unseelie attack?" I asked.

She typed on a blank keyboard wired to the black-box system behind her. "Can't tell. Cameras are down on that side. Security channels are saying it's Eorla's people on the attack."

"Can you reach her?" I asked.

She tilted her head at me. "Not with the lockdown."

"I got through," I said.

She pursed her lips and cocked her head at the spear. "Something tells me that thing goes any damned place it pleases."

I pulled out my cell phone. "I'll try Rand."

"Uh . . ." she said.

I closed the phone. "No signal. Vize and Donor are loose in the building," I said.

She tapped at her keyboard with idle fingers. "Yeah, I've been tracking security movements. They're going up instead of down. I'm betting on the roof. Nice vantage point for an aerial pickup."

I leaned over to see the building schematic on her screen. "That's a pretty strange path."

"But smart. They're sticking to the older parts of the building. The surveillance cameras suck there. When they pass from one section to another, they trip a ward alarm," she said.

"That takes intimate knowledge of the Guildhouse. Someone's helping them," I said.

"Well, it wouldn't be the first time the Guild had a traitor," she said.

"What's the fastest way to the roof from here?" I asked.

"Security's locked the elevators in the lobby. That's manual, so I can't do anything from here. Unless someone flies you up, it's the stairs," she said.

"Not thirtysomething flights," I said.

She pointed at the spear. "What about that thing?"

I knew Donor's and Vize's body signatures. In my mind, I focused on the spear, and the tunnel funneled opened. "Wish me luck," I said.

Meryl jumped from her chair. "Wait! What are you . . ."

She was too late. I was gone, clinging to the spear as it sliced through the darkness. Essence-fire greeted me as I landed in a corridor. I ducked into an office. My head rang with noise, a constant thump against static hiss.

"You're not getting out of here," I shouted.

The spear flared and pulled at my left hand. The damned spear was still bonded to Vize, and he was trying to call it. I tightened my grip, using both hands to hold tight. A sudden release of pressure tossed me against the wall. He wasn't getting it back.

Soft flutterings wafted through the air. They were close if I could feel their sendings. The floor vibrated. I moved away from the door as the vibrations increased and the wall cracked. The building groaned around me. Something was about to give way. I didn't think it smart to stick around and watch. I focused the spear toward Meryl's essence as the floor began to crumble. I gripped the spear and soared through the dark tunnel again.

I fell outside Meryl's office. The spear flew from my hand and rattled across the stone pavers. I grabbed it, afraid Vize would try to call it. Meryl was at my side, helping me up.

"What the hell happened?" Meryl said.

"Donor tried to kill me," I said.

"Imagine that. He took out an entire floor," she said.

I leaned on the spear. "Not him. The building stone was ripped apart. That was dwarf work."

She brushed at my hair. Her hand came away tinged with blood. "Your skin is speckled with blood. Your body can't take the stress of the spear without a shield."

I kissed her on the top of her head. "It'll have to."

I jumped again, seeking out Donor's essence, and this time found myself on a stone spiral stair. Three body signatures trailed upward. I paused. Two, I recognized. I opened my sensing ability. The dark mass in my head sliced down my right arm, keen on the chance to seek out essence. The third essence was dwarven, with a tantalizing familiarity.

The dark mass pressed hard for release, shadow welling out around my hand. It touched the body signatures with a sense of disappointment. They were vapor, residual essence from a person passing through, not enough to sate the desire of the darkness, but enough for me to tag it—Thekk Veinseeker.

I jumped and made an awkward landing on the winding stairs higher up in the towers. I ducked as Thekk swung a fist at me. He missed, punching a hole into the stone wall. As he pulled his hand free, deep orange essence spidered from his fingers, and the wall fell across the stairs.

I scrambled back, holding the spear out to ward off anything thrown at me. "I thought you retired, Veinseeker."

"One never retires from defending one's king," he said. He slapped his palm against the ground, and the steps between us collapsed. I leaned back as pavers slid toward me in a wave. Between his brute strength and raw ability, I wouldn't last against him in a physical fight.

"Don't make me kill you, Thekk. Donor has no escape. Step aside," I said. He answered me with a shower of stone. I wasn't going to kill him. As much as I wanted to, I refused to gut him with the spear. The stone against my back grew hot as his essence poured into it. I had to make a move. Bracing myself for the pain of the darkness, I tapped my body essence and raced toward him as the walls slumped to either side.

I was on him before he realized what I was doing. I grabbed his arm and jumped. We landed beside Eorla on the sidewalk in front of the Rowes Wharf Hotel. Above us, golden essence shimmered in the air. From across the street, elven archers with Donor's insignia threw elf-shot at the shield barrier that Eorla had raised over the hotel. Rand spun toward me, his sword out and bloodied. He relaxed when our eyes met.

"Have you brought help?" Eorla asked.

"No, sorry. Just more trouble for you. Donor's getting away. Can you keep this guy under guard for me?" I said.

Without argument, fine filaments of essence spun from her fingers and wrapped themselves around Thekk. "Of course. What's happening at the Guildhouse? We're hearing reports it's under siege," said Eorla.

"They're saying you're doing it," I said.

She gestured across the street. "I'm otherwise occupied at the moment."

"Donor's got people wearing your colors. He's setting you up to take a fall, Eorla. Whatever you do, stay here. I think Donor's crazy enough to kill you," I said.

She turned away. "I will take that under consideration, Connor. Pray, be safe."

I jumped back to Meryl. She hugged me as I swayed on my feet. "You can't keep doing this," she said.

I held her close, burying my nose in her hair. "One more time, I think. They had Thekk Veinseeker with them."

She spun to the keyboard. "Now the path makes sense. He designed the original building specs." She skimmed through the schematics. "They have a pretty clear path to the roof, but you can make it faster from the tower across from the conference tower. Can you picture it?"

I peered at the screen. "Yep. Got it. It's where Ceridwen held her hearings."

I jumped and landed in the empty hall outside the conference rooms. A broad expanse of windows faced the Guildhouse. Danann fairies filled the sky like angry hornets, their black uniforms darting in and out of clusters of winged solitaries. Down on the street, the elves disguised in Eorla's livery drew the brownie security away from the building. From this vantage point, I realized Donor's strategy: keep Eorla pinned and prevent her from coming to the Guildhouse's defense while making it appear she was actually attacking it. It didn't matter. It was all a distraction for his escape.

Thekk's knowledge of the Guildhouse went stale a century ago. The executive offices were fifty or so years old but still new compared to the rest of the building. He wouldn't know that. I cut across the short bridge to the main part of the building and ran into the stairwell. I jogged up the stairs, taking them two at a time. Shudders ran through the stone, and the lights flickered.

I shouldered through the roof door without stopping, stumbling into bright sun and roaring wind. A jumble of parapets and support buttresses, odd turrets, deep roof valleys, and steep gables spread out before me. The shield dome had parted at the top of the building, and essence-fire was reaching the roof. Guild agents wheeled overhead, trying to contain the damage. I clambered over a low wall and made my way toward the original section of high-peaked slate and verdigris copper.

The conference-room tower was toward the middle of the Guildhouse, rising above older setbacks. Smoke and fire billowed from lower areas near Park Square. The roof vibrated with stress as the essence supporting the more whimsical additions weakened.

The original main tower was about fifty feet away, a broad expanse of pavers surrounded by decorative turrets. I climbed a low parapet. Jumping with the spear such a short distance probably wouldn't hurt too much, but it would hurt. Below me, a series of buttresses like splayed fingers joined the next roof. Heights didn't bother me—even a three-hundred-foot drop. The age of the buttresses without essence support was another matter.

I set my foot on the top of the nearest one, seamed stones

barely a foot wide. It felt firm. I kept the spear ready for an emergency jump, took a deep breath, and stepped from the parapet. Wind tugged at me as I struggled to keep my balance. Someone fired at me, and I lost my footing. I slammed on my back and grabbed the edge as I rolled. The spear flew free, disappearing into the fires below. I swung my leg up and pulled myself back. Elf-shot arced from a nearby tower. I hugged the stone and shinnied down the rest of the way, taking cover under the cornice of the main building. The buttresses swayed and cracked. The conference tower leaned away from me, glass shattering from its windows. Without the help of the faith stone, the Guildhouse was held together with little more than spit and glue.

I climbed the cornice, worrying my fingers in the gaps in the bare strips of stone, and pulled myself over onto the flat expanse of pavers. As I caught my breath, I reached my hand up and said the command for the spear. *"Ithbar."*

With a jolt, the spear appeared in my hand. I leaned on it to get to my feet. Teleporting was tearing my body apart. My joints ached, and muscles burned with exhaustion. Small blood vessels beneath my skin had ruptured, leaving deep red traceries of veins on my arms, probably my face, too.

"Took you long enough," a voice said.

I spun. In the static of essence swirling about, I hadn't sensed Joe at all. He perched next to an ornate chimney pot that belched black smoke. I relaxed and leaned on the spear. "I got sidetracked. Where've you been?"

"Well, last night I was at a party. Can you believe they ran out of seaweed?"

"How'd you know where to find me?" I asked.

"Banjo said it's a day for roofs and that he saw me with some naked guy," he said.

"I hope it wasn't me, 'cause I'm kinda in the mood to keep my clothes on," I said.

"Well, when everything started falling apart, I figured this roof might be the one he was talking about and at least would have an interesting view. Then I found this guy." He fluttered up from the chimney pot. Behind him sat a gargoyle, a chubby naked figure of a man, overly endowed. With a single eye beneath a short spiral horn, he stared with disinterest at the sky. I had named him Virgil long ago when he first appeared outside my Guildhouse office window.

"You can't stay here, Joe. Vize is on his way," I said.

"The last time I left you alone with Vize, he almost killed you."

"Well, this time I'm returning the favor, only I intend to accomplish the goal," I said.

Joe tilted his head with a wry smile. "It's going to be one of those days, isn't it?"

*Touch the sky.*

The words formed in my mind with a dry rasp, like the opening of an ancient vault. Gargoyles didn't talk much, and when they did, the conversation was cryptic. I hadn't figured out what Virgil meant in any of the times he had spoken to me in the past. The common thread in all our interactions was trouble. Something about catastrophe brought him to my side to murmur dire warnings I never understood. Like now, with every gargoyle long gone from the Guildhouse, he alone remained on the roof, the very roof I stood on, the one that Vize and Donor were heading for. How Virgil could predict such a thing had to have an explanation, but one was never forthcoming. Instead, I tried my own gibberish, treating his words like riddles.

"The roof touches the sky," I said.

"Poetic-y," said Joe.

*Hearts like stone. We shall stand and turn the tide in the hour of need.*

The faith stone was shaped like a heart, and the current hour had a lot of need going on. If he was talking about the other gargoyles, they were all hanging out elsewhere. That wasn't going to help me. "Who's standing, Virgil?"

*The circle meets and brings release. The light burns through the dark.*

Joe fluttered up and coughed as a downdraft of smoke hit him. "What the hell are you talking about?"

I gestured at the gargoyle. "Virgil. He's being ominous again."

Joe pulled a long face at Virgil, then turned to me with one eye closed. "You never told me these guys talked to you."

"Virgil does. He's had some good advice," I said.

Joe's eyes went wide. "No wonder you're so screwed up, Connor. The 'goyles are crazy. They've been repeating themselves for a hunnerd years, all stones and hearts and circles."

"You hear them?"

"'Course. We flits all can. Flits ignore them like sane people. They have no brains"—he glanced down—"or clothes."

The words "flits" and "sane" are not often used in the same sentence. Regardless, hearing Joe say that saddened me. I never understood Virgil, and now had an inkling why. If the gargoyles were repeating themselves over and over for years, they were likely nothing more than old recording wards, fanciful ones, but still recording stones. I thought they were sentient. It took the fun out of being one of the few people that heard them.

The tattered shield dome dimmed more around us, the essence prickling off my skin. Guild agents continued their defense above, unaware that the real enemy was trying to escape, not enter the building. Essence-fire was getting through, damaging the towers and supports. More turrets went down in a roar of wood and stone.

A door at the opposite end of the flat roof slammed open. Vize stepped out, intent on the chaos above. I didn't wait for him to talk or make a move. The time for conversation was over, the moment I had always known was coming had arrived. I aimed and threw the spear at him. I aimed to kill. It blazed across the roof, a sliver of white that dimmed the air around it.

Vize sensed it. I expected that. We sensed the same things the same way. I understood that now, but why was a question for another time. Vize shifted his attention to the spear and held out his hand. I expected that, too. He had seen the move work for me. Before he reacted, I let the darkness shoot out from my chest, intent on the essence trail left by the spear. A heartbeat later, I yanked the spear back and watched as the darkness slammed into Vize. It splintered into sinuous lines as it struck an essence barrier.

Donor staggered next to Vize, his body shield hardened, a thick wall of green essence that pushed back against the darkness. He thrust his hand down, a bolt of emerald elf-shot spiking into the roof. Essence spiraled from the point of contact, rippling the pavers. The wave knocked me off my feet, blasting apart the parapet behind me. I clung to the crumbled opening, the darkness snapping back with a painful recoil.

Joe hid behind the chimney. "Good plan, except for the not-killing-him part."

He plunged feetfirst down on my hands. On reflex from the pain, I let go and landed several feet below on the roof of a wide bay window. A stream of elf-shot destroyed the rest of the parapet, showering stone dust down on me. Joe dodged over a valley between two gables. "Hmph. He's not a bad shot for an elf."

"Thanks for the save," I said.

Joe rotated in the air, sniffing. "The barrier's completely down. I say let the big guns up there take the Elven King out, and we go get beers."

"I don't care about the Elven King," I said.

The last of the Guildhouse barrier shield collapsed. A roof slumped on the neighboring gable. The building was shedding years' worth of additions like dead barnacles off a boat. The window bay lurched under my feet as if it had risen a few inches, then resettled itself.

I grabbed the edge of the wall and swung myself over. Donor faced away from me, holding the faith stone above his head. Green light revolved around him in ribbons, wrapping him and Vize in a sphere of bright light. On a gust of essence, they lifted into the air, white light flashing around the sphere, swirling the green ribbons faster. They hovered in place, below the main aerial fighting, essence building around him.

"What the hell is he doing?" I said.

"Oh, that looks bad," Joe said from behind me.

A volley of essence burst from the sphere, streaking like

ball lightning across the sky. The streaks homed in on Guild agents, hit with concussive force, and threw them out of the sky. They weren't stun shots. Appalled, I staggered back as bodies fell limply into the flames below. The remaining agents wheeled away, struggling to regroup.

The air crackled with a sound like thunder. Donor tapped essence as only the most powerful fey can, pulling directly from the air and anything around him. A sustained burst of energy from the bottom of his sphere struck the Guild-house. The roof exploded, slate and stone flying into the air. I ducked as more debris hurtled toward me. Another tower fell, smashing into the one next to it, and both collapsed into the floors below. Donor's sphere grew, solidified into a mass of burning white heat. It expanded, incinerating the building wherever it touched.

Elf-shot came at me and snagged on the tip of the spear. The streamer of essence lashed like a whip slicing through the air. The spear jerked in my hands, and I grappled with it. The streamer flared brighter and spun around me. Joe screamed, and I whirled. The elf-shot wrapped around his legs and flung him about. He struggled against it, his essence flashing as he tried to teleport away. The spear convulsed in my hand, sucking in the streamer of elf-shot. Still bound to it, Joe's body twisted and elongated, then vanished into the spear. Dumbfounded, I stared at the weapon in my hand.

"Joe?" I shouted. I shook the spear, feeling like a fool. It undulated in my hand. Intermittent touches of Joe's body signature danced along its length, then faded into the spear's burning brightness.

Fury raced through me. The darkness leaped within, feeding off my anger. I let it. I let the darkness rise, let it break through my body essence. Streams of black shadow shot from my face and chest, lunging across the fractured roof as they sought the most powerful source of essence nearby. They burrowed into Donor's sphere with ravenous greed. They sucked at the essence, funneling back into me, back into the source of the darkness. I gasped as it coursed through me, through my chest, my face, draining inside me to the nameless dark place. I was a conduit, meaningless in the transaction, as the darkness pulsed and sucked. My feet lifted off the ground as the roof crumbled away beneath them.

The sphere paled, its essence leeching away. Donor realized what was happening and dropped Vize, concerned now for his own safety. Vize plummeted and hit a pitched roof. He flailed as he went over the edge. He fell hard against the remains of a turret and didn't move.

Donor reinforced his body shield, shrugging off the smaller tributaries of my darkness feeding on him. He wasn't strong enough. One of the most powerful fey in the world wasn't strong enough to fight off the darkness. It broke through—*I* broke through. I fed the darkness with all my anger and fury. Shadows coiled around Donor's chest. He fought me as I hauled him toward me. We revolved around each other in a halo of green light and dark shadow. Donor grinned, his teeth framed red with blood. "You think I've never fought this darkness before, Grey? Give in to its desire, let it draw you in close, then strike its vulnerability."

With his fist clutched around the faith stone, he swung at me. I blocked him with the spear in a shower of white sparks. Sensing another source of essence, the darkness coiled around the spear. I was losing control—no—I never had it. The darkness did what it wanted. Donor seemed to sense it and laughed. I didn't have control of the darkness, but I had the spear. I spun my wrist, brought the sharp tip of the spear forward, and shoved it through Donor's shield.

A jumbled kaleidoscope of essence flared as the spear fought against the Elven King's power. Donor swung his fist again. I brought the spear down on his arm, and essence exploded around us. He tumbled away as the darkness snapped free. I fell onto the remains of the roof. Donor landed on his feet, crouching to absorb the shock of the fall. He came up screaming, emerald light bursting from his face in a searing blast.

I threw the spear. It struck the Elven King, the concussive force from the blow flinging me into the air, on a shock wave of essence. I flipped end over end as I rose higher and higher, nothing below but thirty stories of empty air. I rolled in the sky, the explosion expanding into a cloud of wild essence over the Guildhouse. Out of the fireball, a fierce blue light rocketed toward me and slammed into my forehead and

everything

went

white

# 39

White.

Whiteness filled my vision with nothing to break the relent-lessness of it. Above me, the white simply was, as if the air itself was color. Or no color. As if nothing else existed except the white. I hung limp in the air, as if there were no air, no gravity. My head burned, like a cold fire in my mind, blazing against a blanket of night.

Everything is white. I have been here before. This is where it started. Or ended. I don't remember which. Everything around me is white. I stared into a nothingness of white. I am here again. Around me, I see shadows of light flickering in the depths of the white. They spin and whirl, roll and stop, taunting me with patterns that disintegrate as they take shape.

Bursts of color flare in my vision, fireworks against the white, fading to darkness. More, then more, the darkness closing on me, like the slow closing of my eyes. My mind, like my eyes, closing, like my eyes blinking. Like my mind blinking.

My mind blinked.

I jerked my head up, feeling like I had passed out. People

surrounded me, staring at me. Some I recognized, and some I didn't. Their faces held a multitude of expressions—fear and horror and sadness. Then the screams began.

My mind blinked.

Rand stands defiant before me, his clothes in tatters, his face a mix of hurt and hope. "You have to trust me," he says.

"Why? You didn't trust me," I answer.

My mind blinked.

Silhouettes in lavender surround me like shadows in the mist. They do not move. I cannot see their faces, but I know they are waiting, waiting for answers that I do not have, waiting for the inevitable, waiting for . . .

My mind blinked.

Eorla looks at me in surprise and rushes toward me as I lean over the body.

"Tell me what to do," I hear her. I hear her, and I hear fury.

My mind blinked.

I stand on a plain, white grass waving against a white sky. It's not winter, pray, what is this new madness? Where have I come? I turn in place, searching, searching across the plain, searching about the standing stones, but Maeve is not there. Was she? What is this place?

My mind blinked.

The golden-cloaked king shudders into view. "The Wheel of the World turns as It will. It is not mine to lead even a sliver of it."

My mind blinked.

Vize is running. Everything is white. I am running. Everything is white. He looks over his shoulder at me. He looks determined . . . or crazed . . . I can't tell. Everything is white. One minute we were facing each other, and now everything is white. He stops. He looks surprised. There is someone lying on the ground. Something about him is familiar. Everything is white, and there is no ground. There is someone lying in the white. Everything . . .

My mind blinked.

"You can't do this," I shout.

Something is not right. Or different. She doesn't look right. The woman reaches out.

"I must. It's the only way," she says.

I close my eyes against pain, and something black blossoms in my mind. Black like a seed in the white. The woman sings; and then she screams; and then I know what to do.

My mind blinked.

My mind blinked.

. . . the inevitable. A man steps forth, faint spirals of woad pitting the skin above his wide brow, a sudden wind tugging at the dirty drape of cloth over his shoulder. "We shall be as bones, bones of the earth, steadfast and eternal," he says.

"I promise I will try," I say.

"We hear and hope," he says.

My mind blinked.

The wild man returns. "The wielder wheels and is wheeled but chooses his own path. We are the Wheel and Its instrument."

My mind blinks.

He cocks his head as he looks at me, the colors in his eyes shifting like the sea in a storm. "Have you ever met someone and felt like you've known him forever?" he asks.

"No," I say.

He laughs, with a deep rumble in his wide chest.

"Liar," he says. "Liar."

My mind blinked.

Vize looks feverish. "It must happen this way. You must let it happen."

"I won't let you," I say.

He looks frightened yet determined as I reach toward him. "I thought it was me. But it's you. You have to destroy it."

My mind blinks.

The robed man towers up. "The Ways seal and unseal. A needle binds as it pierces."

My mind blinks.

Essence pours out of the sword.

My mind blinks.

Essence pours out of the spear.

My mind blinks.

Essence pours out of the bowl.

My mind blinks.
Essence pours out . . .
My mind blinks.

A blue light burns the sky, a blue so pure it burns white. It hits me in the head like a fist of flame and burns its way in. My head explodes with light and darkness, then everything goes silent. I scream and

everything

goes

white

# 40

Wind roared as I fell through the sky. Smoke and fire blurred around me in a dirty smear of orange and black. I was going to die. No rush of images cascaded through my mind, no marching panorama of my life's highlights. I thought how strangely beautiful the Guildhouse looked as it crumbled in smoke and flame. I closed my eyes, feeling the rush of gravity pull me to the street below. It wasn't going to be pretty. I hoped I didn't hit anyone. At least I was going out in a blaze.

A blue haze of essence around me, the essence of the Dead coming to call me home. My eyes flew open as a turbulent air knocked against me, batting me from side to side. The fractured street pavement grew closer, larger, before wind shear blurred tears into my eyes. Something pressed against my back, like I wasn't falling fast enough and needed a push. The blue essence blossomed around me as I rushed into the embrace of the Dead. The ground moved below, a nauseating shift toward my feet, then flashed by as I skimmed over the street and surged into the air.

*Remain calm,* Ceridwen sent.

I laughed. Remaining calm was so obviously the right course. I had fallen off a burning building and plunged toward my death. I laughed with a sound tinged with madness and disbelief as rough hands gripped my back.

Ceridwen banked away from the smoking building and set down at the opposite end of the square. Chaos filled the streets, people fighting with essence or scattering in fear. Police officers tried to enforce order, only to stare in stark awe when they caught sight of the Guildhouse.

The Guildhouse burned. The upper stories were gone, lost in smoldering stone heaped on the street and sidewalk. Gaping holes belched smoke from where towers used to be. Guild agents swarmed and hovered, darting in to retrieve anyone that appeared in a window or broken opening. The ground trembled, a deep rumble that intensified. The Guildhouse contracted about the middle, a slow, inward shift of wall and tower. With the sound of a raging storm, the Guildhouse shed the remains of its outer walls, pulling the rest of the building with it.

A towering pall of angry gray smoke shot from the implosion. I thrust my hands out, an instinctive warding off of the heat and debris, as a boiling mountain of ash and smoke rolled toward me. My body shield triggered—my full body shield—bursting around me in a crystalline barrier of deep gold. The smoke spilled over me like a wave hitting a cliff, then raced up the street and swallowed the remaining fighters. It passed, becoming less dense, but not dispersing.

My head burned with a cold fire. I trembled with power, but a power I didn't understand. Something had changed. I not only had my body shield back, I could control it. I didn't have time to question it but was glad of it. The dark mass felt different, like it was generating energy instead of absorbing it. My skin danced with an electric sheen.

Ceridwen lay on the ground not far off, no spark of essence in her body. I leaned over and felt for a pulse. She was dead again. I stared for a moment, then left her there. She was Dead. She would wake up in the morning as if nothing had happened.

I stalked toward what was left of the Guildhouse. Fire-fighters wandered through the smoke, empty-handed and helpless, their trucks and gear buried under rubble. Shattered walls rose ghostlike around me. I circled around burning stone to the front entrance. It was gone, nothing left but the fractured remains of the dragon head. The lobby was gone, too, a crater of fire burning where bored receptionists once sat.

Shocked, I fell to my knees. I stared, trying to make sense of what I was seeing—what I was not seeing. Endless piles of stone and fire rose around me. Smoke bled through the filter of my body shield and irritated my eyes. The only sounds were the crackle of fire and the high-pitched beeping of rescue-worker alarms. I don't know how long I sat there before someone touched my shoulder.

"Connor? Are you all right, buddy?"

I lifted my head, the world asserting itself around me like I was waking from a deep sleep. Murdock stared at me, his face filthy and scratched.

"Yes," I said.

"Are you sure? You were screaming," he said.

"She was in the basement," I said.

Horror etched across his face as he stared into the fire. I got to my feet. "I have to get to the subway," I said.

"It's collapsed," he said, his voice rough.

"I have to get to the subway," I said.

I wandered out into the square. Haze filled the air. I didn't remember anything about the walk from Park Square to the Boylston Street T station except stumbling through debris, Murdock beside me like a shadow. Transit workers stood at the entrance, directing people several blocks away to where buses waited. A man stood in front of me as I tried to enter.

"Move," I said. I didn't raise my voice, but it sounded odd in my ears. His face went blank, almost ashen, and he stepped aside. Murdock caught my arm as I walked down the stairs where a gate was open to the platform. I didn't bother using the gap in the fence, but walked onto the tracks and into the tunnel. Smoke trailed along the ceiling. I kept my body shield on until I reached the concrete niche, and we stepped through the glamour.

It was a long, dark walk down the stairs to the tunnel passage. Dim light marked the end, a dull glow of emergency lights. Murdock and I entered the empty office. We stared at dust hanging in air, the computer monitor flickering blue. I went into the outside corridor and froze.

Meryl ran down the hall and into my arms. I hugged her in shocked relief like I had never hugged anyone before. She tilted her face toward mine, surprise coming over her features.

"Holy shit, what happened to your eyes?" she asked.

# 41

I spun a rack of sunglasses and found a pair of designer knockoffs I liked. They covered the upper half of my face with wide dark lenses but didn't make me look like I was on a bus tour for retirees. I handed the vendor a few bills. As I pushed back into the crowded lane, someone stared a little too long. Anxiety twinged at me, but I tamped it down. Everyone stared in the Tangle. It was part of the game. People pretended not to notice each other and avoided conversation but cast sidelong glances at anyone near them.

Intermittent pressure pushed at my mind. Despite everything else, scrying still bothered me. My body shield protected me from the pain, but I hadn't learned to ignore the constant irritation yet.

I reached the end of the stalls and slipped through an essence barrier across a doorway. Silence surrounded me in the empty tunnel. At the exit, another barrier let me through to an outside street. The air held the scent of sea and smoke, but it was fresher than the contained alleyway of the market.

I turned the corner onto the main drag of the Tangle and tugged my hat down.

Within a few minutes, Meryl was beside, matching my stride. She paused to examine some apothecary wares at a decrepit stall. The vendor dressed in rags and spoke in broken Welsh. Meryl bartered with him in his dialect until a stone was exchanged for a small bottle containing deep purple leaves. She slipped it in her pocket.

"He doesn't appear to be a purveyor of fine goods," I said.

She looked at me from beneath her bangs. "On the contrary, he's one of my best suppliers. The look and the talk are all bogus. It keeps the fools and timid away."

I pulled her into the shadow of a boarded-up storefront and kissed her. "I've missed you."

She leaned against me with a smile. "One of these days, Grey, you'll live somewhere with air freshener and maybe a bed, and I'll visit more often."

"I have a bed now," I said.

She tugged at my jacket. "Something bigger than a twin, please."

"Any updates from Gillen Yor?" I asked. Three nights ago, I had snuck into Avalon Memorial for an exam. Gillen thought it best to be discreet. I was a wanted criminal again. MacGoren had accused me of complicity in the destruction of the Guildhouse, and Briallen's denials were falling on deaf ears. I didn't blame her for anything. It was out of her control. It was out of everyone's control.

Meryl gazed at the passing crowd. "Gillen thinks you still have the dark mass. There's something else in there now, a chunk of essence that burns blue. I saw the MRI scan. It looks like a sun in eclipse."

"It's the faith stone," I said.

She gave me a lopsided grin. "Yeah, you have a rock in your head."

I feigned a pout. "Technically, it's a gem."

Meryl tilted her head up. "Take off those glasses."

I pushed them up on the fold of my knit cap. Meryl's eyes shifted back and forth as she stared into mine. My irises had crystallized, facets of light blue framed in lines of white. When the light hit them right, flashes of red, yellow, and blue twinkled. They reminded me of the eyes of an Old One, the sign of long life and ancient ability. Only, I didn't have any ability. The pain of the dark mass was gone, replaced by a cold pulsation. At least my body shield was back—my full body shield. Whatever the faith stone was doing to the dark mass, it was letting me access the shield again. Without other abilities, it was a comfort.

Her smile faded, and she looked away. "Does it hurt?"

I frowned. "Did Gillen say I was dying?"

She dropped her head against my chest. "No, but that doesn't mean I'm not worried."

"It doesn't hurt, at least not the same. I don't really feel it. It's like it's weightless," I said.

"These things tend to be metaphors for the power they represent. It's not really a stone. We see what we need to see to make sense of the ineffable. It's power that was embodied by the stone, but it's all energy now," she said.

I hugged her. "I always get nervous when you get religion."

She giggled. "Nice to know I can make the guy who killed the Elven King nervous."

"I was trying to stop him," I said.

She rose on her toes and kissed. "I know. I was trying to lighten the conversation before I left."

I tugged at her waist. "Do you have to go?"

"I'm still shoring up the power wards in the Archives. I don't want to lose anything else," she said.

Manus ap Eagan had used the faith stone to strengthen the Guildhouse and reinforce the shield dome. When Donor took the stone, it didn't affect the subbasements because they were part of the original design, dug deep underground for stability in the landfill of old marshland. Despite an entire building's collapsing, the Archive storerooms had survived with minimal damage.

"Have you told anyone they're still there?" I asked.

She chuckled. "Nah. I figure I have at least a couple of

months to play before they dig them out. It'll give me a chance to do all the filing I keep not doing." She kissed me again. "Murdock says hi, by the way. He said to tell you this all has a purpose, and it's not for us to judge."

He meant not for him to judge. He wasn't buying the party line that I had destroyed a neighborhood. "He's a good guy."

Meryl danced away from me. "No, he's a *great* guy. And so are you. I'll be back in a few days. Try not to kill or be killed while I'm away."

I smiled. "Will do."

I waited until she disappeared from sight before leaving the storefront. I put my glasses back on and wandered a circuitous route through the streets, weaving in and out of alleys, through basements and abandoned buildings. Finally, I slid through an essence barrier to a room furnished with a table with a few chairs, an old couch, and a—twin—bed. The light from the window shimmered with a sallow tint from the ambient essence endemic to the Tangle.

I slumped on the couch, exhausted. The last week had been filled with running and hiding, dodging everyone from the Boston police to Guild security agents to Consortium warriors. Briallen couldn't take me in without drawing heat down on herself, and we both needed her to be able to operate in the open. My apartment was an obvious no-go zone. Every major law-enforcement agency, fey and human alike, had my face on a wanted poster.

After abandoning one hiding place after another, I had gone to ground in the Tangle, lost among the lost, secure in a nest of criminals and thugs. While the living feared and hated me, the Dead embraced me with open arms. How long that would last, I couldn't guess, but it wouldn't last. Doubt had become the nature of my World.

The Wheel of the World didn't turn, but twisted and spiraled until everything I thought I knew became confused beyond recognition. Friends became enemies, and enemies, friends. Whom to trust and whom to suspect became a game of odds, a precarious knife-edge of uncertain allies, ready to stand by me or not.

Ceridwen entered and placed two stone wards on the table. She no longer looked like the haughty fairy queen who had arrived in Boston determined to take me down. She retained the air of superiority all Dananns had, but months underground and building an army had hardened her appearance. Seeing the transition, I understood now why Maeve appeared to be such a bitch. A fairy at war was a formidable thing to behold. "These will reinforce your security alarms," she said.

"Thank you." I touched her arm, meaning it as no more than to show my appreciation for giving me safe harbor. A jolt went through me as a sliver of white light burned in my head. By Ceridwen's reaction, it happened to her, too. We had both held the spear and bonded to it in our own ways. Something about touching each other called the spear from wherever it disappeared to when it was gone.

The air in the room crackled with the sharp scent of ozone. Essence burst from the ceiling as the spear plunged down and embedded itself in the floor between us. It glowed white-hot, bristling with energy, then sank through the floor, oozing out a pool of essence before it vanished. The pool coalesced into a smoldering amorphous lump of essence that pulsed and shivered.

"The poor thing," Ceridwen said. She stooped and picked up the lumpy mass and cradled it against her chest. The shape burned with intensity but didn't hurt her.

"What the hell is that?" I asked.

Ceridwen shushed me, giving me her shoulder as she hummed under her breath. The shape dimmed and stretched, appendages appearing and flailing at the air. It contracted as she chanted. A burst of pink essence blinded me a moment. When my vision cleared, a sound came out of me, one I didn't hear from myself often. My throat thickened, my chest aching with emotion as I suppressed another sob. "Is he all right?"

wen lowered Joe onto the bed with gentle care.

"He's fine. He needed to remember what he was," she said. He slept, his wings spread flat, his mouth wide open. He looked how he always looked with a hangover.

Ceridwen moved to the window. Beyond the rooftops across the way, a blue haze shimmered to the southwest. "The humans have moved their troops into position on this end of the Weird. Eorla's people are watching the perimeter, and I am maintaining the shield for her. For both of us," she said.

Donor had accomplished his goal. Eorla was being blamed for the destruction of the Guildhouse, with me as her accomplice. They were still counting the dead. The story suited Maeve, and she railed against terrorists in press release after press release. The Teutonic Consortium played the same theme with more emphasis on the role of solitary fairies. For once, both sides acted together.

The official story was that Ambassador Aldred Core died in the collapse. The true story was Donor Elfenkonig, the Elven King, was dead. No one knew outside a small circle of fey and maybe a select human or two. Maeve kept her silence, waiting to see who would take the reins now that her chief adversary was gone.

I tore my gaze away from Joe. "Will you promise not to hurt the humans?" I asked.

Her lips pulled into a taut line. "In war, one can never make such promises."

"You're not at war with them," I said.

She glanced at me with understanding. "I know what you're feeling, Grey. I know what it means to protect people who depend on you. The failure to do so is the pain of leadership, but the Wheel of the World turns as It will. I will do my best to keep this between me and Maeve. That is all I can promise."

I glanced back at Joe.

"That will have to be enough," I said.